MASQUERADE

MASQUERADE

O.O. SANGOYOMI

TOR PUBLISHING GROUP

NEW YORK

This is a work of fiction. All of the characters, organizations,
and events portrayed in this novel are either products of the author's
imagination or are used fictitiously.

MASQUERADE

Copyright © 2024 by O.O. Sangoyomi

A Forge Book
Published by Tom Doherty Associates / Tor Publishing Group
120 Broadway
New York, NY 10271

www.tor-forge.com

Forge® is a registered trademark of Macmillan Publishing Group, LLC.

The Library of Congress Cataloging-in-Publication Data is available
upon request.

ISBN 978-1-250-90429-4 (hardcover)
ISBN 978-1-250-90430-0 (ebook)

Our books may be purchased in bulk for promotional,
educational, or business use. Please contact your local bookseller
or the Macmillan Corporate and Premium Sales Department
at 1-800-221-7945, extension 5442, or by email at
MacmillanSpecialMarkets@macmillan.com.

First Edition: 2024

Printed in the United States of America

0 9 8 7 6 5 4 3 2 1

Memory is Master of Death, the chink in his armour of conceit.

—Wọlé Ṣóyínká,
Death and the King's Horseman

MASQUERADE

1

Each day, countless fleets of camel caravans sailed across the desert sea to reach Timbuktu.

Here, in this port city on the southern edge of the Sahara, waves of men, women, and children flooded the market, searching for supplies. Farmers and craftsmen proudly showcased their wares from behind wooden stands or in front of tents. Threads of dancers wove through cheerful crowds; juggling entertainers could be found on every corner. Travelers' stories of far-off lands rose and fell with the playful chords of musicians. Vibrant colors and savory scents swirled in the air as Timbuktu teemed with the trading, buying, and selling of everything from exotic spices to brilliant fabrics to precious salt and gold.

But today, Timbuktu was still.

I stood in front of a wooden platform, along with what felt like half the market goers. Rain poured from the skies, soaking through my brown wrapper. Thunder rumbled as a Songhai general was dragged onto the platform by soldiers who were not his own.

They forced the general to his knees, the wood beneath him groaning over the incessant patter of rain. His wet robes were stained with blood and grime. Water trickled from his turban, down his bruised face.

A third, smaller man drifted onto the platform. Lines were etched into his face, like ripples in a shadow. Each line marked a history—a birth, a marriage, a death. He frowned as his gaze swept over the crowd, chronicling yet another wrinkle, another event.

He extended his arms on either side of him, and his billowing sleeves crowded around his elbows. "Ọba kìí pòkọrin."

The customary introduction of griots pierced the air. The griot paused, allowing his baritone words to take their place among the crowd, before continuing in accented Arabic, "Gather, gather, hear me now. The Songhai rule this city no more. As of today, Timbuktu belongs to the Aláàfin of Yorùbáland."

The griot gestured to a group of soldiers standing nearby. From within their circle, an old man stepped forward. He wore a red and white kente toga that draped over one of his forearms and shoulders. Beneath the painted white dots covering his body, his skin was as brown and gnarled as an ancient baobab tree. It felt as though time itself paused to accommodate his slow approach.

The griot stepped back as the old man mounted the platform; griots represented nobles and the people, but divine correspondence with the òrìṣàs was left to babaláwos.

The babaláwo looked down at the general and raised a fist. Slowly, very slowly, he uncurled his fingers, uncovering a single cowpea in the center of his palm.

People around me recoiled. I leaned forward. I had heard of the sacred Yorùbá bean, but I had never seen one myself.

Although the general had not flinched, his full lips were clamped thin. From where I stood at the front of the crowd, I saw the fear that flashed across his eyes. He struggled in vain as soldiers pried open his jaw, and the babaláwo forced him to eat the cowpea.

"Great Ṣàngó," the babaláwo cried. His gossamer voice whirled around me, as though entwined in the wind. "This is the man who led your enemies. What is to be his fate?"

There was no answer, of course; the òrìṣàs never personally descended from the heavens to speak to the humans they presided over. Wind howled around us, growing crueler in its acceleration. Fruits were blown off nearby stands; orange sand surged forth. As I shielded my face from the storm, I wondered if all of Timbuktu would be uprooted before the trial ended.

Then lightning ruptured the sky, and the world shuddered under the thunder that followed.

"Ṣàngó has spoken," the griot boomed. He beckoned a soldier forward.

Rage rippled through the fear on the general's face. "This is what you call justice? You Yorùbá are nothing but a tribe of superstitious pagans—"

A soldier plunged a spear into the side of the general's neck. His declaration sputtered into wet gurgling as blood poured from the wound. He fell onto the platform, seizing, until his movements gradually came to a stop.

The babaláwo raised his arms to the sky. "Ṣàngó yọ mí."

"Ṣàngó yọ mí," the crowd echoed. *Ṣàngó saved me.*

The affirmation scratched my throat, threatening to bring more than words with it. But like the rest of the onlookers, I knew to thank the god of thunder and lightning for not condemning me to death instead. His wrath was as deadly as wildfire and just as easily spread.

The griot said, "Nothing about your life in Timbuktu need change. So long as your governor pays tribute to the Aláàfin, he may continue to rule as he sees fit." He turned to a richly-dressed man standing beside the platform in between two soldiers. "Do you accept these terms, or are you determined to follow the fate of Timbuktu's former general?"

The brown seemed to drain from the governor's face. He fell to his knees, his hands clasped in front of him. "I am honored to serve the Aláàfin," he said. Then, in stunted Yorùbá, he added, "An honor."

The griot nodded, and the crowd began to disperse, many of them taking cover from the rain. But I remained rooted in place. I watched as soldiers stepped forward to retrieve the body of the Songhai general. They hauled it onto a wagon like it was a sack of garri, moving with an efficiency that suggested they had done this for years, though they could not have been much older than I was, around the age of nineteen.

"There, there." A robust man slid next to me. He lay a meaty arm around my shoulder, his palm moist against my skin. "I understand your shock. Is it difficult to wrap around your head?"

"I've seen executions before," I said quietly. Though this was true, I had never seen lightning be the final verdict.

"I don't mean the execution." The kindness enveloping the man's words peeled back to reveal impatience beneath. I looked at him and saw that he was pointing at my head. "Your headscarf is the brown of an overripe plantain," he said. "It is old and stiff. Difficult to wear, yes?"

From somewhere within the sleeves of his tunic, he extracted a silk scarf so white that it stung my eyes. "My dear girl," he continued, "your scarf does justice to neither your black nor your beauty. What you need is a bright scarf, for the night sky needs its stars."

It was then I remembered that I did not know this man.

I shrugged his arm off, and as I made my way through the marketplace, other vendors called out to me, also telling me what I needed.

"Come and see your new sandals," called a man with a large beard and a larger belly. "The leather is soft and smooth, but they are strong."

"Fruit directly from the riverbanks of the Niger," proclaimed a woman as orange as the mangoes she held. "The juice can cure the most stubborn of illnesses."

The marketplace's rhythm resumed as though it had never paused. The Yorùbá seizure came as a surprise to no one; Timbuktu sat on agriculturally rich land in a commercially active area. When the Songhai captured the city three years ago, in 1468, they had only been one more addendum to Timbuktu's long history of changing hands. The city's population was not made up of just one people; there were the Songhai and the Yorùbá, but there were also the Fulani, the Moors, the Portuguese, and more. The only thing that unified Timbuktu's inhabitants was a drive for profit. So long as the marketplace continued running, who ruled the city was of little importance.

I had come to the marketplace today with my mother, but in the commotion of the execution, I lost her. Knowing that she would not want me wandering around alone, I decided to head home.

As I rounded a corner onto another busy song-laced street, the Songhai general's execution replayed in my mind. It was an unconventional method of justice, feeding a cowpea to a man then killing him if lightning subsequently flashed or sparing him if it did not. Perhaps the Songhai general was right to call the Yorùbá superstitious, to imply that the will of their god was nothing more than nature's chance. And yet—with it being the very end of wet season, today's rainfall should not have been as heavy as it had been. I could not help but wonder if there was some truth to the common saying that the Yorùbá brought the storm wherever they went.

The rain had dwindled into a drizzle by the time I reached a quieter end of Timbuktu, on the outskirts of the market. The sandy road, less trodden upon here, branched out into evenly spaced compounds. Each were enclosed within waist-high mud-brick walls.

Eventually, I entered the compound of a sun-dried mud house with a flat roof. Its sandy yard was occupied by a handful of women, all of whom wore plain, brown wrappers and headscarves that blended into their skin. Under great plumes of smoke, the women moved between anvils, forges, and furnaces.

Metronomic pings rung through the air as two-handed hammers molded iron and steel into weapons or shaped gold and silver into elaborate designs. One woman sat on a low stool, pounding boiled yam in a wooden mortar for tonight's dinner. I knelt before them all, my knees sinking into warm mud.

"Good afternoon, aunties," I greeted.

"Welcome, child," my aunties chorused without looking up from their work, cuing me to stand.

These women were not really my aunties, but I had called them that for so long that their names had become foreign to my memory. Really, I was unsure if I had ever learned their names—and given that they had called me "child" my whole life, perhaps they never learned mine either.

I made my way to the house. I had just reached the archway when an auntie emerged from inside.

"Why are you going inside?" she asked me. "Is the work at your forge done?"

It was a clear reprimand, for we both knew that the work at our forges was never done. "My mother wants me to take inventory," I said. It was a task I had been given earlier that day.

Her brow unfurrowed; like all the other women here, she might have never fully warmed up to me, but she had nothing but respect for my mother.

She sighed. "You'll have to do inventory another time. I don't want you to wake her."

She gestured over her shoulder to inside the house. Within the dark single room, one of my older aunties lay on a sleeping mat. Although her eyes were closed, beads of sweat ran down her face, and her expression was pulled taut as though sleep was an arduous task. Alarmed, I noted that she was even skinnier than the last time I had seen her.

"She hasn't gotten better?" I asked.

My auntie shook her head sadly. "It is the governor's responsibility to provide for our guild, but even so, he's as stingy with medicine as with the food he gives us. I don't think he wants to waste any resources on an old blacksmith."

I frowned; the woman was not that old. Her sickness might have aged her, but I remembered the unlined, lively face she had worn when she had still been healthy. I had always believed her to be around the same age as my mother.

I shivered, a motion that had nothing to do with my soaked clothes. My mother and I had been blacksmiths my entire life. As unmarried women, it was one of the few ways we could make a living—but sometimes I feared it was what would also kill us. My sick auntie was not the first of us to expire at her forge. Was this to be the fate of my mother and I as well, meeting death exhausted, neglected, and, worst of all, much too soon?

My distress must have shown on my face because my auntie placed a hand on my shoulder. "It'll be okay," she said gently. "She'll wake up soon, and when she does, we should give her something nice. Why don't you take a short break to make her one of your flowers?"

Holding silver and a tweezer, I sat in my usual spot behind the house, my legs tucked to one side of me.

The silver had been shaped into a cylinder. One of the cylinder's ends was open, while the other was fused to a star-shaped sheet of metal. It was meant to be a nearly completed daffodil—or, at least, what I could remember of a daffodil's appearance. I had only seen a real one once, when a trader gifted me the flower.

That day, the trader had arrived in Timbuktu after weeks of traveling with his colorful caravan of slaves, bodyguards, scholars, poets, and fellow traders. Like so many others, the trader had heard of my mother's and aunties' abilities, and he had come to request an iron dagger. My aunties always focused on the orders from generals and kings, leaving less important clientele like him to me. My hands had been less steady than they were now, and my eyes less attuned to identify flaws, yet the trader had marveled at my average dagger.

"My dear," he said in awe, "what is your name?"

Since he already knew my state-given name, I told him my personal name. His eyes widened. "Wait here—I have just the thing for you."

I thought he was one of those people who tried to skip out on payment, and I thought he was doing a poor job of it—as we spoke, his traveling companions had been paying my mother.

He proved me wrong, however, by returning. "A flower for the child whose name means flower," he proclaimed, handing me a flower that was a yellow unlike any gold I had ever seen. "This is a daffodil. They grow in distant lands far, far above the Sahara."

"It's beautiful," I said. Then I grew sad, remembering the flowers I always saw in the market. They bloomed in the day, but after the sun had set and the customers had gone, merchants disposed of wilted petals. "But it'll die."

"Daffodils do not fear dying, for they have conquered Death himself."

"Oh." A pause. Then, "Perhaps you should keep this . . ."

I tried to return the flower to the possibly delirious man, but he only laughed. "Do not be afraid of daffodils, my dear," he said, mistaking my wariness of him for fear of the flower. "They used neither strength nor sorcery to best Death. Just a simple song." He grinned. "From the look on your face, I am guessing you are wondering what that song is?"

I had actually been wondering how a flower could possibly sing. However, the trader was clearly motivated more by his own pride than by my curiosity. So, I simply said, "Okay."

He sang. He could not hold a tune, and he sped up in odd places only to slow much too abruptly. The beginning of the trader's song had since eluded me, and I was no longer certain about its ending. However, what I could remember of the song had burrowed deep into my mind.

The daffodil had succumbed to the desert heat two days later. Since then, I had rebirthed it countless times, using whatever metals my aunties spared me from their work. And with each flower I crafted, I sang the little of the trader's song that I knew, just as I did now.

> *"You listen to her tale*
> *One her teacher always told*
> *Of roads his son walked*

Roads paved with petals of gold
See them bloom, see them shine
See this garden become a sky
With a thousand tiny suns
It's no lie, it's no lie
Light the world through the night
Keep this glow inside your heart
Flowers wilt, lands dwindle
But survival is in the art."

"Beautiful."

In my surprise, I nearly dropped my flower. Ahead of me, a man stood on the other side of the wall. His tattered tunic appeared brown, but when he rested his forearms on the wall and left an imprint, I realized the color was just dirt. He was a culmination of hard lines, from his strong jaw to his broad shoulders. The only soft thing about him was the smile he gave me.

I returned my attention to my flower. The man appeared too poor to place an order with my aunties, and had he meant me harm, he would have done so already. He was just a wanderer; if I ignored him, he would see there was nothing here and drift on elsewhere.

However, my silence did not seem to dissuade him. "The song was nice too," he remarked.

His Arabic was fluent, but he spoke with a strong Yorùbá accent. I curled one of the flower petals up, allowing it to bloom around the cup. Silence settled around me. For a moment, I believed the man had gone. Then—

"What's that you're making?"

I sighed. "It's a flower," I finally obliged, speaking in Yorùbá.

He looked pleasantly surprised. "You're from Yorùbáland?" he asked, switching to Yorùbá as well. In his native language, his voice was deeper and more mellow.

"My mother is. I've never left Timbuktu, but I grew up speaking Yorùbá with her."

"What is your name?"

I hesitated. Then, realizing I had no reason to care about what a beggar thought, I told him, "Òdòdó is the name I have chosen. But the name that was chosen for me is Alálẹ̀."

The man cupped his chin in his broad, bronze colored hand. "*Owners of the Earth*," he thoughtfully repeated my second name, which I shared with my aunties. "Ah. You're a witch."

I narrowed my eyes, peering at him closely. "You seem to have neither the naivete of youth nor the delirium of old age, yet you still believe that blacksmiths are witches?"

His grin widened; he had my full attention now, and he knew it. "You take the ore that Earth gifts us and transform it into deadly weapons or elegant jewelry. That must take magic."

"Because fire is too difficult to fathom."

He laughed. "That's fair," he said. "Although, I think I'd attribute you more to rain. Your voice must be what moved the heavens to tears today."

Living in the desert, I had seen more than my fair share of sunny days. However, as I looked at the radiance with which the man's black eyes shone, I wondered if I had ever seen a light such as his.

I looked at my flower. It still lacked a stem, but the head alone was recognizable enough as a flower. I debated for a moment, then I rose.

As I approached him, the man straightened. There were not many people whom I needed to look up at, but he was an exception.

He allowed my examination with an amused patience. Up close, I saw that he had long curly hair wound into a black knot at the base of his head. A vertical scar ran over his left eye, from above his brow down to his cheek. It was the same mark I had seen on most of the Yorùbá soldiers—the mark of the Aláràá, a clan within the Yorùbá tribe. My mother was Aláràá as well, but since she was neither a man nor born into a prominent family, she did not bear the tribal mark.

There was another, longer scar trailing from the base of the man's neck to beneath his tunic. A token from battle, no doubt. Deep as the wound must have been, the spark in the stranger's gaze made me pity, not him, but rather the man he had fought.

For a vagrant, I decided, he was rather charming.

"Here," I said, holding out my flower. It had been intended for my sick auntie, but I could always make her another.

A dimple sank into the stranger's right cheek as he smiled. "You're giving me your flower?"

"It's not just a flower. It's a daffodil." My interaction with the trader all those years ago surfaced in my mind, and I added, "You said you liked my song. This daffodil may just sing it to you."

He laughed again. This time, I was close enough to feel the joy that emanated from him, warm and encompassing. It was a nice sound.

"In that case, how could I say no?" His calloused hand brushed my own as he accepted the flower.

"It'll fetch a nice price," I informed him. I hoped he would have the sense to trade it for a decent meal. Or at least a bath.

He smiled as he inspected the flower, though when he looked up, his expression had become more pensive. "What do you know of the Aláàfin?"

"The king of kings?"

He nodded, and I frowned. The question was unexpected— but then again, so was this entire conversation.

A falcon cried overhead. I watched it disappear into the horizon as I pondered the question. I knew that the Aláàfin presided over Yorùbáland from his city, Ṣàngótẹ̀. That he led a great army with which he had now conquered most regions west of the Niger.

Even if the stranger did not have a rugged physique, I would have known he was a soldier; every boy in Yorùbáland underwent rigorous military training that lasted well into adulthood. And the Aláàfin was said to be the most skilled fighter of them all. He had taken so many lives in battle that he was often referred to as the Commander of Death.

So, what I knew of the Aláàfin was what anyone else knew. But from the stranger's intense gaze, I gathered these were not the answers he sought.

At last, I shrugged. "When I was a child, I wanted to live in his stables."

The thin shell of hesitancy around the stranger's smile broke, and humor rushed forth freely. "His stables?"

I nodded unblushingly. "They say that the Aláàfin is so rich that he owns ten thousand horses, and each horse has their own mattress. They say that he has hundreds of slaves who keep his stables cleaner than most manors."

I glanced at my sandals. The leather was peeling, and my feet were constantly covered in dirt no matter how hard I scrubbed them—which I did not have time to do very often.

"Even just living in his stables would be better than the life I have now," I remarked softly.

"What if you truly could live with him?"

I looked at the stranger, amused. "What if I could grow a pair of wings to fly me to a bed of clouds?"

I laughed. The stranger did not. He opened his mouth and closed it. Then, he opened it once more. But before he could speak, there came a shrill call.

"Òdòdó."

I looked over my shoulder to see my mother, Okóbí, storming toward us. She was black and stout, like a block of ebony before it was carved. And just like ebony, the dark glimmer of her skin could distract the untrained eye from the resiliency of her rugged muscles.

Instinctively, I bent my knees in obeisance. "Good afternoon, ma," I said.

In response, she grabbed my upper arm and yanked me behind her. Scowling at the stranger, she said, "Our forges are in the front of the house."

The sharpness of Okóbí's voice pierced the toughest of men, but the stranger did not appear fazed. "And lovely forges they are, I'm sure," he replied kindly. "But I am afraid that I am not here for a spear."

"Then you have no business with my daughter."

"I will keep that in mind for when I see her, but in this moment, all I see in front of me are two beautiful sisters."

He winked at me. A smile tugged at the corner of my mouth.

My mother, on the other hand, remained unamused. She had worked with far too many precious metals to be impressed by the silver of the stranger's tongue.

"Come back when you are in need of a spear," Okóbí said slowly, each word dropping with the weight of a stone.

The stranger's smile remained, but an odd glint appeared in his eyes, illuminating them—no, that was not it. There was a light, but it did not make his eyes shine. It made them blacker. Sharper.

It was gone so quickly that I might have imagined it, for in the next moment, the stranger inclined his head. "Of course." His eyes slid to my own, their charisma restored. "Farewell, Alálẹ̀ Òdòdó," he said.

The ghost of *for now* lingered in the air.

He buried his hands into his front pockets, the silver daffodil with them, and as he walked away, he whistled a tune that sounded suspiciously close to the daffodil's song. I found myself disappointed to see him go.

As soon as the man was out of sight, a long exhale seeped out of Okóbí. She whirled around and grasped my face in both of her hands, tilting it down.

"What did he want?" she demanded. Her touch was warm, but it was her black eyes that burned like flaming coals as they raked over my face. "What did he do to you? Did he touch you?"

"I'm fine," I assured her. "I only spoke to the man."

"That's it?"

"That's it."

Her shoulders, which had been steadily climbing to her ears, dropped. "That's it," she repeated, almost to herself.

She reared her arm back and struck me across the face.

The sound whipped through the air as I staggered backwards. I held a hand to my cheek, attempting to numb the pain, but my warm touch only made it worse.

"That's it, she says!" Okóbí cried, her voice muffled by the ringing in my ears. "How many times have I said, do not speak to these beggars? Hm? How many times?"

She lifted her hand again. With a jolt, I quickly responded, "Many."

"Many, many times. Abeg, where do my words go? Do they float in the air until the wind blows them away? What is it about your head that they cannot enter?" she demanded, furiously jabbing two fingers to my temple. "Evil child, is it not enough to cause me misery? Must you allow a man to make your own life miserable as well?

"Listen well—that sorry story does not need to be told twice. I never want to see you so much as look at a man again. And you are *my* daughter, so when I give you instruction, you obey. Do you understand?"

Over the years, variations of this conversation had taught me that were I to say yes, she would accuse me of lying. Yet no was somehow an even worse answer. So, I gave her what she wanted: I dropped my gaze and waited patiently.

Sure enough, Okóbí sighed, like the final hiss of a quenched flame. "Go take inventory."

"Yes, ma."

As I walked away, I heard Okóbí mutter behind me, "She makes that silly flower again and again, yet she still does not understand that it would not have died had it not been beautiful enough to be picked in the first place."

2

Just like blood circulating in the body's veins, iron ore flowed through Earth's core. The strikes of two-handed basalt hammers against blistering metal echoed the cadence of the heart pumping life through the body. The two rhythms were nearly indistinguishable to me, each equally as intrinsic.

It did not matter what a blacksmith called herself; outsiders referred to us all with the same name, as though we were different parts of a single entity: Alálẹ̀. This name marked us as a group who knew the well-guarded secrets behind transforming Earth's most basic resource into objects of utility, empowerment, prestige, and art. There was a sort of magic in the intermingling of the elements of creation that smithing required: fire, air from the bellows to excite it, water to tame it, and earth for its shaper to stand upon.

Any woman deemed unnatural in the eyes of society was called a witch, but the word was especially associated with blacksmiths. And yet, outsiders could not be further from reality when they called us witches. There was nothing mystical about the permanent aches throughout my body from a lifetime of hunching over large flat rocks and hammering metals. There was nothing spellbinding about the burns and scars I had up and down my arms, gifts from molten iron and the fiery lungs of furnaces. But outsiders did not understand the complexity and brutality that was the process of manipulating the Earth, so they feared us. The slur *witch* was their only defense, for they could not get rid of us completely; smithing was necessary for the operation of any empire. And west of the Niger, we were the only ones who could do it.

A dozen machetes that my aunties and I had just forged were lined up in the middle of the yard, their dark iron glimmering in the sunlight. Around me, my aunties rested. Knowing it would not be long before my mother assigned us a new task, most women stayed near their workstations, sitting where they could find shade and passing around skins of water.

I sat in the partial shadow of a large rock. The pile of charcoal next to me was the only one in the yard that was still lit. Last week, when a charming vagrant had visited my house, I had given him the last of my metal flowers. Thus, instead of using this rare free time to rest as my aunties did, I made more flowers.

From a thin sheet of gold, I used a knife to cut out three stars, each about the size of my palm. Their points were curved to resemble petals, and their centers were punctured by a tiny hole through which I would eventually stick a metal flower stem. I cut the remainder of my gold sheet into strips and plied them into short tubes, then centered each tube on a star before using tongs to hold it in the fire next to me. The flames' heat grazed my hands, but I hardly felt it with the sweltering sun beating down on me and slicking my skin with sweat. I slowly rotated the metal flower head until the cup fused to the petals, and once it cooled, I plied the petals upward so that they bloomed around the cup. From there, I inserted iron rods through the petals' base, then used fire one last time to fuse the stems to the flower heads.

I had just finished the last of the flowers when, over the crackle of fire, I heard someone say, "We were witches before, and we are witches now."

I looked behind me. Two of my aunties were huddled together, speaking in low voices. "A witch to the Songhai is different from a witch to these Yorùbá," the second auntie replied. "I cannot help but worry what is in store for us now that Timbuktu is part of Yorùbáland."

Apparently, I was not the only one whose attention had

been caught by their conversation; a third auntie, whose nose was adorned by a golden septum ring, spoke up. "You are right to worry," she said. "Remember, some of our sisters—myself included—are from Yorùbáland. We fled here because as neglected as we are in Timbuktu, it is infinitely preferable to the cruelty faced by witches in Yorùbáland."

The skeptical auntie's stubborn expression remained, but her shoulders sunk slightly, as though she could no longer pretend there was no weight bearing down on her. "But what can we do? There is nowhere to flee, not with the Aláàfin claiming all corners of the Earth."

"Even if there was somewhere else to run, I am not sure I would again," Septum Ring said. "I am tired of running only to be shunned wherever I go. I want somewhere I can stay and live in peace—even if I must fight for that peace."

By now, most of my aunties had paused their work to listen. Some were nodding, as though they were ready to take up arms alongside Septum Ring. But in the faces of most aunties, I saw my own shock reflected. Witches had no allies, and women had no strength; how could we fight the Aláàfin's great army?

"You have made so many weapons that you have fooled yourself into thinking you know how to use them?" a new voice said.

We all turned to see Okóbí walking out of the house, holding the meager medicine for my sick auntie, to come join the conversation. At the appearance of my mother, my other aunties quickly looked away, pretending they had not been listening. However, they stole furtive glances as Septum Ring replied, "I do not mean a physical fight. I just—perhaps there is something we can do to improve our conditions."

"And what do you propose we do?" Okóbí asked. "Speak up, because our voices are so heeded? Exhibit our scars, because the world has always felt so much sympathy for us? Tell me, as unimportant and helpless as you are, what can you do?"

As she spoke, the two aunties who had first spoken lowered their heads, their faces twisted in shame and frustration. Septum

Ring, however, bravely kept her eyes on Okóbí, even as they
filled with tears.

"My sister," she said, "you are cruel."

"I am a mother. And you are filling my daughter's head with
dangerous notions. This is the space we have been given in this
world. No matter how small and how bleak, it is the only one we
have." Okóbí looked around. "Back to work. We need to make
seven iron spearheads. The man who placed the order is expecting them to be ready tomorrow. Let us complete our tasks
so the state will continue to send us food. Each day we survive is
enough of a victory."

Most of my aunties returned to their workstations unfazed; they
had long accepted that hope was not something that belonged to
them. But the aunties who had nodded at the prospect of fighting
now looked defeated. Some scowled at me, and I wanted to tell
them my mother had said that for my benefit but not with my
blessing. However, one look from Okóbí, her black eyes challenging me to say anything at all, stopped me from speaking,
and I quickly made to return to my own workstation.

But no sooner had I stood than a pounding of hooves sounded.
Five men rode horses down the road and came to a stop in front
of our house. Soldiers—recognizable as Aláràá by the vertical scar over their left eyes. They dismounted their horses and
strolled into our yard, all the while chatting among themselves,
as though they entered a public space and not our house.

The men walked around, inspecting our forges and furnaces
with the same appraising looks they gave us, as though we were
a continuation of the equipment. "I'd been excited to make use
of Timbuktu's witches, for I have heard they are one of the most
skilled guilds west of the Niger, and I am in desperate need of
replacing my knife," one man remarked to his comrade. "But
after seeing this hovel for myself, I am no longer sure we can get
what we need."

"I assure you," said the auntie with a septum ring, "we are
more than capable of making a few knives."

The soldiers' chatter lulled as they turned to her. My stomach must have recognized the disgust on their faces faster than my mind did, because I felt it churn before I could fully process why.

The man who had commented about the knives stepped up to my auntie with the septum ring and struck her across the face. The blow was so forceful that she was knocked off-balance. It happened too quickly for anyone to react; the rest of my aunties and I watched, frozen with shock, as Septum Ring crumpled to the ground.

The soldiers laughed. Amidst their laughter, the assailant said, "It is bad enough we must seek out witches. Please, keep our suffering at a minimum and do not speak unless in response to us."

Okóbí rushed to the soldiers and my fallen auntie. I expected her to yell at the soldiers for their impertinence, to subject them to the iron will that made my aunties respect her leadership and that had even cowed customers who overstepped their bounds in the past.

But instead, Okóbí merely helped my auntie to her feet. With her gaze lowered, Okóbí said, "She is sorry, sir. It will not happen again."

"See that it does not, Alálẹ̀. The Aláàfin has been kind to allow you to remain in his new city, but if you continue to disrespect his loyal soldiers, he may very well change his mind."

Okóbí nodded, still looking down. My mother was a short woman, but I had never seen her as small until now. Nor had I witnessed such blatant abuse toward my aunties; we may have been insulted and shunned, but we had never been harmed. We were protected by the state—or at least we had been.

Fear building within me, I looked back to the soldiers. My heart jumped when I met the eyes of a tall, burly man who had been staring at me. He grinned, flashing yellowed teeth that made me flinch.

Somehow, Okóbí noticed the man's interest in me, and she seemed to regain some of her usual intimidating aura as she hurried to me. "Go sell your flowers in the market," she said in a low voice.

"I don't have many flowers right now," I said. "And I don't want to leave you. Those men might—"

Okóbí cut me off with an impatient smack of her lips. "Whatever they do, you cannot stop them. I have one less inconvenience if you are safely away while we take their order."

I opened my mouth to protest again, but Okóbí snapped, "Òdòdó, do not make me angry. I did not kill my mother, so you will not kill me. I said *go*."

The sun was only beginning to color the eastern sky, but the market was already a hive of activity. People swarmed around stands and tents, bartering and buying, singing and laughing.

I had just traded a gold flower for a fair price: a cube of salt roughly the same weight of the flower. Salt was the most valued commodity in the market, even more so than slaves, though those were a close second. Salt was required to preserve and season food, and it was essential for replacing what the body lost in sweat when traveling through the Sahara.

At the conclusion of our business, I said farewell to the salt vendor. As I wove through people and animals to search for a new customer, I passed by the gates of Sankoré University. The institution was what had earned Timbuktu its status as a premier intellectual center, boasting subjects ranging from languages to medicine to law.

Upon seizing Timbuktu in 1468, the Songhai had persecuted scholars in order to eliminate the possibility of them undermining authority. Many scholars had fled, but the newly established Yorùbá rule over the city seemed to have brought them back; the university's campus was the liveliest I had seen it in years.

When I noticed women among the scholars, I could not help but stop and stare. I had heard that women in Yorùbáland could be scholars, musicians—anything except for soldiers. But after living under Islamic law for so long, it was strange to see women other than my aunties outside of a domestic setting.

Nevertheless, I knew I would never be among them. I had neither interest nor experience in scholarship, and given how unimpressive she found my mind, my mother would laugh at the idea of me being a student. No, the best way I could help her was by selling and trading my flowers.

I turned away from the university—only to nearly collide with a wall. When I stepped back, I saw that it was not a wall that had suddenly appeared in my path, but a man. He was as tall as me but twice as wide, and he bore the mark of the Aláràá clan.

When he smiled, I recognized his yellowed teeth—it was the same smile he had given me earlier, when he and his comrades had intruded into my house and assaulted my auntie. Fear gripped me as I realized that he must have followed me from my house to the market; perhaps my auntie had not been enough. Perhaps he meant me harm as well.

And yet his voice was amicable enough as he asked, "What's that you're holding?"

The question caught me off guard, but relieved it was not a threat instead, I held up my last two gold daffodils. "Flowers, sir. I'm trading them."

"Metal flowers made by a young witch." The slur was said with no hostility; he spoke neutrally and with a small nod, as though confirming something. "Come. Let us discuss business."

The statement felt like an order. I had no choice but to allow the man to guide me to a green tent.

As soon as I stepped inside, the shade provided cool relief. Set on the sandy floor were two crates. The soldier waved at one, and I reluctantly sat on its edge, ready to spring up at a moment's notice if needed.

As he poured a pitcher into a chipped wooden cup, he asked, "What will you take in exchange for one flower?"

"Whatever you can spare, sir," I said. I was not always so in-different to the price of my labor, but I knew what I needed most from this trade was to leave unharmed.

"For someone living in Timbuktu, you do not drive a partic-ularly hard bargain," he said with a chuckle.

When I did not share his amusement, his smile softened. To my confusion, something like sympathy colored his gaze.

"Very well then," he said. "In exchange for one of your flow-ers, I give you this refreshment."

He offered me the wooden cup. Although it pained me to complete such an unfair trade, I nodded stiffly, handed him a flower, and accepted the drink.

I made to leave the tent, but the man said, "Won't you hu-mor me by telling me how it tastes? It is a recipe of my own creation."

I hesitated, but under the man's mostly friendly, slightly pity-ing smile, I nodded. I took a sip—only to pull back in surprise. It was as though the drink had expired; it slithered down my throat, sticking at points along the way.

I looked up at the soldier. This simple motion sent the world spinning. The man watched me intently as he swayed side to side—or was I the one moving?

Black curled around the edges of my vision, dimming sound as well as light. I vaguely acknowledged that the cup had slipped out of my hand, though I was not sure when.

"Wait," I managed, but it was too late. I was already falling.

My senses returned one at a time. The swirling sound of un-obstructed wind tumbling across the world. A vaguely rotten stench that coated my nostrils. Soft, damp ground beneath me, and rough bark digging into my bare shoulders and upper back.

I opened my eyes. Sand stretched endlessly in front of me, curving in the distance to meet the ink-black sky.

I shivered; the Sahara's nights were as cold as its days were hot. Voices brought my attention to a small lake nearby. Standing at its moonlit shore were two men. Neither were the soldier who had tricked me. They wore the long woolen robes of travelers—which were caked with grime—and each of their heads and faces were covered by a litham so that only their eyes were visible. Judging from how they waved their hands about them, they were discussing the next steps of their trip— but to where?

Panic welled in my chest. I hauled myself to my feet with the help of the palm tree behind me, but as I looked around, any hope of escape shriveled. Beyond the island of green on which I stood was an endless sea of sandy dunes. I would not last long outside of this oasis.

A shout launched my heart into my throat. The men had noticed I was awake—one pointed at me. He crouched and, with his face turned to me, slowly scooped a waterskin in the lake, as if to make sure I did not miss a thing. Then him and the other man climbed up the short but steep lake bed. In my fright, I could only watch as they drew nearer until they were close enough for the first man to extend the waterskin to me.

"Water?"

I did not move; accepting a drink from a stranger was what had stranded me here in the first place. As if he could hear my suspicion, the man grunted and waved a hand behind him at the lake.

I realized he was right—this time, at least, I was certain of what he offered me; I had watched him collect the water myself. Cautiously, I took the waterskin and drank, draining the skin in two large gulps.

Wiping the back of my hand over my mouth, I returned the waterskin to the man. "Who are you?" I asked.

One man began speaking in a melodic language that was neither Arabic nor Yorùbá, the only two languages I spoke.

"I can't understand you," I interrupted. "Are you able to speak something else?"

I asked in Arabic, for that was what he had first spoken to me in, and I hoped he would return to it. But the two men merely looked at each other. Because their faces were covered, their bemusement was shown in other ways—the flick of one man's hands, the tilt of the other's head. Then, as one, they shrugged and turned back to me.

"Water," the first one repeated. The other nodded in agreement.

Of course—the stained woolen robes, the foreign tongue. These men did not just travel through the Sahara; they lived here.

I had heard of the desert nomads, the only people in existence who could navigate the desert using the position of the stars and the patterns left by the wind. Several kingdoms below the Sahara relied on them to uphold the vital trade of salt from their mines in Taghaza.

Taghaza. A chill ran down my neck. That must be where these men were taking me, to that desolate city in the middle of the Sahara. I knew criminals and captives were sold to Taghaza, but I never thought nomads *took* slaves themselves.

I could not survive a week in Taghaza. Even for men much stronger and healthier than I, the salt mines were a death sentence.

I took a slow, shaky breath, and I released it just as slow. Then, I launched into a sprint.

The nomads were faster. I had not taken more than a couple of steps when my wrist was yanked back. Caught off balance, I stumbled back into a torso and a pair of arms snaked around me.

"No!" I shrieked as I struggled against my captor in vain. "Let me go!"

A guttural sound vibrated within the man's chest—a command. I kicked and screamed, but that did not stop the second man from smashing a wet, dirty cloth against my face.

An acrid scent stung my nose, burning a path to my temples.

My vision blurred, sharpened, then darkened. Gradually, my body failed to obey my screaming mind.

The last thing I saw was the nomad. His voice was a distant buzz, and his free hand waved next to him as he and his companion continued discussing their travel plans while I blacked out.

When I next regained consciousness, the men were gone.

Traces of whatever herb had been on the nomad's cloth lingered in the back of my mind, pressing dully against my eyes. I lifted myself from scarlet cushions to observe my new plush surroundings. I had seen enough rich men to know that I was in a palanquin, though until now, I had never seen the interior of one. They were gallant displays of wealth—and a rather inefficient method of travel for a journey to Taghaza.

I pulled back a netted curtain, and sunlight poured inside. I blinked rapidly, hoping that each time my eyes opened, my mind would be better able to make sense of the sight before me.

A polished stone road gleaming in sunlight. Patches of green grass overflowing with colorful flowers. Towering mud buildings with gilded accents creeping up their sides like golden vines. Older men in fine tunics, gold woven in their curly beards. Clusters of giggling women dressed in vibrant wrappers and dresses. Music drifting lazily over tall trees that waved at me with green fingers.

The heat here was heavier. I was not in the salt mines, but I had not returned to Timbuktu either. I had only heard storytellers speak of one city so lush: Ṣàngótẹ̀, the city in which the Aláàfin of Yorùbáland resided.

Panic twisted my insides. Ṣàngótẹ̀ was in the Sahel, the shores of the Sahara; why would I be deposited in the south when that only prolonged the journey north to Taghaza?

Eventually, the palanquin came to a halt before a massive

stone barrier. Parapets and towers dotted the very top of the
wall, where bowmen stood watch next to white puffs of clouds.
A man yelled, my dread muddling his words in my ears, and a
loud creak ground through the air. The gates opened inward,
but not before I saw a bronze emblem engraved into them.

The emblem was the silhouette of three elephant heads: one
looking to the past, one to the future, and the middle one facing forward, looking directly at the present. Their trunks were
curved upward, their mouths open in a silent war cry. The
image was so widespread that it had been well-known in Timbuktu even before the Yorùbá had captured the city. Every man,
woman, and child west of the Niger knew it. It was the pin that
held soldiers' capes; the imprint in the wax that sealed official
envelopes; the design that could be found on pots and rugs on
every street corner.

It was the symbol of the Aláàfin.

I sat, numb with shock, as the palanquin proceeded through
the gates. So great was the Aláàfin's compound that they did not
call it a palace, as with other kings, but rather *the royal city*.

Stretching all around me were stone paths, of which every
other brick was paved with bronze. The paths cut through
trimmed grass fields that held elaborate mud buildings, each
with domed roofs and doors accented by gold and bronze. The
scene shone so brightly that it was difficult to tell if it was the sun
that illuminated them or the other way around.

There were barracks for soldiers and living quarters for slaves.
There were entire houses, complete with gates and gardens, for
the Aláàfin's court to live in with their families. I passed storehouses of food, fabrics, and weapons. I glimpsed mountains of
copper, cowrie shells, and bronze within treasuries that were
heavily guarded by soldiers with iron spears. At some point, I
heard scattered brays and a faint pounding of hooves, but before
I could peek out the other side of the palanquin, I had turned the
corner to begin down another vast path.

The splendor was as unsettling as it was astonishing. By the

time the palanquin finally came to a halt, I was cold with fear.
I was lowered to the ground slowly—though my stomach still
dropped abruptly—and two of my carriers came around to
pull me out. They guided me up a short flight of ivory steps
leading to a lavish curtain draped over the entrance of a stone
building. Four women waited in front of it, their humble attire
indicating that they were slaves.

The men handed me off to the women, who respectfully knelt
on the ground—thanking the men, I assumed—before ushering
me into the building. Immediately, a cloud of steam bestowed
damp kisses on my skin. High walls, some lined with latrines,
were without a ceiling to connect them, allowing sun to stream
freely onto the pool at the center of the room. My disrobing was
strikingly efficient, and I was soon lowered into the sparkling
water and immersed in the scent of jasmine as well as the women's
incessant stream of compliments.

"You're gorgeous, my dear—isn't she gorgeous?"

"Yes-o, see how smooth her skin is!"

"Such beautiful brown eyes!"

Standing around me in their smallclothes, the women loosened my cornrows so that my hair floated in a massive black
cloud around me. They scrubbed me from scalp to sole, their
black soap and netted cloths stripping away layer after layer of
grime.

Their overlapping voices and the overwhelming perfume
made my head swim. I could not understand why the women
were being so kind. As they guided me out of the water,
wrapped me in a silk robe, and slid my feet into soft slippers,
I thought of Okóbí. My mother never liked me out of her sight
for long; what did she make of my absence? Even if she somehow discovered I had been sold into slavery, I did not know if
there was anything she could do about it—I did not know if
there was anything she *would* do. All I had ever caused her was
grief. Maybe she would think it was better this way.

The women ushered me out the bathhouse, to a large field

bordered by a mud wall. Guards posted at the opening of the
wall nodded to us as we walked through. Within was yet another one of the royal city's neighborhoods, made up of large
mud-brick huts. Groups of richly dressed women paused in their
conversations to stare as I walked by.

I was saved from their scrutiny as the slave women brought
me into a hut. The single room was more spacious than any
other hut I'd ever seen; nearly the size of a small house, it easily
held a velvet divan, a fine wooden table and stool, and a handful of small bronze statues. There was even a bed, its raised
wood frame supporting a wool-stuffed mattress swathed in linen
sheets. On one end of the bed sat a curved wooden headrest, the
base of which was lacquered with gold. I knew this could not be
my dwelling; as rich as the Aláàfin was, it was unlikely he would
spare the luxury of furniture for a slave.

The women nudged me onto a stool then walked to a table
laden with glass containers of varying shapes, sizes, and colors. I
was unsure what to make of them until the women each grasped
two and turned to me.

Still showering me with compliments, they navigated around
my robe to work oils, butters, and perfumes into my hair and
skin until my limbs glowed black. A butter that smelled like ripe
mangoes was massaged into my face, and the scent was sweet
enough to renew my hunger pains.

"This is her?" a soft voice cut through the chatter.

A new woman had entered the room. She was shorter and
skinnier than me, but the lines that crinkled at the corners of
her eyes told me she had been smiling for longer than I had been
alive. Hanging from one of her arms was a dress made of aṣọ òkè
fabric. She carefully placed it on the table before turning back to
me. She held up a hand, and, as one, the other women stepped
back, suddenly quiet with their heads bowed.

"I am Ìgbín, the tailor who attends to the women of the royal
city," the newcomer said. Her words came quickly but were not
rushed; she spoke with the speed and precision of someone who

knew exactly what they wanted to say and who intended to say only that, not a breath more.

Ìgbín raised a jumble of fabric that unfurled down into a long blue strip. "May I?"

I eyed the cloth warily, but when I looked back at Ìgbín, my apprehension eased. Her smile was kind, the first humanizing encounter I had since arriving. I realized that over the course of the past few days, I had somehow been attended to the point of neglect.

My shoulders lifted, and my head jerked forward. Accepting this cross of a shrug and a nod as consent, Ìgbín began wrapping the strip around my waist, arms, shoulders. I felt nothing; I only saw flashes of blue winding around me.

"Typically," she said as she worked, "I will attend to you first thing in the morning, so please forgive my tardiness today. I was not informed of your existence until moments after your arrival."

She stepped back and began rolling the strip into a ball, apparently finished, though I had not seen her write anything down. "Because I am not yet familiar with your tastes," she continued, "I have brought you one of my previous pieces, recently worn for the same occasion. I will make adjustments for you now."

Ìgbín was silent for a moment. With a jolt, I realized that she awaited a response. I gave her a stiff nod, and she raised a brow, her brown eyes searching.

Then she said gently, "I am sure this is scary, but have no fear. You will make a lovely bride."

My heart came to a grinding halt. *Bride?*

Ìgbín met my blank stare with a smile then turned to the dress she had brought. It took a few beats before my heart was able to restart, and my mind with it.

"What do you mean, *bride*?" I asked hoarsely.

Behind me, a murmur passed through the women who had attended to me. Ìgbín looked at me, and when she saw the sincerity in my face, her disbelief grew.

"You are unaware?" she asked, slightly incredulous. Her eyes darted to the women, and I followed her gaze. I briefly caught the varying expressions of humor and horror my attendants wore before they saw that I was looking and wiped their faces into polite, blank smiles.

Ìgbín's hands closed around one of my own, bringing my attention back to her. There was sympathy in her smile now.

"My dear, you are to be the bride of the Aláàfin."

3

Bride of the Aláàfin.

As I was carried through the royal city in a palanquin, I stared numbly at the velvet interior, trapped in a dreamlike state. No matter how hard I tried, it seemed I could not wake. *Bride of* the *Aláàfin*.

The palanquin stopped at a field. This time, when one of my carriers came to the curtain, I allowed him to help me stand up. Partly because I did not want to be dragged out again, but mostly because I did require his help; my new dress complicated an action as simple as standing.

The vivid red garment glittered violently in the sunlight. Silver accents dripped over the aṣọ òkè material in elegant designs and lined my flared sleeves as well as the hem of my dress. Thanks to Ìgbín's adjustments, the dress clung to me like a second skin, leaving me little choice but to stay still once guards positioned me under a tree's shade.

My hair had been redone into one long cornrow, wound around my head and pressed flat against my scalp to accommodate my enormous gèlè. The headpiece's weight was so great that I was half convinced it was real silver. I feared that tilting my face too far to one side would unbalance me entirely—though perhaps the large beaded necklaces looped several times over my neck would serve as a decent counterweight.

There was a waist-high stone wall ahead of me. Behind it, on lower ground, loomed a colossal mud structure. It had large, gaping archways spaced along its front, each one under a high dome.

Stemming from within the magnificent edifice were shrill roars that sent tremors through the ground beneath my bejeweled slippers. Whether they came from man, beast, or both, I could not tell.

My unease was only heightened by the soldiers along the perimeter of the field. Each man wore only cotton breeches, emphasizing builds so tall and muscular that their spears seemed unnecessary. I could not shake the feeling that their task was to keep me safe as much as it was to keep me from running.

"The Aláàfin approaches!" cried one soldier. The rest snapped into attention.

The racket seemed to grow louder, and fear twisted my stomach. Was it a creature in there, making that noise, or the Aláàfin? Were they one in the same? A scream sounded. I felt the urge to run, but I could not move, even as the commotion grew louder, and louder, and—

"It is customary for subjects to kneel before their king," a voice whispered in my ear. "Or at least look at him."

I whirled around. When I saw the man who grinned down at me, the air vanished from my lungs.

It's my dehydration, I reasoned. *My eyes are playing tricks on me.*

But even as I thought this, I knew it was not true. I was no longer in the desert, and this was no mirage. The man before me now was indeed the same stranger whom I had met over a week prior; the vagrant to whom I had given a flower.

Except he did not look remotely homeless now. In place of torn, dirty clothes, he wore a billowy white shirt and slim-fitting trousers that shone against his bronze skin. His black curls were now clean and divided into small individual braids that reached past his shoulders. Many of the braids, I noticed, were decorated with gold cuffs and cowrie shells.

But his smile—it was the same radiant smile I remembered, one that somehow glowed brighter than his attire. In my shock, I meant to take a step back, but the world had become off-balance, and I stumbled instead.

Before I could fall, the man was at my side with a steadying hand on my back. "Alálẹ̀ Òdòdó," he uttered as one did a prayer. "Hello."

"Hi," I said, my voice small and breathless.

A pause.

"You're—?" I began, but disbelief tangled my words together.

His smile widened, summoning a single dimple on his right cheek. "I have many names. You need only call me Àrẹ̀mọ."

I stared. This was *absurd*. He was a begger, a low-ranked soldier at best. He was not—he simply could not be—

"My king!"

I quickly stepped away from Àrẹ̀mọ as a man hurried toward us. The man's skin was the smooth brown of a bitter kola nut, and a floor-length indigo robe dangled off his gangly frame. A matching soft fez cap was perched atop his long individual braids, which were as gray as his braided beard. Four slaves followed him, each carrying a large wooden chest.

"My king," the man repeated as he halted near enough that I could now hear the scorn in his deep voice. "I must admit I am rather uncomfortable with this ordeal. Your mother and the princess are still away at a party—at least wait for their return."

Àrẹ̀mọ raised a brow. "I do not require their permission, Gassire."

"No, of course not," Gassire agreed quickly. "I only meant— perhaps you would like to include them in your sudden plans to parade your future wife around the capital. Or at least inform them that you now *have* a future wife."

"I plan to tell everyone—at a feast. How does a feast sound?"

Gassire pinched the bridge of his broad nose. "Like a spontaneous end to a day chaotic even by your standards."

"Excellent, because I've already informed the cooks. Gather the court. Let them know that, in honor of my beautiful bride, there will be a feast after the parade—speaking of which, where is Ajá?"

Àrẹ̀mọ looked at me expectantly. I did not know whether to laugh or cry.

"Parade?" I echoed, slightly dizzy. "Through Ṣàngótẹ̀?"

A nearby soldier stepped forward. "I've sent two men to wrestle with Bínú," he told Àrẹ̀mọ, gesturing beyond the wall. All at once, I became aware again of the ongoing racket from within the building.

A shadow crossed Àrẹ̀mọ's smiling face. "And Ajá?"

The soldier faltered. Gassire, on the other hand, said, "Oh give the man a break. No sane person would willingly approach Ajá."

Àrẹ̀mọ considered the soldier, rubbing the ring on his thumb against his chin. After a moment, his attention shifted to Gassire, and I swore I heard the soldier give an almost imperceptible sigh. I wondered how terrible Àrẹ̀mọ's temper was that the soldier was so relieved to have avoided it. Then I wondered who Gassire was that his comment had not wrought Àrẹ̀mọ's ire onto him instead.

"Bínú is too difficult," Àrẹ̀mọ said. He gestured at the shaking building, as if it proved his point.

"And Ajá is too dangerous," Gassire countered.

"Bínú was loyal to my father. He followed him everywhere—I expect Bínú will soon follow him to the grave as well." Àrẹ̀mọ turned away. "Ajá represents the current Aláàfin. If no one else will get him, I'll do it myself."

Gassire and the soldiers called out, but Àrẹ̀mọ had already hopped over the wall. He walked to one of the building's archways and yelled, "I've grown weary of your incompetence. Leave him."

Two soldiers emerged from the building. The silence that followed them was overwhelming in its abruptness. Upon seeing Àrẹ̀mọ, they dropped to their knees, their heads bowed in shame. Àrèmọ paid no heed to their muttered apologies, continuing down the length of the building until he came to a halt in front of a different archway.

"Ajá," he called, patting the wall twice. "We're going for a walk."

He stepped back then clasped his hands behind him, waiting. The groveling men jumped to their feet and made a beeline to the wall, scrambling over it with the help of the soldiers on this side of the wall.

This miserable day had already overwhelmed my capacity for confusion; whatever monster lurked in the bowels of that building could not surprise me. I expected Ajá to be a beast with a dozen heads and a single eye, or even the trickster òrìṣà Èṣù, who had descended from the heavens to personally deliver the final punch line of this joke that everyone except for me seemed to be in on.

What I had not expected to emerge from the shadows was an elephant. Bit by bit, sunlight illuminated its black skin. Large ears flapped around its head as it approached timidly. When it saw Àrèmọ, it paused and tilted its head curiously.

Then it charged.

Its thunderous gallop shook the ground. A furious trumpet erupted from it, dwarfing the yells of the soldiers who stood at the wall but did not dare go over it themselves. Beside me, Gassire watched with wide eyes, muttering curses around his knuckles held between his teeth.

Àrèmọ was the only one who was calm. As the elephant neared, he merely smiled. He was very brave. Or, perhaps, very foolish.

Either way, he's going to be trampled. The realization carried with it a twinge of fear; if he died, there would be no one to marry. I would have to leave this world before I even entered it.

I wondered if I should feel guilty about the inconsiderate and possibly ludicrous thought, but I was not left to wonder for long;

just as the elephant came within an arm's reach of Àrèmọ, it suddenly stopped. Its ears flared around its raised head, and its ivory tusks glimmered dangerously.

After a moment, it ambled the rest of the way to Àrèmọ, the murder gone from its amber eyes.

Laughing, Àrèmọ wrapped his arms around one of its great stubby legs. "Good to see you, my friend."

In response, Ajá snorted.

Àrèmọ gave his elephant a pat before walking to the wall. As he smoothly lifted himself back over it, he said, "Remove the ornaments from Bínú's stable and put them on Ajá."

When no one responded, Àrèmọ looked up from brushing dust off his shirt. I glanced at the men and saw my own amazement reflected on their faces.

Àrèmọ propped his hands on his hips and turned to his elephant. "Ajá is always less fickle after he's gotten his tantrum out, but it's difficult to say how long his good mood will last. It's best to take advantage of it." He turned back to the soldiers. "Quickly."

The men sprang into action, clearing the wall and jogging to the first archway. I watched in bemusement as they retrieved a large square saddle and various cloths then placed them around Ajá, who pawed at the ground.

"If you take her beyond these walls," Gassire said quietly, bringing my attention to him, "if you announce a new bride, that makes this engagement official. Are you certain that you wish to proceed?"

An intense gleam flashed across Àrèmọ's black eyes. "I am."

I cleared my throat. "Can I ask—?"

"Very well then," Gassire said, cutting me off. "But if you insist on doing this, you will do it properly."

He snapped his fingers over his shoulder. His slaves started forward as he continued, "You must get dressed. Do not embarrass your subjects by looking like an ordinary man."

I frowned; Àrèmọ looked clothed to me. But not enough,

apparently, for the slaves set the chests before us with heavy thuds and threw back the lids, revealing fabrics of endless colors and piles upon piles of jewelry.

Silently and efficiently, the slaves transformed Àrẹ̀mọ before my eyes. They layered onto him tunics embellished with tassels, then jackets made of the finest cloth, then draperies embroidered with vivid artwork of animals and beans and plants. They slipped his feet into vibrant slippers with jewel-encrusted shin guards. They wrapped his neck with necklaces of gold and bronze and wood that were so long they needed to be looped over his head three times each. They poured rings with bulging gemstones onto his fingers, and they clasped so many bracelets on his arms that he rang like a bell from the slightest movement.

By the time they were finished, Àrẹ̀mọ's form was completely obliterated under color, jewels, and baubles, converting him into a kaleidoscopic entity.

"Then it's true," I said, in amazement, in terror. I had figured out as much, of course, but looking at this half man, half god in front of me, only now did it fully hit me. "You're the Aláàfin of Yorùbáland."

Àrẹ̀mọ smiled. Gassire, on the other hand, cast me a withering look before turning back to Àrẹ̀mọ. "And of course, you must wear your crown," he said.

A slave set a long, thin wooden box on the ground. From it, he extracted a conical headpiece that was nearly as long as my arm. It was made entirely of bronze, and red and white beads coiled around it all the way to its pointed top. Strung to the crown's brim was what must have been hundreds of long white beads, rustling softly.

"My king, Ajá is ready," one of the soldiers called.

The elephant was now as richly garbed as his owner. A shining bronze plate was fastened to his face, tapered on the bottom to fit the base of his trunk. His back was covered by a massive red caparison that had bronze tassels dangling from its edges. Atop the rich cloth was a large wooden saddle chair secured by rope looping under the elephant. The soldiers gave Ajá a wide berth; two were crouched around one other, who seemed to have been knocked unconscious.

"Excellent." Àrèmọ smiled at me and held out a glittering hand. "Come. So many wonders await beyond that wall. And I want them all to see you."

Boom. BOOM. Rat-tat, boom.

I clutched the saddle's railing so tightly that the wood nearly cracked, but I dared not ease my grip as I shifted left then right then left again, swaying on Ajá's heavy, uneven stride.

Although the stone gate before me was different than the one through which I had arrived, it was just as massive. One of the soldiers escorting Ajá yelled up to the men standing on the parapets, and a moment later, the gate parted.

The ceaseless drumming swelled and streamed in through the opening. Above, clouds had started to congregate, threatening a storm. Outside the royal city, illuminated by the day's gray light, stood a block of men. Each had a djembe drum strapped to his front. They began marching forward as one, their feet in time with their beat. I lurched forward as Ajá strutted behind them, his trunk held high for the colorful crowd that stretched from the gates to far down the street. The mix of pounding drums, cheering voices, and wonderful fragrances all soared wildly above Sàngótẹ̀ as our procession sailed through the sea of people.

I braved a glance over the side of Ajá. Far below me swam excited faces—young and old, man and woman. A group of children shrieked with delight when my gaze fell onto them. One little girl—her afro as big as her body—waved vigorously.

"You can wave back, you know," Àrèmọ's amused voice grazed my ear. He sat behind me, his robes swirling around us and spilling over the sides of the saddle.

"I'm not letting go."

My voice was hardly more than a whisper, but Àrèmọ must

have heard me, because he chuckled. "You won't fall. I would never allow it."

He placed his hands beside my own. I looked over my shoulder and my gèlè brushed the white beads streaming from his crown, which completely replaced his face with a white wall.

As the beads rustled in my ear, my curiosity piqued. "Why do you wear that?"

"You don't know that kings wear crowns?"

"I do, which is why I asked why you're wearing *that*."

Àrèmọ laughed again. Despite my fear, I could acknowledge how lovely of a sound it was.

"My face is of little importance to my subjects," he explained. "It is only my title they know, something the crown assures. It is the glue that stretches over generations and merges every Aláàfin—past, present, and future—into one ruler."

One ruler, I reflected silently, watching the screaming faces below. When they looked at Àrèmọ, all they saw was a beaded mask, constant in the face of time. For all they knew, the Aláàfin was a single undying king.

Silence twined between us. But as we turned a street corner and were greeted by another enthusiastic crowd, Àrèmọ pulled the silence apart.

"Does that unsettle you?" he asked.

In truth, the Aláàfin's unique immortality did not distress me nearly as much as my sudden engagement to him. But I dared not say anything that might provoke him—especially with the fall to the ground being so far. I merely shrugged.

"Look at me," he said. When I hesitated, he added, "Please."

Reluctantly, I looked. He parted his crown's beads, just enough to unmask his face.

"Crown or not, I'm me."

I held his tender gaze for a moment before facing straight ahead. His words were clearly meant to put me at ease, but they did not change the fact that my mother was most likely worried out of her mind about me. They did not change that now, standing on the precipice of the better life I had always wanted, I was filled with doubt about making the jump, unsure if it was even real.

No, his words did not calm me—but his smile. His smile did. Because for a moment, the noise had faded, and the extravagance had melted away. For a moment, he had once again become the ragged traveler with a dimpled smile to whom I had gifted a silver flower.

It was not exactly comforting, but it was familiar. And I did not know how badly I needed familiar until now. As Ajá continued through the capital, I found myself leaning into Àrẹ̀mọ. When he wrapped an arm around my torso and pulled me closer, I let him.

His embrace immersed me in a faint scent of rain. The one right before the sky ripped open, and water poured down.

B y the time we returned to the royal city, cold rain sprinkled
from the sky.

After Àrèmọ shed his crown and most of his layers, we
left a restless Ajá with frightened stable hands and were carried
via palanquin to a massive mud building. As we made our way
up the great ivory steps—trailed by soldiers and slaves—and
passed through a tall archway, I saw that this Èṣù-harassed day
was far from over.

Positioned under large windows were gilded braziers with
crackling flames. The brown walls were decorated with rock
paintings—silhouettes of valiant warriors; herds of antelope;
side-facing women with hair larger than their heads; rhinocer-
oses that stretched from the floor high up to the ceiling.

At the center of the room was a long table of polished wood.
Men and women were seated around it, their high backed chairs
trimmed with gold. The diners' colorful ensembles and abundance of jewels did not equal Àrèmọ at his height of opulence,
but they certainly came close. Their conversation was backed
by the lively music played by drummers in a corner of the room.

Gassire, who stood next to the entrance, was the first to notice
our arrival. He nodded at Àrèmọ before turning to the musicians, and, with a raised hand, he silenced them mid song.

"Ọba kìí pọ̀kọrin," Gassire boomed, his arms held wide.
"Àrèmọ Tèmítọ́pẹ́ Ológun Babátúndé Gbekude, Aláàfin of
Yorùbáland, King of Ṣàngótẹ̀, Leader of the Aláràà, Son of Àgò,

Descendant of Ṣàngó, enters with his soon to be wife, the Alálẹ̀
called Òdòdó."

Applause burst from the table as the musicians picked up a
new merry song. I eyed Gassire with a newfound understanding.

"He's your griot?" I whispered to Àrẹ̀mọ.

"Yes, Gassire is the royal griot." Àrẹ̀mọ did not bother whispering in return, and I winced as Gassire scowled at me from
where he stood just a few paces away.

"His parents were very original, naming him after the very
first griot, just as so many other griots have been named," Àrẹ̀mọ
continued absently. He seemed distracted; his eyes roamed over
the slaves who stood on the outskirts of the room.

Then he gave me a brief smile and took my hand. "Come.
The feast cannot begin until we sit."

As he guided me forward, I felt the heat of dozens of eyes searing into me. I kept my gaze down, wishing we could move faster,
but Àrẹ̀mọ could not go more than a few steps without clapping
a man on the shoulder and greeting him.

But once Àrẹ̀mọ and I reached the head of the table, my
discomfort was forgotten; the moment we sat, slaves launched
forward, bearing an extravaganza of food. Fresh crayfish and
spinach swelled in thick ẹ̀gúsí soup. Orange jollof rice swathed in
diced tomatoes, onions, and peppers gleamed on silver plates. Savory scents wafted from steaming vegetable stews of beef, chicken,
and goat. Heaps of sweet plantain slices, piles of crunchy bean
cakes, and mounds of golden meat pies were stacked high between
the abundant entrees.

I eagerly reached for the nearest plate, but Àrẹ̀mọ stopped
me. He beckoned to a slave, who served me a bowl of stew and
a plate of yam that was pounded and crushed into a doughlike
consistency. When I looked at Àrẹ̀mọ questioningly, he explained in a low voice, "Eating this will secure your place here."

I did not know what he meant, but I had no intention of refus-
ing the food; my hunger pains, having been forgotten amidst the

chaos of the day, now returned tenfold. My stomach was nearly as loud as the storm brewing outside.

My mouth watering, I tore a piece from the ball of pounded yam, dipped it in the stew, and ate it. The yam was so soft that it melted away, and the stew heated my stomach in a welcoming embrace. From the golden goblet before me, I gratefully drank a creamy millet beverage. Growing up as a blacksmith provided for by the city of Timbuktu meant that I had never gone hungry, but I had never been presented with such an excess of food either.

Some bites were lumpy, but I was more than familiar with semi-mashed yam, and it was delicious all the same. As the food settled my stomach and my nerves with it, I chanced a glance around the room.

Àrèmọ conversed with a bearded man on his right. The nobles spoke among themselves, though their conversations did not seem very engaged. Despite their smiles and the musical backdrop, a certain tension pulled the air taut. More than once, my eyes met someone else's only for theirs to dart away. One man, however, did not avert his gaze when I caught him looking at me.

Beautiful.

The word surfaced in my mind unwillingly. The man's tunic and trousers were plain black, and he wore no jewelry other than a single gold earring. His simple attire only enhanced the reddish hue of his brown skin, like a flame against the night. His black curls were close cropped to his scalp, and stubble covered his high cheekbones, except for a portion of his right cheek where three vertical scars ran down to his chiseled jawline, as though he had been clawed at by a wild animal. The mark of the Ẹgbẹ́-Ọdẹ clan.

His large eyes, rimmed with full lashes, were unlike any I had ever seen, made up of shifting browns and greens so soft that they were liquid—and they blazed with rage.

Had it been anyone else, I would have cowered from such a

blatant display of fiery hatred. But the man was so attractive that, somehow, the prospect of getting burned did not seem so bad.

Women sat around him, pawing at his arm or trying to feed him, but his attention remained on me. I hesitated, then I lifted a hand to the man. Shock flit across his face, as though the small wave had carried with it a great audacity. Then his anger returned, burning hotter than before. In one smooth motion, he pulled a hunting knife from somewhere on his person and drove it into the plate in front of him.

The crack of the clay plate startled most of the diners, worst of all the women fawning over him. I eyed the knife with interest; the blade was of handsomely forged bronze.

Àrèmọ raised a hand, silencing the musicians. Now that the music had stopped, I could hear that the weather outside had escalated into a full thunderstorm.

"Something on your mind, Ọmóṣẹwà?" Àrèmọ asked the man.

"Now you wish to hear my thoughts, my king?" Ọmóṣẹwà asked. His voice was surprisingly soft, more in accordance with his delicate appearance than his coarse manner.

"Not particularly," Àrèmọ replied, "but I'd rather you release whatever's troubling you instead of taking it out on my mother's favorite plates."

The plate had a silver coating, I could not help but note. The knife had to be incredibly sharp to cut the plate in half so cleanly. The work of an expert blacksmith, I was sure.

"Whatever's troubling—?" Ọmóṣẹwà repeated indignantly. "My king, *she* is what is troubling."

He brandished a finger at me, and all at once, the nobles' attention was thrust onto me, as though they had been waiting for an excuse to look. Outside, thunder rolled through the sky. Shifting in my seat, I glanced at Àrèmọ, who smiled at Ọmóṣẹwà.

"You want to be careful with how you speak of her," Àrèmọ said pleasantly, "because I may just forget that we are friends."

The nobles exchanged uncomfortable glances. Ọmóṣẹwà wavered, but only for a moment; he leaned forward, his hand resting on the hilt of his knife, bringing my attention to the carvings in the wood.

The way that Ọmọ́ṣẹ̀wà had to adjust his grip around the carvings meant that they were for decoration, not function. Not many blacksmiths would waste time on such frivolities; not unless the order was for a person of great importance.

"You plucked the girl off the streets," Ọmọ́ṣẹ̀wà pressed.

"You," Àrẹ̀mọ said, "have found wives under more questionable circumstances."

Some of the women around Ọmọ́ṣẹ̀wà fidgeted. Through gritted teeth, Ọmọ́ṣẹ̀wà said, "I have never sunk so low as to seek out a *witch*."

Murmurs rippled down the table. He seemed so disgusted by witches, and yet . . .

I cleared my throat, drawing the men's attention to me. "Though it was a witch who made that hunting knife you seem to love so much."

To my surprise, there came a smattering of chuckles. Out of the corner of my eye, I saw Àrẹ̀mọ grin at me.

Ọmọ́ṣẹ̀wà looked murderous. He uprooted the knife and threw it onto the table with a clatter as he stood. "You have my unconditional loyalty, my king, but I simply cannot watch you marry that girl."

He moved to leave, but before he could take more than a few steps, three soldiers rushed forth and raised a hand to his chest.

Ọmọ́ṣẹ̀wà swatted their hands away and whirled around. "What is this?"

"I would prefer if you stayed," Àrẹ̀mọ said with a lazy flick of his goblet. "Partake in my joy, my friend."

Ọmọ́ṣẹ̀wà wrenched his mouth open, but before he could respond, a noblewoman sighed. "Oh, Ọmọ́ṣẹ̀wà, enough with the dramatics. Leave the entertainment to the musicians."

"Was a single cup of palm wine too much for him?" another woman asked. "It's no wonder soldiers are forbidden from drinking . . ."

Another, healthier round of laughter went around the room, only further infuriating the man. A growing panic prevented me from joining in; they could tease Ọmọ́sẹ̀wà now, but if he continued to oppose my engagement to Àrẹ̀mọ, others may begin to agree with him.

Àrẹ̀mọ had said that eating this food would ensure I stayed. I took a piece of yam, inspecting it closely. It was another lumpy piece, the sixth or seventh I had encountered. This time, I noticed a minuscule brown spot within the cloud of white. As I picked away the yam, the spot grew. My pulse slowed. By the time I had completely uncovered the spot, my heart had come to a halt.

It was a cowpea.

The rest of the room seemed to fade, a white noise clogging my ears. I had thought Àrẹ̀mọ was impulsive, and perhaps a tad slow, but now I realized just how meticulous he was. I should have been frightened; I should have leapt from the table and flung the cowpea far, far away.

Instead, I slowly raised it. Hesitated. Then, I ate it. The bean seemed to crackle in my mouth, each bite sending a spark through me.

I could not think about what I was doing; if I did, I would lose my nerve. I sifted through the yam until I discovered another cowpea. But I had barely raised the bean to my mouth when it was slapped out of my hand.

"*Cowpea!*" yelled the diner next to me.

He pulled me away from the table. As other diners shouted and scrambled to their feet, it fully hit me: I had eaten cowpeas. *I had eaten cowpeas.*

My heart racing, I looked out a nearby window. It rained so heavily that it looked like shadows were falling from the night sky. My numbness was punctured by a sharp panic. The general in Timbuktu had eaten one cowpea, and when lightning flashed thereafter, he had been sentenced to death. What were the odds the Yorùbá would let me survive a trial before Ṣàngó, during a storm, after I had eaten *six* of their sacred beans?

Laughter sounded among the yells of terror. I looked to see Àrèmọ grinning at me, his eyes alight with chaos. Before I could react, he closed the distance between us and scooped me into his arms. More shouts sounded, but Àrèmọ had already jogged outside, into the storm.

Above, navy clouds caged the moon. Wind whirled around us, extinguishing the torches that bordered the field. Àrèmọ set me down in the grass, but my legs no longer supported me, and I fell to my knees.

Àrèmọ circled me, his arms stretched out on either side of him as he yelled to the sky, "Ṣàngó! I come to you as your devoted descendant, seeking your blessing for this union. If this girl is unworthy of marrying the Aláàfin, let your disapproval be known!"

Violent gales pulled at my clothes and sliced my skin, snatching away my breaths as soon as they had been expended. I could not run; even if my legs worked, the Aláràá would be quick to catch me. *What* had I been thinking when I dared to summon a god's attention?

But no sooner had I asked did images flash before my eyes—the scars covering my arms; my mother's weary face, and my sick auntie who we all knew would never get better; my auntie falling after that man had hit her. A man who had sought our help and threatened us in the same breath.

Anger blazed through my fear. Perhaps this was the part where I begged for mercy, but I could not bring myself to do so. I had been given a chance to escape the pathetic life of being a witch, and I took it. I did not regret that.

All it would take was for one flash of lightning to appear in the sky, and I would be condemned to death. Or perhaps in his wrath, Ṣàngó would strike me down directly. With each distant growl of thunder, I tensed, preparing for the damning verdict.

But lightning never came. Gradually, the wind slowed until

the night was still. I lifted my head shakily; the sky was clearing. The moon emerged from behind the clouds, serene and watchful.

"Ṣàngó yọ mí."

The grave prayer sounded behind me. Gassire, the slaves, soldiers, and nobles were all gathered in the archway. In the moonlight, I could just barely see their horror and rage.

"You have all borne witness to Ṣàngó's decision," Àrẹ̀mọ boomed. He was smiling, but a storm brewed behind his gaze. "Alálẹ̀ Òdòdó is to be my wife—to question this now is to question Ṣàngó himself. Who dares defy the will of a god?"

A gentle breeze floated through the air—the only response that Àrẹ̀mọ received.

I was carried back to the hut I had been clothed in.

There, my handmaids exchanged my dress for a sleeping gown, a silk robe, and a headscarf with tails that hung over my shoulder. After saying cheerful good nights, they left me alone in what I now knew to be my quarters. It was larger than my home in Timbuktu, which was a single room I had shared with my mother and all my aunties. Our work was endless, and anyways, the desert heat did not allow us to stay indoors for long.

Ṣàngótẹ̀'s heat was only slightly kinder, but staying in this hut would not be an issue. Even with the wooden door sealing the entrance, the windows curving with the round walls permitted a pleasant circulation of air.

I sat on the large woven rug in the center of the room, my legs tucked to one side of me. My hand absently traced over the three-headed elephant emblem embroidered into its center. I had almost died for this rug, I realized. Had my mother been here, she would have called me a fool. She would have every right to; I had been ill-prepared to face how big the world was—or perhaps how small I had always been.

But even so, this one rug was worth more than everything I had ever owned, and I had managed to grab hold of it. Despite my terror, as I watched the colorful fibers shift under my touch, I was uncertain if I could ever bring myself to let go.

My uncertainty of what to do next became so overwhelming that when a knock sounded at the door, I was relieved. That ease quickly subsided when it was Àrèmọ who entered.

"Òdòdó," he greeted. He took a step toward me. Paused. Seemed to think better of it. Then he walked to a divan, examining his hands as he sat.

After a moment, he said, "I wanted to apologize for Ọmóṣẹwà's attitude toward you. He's Ẹgbẹ́-Ọdẹ—they're quick to declare something as witchcraft. By far, they're the most superstitious clan of the Yorùbá tribe."

I tilted my head in disbelief. Àrèmọ sighed, scratching the back of his neck.

"Also," he added reluctantly, "I apologize if I scared you with the cowpea."

"Scared me? Your trick could have *killed* me."

"I know you realized those beans were in your food. Yet you continued eating anyways." When I did not respond, he took my silence as a confirmation and continued, "You understood as well as I did that extreme measures were required to prevent interference in our union. You ate those cowpeas because this is the life you want, as you once confided in me."

"I also vaguely recall that I asked for a bed of clouds, because that is the kind of absurdities that are spoken of in short, meaningless conversations with strangers."

Àrèmọ chuckled, still looking at his hands. I opened my mouth to say something, anything, that would wipe away his flippancy—but then I saw a flash of silver. My eyebrows unknitted slowly as I realized what he held: the flower I had given him when we first met.

"Perhaps our interaction was meaningless to you," he said quietly, "but you've ruined music for me. I've hired a dozen different musicians. None suffice. Every song that I've heard since yours has sounded just slightly out of tune."

Maybe it was my near encounter with death, or maybe it was the faint smile on his face that was the one straw too many piled onto an already loaded day, but I felt something inside me snap. Anger and frustration flooded through me, and the next thing I knew I was on my feet.

"You did all this for a *song*?"

He stood as well. "Òdòdó—"

"I never would have eaten cowpeas had you not presented them to me. Is that the game you are playing, one that uses my desperation as your entertainment? Did you enjoy watching me be nearly sentenced to death? Was it thrilling to pay nomads to transport me across the desert like some commodity? Most of all, have you finished having your fun now, my king? Because I am a very long way from home, and I am very tired, and I still do not understand what it is you want or why you think it is me who can give it to you."

With each question, I had drawn nearer to him until our faces were inches apart. He stared at me. I glared back.

After a moment, he dropped his gaze, rubbing his chin with one hand and twirling the flower in his other. "When I was a boy," he said at last, "I always made the royal babaláwo tell me the story of how humans were created. I'm sure you're familiar with it—Obàtálá journeyed down to Earth, where he constructed clay figures in his likeness. These became our bodies, into which supreme ruler Olódùmarè breathed souls, àṣẹ. And so our spirits came to wear these temporal masks during their time on Earth.

"Was it possible, I wondered, that two people could be molded from the same block of clay? I asked again and again. People dismissed my intrigue as childish curiosity, but the question only grew more potent with age. Then, just a few weeks ago, the òrìṣàs took pity on my lifelong conflict and finally answered me."

"They spoke to you?" I asked, grudgingly impressed. I never knew the Aláàfin had the divine privileges that babaláwos did.

But Àrèmọ shook his head. "They sent me a dream."

"So they spoke to you in a dream?"

"I do not know. I forgot the dream as soon as I woke up. But—
but," he repeated louder, over my scoff, "what I do remember is
that when I awoke, I had a hunger unlike anything I had ever
experienced. Nothing the cooks concocted could satisfy me. I
visited brothels, I sought the words of learned men. I fed every
appetite I could think of, traveling for days on horse and foot. I
could have consumed the entire world and still died famished.

"Just when I was about to burst from the emptiness inside me,
I joined my men in their final push to capture Timbuktu. And
there, I saw you. The moment I heard your song, I could breathe
again. I could feel."

Àrèmọ raised his hand, his palm facing me. My eyes flickered
between him and his hand. He watched me patiently.

Slowly, I mirrored the movement, lifting my own hand. After a moment of hesitation, when he still had not moved, I put
my hand to his. His hand curled over mine, our fingers locking
together.

"You see?" Àrèmọ whispered. "You see how naturally we fit?
As though the human body was created for the sole purpose of
completing another. If a person requires another to be whole,
then it is you who I want to complete me, Alálè Òdòdó."

I nearly flinched from the intensity in his gaze. It was the
same gleam that had briefly shone in his eyes when we first met.

I looked around at the spacious hut and its expensive furniture. It was almost what I had always dreamed of—almost.
There was one crucial piece missing. Although a part of me was
compelled to accept this life, no matter the cost, a larger, heavier
part of me knew that what was missing was too valuable to go
on without.

I extracted my hand from Àrèmọ's, my skin immediately cold
without his touch. "As questionable as your offer is, my king, I
thank you for it," I said. "Truly. But I must refuse. This is what
I have always wanted for myself—and for my mother. I cannot
marry you and live here, in the royal city, while she remains in
Timbuktu, slaving over a forge."

"Then I will bring her here to live with you," Àrẹ̀mọ said at once.

I chuckled humorlessly. "Your court was so delighted when you told them one witch would be living among them. I'm sure they'd be positively elated to have two."

"My nobles are as annoying as a pack of hyenas, but they cannot disobey me. None of them will pester you or your mother, I will make sure of it. And to prove my love for you, I will not force this marriage upon you. We will wait until your mother is here to give us her blessing."

I crossed my arms over my chest. Àrẹ̀mọ's expression contained no trace of humor; there was not even lust. The all-powerful Aláàfin was completely sincere about loving me. *Me.*

"You're serious," I said in wonder. "You really believe you've fallen in love with me? So soon?"

Àrẹ̀mọ shrugged. "What is love but a choice? I do not need to fall in love with you. I have chosen to step into it—and I pray that you choose me as well."

He pressed a kiss to my forehead. I was too tired to pull away.

"I will send for your mother first thing in the morning," he said, tucking the silver daffodil into his pocket as he made his exit. "Sleep well, my flower."

5

After Àrẹmọ left, I ran my hand over each intricate statue, each polished table, each smooth wall. The first time I circled my hut, it was with a mounting horror as I fully understood the life I had agreed to. The second time, it was with a blossoming joy as I realized that this was all mine.

The third time around, guilt and fear struck me so deeply that I made the abrupt decision to leave and return to my mother. However, I only made it as far as the guards at the entrance of the women's compound when I turned back around. There were guards everywhere in the royal city, all reporting to the Aláà-fin. And as determined as he seemed to please me, I doubted he would let me simply walk away.

Anyways, it was not uncommon for rich men to marry pretty girls who they had only seen once. Sure, the man usually needed to beg the family's blessing with gifts and gold, but I supposed the Aláàfin need not beg. A man of his status could take anything he wanted.

And, I reminded myself, this was what I wanted too. If Àrẹmọ kept his word, then I would finally save myself and my mother from a life of hard labor and disrespect.

It was this thought with which I tried to comfort myself as I finally crawled onto the bed. Outside, the sky was already tinged with gray. I did not think I would be able to fall asleep, but I must have, because the next thing I knew a slam jerked me from a dreamless slumber.

Lively voices trilled painfully off my mind. I peered blearily at the sudden flock of women flitting around. With a groan, I coaxed sleep away from my eyes with the heel of my palms as their chirping and twittering filled the room.

"And replace the bronze statues with gold," the haughty voice of an older woman was saying. "Bronze is too valuable to be in the hands of a commoner."

"Yes, Mama Aláàfin," came a high-pitched response.

"Oh!" the first woman gasped. "Have these people tracked dirt onto my rug already? Take it outside and beat the dust from it."

"Yes, Mama Aláàfin."

"While you're at it, replace it with one from our local collection. Actually, a rug from one of the horses' stables should do and do you plan on staying in that bed all day or will you ever come greet me?"

The room quieted. With a jolt, I realized that the abrupt question was addressed to me. Now fully awake, I removed my hands from my face.

My handmaids and another set of slave women were scattered through the room, holding statues or else standing around the rug now rolled into a large cylinder. As my gaze met each of theirs, they sank to their knees and bowed their heads as they said a cheerful "Good morning, my lady" before diving back into their tasks.

One woman, however, did not move. Her hands, clasped in front of her, were concealed by sleeves that flared at her elbows and dripped down to her knees. Her lace dress was as silver as the beaded cornrows that zigged and zagged over her head in complicated patterns then cascaded down to her full hips. The woman looked at me expectantly, encasing me in her hard amber eyes.

Mama Aláàfin, they called her, I reflected. Then I saw it—the same strong jaw, the same broad nose, the same unbent posture.

There was no denying it. This was Àrèmọ's mother.

I slipped out of the bed. Before my feet touched the ground, a handmaid placed slippers in front of me, giving me a soft landing. Another handmaid appeared at my side to wrap my silk robe around me.

I blinked, but they had already returned to their work. As the shock of their efficiency wore off, I approached Àrèmọ's mother. Although I was a good head taller, her severe gaze made me feel like I was the smaller one.

"Good morning, ma," I said, kneeling before her. Normally, I was good at paying obeisance, but nerves made me shaky.

She noticed; a crease appeared between her brows. I knew that it would not stick. The smoothness of her skin meant she had never had a reason to frown for long. And from its sandy complexion, I deduced that she had never been made to spend long periods of time in the sun either.

A single knock sounded at the door. Ìgbín slipped inside, a rich purple wrapper draped over her arm.

She knelt on the ground. "Good morning, ma."

"Ìgbín," Mama Aláàfin greeted. "You've come to clothe the girl?"

"I'll take her measurements first, if she does not mind."

Ìgbín offered me a small smile, patiently awaiting my response. I nodded; Ìgbín was kind enough that I did not mind her taking my measurements again, though she had just done so yesterday.

As the tailor's nimble touch fluttered around me, Mama Aláàfin said, "Good. Perhaps once the girl looks like a noble, the manners of one will seep into her."

Her gaze was pointed. I looked away, heat blooming on my cheeks.

"Abeg," Mama Aláàfin continued, "I do not know what that boy was thinking. He could have named anyone else as his bride—the daughter of a general, of a king."

"He has been approached by such women before, my lady, but if I recall correctly, you were displeased with them as well," Ìgbín remarked, faintly amused.

"Still, they are better than a witch!"

Mama Aláàfin delicately collapsed onto a divan and held out her hand. Half of a breath later, a handmaid was at her side, giving her a golden goblet of palm wine.

Mama Aláàfin said, "And why just one woman? By the time Àrèmọ's father was twenty-five, he was on his fourth wife and sixth child. Àrèmọ barely has one wife! And now her," she added, gesturing toward me. "Do you know how odd that looks?"

"General Rótìmí just turned thirty. He has no wives or children, and he's highly respected."

"Is that supposed to make me feel better? I've heard the rumors about Rótìmí . . ."

"The Aláàfin is still young," Ìgbín assured her from where she squatted at my side, measuring the length of my leg. "The only thing youth dream about is finding love, but he'll outgrow that soon."

"How soon? I want to be here to see my grandchildren, Ìgbín."

"She will be able to bear children—look at the strength in her arms."

"No, I'd rather not have to look at those hideous scars. How she ever caught the attention of my son with marks like those truly mystifies me." Mama Aláàfin paused. Her eyes ticked over me, checking off different points of my appearance. "It must have been her face," she said thoughtfully, rising and walking up to me. "It's distracting, don't you think?"

Ìgbín stood, rolling up her measuring strip. "She's pretty."

"Yes, that is what has blinded him. But pretty or not, she will never be anything more than a witch." Mama Aláàfin gripped my chin. "And I intend to make him see that."

I shrunk back from her, but her small grip was firm. Her nails dug painfully into my skin, and for a moment, I thought she would squeeze until she drew blood.

The fear passed as quickly as it came, for in the next moment she released me. "Until then, I am obligated to humor my son's whims," she said. "Àrẹ̀mọ has not stopped speaking about your voice—the makings of a musician, allegedly. Can you read music?"

The abrupt shift from speaking about me to speaking *to* me caught me off guard; my jaw worked through the motion of speech twice before my words could come.

"I can't read."

Ìgbín turned away abruptly, clearing her throat. Mama Aláà-fin stared at me for a long time. Long enough that I wondered if I should say something more.

She downed her goblet in a single gulp and held it out to the nearest handmaid. "More wine."

A slave arrived with a bowl of ògì. I breakfasted on the hot, sugared millet pudding as I listened to Mama Aláàfin arrange my new life.

"She will have to learn how to read," she told no one in particular; although her handmaids nodded enthusiastically, they seemed to serve little purpose beyond keeping her goblet full. Absently waving a finger covered in rings, she continued, "Nobles cannot be as illiterate as the masses—especially not noblewomen. I cannot have her embarrassing my son, even if her place here is only temporary. She will take lessons during the day, and in the evenings, she will practice music. But the first thing she must do today, of course, is complete her morning exercise. Take her to our field. Now that the sun is up, I'm sure everyone will already be there."

I paid no mind to Mama Aláàfin's thinly veiled threats to drive me out of the royal city. Despite her many complaints about me, she nevertheless constructed my daily routine, no doubt under the orders of Àrẹ̀mọ. It was clear she was unwilling to go against her son; so long as the Aláàfin wanted me here, how could she possibly be a threat?

With my belly warm and my lack of sleep catching up to me,

I felt too untroubled to respond to her assessment. As I was shuf-
fled off in a palanquin, it was all I could do to keep myself from
dozing off on the velvet cushions. But before long, loud voices
jerked me out of my stupor.

Alarmed, I peered through the curtains. The burgeoning sun
painted the sky with strokes of pink, lavender, and orange. In
front of me, groups of women were dispersed throughout a massive field.

There were women wrestling in the grass and others running
a ball from one edge of the field to the other. Women flipped
through the air in amazing acrobatic feats or else trotted lei-
surely on sleek mares that had ribbons woven in their shiny
manes. Several women, just as old or young as the rest, sat on
the edges of the field, clutching their swollen bellies.

The more of the scene that I drank in, the more I relaxed.
The yells were not of fear, but of joy.

My palanquin was set down, and a woman appeared before
me, as though she had materialized from the soft light of dawn.
Her skin shone like liquified sunlight that had been simmered
with honey. She wore the same cotton dress as me and the other
women, but on her tall willowy frame, the simple dress was
transformed into a bold fashion statement.

She seemed so much like something out of a dream that I was
half convinced I had fallen asleep after all. That was, until she
asked, "Òdòdó?"

I nodded numbly. She smiled, adding more light to the day.
There was a gap between her two front teeth.

As I stood, I noticed that my forehead came up to her chin;
she must have been as tall as Àrẹ̀mọ. Perhaps even taller with
her large bantu knots, each of which had fine gold strands spiraling around it.

She pulled me into a cocoa butter-scented embrace. "I've
been looking forward to meeting you, little flower."

I could not return the sentiment, but luckily, she did not give me time to form a response; she took my hand and guided me across the field.

"I don't know why I fooled myself into believing I could return to the royal city by sunset yesterday," she said casually, as though this was just one of many conversations we had had. "Bùnmi told me that her party would start at midday, so I should have known people would not arrive until the sun had already set. I apologize for not greeting you, but by the time I got back, I was told you had already retired. In my defense, though, that is also when I learned of your existence."

"That has been a common thread," I muttered, slightly out of breath—my strides were awkward and clunky alongside her long legs, which seemed to glide her across the grass.

"Here is good." She tugged me to a stop under a palm tree. Two women were already lounging in its shade, but upon seeing us, they dipped their heads and stood.

I watched, puzzled, as they walked away. My guide, however, merely sat in the grass and looked up at me. After a moment, I followed her lead. My body was stiff as I did so, as though her dark gaze petrified my muscle into bone.

"I think I'd like to run today," she said, extending her legs and reaching for her sandals. "Would you like to be at my side?"

"I'm not sure if I can," I admitted. I had completed my mother's and aunties' errands all my life, but even so, multiple trips from our house to the market still winded me.

"It's the dress, isn't it? I know, I found them so annoying at first. I don't know why they give us these silly things. Here—" She straightened and snapped her fingers.

A nearby guard jogged to us. "Yes, your majesty?"

"Give Òdòdó your trousers."

"Yes, your majesty." He began unraveling his drawstring.

"Wait," I said quickly. "That's fine—I don't want his trousers!"

"Are you sure?" the woman asked. "It's not like he needs them."

I eyed the stone-faced soldier; the only other thing he wore besides his trousers was a spear in his hand. "I think he needs them more than me," I said warily.

"You think? I've always thought it wouldn't make a difference, since, you know . . ."

She held up two fingers and brought them together in a sharp snipping motion. When I only stared, her eyes widened, and her hand flew to her smile. "Oh, you don't know?"

To the soldier, she said, "Never mind. I apologize for disturbing you."

"It's always a pleasure." He bowed then jogged back to his post, where he reverted into a statue.

The woman leaned into me, and in turn, her mischievous smile pulled me toward her. In a stage whisper, she said, "He's a eunuch."

Shocked, I asked, "How do you know?"

"All the slaves guarding us are."

I looked at the men stationed along the perimeter of the field. They blended in with their surroundings, keeping a watchful eye over the women.

"But, why would . . . ?"

The woman laughed. "Isn't it obvious? A farmer is protective of his cows. Just imagine the possessiveness of powerful men. Since their wars keep them from watching us at all times, they must go to extremes to keep track of their wives and daughters, both for our protection and our surveillance."

Her words made me realize that since coming to the royal city, there had never been a guard too far behind me. I knew they kept watch over me, but it never occurred to me that they might be *watching* me. Discomfort crawled over my skin; surely I misunderstood the woman. She made it sound as though the guards spied on us, but there was no reason for that.

Us. The realization that I had grouped myself with the woman drew my attention back to her. "What brings you to the royal city?" I asked.

"Pardon?"

"Are you here with your husband or your father?" I asked. As comfortable as I had become with the woman, I still had no idea who she was. I scrutinized her tribal mark—two parallel lines across her left cheek, from her nose to her ear—but it was of a clan with which I was unfamiliar. "Who are you?"

"Oh! This whole time—?" she asked, surprised. "Well, in any case, I'm Kòlò."

She said nothing more, seeming to believe that answer sufficed. When she saw that I still waited expectantly, however, she added, "Daughter of King Adéjọlá."

I gazed at her in awe. "You're a princess?"

"Hm," Kòlò said, her smile fading. "When I heard that Ọmóṣẹwà had thrown one of his tantrums, I thought he was just upset that he had not gotten to you first. But you really are a commoner, aren't you?" She put a hand on my knee. "Well, not anymore, I suppose. Soon, you'll join me as the wife of the Aláàfin."

Realization dawned on me. The women from earlier—rather than sharing the shade with us, they had left immediately. I had assumed we bothered them, but now I saw it was quite the opposite; if a woman's authority was in conjunction with her husband's status, Kòlò had to be the wife of the most important man here to garner such a reaction.

I looked around the field with new eyes, noting the distance the other women kept. When I made eye contact with any, they bowed their head courteously and quickly turned away, even the women much older than I.

In a matter of days, I had gone from living as the state's drudge to receiving the respect of women whom I had never even met. The change was so abrupt that it dizzied me—but it was a pleasant dizziness.

Kòlò tilted her head, her almond-shaped eyes shining. "I suppose you hate me now?"

"What?" I asked, taken aback. "Of course not."

"I know how terse things can be between wives. I watch that

tired show every day . . ." She waved a vague hand around the field.

"No, I don't mind," I assured her, and I meant it. Jealousy would have entailed me caring for Àrèmọ, but Kọ̀lọ̀ had made a much better first impression. "I'm just shocked. The way Àrèmọ spoke, it was as though he had never found love."

"Well, he hasn't. At least, not until he met you." She smiled at my surprise. "He and I are hardly married. Our union is political, on behalf of Ọ̀yọ́."

My eyes widened—that was why I did not recognize her tribal mark. I had never met anyone from Ọ̀yọ́. Although the Ọ̀yọ́ were a clan of the Yorùbá tribe, they remained independent of Yorùbáland. Not that the Aláàfin had not tried to bring them under his rule; Ọ̀yọ́ and Ṣàngótẹ̀ had been at war for generations. For all the lands the Aláràà had conquered, they could never secure Ọ̀yọ́. It was protected by the Ahosi of Dahomey, a legendary regiment of woman warriors who roamed the rainforests of the south.

It was unbelievable that women could triumph against armies of men, but it must have been true, because two years ago the Aláàfin finally put an end to the war—not with a victory but with a truce. I assumed that would have been under Àrèmọ's rule; his marriage to Kọ̀lọ̀ must have been part of the treaty.

"So you see," Kọ̀lọ̀ continued, "you need not compete with me for Àrèmọ's affection. You have already won. In fact, when our wedding night did not yield any children, I suppose he was so distraught at the prospect of having to lay with me again that he went to find a better wife to give him sons."

"Don't talk like that," I said, scandalized. "You were born a princess, and you're beautiful. Whatever drove Àrèmọ away was no fault of yours."

Kọ̀lọ̀'s expression shifted, a nearly imperceptible change. Suddenly, I had the feeling that her smile had been insincere up until this point, a mask I had not noticed until it was gone.

"You're a sweet little flower, aren't you?" Her voice was softer now, more pensive. She looked at me a moment more. "Perhaps we will get along after all."

She stood and stretched her long arms toward the sky before offering a hand to me.

"Come, let's run before the heat drives us indoors. It'll be fun."

It was not fun.

Within my first few steps, my body begged me to stop. My lungs shriveled; my vision flooded with sweat. My legs became so heavy that I was sure I was sinking, but I forced myself to keep up with Kọ̀lọ̀.

Her moderate pace never wavered; I was not even sure if she felt anything. She maintained a constant stream of commentary on the various noblewomen we passed. Upon completing our third lap around the field, Kọ̀lọ̀ slowed. I stumbled as I tried to do the same, as though I had forgotten how.

As soon as I came to a halt, a pain so severe gripped my legs that I nearly fainted. Dizzy, I moved to sit, but Kọ̀lọ̀ wrapped an arm around my shoulders, nudging me onwards.

"I know it hurts to keep going, sweet flower," she said, "but it hurts even more when you stop. The only way for it to get better is to continue moving forward. The first run is always the hardest—not that it gets any easier. But the more you run, the more capable you become at handling that type of stress. I'm sure you'll notice improvement tomorrow."

"You," I panted, "expect me to do that again?"

"Sure. If you want to get better, you must run every day."

I really did faint then.

When I came to, Kọ̀lọ̀ was gone. I sat in the hot, perfumed pool of the bathhouse, my handmaids scrubbing away my fatigue with black soap. As I finished my bath, the rest of the noblewomen arrived for their own baths.

My handmaids took me to my hut, where they oiled my skin and cornrows then clothed me in the purple wrapper that Ìgbín had brought earlier. The deep yellow accents that sprawled across the fabric matched the scarf they tied over my head. Five tiers of gold necklaces were looped around my neck, the lowest of which had a tail that dropped to the center of my chest. A gilded cuff was snaked around my upper arm.

Under my handmaids' cheered encouragement, I circled the room, trying to adjust to the heavy but pleasant weight of so much jewelry. A knock sounded at the door. One woman opened it and sank to her knees when Gassire stepped inside. The rest of the women followed her lead. I was wondering if I was supposed to kneel before the royal griot too when he answered my question for me.

"My lady," he said, bowing his head, albeit stiffly. "The Aláà-fin's mother has informed him that you are in need of fundamental instruction."

Tucked into the crook of his elbow were manuscripts similar to those I had seen carried by scholars in Timbuktu. "You are to be my teacher?" I asked, confused.

Griots tracked every wedding, every birth, and every death in their region. They were the keepers of histories and traditions dating back to the beginnings of empires, a repository of information they tapped into to fuel social and political events. Their knowledge was well-guarded and passed orally only to their successors. They were not teachers.

From the disgruntled look on Gassire's face, he was all too aware of this. Àrèmọ must have insisted he be the one to instruct me, and the word of the Aláàfin trumped even the royal griot's pride. So, instead of commenting, I merely gestured to a circular table. With a sigh, he placed his manuscripts onto its surface before settling into a chair. I sat next to him.

"Because you need to be well-versed in the current affairs of Ṣàngótẹ̀ anyways," he said, "your literacy lessons will be used as an opportunity for review."

He unfurled a large map and pointed to just below the bend of the Niger River, his finger as gnarled as the calf skin parchment.

"Here is Ṣàngótẹ̀, the city of the Aláràà clan. It is the seat of the Aláàfin's power, the capital from where he presides over Yorùbáland. With Ṣàngó as our patron òrìṣà, and the Aláàfin as both our general and king, we have had the strength to expand our influence to how many major cities other than the capital?"

"Oh!" I started. "Um—"

"Six. Koumbi Saleh, Ògúndélé, Ilé-Ifẹ̀, Ayédùn, Ìlọ́dẹ, and Wúràkẹ́mi. The last two were taken under the current Aláàfin's reign. Not only does Wúràkẹ́mi extend the Aláàfin's rule to the ocean, but it also contributes handsomely to our supply of gold.

"Now, Yorùbáland extends from left of the Niger to"—he dragged his finger to Wúràkẹ́mi—"the Gold Coast to"—he dragged his finger to Timbuktu—"the southern edge of the Sahara. The Aláàfin presides over these areas and every town, trading post, and backwater village in between, which all act as vassal states to Ṣàngótẹ̀. The current Aláàfin has sent at least one of his half siblings and their mothers to each court. In exchange, one member of their own ruling family comes to live here in the royal city. Why?"

"Mmm—"

"This cements our relations with these regions," he answered his own question. He did not seem to require my input. "Although, of course, it is also wise of the Aláàfin to place his siblings' ambitions far from his throne, especially given that he is one of the youngest among them.

"For the men of conquered clans who refuse to acknowledge their new ruler, they and their families are taken as slaves, or they are executed. Otherwise, every boy and man are welcomed as a soldier to fight for Ṣàngótẹ̀. And this results in?"

This time, I did not bother trying to answer.

"The strength of our army being augmented with each battle won. Currently, the Aláàfin commands around three hundred thousand men—"

"*What?*"

I supposed it made sense that Àrẹ̀mọ commanded so many

men, considering he was the Aláàfin who had expanded
Yorùbáland the most in such a short amount of time. But so far,
all I had seen of him was either a flirtatious vagrant or a lovesick
lunatic. It was difficult to connect these two men with the Commander of Death.

Gassire stared at me, irritation curling his upper lip. I felt my
cheeks heat. "I just didn't realize how large the army is," I muttered, fiddling with my armlet.

As if to shake off the interruption, Gassire lifted his chin.
"Yes, well, of course the Aláàfin cannot watch over his entire
army. There are men who watch over their own unit, and men
who watch over those men, and so on until you reach the six
generals, one for each major city.

"Their seconds-in-command oversee their armies from within
their cities, while the generals themselves direct their men from
here. Distance from their cities is necessary to make sensible decisions about the whole of their army. Living here also allows
them to report directly to the Aláàfin and provide him with
counsel. Speaking of which, you'll need to know these men.
There's General Balógun of Koumbi Saleh; General Ọmọ́ṣẹ̀wà
of Ìlọ́dẹ—you became, ah, acquainted with him last night.
There's General . . ."

A butterfly fluttered over our table.

Gassire did not notice; he was getting into his stride now,
moving his hands about him to punctuate his words. The butterfly's green-yellow wings flapped incessantly. The gentle beat was
so faint that I had to concentrate to hear it, the small sound accented by the tinkle of Gassire's golden bracelets.

Bum clink. Bum clink. There was a brown spot, I noticed, on one
of the butterfly's wings, like an eye. It winked in the flashes of
sunlight reflected from Gassire's bracelets. *Bum clink. Bum clink.*
My legs were so heavy from my run. Everything was heavy, and
the heat wrapped so comfortably around me—

A thud jerked me out of my daze. My eyes flew open, though
I had not realized they had been closing. Gassire scowled at me,

gripping the stack of manuscripts he had slammed onto the table.

"If you find it tedious to educate yourself on the kingdom your future husband controls, my lady," he said, "we can go ahead and skip to the literacy lessons. Pay close attention—I expect you to copy every single passage I read."

After hours of mimicking the shapes of words onto parchment, my hands spasming from having grasped a reed stylus for so long, I was taken to my music lessons.

They were held in the field from this morning, except this time the expanse of grass was lit by the waning moon. Flaming torches formed a large circle in the center of the field. The smell of dew and smoke mingled with the laughter of women dancing at the center of the circle. Music, gleeful in its chaos, swelled from the tapping of mallets against the wooden keys of balafons, the strumming of the double strings of gold and silver guembris, and the hypnotic drumming of djembes.

I sat with Kọ̀lọ̀, whose long, toned torso was showcased by a red bandeau top with triangular orange patterns. She wore brown trousers, and though it was more common to see women wearing wrappers or dresses, she wore them well. I only hoped she had not gotten them off a guard.

My music lessons were a lot less formal than my lessons with Gassire. Three other noblewomen joined us, and after a round of introductions—during which I learned two were wives of a noble and one was a daughter—the women indulged in conversation, their instruments sitting untouched beside them. Under the cover of the loud music that prevented guards from overhearing them, they seemed to speak freer.

"My husband tells me it is planned for the second full moon in wet season this year."

"That's what I heard too. You wouldn't believe how excited my son is for it. The boy forgets he could die."

"Oh, let him be excited. Every man dreams of his crowning."

"What is that?" Kòlò interrupted. I was glad, because I did not know either.

"Ah, your majesty, you fit in so well here that I sometimes forget you're not from Ṣàngótẹ̀. A crowning is an Aláràá soldier's first real battle. It's a rite of passage a senior trainee must take before he can officially join the Aláàfin's army."

"All of them, at once?" Kòlò asked. "But won't that leave Ṣàngótẹ̀ temporarily defenseless?"

"Well, the city guard will still be here."

"But it is still a gamble to have so many skilled soldiers gone," another woman chimed in. "That's why the crowning is always at a different time than it was the previous year, so no one can predict it."

"Also, it's technically a secret. I'm not supposed to know—I only overheard my husband telling his friends."

"And men say women can't keep secrets?"

"Imagine!"

They laughed. I did not. I had tried to stay engaged and enjoy the uselessness of the conversation, for it was certainly more enjoyable than working at a forge. But ultimately, when I could not stop staring at the array of instruments brought by slaves and our guards, I tuned out the women and allowed myself to explore the mechanisms of a talking drum.

The hourglass-shaped device had two goatskin drumheads, one on either end, that were connected by cords. A rope wound around them so that they caved inwards, curving with the drum. I positioned the instrument under my arm, tapping out notes with a curved stick. When I squeezed the drum and its cords, I got higher notes, and loosening my grip yielded lower sounds.

Its closeness to the sound of a human voice entranced me. I had nearly figured out how to make it hum my daffodil song when a surge in voices shattered my concentration.

Slightly annoyed, I saw that the disruption was caused by the arrival of a dozen men, some still shirtless from their daylong

training. Women ran to greet them. I glimpsed a grinning
Ọmọṣẹwà twirling one woman with a hand over her head, his
other arm wrapped around another woman's shoulders. These
must be their husbands, meaning they were not just soldiers, but
nobles and generals. Which meant . . .

Àrẹ̀mọ plopped down onto the grass next to me.

"Husband," Kọ̀lọ̀ greeted cheerfully. "What a pleasant surprise."

Àrẹ̀mọ gave her a brief smile then he turned to me. "Òdòdó,
my flower," he greeted, a true smile lighting his face.

I glanced at Kọ̀lọ̀. With a small shrug, she stood, and the
three other woman who had sat with us followed her lead. As if
she sensed my guilt, Kọ̀lọ̀ lightly brushed my head as she and the
women walked away to join another group.

Àrẹ̀mọ did not seem to notice Kọ̀lọ̀'s departure. "How has
your day gone?" he asked me. "Other than attempting to steal
your guard's trousers, I hope you have been staying out of trouble?"

The mention of the occurrence from earlier today took me
by surprise. Àrẹ̀mọ had not been there for it, yet he knew about
it. He had commanded his mother to oversee my schedule, but
Mama Aláàfin had not been present for that either.

Kọ̀lọ̀'s comment about the women of the royal city being
monitored resurfaced in my mind, bringing with it the same discomfort I had felt when I first heard it. If our guards really did
surveil us, then only now did I realize that it would be Àrẹ̀mọ to
whom they reported.

Suppressing my shock, I replied, "No, I have not attempted to
steal any more trousers."

Àrẹ̀mọ laughed, louder than I thought necessary, for I did not
think my words had been very funny. "Good," he said. "Tell me
about the rest of your day."

I frowned; what was the point? He clearly already knew how
my day went—and I could guess how his day went as well. He
wore the smell of blood and sweat like a perfume.

Three hundred thousand men under his command . . .

I suppressed a shiver. "Maybe later," I said. "I was in the middle of a song."

"Excellent." Àrèmọ reclined onto one elbow. "Let me listen to you play."

I looked at him uncertainly; surely the Aláàfin had better ways to use his time. But when Àrèmọ only smiled, I turned back to my talking drum. Tentatively, I tapped out notes, expecting Àrèmọ to become bored with my struggling song at any moment. However, when I chanced a glance at him, his eyes were closed and his face was tilted to the sound, as though the disjointed notes were a masterful composition.

6

The next morning, I was awoken by a clap of thunder.

As I was informed by Ìgbín upon her arrival, this was predicted to be the last rainfall before dry season officially arrived. Each year, during rainy season's final storm, it was believed that Ṣàngó bestowed a parting message of wisdom onto his city, speaking through the royal babaláwo. And as the future wife of the Aláàfin, I was expected to bear witness.

I was clothed in a gray wrapper with swirling stark white designs, a white headscarf, and an abundance of silver jewelry. Afterwards, I was carried to a small stone building. I walked through its archway, down a narrow sloping tunnel.

I emerged into an arena that looked like it had sunk into itself. Above, what must have once been a floor was a jagged and open ceiling. Gray light and rain fell freely onto the center of the room, where there sat a man covered in the white painted dots sometimes worn by babaláwos. Countless brass chains of red and white beads looped over his kente toga. Behind him stretched a long table holding miniature ebony statues of humanlike icons—the òrìṣàs. Scattered among them were kola and palm nuts, cowrie shells, and cracked rocks that were so unnaturally dark they looked as though they had been struck by lightning.

Nobles sat on tiered stone benches that lined dirt walls, low conversation buzzing among them. They seemed to be seated by family; most men were surrounded by women and children. Eyes pressed into me as I joined Kòlò and Mama Aláàfin where they sat on a balcony somewhat separated from the other nobles.

"Good morning, ma," I said, dipping my head to Mama Aláàfin.

Her lips twisted, as though the very sight of me soured her tongue. But Kòlò patted the bench next to her and said, "Good morning, little flower."

As I sat beside her, I asked, "Where's Àrèmo?"

"Observing one of the royal city's barracks. He likes to personally ensure that his soldiers' training is coming along well."

"The soldiers have to train today?" I asked, surprised. "Even in the rain?"

Kòlò laughed hollowly. "Rain is nothing to them. The way he works those soldiers, they've lived on the edge of death their entire lives. There is nothing he cares about more than ensuring his great army stays great."

When she saw my frown, she smiled and put her arm through my own. Her cocoa butter scent was less sweet now that I had glimpsed the bitterness that lay beneath.

"Look, he's starting," she said, putting a finger to her lips as though I was the one who had been talking.

Below, the royal babaláwo was moving to the table. "Ṣàngó yọ mí," he greeted.

I should not have been able to hear his brittle voice so clearly, but I did. So did the rest of the room, for the affirmation was said back to him. As the solemn harmony echoed around us, the babaláwo plucked a palm nut from the table and rubbed it in his palms vigorously as he began to pray.

He prayed to his ancestors and to the supreme creator Olódùmarè. He prayed to Èṣù, the trickster òrìṣà and divine messenger between heaven and Earth; to Ògún, the warrior and master blacksmith; to Ọya, the fierce goddess whose whirlwinds could ravage the landscape; to Obàtálá, the patient and wise father. He prayed to those òrìṣàs and more, ending with the òrìṣà who had gathered us here today.

"Ṣàngó," he said, "we give thanks for the storm and the water that it brings our crops. We pray that your city continues to represent your power. We pray that—"

He stopped suddenly, both his words and his hands. A prickle went down the back of my neck; it looked wrong. Nothing, living or inanimate, should be that still—yet there the babaláwo stood, like a tear in the fabric of reality.

Murmurs sounded but were quickly hushed. Nobles shifted, as if to make sure they still could. Beside me, Kòlò uncrossed and crossed her legs. I leaned forward, not quite sure if there was anything to see but not wanting to look away.

"There is but one home to the snail," the babaláwo said suddenly. His voice filled the room now; it had grown bigger. Not louder—it was simply more. "There is but one shell to the àṣẹ of the soul. Be as water, always knowing the right direction, and the world will never be off course."

We held a collective breath, waiting. But that appeared to be the only thing that the babaláwo had to say. He relaxed, dusting what remained of the palm nut from his hands, and declared, "Ṣàngó has spoken."

Around the room, men grumbled. Women rolled their eyes. Even Kòlò was frowning.

But I slumped back against the wall in relief. To some subconscious degree, I had believed the storm was for me, the revocation of Ṣàngó's blessing for my marriage to the Aláàfin. Now, though, I was sure it had not been an oversight. My impoverished days were truly over, and soon I would be able to save my mother from her toil as well.

Above the arena, rain fell slower, then not at all. Weak beams of sunlight found their way through the gradually dissolving clouds.

Afterwards, outside the arena's stone entrance, Mama Aláàfin informed Kòlò that she would be taking her to a naming ceremony being held in Ṣàngótẹ̀.

"You would like me to accompany you?" Kọ̀lọ̀ seemed surprised.

"Of course. The entirety of the Aláàfin's family has been invited."

"Am I coming as well, ma?" I asked.

Mama Aláàfin's smug expression made me think that she had been anticipating that question, had even been trying to prompt it from me. "As my son has yet to marry you, the invitation to the Aláàfin's family does not extend to you," she said. "They are expecting to receive his wife and his mother. Meanwhile, you will be attending your lessons with the griot."

My face warmed. I knew that I did not technically have a place in the royal city yet, but as I realized with a surprising amount of disappointment, I had been hoping those around me had not noticed.

As if she knew what I was thinking, Mama Aláàfin placed a hand on my shoulder, much to my surprise. "It will take some time before you can fulfill your role here," she said softly. "Perhaps something that will help you adjust is knowing you are not alone. The royal city has its own witches—blacksmiths, I mean. Over where the forges are. Why don't you go meet them before your lessons today?"

She offered me a smile, the first one she had ever given me, and I felt my spirits raise. We had gotten off to a rough start, but it seemed she was beginning to warm up to me at last. And she had a point—I had spent my entire life being around blacksmiths. Perhaps knowing that world was not far away would help me be more at ease in this one.

"I will. Thank you, ma," I said.

Mama Aláàfin nodded then took Kọ̀lọ̀'s arm and began leading her away, their guards following behind them. As they walked, Kọ̀lọ̀ glanced over her shoulder at me, a slight frown on her face. I smiled at her to assure her that I was no longer upset about being left behind, then I turned away to begin my own day.

Slaves tried to bring me my palanquin, but I waved it away, deciding to walk to the forges. Now that I was certain that this was my home, I wanted to learn how to navigate it.

But even with help from my handmaids and two guards, the twists and turns of the royal city alluded me. At one point, I ended up on a path that led to the horses' stables. To my delight, I found that the tales I had heard growing up failed to do the stables justice. Not only did every horse have its own mattress, but they also each had a silk rope for a halter, a copper container strapped to their undersides as a urinal, and three stable hands attending to their every need. A patchwork of horses— rich chestnut and soft gray and jet black—frolicked in an open field, strands of gold glittering in their manes. I even spotted some horses tethered to large gold nuggets functioning as hitching posts.

As I walked through the royal city, slaves, soldiers, and even some nobles fell over themselves to please me. They offered funny stories to make me laugh and volunteered to be my personal tour guide and "It would be no trouble at all to carry you, my lady, are you certain that you want to walk?" The same dizzying feeling from yesterday filled me until I was more so floating than walking.

By the time I arrived at the royal city's forges, the sun had hooked itself to the highest notch in the sky. The forges were located near the barracks and training fields, an area I had never had reason to visit until now.

Despite the opulence of the rest of the royal city, the blacksmiths' workspace looked similar to my home in Timbuktu. The only differences were this space was larger, and it was positioned under a pavilion. About a dozen women—each wearing the stained and singed wrappers with which I was so familiar— were at work. Some sat at the furnaces, diligently working the bellows. Others worked in pairs, one using tongs to hold incandescent metal on the surface of a large flat rock while the other struck it into shape with a basalt hammer. The rhythmic beating

pulsed in the air, a cadence that lulled me into an ease I had not
felt anywhere else in the royal city.

As my retinue stepped into the cool shade of the pavilion, the
women paused to watch us. I knelt before them and said, "Good
afternoon, aunties."

I waited, but the only sound that met my words was the crackling flames of the furnaces. Confused, I looked up. Many of the
women watched me in bewilderment. However, when I met the
eyes of one girl, she seemed to snap out of her shock.

"You are welcome," she said, striding forward. "You must
forgive my aunties and I for our silence. We have never been
greeted by a noble, much less by a bride of the Aláàfin."

The girl proffered her hand to me. Her skin was a brown so
cool that it almost seemed tinged with silver, but when I took her
hand, her calloused touch was warm. She helped me to my feet,
and standing, I was nearly a whole head taller than her.

"Before I was called the Aláàfin's bride, I was called Alálẹ̀,"
I said.

The girl did not smile. I doubted she did so very often; her
facial features were so sharp that they looked as though they had
been carved, like etchings in stone. However, there was amusement in her voice as she replied, "Yes, we are familiar with your
story."

The longer I looked into her eyes, the more disconcerting I
found them. Most people's eyes were windows through which
their inner thoughts and feelings could be seen. But gazing at
her, I felt that I saw myself more than her, with her eyes being so
dark and large that they reflected my face.

It was then that I processed what she had called the other
women—not her sisters, as most blacksmiths called each other,
but her aunties. The same thing I called the blacksmiths I
worked with, because of the notable age gap I shared with all of
them—an age gap, I now noticed, that she also seemed to have
with the women around her.

She looked around nineteen, my own age, making her the youngest blacksmith I had ever met other than myself. Most blacksmiths were at least middle-aged; by then, they'd had enough time to prove that they were of no use to society. Blacksmithing was not a profession that women chose. It was one they fell into after their parents deemed them failed daughters, or their husbands deemed them failed wives and mothers. It was this, even more than our seemingly mystical abilities, that made us so despised; our largest crime was being, not just women, but women without a man to belong to.

I was one of the few blacksmiths born into the profession because my mother befell this fate while she was pregnant. I did not ask the girl if she shared a similar story; most women did not talk about the circumstances that had led to them becoming a blacksmith, and it was an unspoken rule to not inquire.

"My name is Dígíọlá, but you are my sister, so you will call me Dígí," the girl continued. She glanced over her shoulder, at her forge, then turned back to me and took my hand in both of her own. "We must resume our work, but thank you for coming to greet us. We are proud of you, how high you have flown from your humble beginnings. Please come see your sisters again soon."

Dígí's permanently neutral expression added sincerity to her words. She did not care to please me; she was simply speaking her mind. And the minds of the women around her, apparently, for as I looked around, I saw the other blacksmiths nodding at Dígí's words.

My heart swelled. "Thank you," I said. "I will."

With a final dip of my head to the room at large, I left the pavilion. As my retinue and I embarked down a stone path, I felt imbued with happiness. Mama Aláàfin had been right; it was reassuring to know there was at least one place in the royal city where I naturally belonged.

The heat of the sun was relentless now. One of my handmaids

had just unfolded a parasol to hold over me when, on the path running perpendicular to ours, came a boisterous man nearly as wide as he was tall. He jabbered away to a skinnier man, who nodded with the stiffness that came with civility rather than genuine interest. The big man glanced my way and back to his companion. Then, apparently processing who he just saw, he turned to me entirely. A grin cracked across his face, like a crooked crevice in a stretch of wood.

"The lovely Alálẹ̀ Òdòdó!" he boomed, striding up to me so that my retinue had little choice but to stop. The man towered over me, making my parasol temporarily redundant. He took my hand and pressed a sweaty kiss to it. "I was warned of your beauty, but even so, you've left me defenseless."

"Thank you," I said, tugging my hand free and discreetly wiping it against my wrapper.

The man placed one massive hand on his balding head and one on his hip, looking back the way I came. "Where are you leaving? The only thing down that way is the witches' place."

"That is where I am coming from, visiting the royal city's blacksmiths," I said, subtly correcting his label. "I wanted to say hello."

"Is that so." The man's beady eyes narrowed, and for a moment, I thought I had offended him.

The feeling subsided as soon as it had come, for when he turned his attention to my guards, his friendly air was restored. "So, these are the slaves tasked with your protection." He leaned in and asked, "Tell me, my dear, have they tried to seduce you?"

"No," I said slowly. I often forgot my guards were even present because of their subdued manner—a manner I wished this man would adopt.

He clicked his tongue in disapproval. "The job is wasted on eunuchs. Lucky bastards don't know how good they have it. How I'd love to do nothing but watch a beautiful woman all day."

I did not know what to say to that, so I said nothing.

The man flashed me a smile before looking at my guards. "Fẹ́mi, Wọlé," he said, and I only realized those were my guards' names when they snapped to attention. "You protect this woman with your life, you hear me? Do whatever it takes to ensure that she stays safe and pure."

"Yes, Captain Kiigba, sir!"

"Captain Kiigba?" I echoed, for the name struck a familiar chord in my mind. I realized it was a name the royal griot had made me write again and again yesterday.

I eyed the scar running over his eye in a new light; Kiigba was not just any Aláràá soldier. He was the second-in-command to the Aláàfin, the voice of Ṣàngótẹ̀ when the Aláàfin's focus needed to broaden to all of Yorùbáland. That made him the second most powerful man in the capital . . . And yet, while Àrẹ̀mọ could command a room with just a look, the man before me was entirely underwhelming. It made me wonder why Àrẹ̀mọ would keep a man like this so close to him.

Kiigba seemed delighted that I recognized his name; he wiggled an eyebrow. "Do not be intimidated," he said. "I am only the captain to my soldiers. To you, I can simply be Kiigba. That is what my wives call me."

To my relief, the other man present stepped between us. "Though I also call him that," he said, "so do with that information what you will."

With a bow, the man continued, "It is my pleasure to finally make your acquaintance, my lady. I am General Rótìmí."

Rótìmí, I recalled. *The general of Wúràkẹ́mi.*

Even before Gassire's lesson, I had heard countless merchants speak in revered tones of the mines of Wúràkẹ́mi. Ṣàngótẹ̀ had had its own mines before, but since acquiring Wúràkẹ́mi, Yorùbáland was now practically drowning in gold.

General Rótìmí certainly represented the Gold Coast well; massive gold rings gleamed on his hands, and gold foil flaked the trim of his brown tunic. Thin gold strands were woven in his chin-length braids, which ended in columns of gilded beads. As Rótìmí straightened, I saw that even his brown eyes were dotted with yellow, like specks of gold floating in syrup.

A vertical scar ran under each of Rótìmí's eyes, down his ginger-brown cheeks—the mark of the Òòrùn, Wúràkẹ́mi's predominant clan. His gaze was level with my own, and I saw that a small smile lifted a corner of his mouth. I had the sudden urge to ask what, exactly, was so amusing, but as soon as I had the thought, I acknowledged how childish of a question it was. And anyway, his smile was so vague that I could not be certain I was not making it up.

"I spotted you playing the talking drum last night," Rótìmí said. "You're a natural talent. We simply must play together."

I hesitated, but I did not want to be rude. "Sure," I said reluctantly.

He sighed. "Our music session will not be any time soon, though."

Then why did you suggest it in the first place? I could not help but think.

Rótìmí went on, "My schedule is very hectic, and I can only imagine how busy you must be as the next wife of the Aláàfin."

I held my chin higher, not completely sure why I did so. He sounded kind, but something about his expression made the underside of my skin itch. "I am," I said. "I have lessons."

There was no denying the smile on Rótìmí's face now. "Of course." He bowed again then clapped a hand on Kiigba's shoulder. "We have taken up enough of your time. I wish you the best of luck with your *lessons*, my lady."

Kiigba also bowed in farewell. As he straightened, his black eyes traveled over me uncomfortably slow, pausing at my chest. I was not so foolish as to think that he was admiring my necklaces.

"I hope to see you again soon," he said.

"Yes . . ." I began, but I trailed off, unable to truthfully return the sentiment as he and Rótìmí went on their way.

Rótìmí's smile lingered in my mind, and I groaned. I had not been ashamed of not knowing how to read, but for some reason, now that he knew I needed lessons, I found the whole ordeal embarrassing.

When I reached my hut, I found Gassire waiting at a table, manuscripts stacked in front of him. The griot acknowledged my arrival with a curt, "You're late."

"I'm sorry," I said, quickly taking the seat next to him. "I lost track of time exploring the royal city, but it won't happen again."

"I should hope not. We are beginning your lessons in strategy, a particularly complex subject. If you ever hope to become learned in it, you must be more dedicated than what I have seen from you thus far."

"Strategy?" I asked, confused. "Is that why I've been exercising each morning, to prepare for combat training?"

Gassire's annoyance melted into amusement. "My dear, there are no Ahosi warriors in Sàngótè. Aláràá women do not fight— your exercise is to make you stronger for childbearing." He laughed at my stunned expression. "We all must serve the Aláà- fin. A man by being the best soldier he can be, and a woman by birthing those healthy soldiers."

I felt myself deflate. As a blacksmith, my value had lain in my ability to produce for the state. And now, according to Gassire, my value as a noblewoman would lay in . . . my ability to produce for the state.

But no—I had seen the glamour of the royal city, the softness with which the wives of rich men lived. It was a life incomparable to the laborious reality of a blacksmith. No matter what Gassire said, I refused to believe my new status as a wife would not be a vast upgrade from being a witch.

"Strategy," Gassire continued, pulling me from my thoughts, "is a fundamental part of every noble's education, even noblewomen. After all, the Aláàfin's army is such an integral part of Aláràá pride that to understand it is to understand the Aláràá people.

"But training so many men would be useless without knowing

how to use those skills, hence why officers spend as much time being taught strategy as they do on the training field. For your instruction, we can begin with one of the most basic principles: deception. You are from Timbuktu, yes?"

"I am," I responded enthusiastically, for it was the one question he had asked thus far to which I knew the answer.

Gassire nodded. "Then you know that deception is a tool the Sahara uses well. Heat is the desert's strength, but mirages are the strategy it utilizes to make its enemies succumb to that power.

"What is the key to deception?" Gassire asked. "The key is to condition the enemy to see only what you want them to see. Thus, when a unit of soldiers is weak? They must appear strong to prevent a quick defeat. And when they are strong? They must seem weak to lure in the enemy. The Aláàfin was particularly successful in applying this tactic in the Battle of—"

A sudden clamor of voices drowned out Gassire's lecture. The scowl he gave me was so accusatory that I quickly said, "It's coming from outside."

He stood and swept out of my hut. Curious, I followed close behind him. Other women were emerging from their huts, confusion plain on their faces. Gassire and I joined them as they walked through the gates ahead.

On a nearby field stood at least a hundred men, scattered in pairs. They wore nothing but loose, knee-length cotton breeches and sandals. Each held long wooden sticks crossed over their partner's, and at the commands of an unseen man, they pulled back, struck, pulled back, struck.

From the amazement of the women around me, I garnered this was not a common sight for them. I was wondering what had made the soldiers train here today when a shout sounded, one removed from the stream of commands.

The soldiers moved out of their pairs into one large arc that faced the women's compound. A man stepped forth from the ranks and handed his stick to one of his companions, who in turn gave him an iron-tipped spear and an oval shield. I had seen similar brown shields traded in Timbuktu; they were made with the rough hide of hippopotamus and were used by soldiers during battle.

A second man joined the first, and cheers surged forth. I could easily see over the heads of the women around me, but I still craned my neck for a better view, hardly believing my eyes.

The new man wore the same cotton breeches as the others, though his were black instead of brown. His bare torso rippled with muscle and was crisscrossed with scars, like a carefully forged, but scratched-up, bronze statue.

So far, I had seen two sides of my future husband: the good-natured Àrèmọ, a pining fool, and the opulent Aláàfin, an influential noble. Now I saw his third side, the side I had not realized I had been waiting to present itself until it did: the Commander of Death.

From the holsters attached to his leather belt, Àrèmọ extracted dual double-sided axes. It was the same weapon of choice as his ancestor, Ṣàngó.

I watched in fascination. For once, there was no hint of amusement on Àrèmọ's face, his bronze axes poised in front of him. His opponent aimed his spear tip first at Àrèmọ, his other arm bearing his shield. Amidst the cheers of the watching soldiers, a yell sounded. The two men circled, neither taking their eyes from the other. Then, Àrèmọ's opponent lunged forward. A sequence of flashing metal was initiated. Each step was feather light, already on to the next as soon as the previous had happened. One man moved forward, the other moved back. Their bodies twirled; twisted over, under; swept from side to side.

It was a dance. A vicious yet captivating performance, the ringing of metal on metal a unique kind of melody.

His opponent stumbled. Almost faster than I could follow, Àrèmọ knocked the man off his feet. The latter fell flat on his back, his spear and shield knocked askew. One of Àrèmọ's axes hovered over his neck.

Applause erupted. Àrèmọ helped the fallen man stand and gave him an amicable clap on the shoulder. Then, shielding his eyes from the sun with an ax, he scanned the women gathered in front of our compound. His eyes met mine, and a grin lit his face. Annoyed by the realization this was what he had disrupted my lessons for, I did not return his smile. His only widened.

Half exasperated and half amused, Gassire remarked, "It would appear the Aláàfin seeks to impress you, my lady. Are you impressed?" Gassire glanced at me, and apparently misreading my discontent, he added, "Or are you now having misgivings about your engagement?"

"Not at all," I said quickly. "The training session caught me off guard, but yes, I suppose it was admirable."

Gassire returned his attention to the field. As we watched Àrèmọ pick out another man to duel, Gassire said, "In oral tradition, the Aláàfin is said to be a warrior hero, a grand and undefeated force of nature. But you, my lady, are from Timbuktu, a city that was long ruled by the Aláàfin's enemies. In their history books, the Aláàfin is written as a cruel and capricious tyrant. It would make sense if you saw him as a monster."

I frowned, unsure why Gassire would tell me this. It felt like another one of his tests within a lesson, but I was even less certain about how to respond to this one than the others.

At last, as a new fight began, I said honestly, "I have heard of the Aláàfin's brutality, of course. I have seen how children cry when those stories are told. But I have also seen the awe— grudging or otherwise—sparked in men as they speak of the empire he is building. Sometimes stories make him a hero, and sometimes they make him a villain, but all of them say he is great. And that is admirable, isn't it?"

Gassire did not immediately respond to my genuine question, merely holding my gaze for long enough that I began to wonder if I had said something wrong, or perhaps too obvious.

Just as I was reaching peak discomfort, Gassire said quietly, "How quaint. It seems the monster has indeed found his heart."

He turned to reenter the women's compound. "Let's finish your lessons, my lady."

As I made to follow him, I glanced back at the field in time to see Àrẹ̀mọ's ax graze his opponent's arm. The move was met by raucous cheers. It was unclear whether it had been an accident, but either way, red droplets of blood spattered against the grass.

7

Soon after Gassire and I returned to my hut, the noise faded; training had been moved elsewhere. After my lesson finished, I found myself standing at my window. Partly to keep out of my ladies' way as they tidied my room, but also to gaze at the cloudless sky.

My mother and I had never enjoyed sunny weather; it made working in the sweltering heat of Timbuktu worse. It was only now, resting under a gilded roof, that I could appreciate the beauty of a clear sky. If my mother could stand where I stood now, I was sure she would have a new love for the radiant blue as well.

Behind me, I heard the door open and close. I turned to see my ladies kneeling before the Aláàfin as he walked into my hut. His axes were sheathed now, hanging at his sides from the holsters attached to his leather belt. As he approached me, his hands behind his back, his smile was so large that his eyes crinkled at the corners. "I have a gift for you," he announced. "My pages had to outbid all sorts of merchants to secure it at auction."

With a flourish, he draped a fur over the windowsill. It was as orange as the sunset, with white edges branching out into a stubbed limb on each corner. Black stripes unfurled over it like spilled ink.

"A discolored zebra," I observed, nonplussed.

"Actually, this is an animal from Asia."

"Oh. A discolored *exotic* zebra."

Àrèmọ laughed. "Fine, you are unhappy with the fur. What would you like, then?"

I looked at him in confusion; I did not think anyone had ever asked me that. "I can have anything?" I asked.

Àrèmọ wrapped his arms around my waist. Though he sparkled with sweat, it was not entirely unpleasant as he pulled me into him, enveloping me in a smell like the promise of rain.

"Anything," he affirmed, swaying us from side to side. "Would you like me to capture the southern winds and bottle them in a crystal vial? Would you like me to pluck the stars out of the sky, one by one, so that you may adorn your braids with them? Say it, and it is yours.

"I can provide you with whatever you desire," he continued. "And I hope that will be enough to prevent you from returning to your life as a witch."

As he spoke, a smile had been spreading across my face. But at this, it stalled. "What do you mean?" I asked. "I have no intention of taking up blacksmithing again."

"Were you not at the forges today?"

Though his voice was soft, I went rigid. No doubt it was my guards who told him. I had come to accept that Kòlò had been right; my guards likely kept him updated on my movements. But there was no reason to let that bother me. It was for my safety, and besides, nothing about my daily routine needed to be kept secret.

So, I honestly replied, "Yes, I went to visit the royal city's blacksmiths. I thought it would be nice to meet them."

"Why," he said, his voice still incredibly soft, "keep the company of witches when you are no longer one yourself?"

Turned away from him, I could not see his face, but the shift in his mood felt like a sudden heaviness in the air. My anxiety spiked; I thought of the blacksmiths' shock when I visited them, of Kiigba's expression when he saw me leaving the forges. Only now did I realize how strange it must have seemed for the Aláà-fin's wife to be there.

I did not know why I thought to do that—but suddenly I remembered, I had not been the one who thought of that idea.

It had been Mama Aláàfin who had given me that advice so kindly, though she had never been kind to me. She must have known it would make me seem as though I favored my old life over the Aláàfin's proposal.

I considered telling Àrèmọ it had been his mother's idea, but she had already gotten what she wanted; his trust in me was cracked. That fracture might only grow if I were to criticize his own mother.

"It was a lapse in judgement, one that will not happen again," I assured him. "I know the blacksmiths have nothing to offer me."

Dígí's offer of friendship surfaced in my mind, and, with a twinge of guilt, I pushed down the memory. It was true I had looked forward to having a friend in the royal city with whom connection came naturally, but if it made Àrèmọ doubt me in any way, then it was not worth having.

After a moment, I felt him relax. "Sure, my flower," he said. "I only worried you were having second thoughts about our union. You have not even accepted my proposal yet."

I allowed myself to exhale, easing back into his embrace; perhaps I had only imagined the tension. "But I will," I said. "I just want my mother to be here when I get married."

Àrèmọ rested his chin on my head. "I know. Do not worry. She will be found."

"Found? She's not lost." When he did not answer, I pulled away from him to meet his eye. "Àrèmọ?"

He sighed, running a hand over the fur. Even when he was dressed for combat, I noticed, his fingers still shone with clusters of rings.

"I received a messenger earlier," he said. "My men arrived at your home in Timbuktu to retrieve your mother, but they found your house completely empty. Your mother and all the other blacksmiths are gone."

"Gone?" I asked, alarmed. "But we've lived in that house my

entire life—there's no reason why my mother would go any-where else. What could have happened to her?

Àrèmọ took my hand and gave it a reassuring squeeze. "Òdòdó, there is no way an entire guild of blacksmiths befell misfortune, especially when there is no sign of conflict. Your mother and her sisters willingly left Timbuktu."

"I have never known a blacksmith guild to leave their forges," I said, dazed. I did not even know it was possible.

I recalled the conversation my aunties had shortly before I was taken from Timbuktu, when their discontent pushed them to consider resisting their conditions. But—they could not have actually gone through with that plan, could they? Although on the rare occasion a blacksmith might leave, for a whole guild of blacksmiths to vanish was unheard of. The state depended on us, and in any case, there was no alternative for us to make a living.

"Neither have I," Àrèmọ said grimly. "But it does not matter. I will find your mother, and she will give us her blessing."

There was a glint in his black eyes. It was the same one he had when my mother told him to go away. The same one from when the nobles challenged his intention to marry me.

I had not been able to name it before, but now I thought I un-derstood it better—it was the look of a man who had never been denied something, at least not for long. Whether because it had been granted to him, or he had taken it himself.

At last, I nodded. "I trust that you will."

Surprisingly, I meant it. He may not have cared about my mother's well-being, but he was set on marrying me. And despite his flippant attitude, I knew he was a man who would do any-thing to get what he wanted.

The next morning, after my run with Kọlọ, my handmaids whisked me off to the bathhouse with the velocity of a leaf swept up by a sudden gale.

I would need all day to prepare for tonight's celebration, they
explained excitedly. But as to what kind of celebration was taking
place, none of the four women could provide a clear answer. Apparently, parties in the royal city were so common that question-
ing why one was happening was as useless as asking why the sky
was blue. It just was.

My handmaids bathed me before escorting me back to my
hut, where they worked oils and butters into my skin and hair.
Ìgbín soon arrived to clothe me in a traditional ìró and bùbá
ensemble.

The blouse and wrap skirt were sometimes a pale pink and
sometimes gold, depending on how the light hit the shimmering
aṣọ òkè fabric. A crisp white shawl was folded in half and draped
over my left shoulder, the ends of it resting against the fronts and
backs of my knees. My feet were slipped into fine leather sandals
with rich brown straps that laced up to my midcalf.

The moment she finished, Ìgbín left to dress another noblewoman, leaving my handmaids to drench me in jewelry. Thick
wooden bangles were piled onto my wrists, as dark of a brown as
the leaf-shaped earrings that were clasped to my ears. My neck
was adorned with necklaces of wooden beads, and copper rings
were stacked onto my fingers.

My handmaids sat me on a cushion in front of the mirror—its
edges lacquered with spiraling golden designs—and began re-
braiding my hair. This time, my cornrows were braided in very
small, very neat straight lines from the front of my head down
to my midback.

As my ladies added a dozen wooden beads to each braid, I
looked at my reflection in amazement. My skin glowed black;
my clothes sparkled at the slightest movement. Every part of me
glittered in a way I had only ever seen from the wives of wealthy
merchants and governors. There had been something ethereal
about those women, like the patterns woven in their dresses were
threaded with daydreams.

I wondered—would I now fit in with them? If I walked

through Timbuktu, would children stop in their tracks to watch me go by? Would traders offer me their wares for free, desperate for only the payment of my smile? Would my aunties even recognize me?

No, I did not think they would—not even the me who had been a blacksmith, who had performed backbreaking labor each day, would recognize the woman I saw in the mirror. The thought filled me with warmth.

Kòlò entered my hut, wearing a cobalt ìró and bùbá. Her shawl was as golden as the jewels cuffed to her bantu knots. A chain hung from her center knot, ending in a clear gemstone that dangled over her high forehead. I watched her glide toward me, somewhat transfixed; it was like watching the sun rise for a new day.

"Little flower," Kòlò greeted. "It occurred to me that I should act like the senior wife I am and help you get ready." Her eyes flicked over me before she shrugged, her many bangles clinking together with the raise of her arms. "It would seem the thought occurred to me too late. Well, I can at least add the finishing touches."

A knee brushed my back as the women braiding my hair stood so Kòlò could take their place. They dipped their heads before exiting the room, leaving us alone.

"You'll have a great time tonight," Kòlò promised. "There are many things the Òyó do better than the Alàràá, but even I must admit, parties are not one of them."

"Your father's parties must have been extravagant, though," I said. Yorùbáland was overladen with festivities, and I had no doubt they extended to Òyó as well.

"My father?" Kòlò asked, her voice high as though the question had caught her off guard. "Ah—King Adéjolá hosts many celebrations, yes, but the life of Òyó does not bleed from the splendors of nobles. The land itself is the heart of the city.

"Green was invented there, little flower. There are more trees than you could imagine. It is a jungle that is always moving, with chattering monkeys swinging overhead and leopards prowling in the undergrowth and water—oh, the waterfalls! Imagine, freshwater cascading over rocky cliffs into crystal pools below. Does that not sound amazing?"

"It does," I said. It should have sounded absurd, but the passion with which Kòlò spoke made even flying water sound like something to dream of. "You must really miss it."

"I left half of my heart there. If I could be granted anything, I would just want to be whole again."

She swept my cornrows over one of my shoulders. As she admired her beaded work, I remarked, "All I know of Ọ̀yọ́ is the Ahosi women warriors who defend the city. Many of their stories have reached Timbuktu—is it true what they say, that the Ahosi fight as well as men?"

"Better." She leaned down so that her face was next to mine. Smiling at me in the mirror, her voice took on a mystical note as she continued, "After all, a man is more likely to be faster, and stronger. But a woman? She can take her opponents out of the race altogether."

I returned her smile, but my amusement faded as I recalled the events of the past few days. "That is a truth I may be victim to, if I keep falling for Mama Aláàfin's attempts to get me expelled from the royal city."

"Do not mind her," Kòlò said. "Because she cannot marry her own son, she resents any woman who can."

"She does not seem to resent you," I pointed out.

"Only thanks to you. Before your arrival, she tormented me in the same way. So, you simply need to wait until Àrèmọ finds a third wife, for then his mother's ire will turn to that woman."

It was clear Kòlò meant it as a joke, but I did not find it funny. "Do you really think he would take a third wife?" I asked, the thought bringing with it a surprising amount of dread. Although I did not yet love Àrèmọ, it was clear he loved me. I had become so used to his affection that imagining a life without it felt emptying.

Kòlò's smile faded. "I do not know. If I were his second wife, the answer would be a definitive yes. But you are his second wife, and I have never seen him more content with any woman like he is with you."

The sadness in her voice made me suddenly realize how insensitive my question had been. "I am sorry," I said, turning to face her. "I have no right to worry you about another woman becoming Àrẹ̀mọ's favorite when that is what I did to you."

"You did no such thing. I am his first wife, but I have never been his favorite. He cares for me as much as he does any political agreement." When I did not look convinced, Kọ̀lọ̀ cupped my cheek. "Truly, sweet flower, save your pity. Though I may not have the Aláàfin's affection, I am still allowed his resources. He is richer than my father, and, as his wife, I have been able to send incredible gifts to my family and our friends. I only wish I could send the gifts more regularly, but because Àrẹ̀mọ's feelings for me are limited, so is the number of things I can ask for in his name—but I am sure that is a problem you do not face. Let me stop bothering you with it."

"You are not bothering me. You are my friend, so your worries are my own," I assured her. I recalled the promise Àrẹ̀mọ made when he gifted me the fur yesterday, and an idea occurred to me. "No, I do not face the same issue," I continued, "and that allows me to help you. Perhaps I could ask for more gifts. Then I'll pass those onto you, so you have more to send to your family."

Kọ̀lọ̀ beamed. "Would you do that? Thank you, that would mean so much to me. I am especially partial to the royal city's aṣọ òkè, for I have not found fabrics woven as expertly anywhere else."

She stood and proffered her hand to me, her smile as warming as the sun's rays. "But we can continue discussing this at a later time. Tonight, we have a party to attend."

8

The party was held in a garden of the royal city.

Hedge walls bursting with brilliant flowers bordered a massive vine-covered terrace that pulsed with lively music. Spaced along the perimeter of the terrace were shorter hedges shaped into neat squares. Each one enclosed a clay statue of an elephant with its trunk raised high. Sweet floral and citrus fragrances floated through the garden, and merry fires crackled in bronze braziers, rivaling the countless twinkling diamonds encrusted into the overhead blanket of black.

The heat would do away with all this green in the next few days, of course. But for tonight, the royal city gorged itself on the reckless extravagance.

Àrèmọ sat on a decorated chair positioned on a stone platform at one end of the terrace. Slaves stood on either side of him, fanning him with large palm fronds. He had donned the mantle of the Aláàfin; his body was spun in rich robes that spilled over his seat, and his face was masked by his towering beaded crown. Occasionally, he waved a bejeweled hand in acknowledgment of the circulation of nobles who prostrated before him, bearing lavish gifts. Otherwise, he sat perfectly still, the very picture of an idol surveying his devotees.

I found myself on the outskirts of the terrace, next to tables that creaked under heaps of food. There was charred tilapia immersed in savory stews, and steaming balls of ọfadà rice served on large uma leaves; spicy pepper soup teeming with chicken and goat, and watermelons carved into flamingos that were perched atop nests of berries and cream.

I sampled a skewer of súyà. The dried beef was so spicy that it was hot to the touch. My mouth felt as though it were aflame, but I enjoyed it all the same. As I reached for another, I noticed Rótìmí approaching.

He bowed. "My lady."

As his eyes swept over me, I was unsure of what it was flickering behind his expression, only that I found myself tensing.

When Rótìmí's eyes found mine again, however, all he said was, "You look radiant."

"Thank you," I said stiffly, taking in his light blue agbádá. The loose sleeveless gown and long-sleeved undershirt suited him, though his matching fez cap sat slightly crooked atop his braids.

Rótìmí waited. After a moment, I remembered to say, "You look nice as well."

He laughed. "Please, you need not strain yourself reaching to return the compliment. I have already accepted I cannot compete with your beauty."

"There you are."

A man with very long, tied-up braids appeared next to Rótìmí. He wore a tunic and trousers, an outfit plainer than the agbádás most of the noblemen wore tonight. He slung an arm around Rótìmí's shoulders, and to my surprise, the general allowed it.

"The serving woman didn't want to give me any more palm wine," the man said, raising a goblet in his other hand. He shared Rótìmí's flat, drawn-out way of speaking, as well as the vertical line under each of his eyes. "It took much more effort to convince her than I thought it would."

Rótìmí said, "Be careful, the Aláàfin is strict about how much he allows his soldiers to drink. It would be quite a pain if you got on his bad side."

"If I do get into any trouble, I know you'll just get me out of

it. You owe me, after all, for all the times that I've done the same
for you."

The general rolled his eyes, but he did not truly look annoyed.
He noticed my curiosity and explained, "Òdòdó, this is Captain Ìlérí, my second-in-command. Ìlérí, Òdòdó is the Aláàfin's
bride-to-be."

Ìlérí took my hand and pressed a kiss to its back. "It is my
pleasure to make your acquaintance, my lady. If I had known
how beautiful you were, perhaps I would have decided to stay in
Sàngótẹ̀ for at least one more night."

"You're leaving?" I asked.

"Right after this party. My dear general cannot wait to be rid
of me."

"You are overdramatic—you know I need you in Wúràkẹ́mi,"
Rótìmí said. To me, he explained, "Ìlérí is a very talented strate-
gist. Neither our king nor our army could function without him."

Ìlérí raised his brow. "That sounded like a genuine compliment."

"His mind is sharper than my finest blade, even though he
may not look like it."

"Ah. I spoke too soon." To me, Ìlérí said, "It was a pleasure
making your acquaintance, my lady, but I am sure you've been
subjected to my general's presence enough. Allow me to put you
out of your misery by taking him away—he has been longing to
visit the dance floor."

"That is not true," Rótìmí said.

"You dance, Rótìmí?" I asked.

"No."

"He's the finest dancer in Wúràkẹ́mi!" Ìlérí said. "He's just
being modest. Or perhaps his memory is short, but lucky for
him I have been by his side for years and am always willing to
remember."

"She has no interest in any of that," Rótìmí said.

"Actually," I said, smiling slightly, "I am very interested."

Ìlérí grinned, flashing a gold tooth. "Let me tell you about the time we were stationed along the Senegal River. We were on a mission for . . ."

Ìlérí continued his story, but my attention was on Rótìmí. I wondered if he was aware of the smile slowly spreading across his face as his second-in-command spoke. A smile that, for once, had no caustic layers. It changed him into an entirely different person—and I found I liked this man much better.

When Ìlérí finished his story, I said softly, "It sounds like you two make a good team."

Rótìmí looked at me in shock, as though just remembering I was still here. Behind his expression, a wall rapidly rebuilt itself—but not before a small smile slipped through.

Suddenly, a mellow sound splashed into the music. As it rippled through the garden, the party grew quiet.

Àrèmọ sat as still as ever in his chair. In front of his platform, Gassire now stood next to a seated musician. A large kora was positioned in front of the musician, and as she ran her hands across its many strings, another wave of tranquility undulated through the air.

"Ọba kìí pòkọrin," Gassire boomed, his voice wrapping around the garden. "Gather, gather, come and see. I now tell you the story of how Ṣàngótè came to be."

Ìlérí offered me his arm. I glanced at Rótìmí, and when he gave me a small nod, I took it. The three of us joined the stream of nobles pooling around Gassire, who swayed side to side, caught in the hypnotic strumming of the kora.

"First, know the story of great Ṣàngó, the fourth Aláàfin of Ọ̀yọ́," he began. "There came a day when Ṣàngó sat experimenting with a divine leaf. But in his tinkering, he summoned lightning, setting his bronze palace ablaze and killing his family, plunging himself into grief."

Gassire was not just speaking; his voice swelled and decrescendoed with the music, building and molding the tale into something tangible. I listened, transfixed; just as I was a craftsman of metal, the griot was a craftsman of words.

"Great Ṣàngó left his city. He hanged himself with a glittering bronze chain. But before he did, he looked to the clouds and made this humble vow"—Gassire's voice broadened, rising into the character of Ṣàngó—"'I have wrought destruction, I have wrought death! I have killed those whom I love! For misusing the òrìṣà's power, I must become lightning itself!' And so he became an eternal moral presence, rumbling high above.

"Generations later, the Aláàfin birthed a sickly heir. But the heir's junior brother was strong, and the junior brother was clever, and so maybe, the whispers said, for the choice of the next Aláàfin, the junior brother would be better.

"The heir was sickly, not deaf, and he grew very angry. He said to himself, 'My brother means to take what is mine. What to do, what do I do?'" Gassire sat, his chin on his hand and his brow furrowed. "He thought. And thought. And thought. And he realized there was only one thing he could do.

"That night, great Ṣàngó came to the junior brother in a dream. 'Your brother plots your murder. Tonight you must flee,' he told him. 'But I have seen your heart is gold, so I will guide you to your own city, your own empire, that you will name after me.'"

A movement in the corner of my eye broke the griot's spell on me. On the edge of the terrace, a woman stood listening to Gassire. After a moment, I realized that woman was Kòlò.

Except she looked nothing like herself. Her face, normally calm and playful, was distorted by a rage that sent a chill down the back of my neck. I followed the trail of her gaze to where it ended at Gassire. I frowned; what could the royal griot have done to incur her wrath?

I glanced again at Kòlò, only to see the reason I had been drawn to her direction in the first place: Dígí stood behind her. She stood mostly concealed within the plant wall, but when I met her large dark eyes, she emerged ever so slightly, beckoning me with a subtle move of her hand.

"I'll be back in a moment," I whispered to Ìlérí, disentangling my arm from his.

He and Rótìmí gave me a curious glance, but they nodded. With everyone focused on Gassire, no one paid me any heed as I moved to the other side of the terrace and squeezed through a narrow gap in the hedge wall.

This part of the garden was less polished than where the party was being held; the stone floor had turned to dirt, and vines grew wild, unobstructed by decorations. Without braziers, I had only starlight to guide me as I navigated the hedges.

"Dígí?" I asked quietly; Gassire's resonant voice had faded, but I still did not want to speak too loudly in case I drew the attention of the partygoers.

I jumped in surprise as a shadow broke off from the darkness— Dígí. She rushed to me and grasped my arm. "Òdòdó, my sister, I don't have much time. I just needed to see you before it began."

"What?" I asked in place of a thousand questions. What was she doing here? What did she mean she did not have much time? *What* was going to begin?

"We are leaving very soon," she said, which only left me with more questions. "Some are going as far from here as they can manage, and I do not blame them. But I will stay in Sàngótè, for you. There is a ceramics shop near the royal city's west gate, where a potter is providing me with refuge. If you ever need me, find me there. And thank you, Òdòdó."

Before I could begin to make sense of Dígí's words, twigs crunched behind me. My heart leapt as I whirled around. A large man stumbled down the path in my direction.

"Captain Kiigba," I said. I glanced behind me, but there was only empty space, as though Dígí had never been there.

"You shouldn't go wandering off like this," Kiigba said, bringing my attention back to him. "You never know what dangers lurk in the dark."

"Yes, well . . ." I glanced behind me once more, then shook the strange encounter from my head. "I was just heading back to the party."

I moved to step around Kiigba, but he put a massive hand on

my shoulder. "Wait, wait, wait," he said, chuçkling. "There's no rush. I can keep you safe now that I'm here."

His hand slithered down my arm, summoning unpleasant goose bumps even through the sleeve of my blouse. I stepped back, clutching my arm protectively.

"That's not necessary," I assured him.

I tried to get around him again, but he yanked my arm, causing me to slam into him with enough force that the breath was knocked from my lungs.

"You doubt me, is that it?" he asked, so close that a mist of palm wine settled on my face. "You think it's only your Aláàfin who knows how to keep a woman safe?"

"No, of course not," I said quickly, my words tripping over my growing panic. "Captain Kiigba, please—"

His hand fastened around my neck. My plea broke into a choked sob. I tried to push him away, but it was like attempting to move a mountain.

"Your Aláàfin doesn't even know how to properly claim a woman that's been all but handed to him." His breath was moist on my ear. His free hand trailed along the curve of my hip, bunching the fabric of my dress. "I may be his second-in-command, but I'll be the first to his bride."

His lips crashed into mine. I tried to scream, to pry his hands off, but his grip around my neck tightened. The edges of my vision blackened; the only thing I could register was the overwhelming scent of palm wine.

Then he was gone. I took an involuntary shuddering gasp, my body hunched over in its attempt to relearn how to take in air.

A hand landed on my back. I jumped, my pulse pounding in my ears.

It was only Kòlò. In my frenzied turn, my beaded braids struck her face, and she flinched so hard that I flinched too. My eyes widened at the two horizontal scars on her left cheek, which were now pinkish and swollen. Had I hurt her?

"I'm sorry," I choked, my head whirling. "I didn't mean to, I didn't—"

"Don't. It wasn't you—my tribal mark never healed right. It flares up sometimes." Kòlò pulled me into an embrace, her cocoa butter scent as soothing as the small circles she rubbed in my back. "Hush now. You're okay."

I became aware of yells. My breaths came sporadically as I looked around; Kiigba was on the ground, clutching a dagger sticking out of his side. Standing above him was Rótìmí, whose arms were outstretched to Àrèmọ. The latter had shed multiple colorful layers for mobility, and he had removed his crown, unmasking a murderous expression.

"You've done enough damage," Rótìmí was saying. "Anymore and you'll kill him, and I am sure you understand the consequences of that."

The air around Àrèmọ seemed to waver, as though melting from the heat of his anger. "Get out of my way, or I'll kill you too."

"Òdòdó," Kòlò said sharply, cupping my chin and jerking my face to her. "I said you're okay. Enough with the crying."

Her hands swiped over my cheeks, discarding tears I didn't know I had. She bent down and picked up my shawl; it must have fallen during Kiigba's attack.

"And since you're okay," Kòlò continued, folding my shawl onto my shoulder and straightening my blouse, "we will return to that party, where we will smile. Because regardless of whether she's happy or sad, a good wife is expected to always smile. Okay?"

"My king," Rótìmí yelled.

I looked to see Àrèmọ disappearing around the bend, pushing a disorientated Kiigba in front of him. Rótìmí groaned and rushed after them.

"I said," Kòlò prompted, her grip on my chin tightening painfully, "okay?"

I could not stop sniffing. Kòlò's eyes burrowed into mine, digging for a response. After a moment, I gave a shaky nod.

"Good girl." She released my face and took my arm. We followed a trail of Kiigba's blood back to the party. As we stepped onto the terrace, Kòlò whispered in my ear, "Smile."

My face protested, but I did as she said. Every noble and slave faced the center of the room. As Kòlò and I joined them, I saw they were no longer listening to Gassire; there was a new show happening.

"Captain Kiigba has graciously volunteered to demonstrate his mastery of combat," Àrẹmọ announced, gesturing to a half-conscious and kneeling Kiigba.

Most of the attendees were residents of the royal city, but for the few who were not, their eyes were round with fear and awe as they beheld the Aláàfin's face. They had never seen the king without the mask of his crown; for all they knew, this was the face of Ṣàngó himself.

There was certainly a godlike fury clouding around Àrẹmọ as he declared, "Kiigba will need a weapon—one that's not sticking out of his gut."

The crowd laughed loudly, each noble more determined than the last to show the Aláàfin they were entertained, determined to stay on the right side of the joke. Kòlò jammed her elbow into my side. I forced myself to laugh.

Àrẹmọ snapped his fingers. A guard rushed forward, holding a spear. Àrẹmọ took the weapon then tossed it. With a clatter, it slid across the ground to Kiigba.

"And you know what?" Àrẹmọ asked, making a show of thinking. He tapped a finger to his chin, leaving a red spot of Kiigba's blood on his face. "Because I am kind, I think I will help him with his exhibition."

He held out his hand. Another soldier placed one of his dual axes into his grasp. Àrẹmọ rested the ax head on his shoulder, sizing up the wounded captain.

"Pick up the spear, my friend," Àrẹ̀mọ said gently, as if coaxing a child. "Let's spar."

Kiigba looked around, his eyes wide with fear and glazed with pain. When no one came to his aid, he stretched a bloody hand to the spear.

In the same moment, Àrẹ̀mọ kicked it away, sending it spiraling across the floor. "Such poor dexterity!" he said. "Try again."

Kiigba began crawling to the spear. Àrẹ̀mọ laughed with the other nobles. He could have looked amused had it not been for the tempest whirling in his eyes.

Àrẹ̀mọ turned to the men standing guard over the garden, his arms wide in display. "You see what happens when you're not strong enough to resist the temptation of alcohol?" he asked them. "Be grateful to Captain Kiigba for teaching you this important lesson: alcohol makes you useless." When he turned back to Kiigba, his smile had vanished, any attempt to conceal his blazing anger melted away. "And there is no room in my army for a useless soldier."

Àrẹ̀mọ stepped up to Kiigba—who had nearly reached the spear—and he brought down his ax. I forced myself to keep laughing.

Kiigba's body swayed precariously before collapsing in one direction, his head falling in the other. I forced myself to keep laughing.

The head rolled across the grass and bumped into my feet. Its unseeing eyes were stretched wide with permanent horror.

I forced myself to keep laughing.

Soldiers escorted me from the garden. They returned me to the women's compound, where my handmaids waited for me outside of the bathhouse.

I was stripped of my aṣọ òkè, which now shone with flecks of blood, and lowered into a warm pool. As my handmaids scrubbed me, I kept my hands protectively over my neck, just in case. Kiigba was gone, and I knew my handmaids would not do such a thing, but still. Just in case.

The curtain over the bathhouse's entrance swished, and Àrẹ̀mọ entered. Although veils of steam wavered between us and the water was opaque from soap and perfumes, he kept his eyes on the sky above as he sat on a bench behind me so we both faced the same direction.

My handmaids climbed out of the bath and respectfully knelt in front of their Aláàfin, their heads bowed, before they silently filed out of the bathhouse. After they had gone, Àrẹ̀mọ said, "I apologize for the intrusion. This was the only moment I had to spare tonight, and I needed to check on you before you retired.

"More than that," he went on, "I need to know what you were doing in the gardens, so far away from the party. Some of my men think I acted too impulsively, killing my second-in-command. But after what he did, I am certain there was no other position I could take. I just need to know why I was put in that position in the first place."

I said nothing at first, watching the steam rise from the water with unseeing eyes. I could not tell him I wandered off to speak with Dígí, a blacksmith. Not after he had expressed his displeasure about me associating with my old life; not after I had watched him cut down his own second without hesitation.

"I went to look at flowers," I said at last, and it almost startled me, the emptiness in my voice. "There were so many brought for the party I had never seen before. Then Kiigba came."

A long exhale seeped out of Àrẹ̀mọ. "I see. I am truly sorry for what happened to you tonight. I should have been able to prevent it. I just never anticipated anything like this—especially not from one of my best men."

It took me a moment to realize he was referring to Kiigba as one of his best men. Kiigba, the man who had proven to be crude, clumsy, and unremarkable from the moment I met him.

Once again, I wondered how the man had risen to such a high position in the Aláàfin's army.

"This cannot happen again," Àrẹmọ continued. "If tonight has taught me anything, it is that, try as I might, I cannot always protect you. The only solution is for me to train you so that when I am not with you, and your guards are too slow, you can protect yourself."

"Train me?" I echoed, my shock bringing me out of my numbness. I turned to look at him. He was still looking straight ahead, his jaw set with resolve. "But Gassire told me Aláràá women do not fight."

"They do not, but no one will know about this. I will personally teach you, and we will only train at night—starting tomorrow." He stood. "Good night, my flower. I must return to cleaning up the mess I have made, but I hope that you, at least, are able to find rest tonight."

9

T hat man is not serious."

Startled, I looked at Mama Aláàfin, who chased this sentiment with a sip from a golden goblet. It was only breakfast, but that did not matter; she drank wine with every meal. And when there was not a meal.

For a moment, I believed she had somehow discovered Àrèmọ's plan to train me. But then she continued, "I heard Kútì just took a new wife last month."

"Yes, and the potter's daughter had heard it too," Kòlò said from across the table, her chin raised as her slave dabbed the corners of her mouth with a napkin. "When Kútì tried to court her, she asked him how many wives he had already. But he became offended, telling her, 'That's a personal question.'"

Relieved, I returned to watching my handmaid pluck the seeds from a slice of melon for me. My daily breakfasts with Kòlò and Mama Aláàfin were already stressful because of the potential threat posed by the latter. Ever since she tricked me into greeting the blacksmiths, I had been vigilant for any other attempts she might make to undermine her son's trust in me. Nonetheless, I was even more on edge today, nervous about my lessons with Àrèmọ tonight.

Kòlò rested her chin on her hand, then promptly pulled away, as if she had been burned. I noticed her tribal mark was red, still inflamed from yesterday.

Mama Aláàfin noticed as well. "That old thing is still bothering you, even to this day?" she asked. "A shame you're Òyọ́. I

have never seen the Aláràá botch a tribal mark. Our process is
so efficient that the babies hardly cry."

The corners of Kòlò's mouth tilted upwards, but she did not
smile. "Yes, thankfully, our clans do things very differently. By
the way, have you heard of the thief that the Lawals caught sneaking into their estate? They mean to put the man to death for it."

Kòlò said this very quickly, as though diverting the topic before Mama Aláàfin pushed her to say something she might regret. Lucky for her, Mama Aláàfin was as fond of gossip as she
was of wine. With a sniff, Mama Aláàfin replied, "Good. He
won't do it again."

"Àrèmo?" I said in surprise, interrupting their conversation.

He was approaching the pavilion under which we sat. As we
turned to him, he smiled and said, "I come bearing gifts."

Behind him trailed four slaves. They deposited two open
wooden chests between Mama Aláàfin and me, which overflowed with bronze and beaded necklaces, large gemstones, and
various fabrics.

A fifth slave gave Kòlò her gift: a sparkling emerald necklace
and matching dangling earrings.

"Thank you, husband," Kòlò said, but as soon as he turned
away, her smile fell.

She stood from the table. On her way out, she paused near
the edge of the pavilion, glancing at the treasures next to Mama
Aláàfin and I, before inspecting her own necklace and earrings.
Then she left, abandoning her small gift on a table. I was the
only one who seemed to notice.

"Which one is mine?" Mama Aláàfin asked, looking between
the two chests the slaves had brought.

"Whichever one you choose, they are both the same," Àrèmo
said.

Mama Aláàfin raised a brow. "The same? Even though I am
your mother?"

"You are my mother, and Òdòdó is my bride," he said hap-
pily. "The two most important women in my life."

"In what order?"

But Àrèmọ only laughed. Mama Aláàfin looked at me, and
I knew that if it had been a man who regarded me like that,
Àrèmọ would have held another execution. But as it was, not
even my guards seemed to sense her malice toward me. It was
only I who felt a chill, fearful of what this old woman might do.

To my relief, after a moment, Mama Aláàfin turned back to
her son. "Sit down and eat," she said, gesturing to the breads and
bean porridge set on the table before us. "You need the energy."

Àrèmọ shook his head. "I must return to training and determining if any of Kiigba's sons are good enough to replace him. I
only came to drop these off."

"You have a new scar every day. Are you sure you're not
training too much?"

Mama Aláàfin reached up and cupped his face, inspecting
him with a fondness that she reserved solely for him. I had come
to learn that there were only two things in this world Mama
Aláàfin cared about: her son and opulence—and perhaps she
loved her son mostly because he was her gateway to opulence, a
privilege she wanted to keep as hers and hers alone.

Chuckling, Àrèmọ took his mother's hand and kissed the
back of it. "Better too much than too little. I will see you later."
He moved around the table to where I sat and pressed a kiss to
my cheek. "And you, my flower, I will see tonight," he whispered
in my ear.

As he made his leave, trailed by slaves and guards, I looked at
my new chest of treasure, any unease I had felt fading as I was
overcome by awe. The gems and jewelry glimmered so brightly
in the morning light that they seemed to be wriggling.

"Where am I supposed to put this?" I wondered aloud.

With Àrèmọ gone, Mama Aláàfin's expression had soured.
"Put it on my head," she replied curtly, rising from the table.

She snapped her fingers. Her personal guards rushed forward,
each man grasping one end of a chest. Hauling it onto their
shoulders, they followed her away from the pavilion.

Breakfast was over then, I presumed. It was time to join the other noblewomen in the field so I could run, but it would take a while to drag this chest all the way back to my hut. Well, I supposed the sooner I started, the sooner I would make it to the field.

With a sigh, I rose from my chair and grabbed the chest's handles. My days of hammering metals until my arms ached not too far behind me, I was able to lift it by myself. But no sooner had I done so than my guards rushed forth, causing me to drop the chest in surprise.

"Apologies, my lady," one said quickly as they bowed. "We must have missed when you signaled us to carry this. Please forgive us."

I stared. "There is nothing to forgive. I did not signal for you."

"Have we caused you offense?"

"What? No, of course not."

"Then why did you not call on us?"

"I don't know, I hadn't thought of . . ." I trailed off under their confused expressions, suddenly feeling silly.

Had I not just seen Mama Aláàfin's guards rush to her aid? But then again, she was *her*. She was familiar with this way of living. Meanwhile, not two weeks ago, I was still laboring alongside my aunties.

"I would not want to bother you with such a trivial matter, anyways," I said, hoping to distract from my clear lapse in judgement.

"There is no task too big or too small, my lady. Give us a command, any command at all, and we'll do it."

"Would you leap from a balcony if I told you to?" I asked jokingly, offering a nervous chuckle.

The men did not laugh. They did not even smile. Their faces deadpan, they replied in unison, "Yes."

Silence settled between us. After a moment, I realized the two men were still awaiting my orders.

"Er—can you take this to my quarters? Please?"

"Yes, my lady."

They bowed then picked up the chest. Although they grunted from the effort, they did so without complaint. I watched them leave in amazement. That was the first time I had ever given an order; I could not believe they had done as I said.

No—of course they had obeyed. I was the Aláàfin's future wife. Regardless of my past, this was my life now. It was natural to be served; next time something like this happened, I would make sure to not be surprised.

Holding my head higher, I gestured to my remaining two guards, and they followed me to the field. The soft dawn illuminated the women exercising, their joyful cheers mingling with the birds' morning songs. I looked for Kòlò and found her walking some distance away.

As I caught up with her, I said, "I'm sorry about the small present that Àrèmo got for you. It wasn't very kind of him."

"Not everyone is as kind as you are, sweet flower," Kòlò said, waving a hand dismissively.

"Do you want something from my chest? My offer from yesterday still stands."

Kòlò's brave face softened into a smile. "That is very thoughtful. Sure, I will come by your hut after our run."

I nodded, glad I could at least do that for her. As we walked, I watched a race occurring between two women. A cheering crowd had gathered around them. I frowned; something felt off. After a moment, I realized there were about ten less women present than normal—Kiigba's wives and daughters.

"Where is Kiigba's family?" I asked.

Kòlò looked around, just now noticing their absence too. "I suppose now that he's dead, they need to find somewhere else to live."

"But aren't his sons still here?" I asked, remembering what Àrèmo had said earlier.

"I don't doubt it—they still need to serve in the Aláàfin's army, after all. But if I recall correctly, none are old enough to be the head of his household, since they're not done with their training. So, the women in his family will need to find another man to live with."

Shocked, I looked around at the noblewomen. As usual, they completed their exercises with such grace that they looked otherworldly. They should have been untouchable—and yet, in just one night, the lives of the women in Kiigba's family had changed forever.

"Ah, look," Kọ̀lọ̀ said, oblivious to my troubled thinking. "Our guests are here."

We had come to a palm tree, under which sat two women. I had never seen them before; they wore the same plain exercise dresses as myself and the other noblewomen, though they also wore low turbans on their heads.

"These are the wives of Sheikh Omar al-Hakim, one of Yorùbáland's newer governors," Kọ̀lọ̀ explained. "The sheikh is sojourning in the royal city while he petitions the Aláàfin for new policies. And because I know how dull it is to have to sit and wait for your husband, I invited these women to run with us today."

"Peace be upon you, my lady," the older of the two women said to me in accented Yorùbá. She dipped her head, and I did the same.

The younger woman said, "Thank you again for inviting us, your majesty. I'm excited to run with you—it'll be good preparation for our journey."

"Journey?" I asked.

"Yes, our sons are now old enough, so we're embarking on a trip right after we leave Ṣàngótẹ̀. I'm afraid I can't say much more than that. Our husband doesn't want anyone to know—I probably shouldn't even have mentioned it."

"Mentioned what?" Kọ̀lọ̀ said, and the two women laughed.

As we began stretching, angry shouts drew our attention. It was not coming from the other noblewomen; even they had paused their various activities to see what was happening.

A dozen women were walking past our field. They wore tattered cloaks fastened by the Aláàfin's three-headed elephant
emblem, and there were scars on their arms. The royal city's
blacksmiths.

Dígí was among them. No sooner than I saw her did her eyes
find me as well. I frowned, trying to silently ask her the reason
for this. But she only gave me a firm nod before looking ahead
once more.

A handful of nearby soldiers began jeering at the blacksmiths.
It was then that I noticed the ill-concealed disdain with which
the noblewomen around me watched the scene. I scanned the
field, pausing when my gaze landed on Mama Aláàfin. While
everyone watched the blacksmiths leave, Mama Aláàfin watched
me with narrowed eyes. Scared she had seen the brief silent
exchange between Dígí and I, I quickly looked away from the
procession.

"You said you have sons?" I asked, turning back to the sheikh's
wives. "You must tell me about them."

The sheikh's wives did not make it very far before they tired.
After thanking Kòlò and I, they returned to their lodging while
we ran onwards.

Once we were done and had both cleaned up, Kòlò came
to my hut. Even after giving her a dozen jewel-encrusted ornaments, the wooden chest Àrèmo had gifted me remained nearly
full. For good measure, I also had my handmaids find Ìgbín and
retrieve from her two bundles of the aṣọ òkè that Kòlò had expressed interest in yesterday. The items were placed on a wooden
cart in preparation for slaves to move them out of the royal city
and deliver them to Kòlò's family.

"You are the kindest friend I have made in Ṣàngótè," Kòlò
beamed, and when she pulled me into her warm embrace, I felt
as though I could say the same about her.

Soon after she left my hut with the presents, Gassire arrived for my lessons. Helping Kòlò had distracted me, but once I was able to sit still, I found myself worrying about my impending training session with Àrèmọ. The royal griot was not impressed by my absent-mindedness; when he saw that his lessons were not sticking, he made me copy an entire manuscript. Working with the reed stylus still felt unnatural, but at least I was beginning to be able to recognize basic words.

By the time I returned from my nightly music session, my stomach was twisting itself into knots. I had not seen Àrèmọ since morning; what if he had changed his mind? What if he had forgotten? What if—?

A knock.

I stopped pacing, looking at my door intently. When another knock came, I accepted I had not imagined the sound.

I opened the door, and there stood the Commander of Death. He wore his training outfit—black trousers and his axes hanging from his belt. I suddenly felt ill-prepared in my green wrapper.

But if Àrèmọ thought anything of my choice of attire, I could not tell; his face was unreadable as he jerked his head to the side. "Come."

I followed him, but he had taken only a few paces when he came to a halt and turned around. "Your services are not needed tonight," he said, his eyes over my head.

I glanced over my shoulder in time to see my guards give him a solemn nod before returning to their posts outside my hut. When I faced forward again, he was already halfway to the gate of the women's compound. I jogged to catch up.

This late at night, the only people moving through the royal city were slaves and patrolling soldiers. As we walked down path after torchlit path, a silence thicker than the humidity bloated between us. I watched his stoic expression from the corner of my eye, wondering if I should have felt more frightened.

Once we neared one of the great walls bordering the royal city, Àrèmọ stepped off the stone path onto an open field. We made our way to torches at the center, grass crunching beneath our sandals. As we stepped into the circle of light, Àrèmọ turned to me.

"Before we begin," he said, "I want to make it clear that there will be limitations to your training. Men begin their military training at age seven. They are underfed for years in preparation of the hunger pains that may come during deployment. They march barefoot until the bottoms of their feet are stone. They're moved to the front lines once a year until they retire. These are things I will never put you through, but this protection comes at a cost—you will not be as skilled as most attackers you may encounter."

I hesitated, then asked, "Is that why you're upset with me?"

Àrèmọ looked shocked. "What do you mean?"

"You've been quiet since you came to get me, so I assumed you're having second thoughts—though I'd like to remind you this was your idea, not mine."

For the first time tonight, a small smile appeared on Àrèmọ's face. "And I stand by it. I have not changed my mind, but I apologize if I've been cold, my flower. I am still thawing from my irritation with this Èsù-harassed day. This morning, all my blacksmiths left the royal city. They still have not returned—I do not think they are going to. None of my men realized this, and so the fools simply allowed them to walk away."

Suddenly, I remembered my encounter with Dígí at the party last night. In the mayhem that had been Kiigba's execution, I had all but forgotten. This must have been what she had tried to warn me of. *But I will stay in Sàngótè, for you*, she had said. I needed to find a way to meet her without my guards knowing; I needed to know what the blacksmiths were up to.

In his venting, Àrèmọ did not notice my sudden stillness. "But even more vexing than that," he continued, "I have been fighting a new petition all day."

Pulling my mind away from the blacksmiths, for now, I thought back to earlier today. "The petition made by the sheikh?" I asked.

"Yes, he wants me to lessen the number of soldiers at our

borders and instead deploy them throughout Yorùbáland. He claims this would enable better protection for merchants and thus facilitate more trade. Of course I acknowledge the importance of merchants, but if I allow my war efforts to stall now, Yorùbáland will never become as large as I know it could be. Nonetheless, there are already those in my court who have always been hesitant to expand further, and they are using the sheikh's petition to further their own motives. The more supporters the sheikh gains, the harder it becomes for me to dismiss him."

"If he's the main advocate for the change, and its support would evaporate without him, why not just draw out the final decision until after he's gone? He's leaving in a few days for his pilgrimage."

Àrèmọ frowned. "Why would he take a pilgrimage? He has been vocal of his conversion to the Yorùbá religion ever since he swore allegiance to me."

"Well, his wives did not explicitly say they were going on a pilgrimage, but that is what it sounded like." I thought for a moment and added, "They also said their husband had not wanted them to tell anyone about it. Perhaps this is why."

"So his faith wouldn't be used against him," Àrèmọ said slowly, his expression clearing. "You learned all this from the man's wives?"

"Well, yes," I said, somewhat uncertainly. It was just trivial gossip, after all.

But apparently Àrèmọ did not find this information so trivial. "I suppose that women are often exposed to the affairs of their fathers, husbands, and sons," he mused, as though he had never considered the thought before. He had become contemplative, regarding me with his head tilted to one side.

After a moment, he said, "Sometimes, I almost regret my rash decision to kill Kiigba."

I flinched, but Àrèmọ placed a calming hand on my arm.

"I said almost," he said gently. "Of course, I would do it again.

He hurt you, and that is justification enough to take any man's life, no matter who he is. But there have been times when I am overwhelmed about how to fix the hole in my ranks left by my second."

"Was he that good of a soldier?" I asked, confused.

"No. In fact, Kiigba was terrible at combat," Àrèmọ said, confirming what was evident to anyone who had merely looked at the man. "It is possible he had been skilled once. But as an older man he had lost his agility, and as a rich, successful man, he had lost his drive.

"However, he was useful in other ways. Most of the high-ranked soldiers are at least a couple years my elder. To earn their respect, I had to do no less than conquer one of the great cities my ancestors failed to. When that did not work, I conquered another. Even now, I still work to prove my age does not inhibit my rule. But Kiigba was my father's second-in-command. He had more friends than I do, and thus he was better informed about the happenings in my court."

"He was a means of information for you," I realized aloud.

I had never understood why Àrèmọ kept a man as average as Kiigba so close to him—but now I saw that averageness was exactly what made Kiigba useful. His simple air, combined with his extensive experience in the Aláàfin's army, had given him an approachable disposition that loosened tongues.

I recalled the first time I had met Kiigba, how he had known the names of my guards, who were so often smeared into the background. I thought it had been my guards who told Àrèmọ of my visit to the blacksmiths, but now it occurred to me that it was more likely they had reported to Kiigba.

Àrèmọ nodded. "And now that he is dead, I feel as though I am missing an ear in my own court. I had thought with Kiigba gone, I would need to earn my nobles' trust myself, that it would take years before I was again privileged to the kinds of information he brought me. But now I see that won't be necessary, not when I have access to the innermost part of their lives: their women. Or, at least, I could." His hand moved from my arm to my chin, tilting my head up. "Would you do that for me, my flower?"

I hesitated. Not because I did not want to say yes, but because I was not sure if it was even in my power to make such a decision. "I couldn't replace your seasoned advisor," I said. "I wouldn't know what to do with the information I manage to collect."

"You do not need to worry about how to use it. Just tell me exactly what you hear, and I will determine its value."

Although I was still reluctant, I said, "I suppose I could do that."

The warmth of Àrèmọ's smile melted the edge off this conversation. "Thank you," he said, and I smiled as he kissed my cheek. "I look forward to hearing what you have for me. But for tonight, let us begin your training."

I watched as he walked around me and extracted his double-sided axes from his belt.

"Are you going to give me one?" I asked curiously.

"Firstly, please do not insult my axes by implying that I would fight with one without the other. Secondly—" he dropped the axes to the ground, where they landed with a thud "—there is nothing to teach about swinging an ax. What every warrior must first learn is his way around the body."

He took my wrist and gently raised my arm, his hand brushing along the underside of my bicep. "A cut here could be fatal if your enemy doesn't get help in time. But more often than not, it only results in a mess of blood."

He placed his hands on my waist, smiling slightly, as though he knew my heart was racing. "Aim here," he said, dragging a hand across my lower abdomen, "and you pierce an organ. Most do not heal from that, but they die too slow for my liking. That's why I prefer . . ." He leaned down until his eyes were level with mine and grasped the inside of my thigh. "Here," he said softly, over my sharp intake of air. "The only catch is that there is no room for error. You must strike deeply enough the first time around."

His grip tightened for just a moment before he released me.

I suppressed a shiver as his hand slid up my front slowly and stopped under my collarbone. "The heart is a safe bet. Break a man's heart, and you've broken him completely."

Àrèmọ moved behind me. The smell of rain danced around me. I closed my eyes as he put his hands on either side of my head. "Even more of a guarantee is the head. But the absolute best way to kill a man . . ."

He tilted my head and brushed my hair aside, exposing my neck. Very slowly, he dragged a finger from one side of my neck to the other.

"This," he whispered, his cheek brushing against my ear, "is by far the most vulnerable part of the body. When used correctly, it leaves no chance of survival. You hold their life in your hands."

The warmth behind me vanished. I blinked my eyes open to see him walking away. While his back was turned, I fixed my hair, not entirely sure why it was difficult to breathe.

Àrèmọ picked a long wooden stick off the ground and tossed it to me. Miraculously, my hand closed around it in time.

"Now that the foundation has been set," Àrèmọ said, "the only thing left to do is build."

"You want me to hit you?"

He grinned, picking up his own stick. "I want you to try."

I looked between him and the stick uncertainly. He waited patiently, his stick resting on his shoulder. With a shrug, I walked up to him. He did not move. Was he going easy on me?

I raised the stick over my head and aimed for the side of his torso, one of the deadly spots he had taught me. I did not see him move, only felt my stick ripped out of my grasp midswing. Shocked, I watched it fall to the ground a couple paces away. When I turned back, Àrèmọ's stick was next to my head.

"Dead," he said softly. He flipped his stick back onto his shoulder.

My eyes narrowed, but he only smiled. Shaking out the sting in my hands, I retrieved my stick. I took a deep breath then swung around quickly—only to have Àrèmọ's stick prod my stomach.

"Dead." He reset his position.

I aimed for his heart. He got to mine first. "Dead."

Frustrated, I swung with as much force as I could. Àrèmọ ducked and darted toward me. There was a shove in my shoulder and a foot behind my ankle, and the next thing I knew, I was falling.

Pain shot up my spine as I hit the ground. Before I could catch my breath, Àrèmọ was standing over me, his stick at my throat. "Extremely dead."

"This is useless," I huffed, pushing the stick away. "I'm not learning anything."

"Nonsense. You're doing a wonderful job learning how to die." He proffered his free hand to me. "And once you can recognize death, you understand what to avoid."

I looked up at him. The twinkle in his eyes rivaled the stars shining behind him.

With a sigh, I took his hand.

10

Each night, Àrèmọ came to my hut to fetch me for training. Our original plan was that I learn the basics of combat, just enough for me to be able to defend myself.

But then the blacksmith strikes began. As it turned out, the royal city's blacksmiths had not been alone in walking away from their forges; blacksmiths throughout Yorùbáland were disappearing. I wondered if my mother was among them, but I had no way of knowing; there continued to be no sign of her, no matter how far Àrèmọ extended his search.

The more blacksmith guilds that mysteriously abandoned their posts, the more I knew I needed to visit Dígí. I needed to know why they were behaving like this, but more than that, I needed her help in finding my mother. If the blacksmiths were all moving as one, then perhaps Dígí had resources for finding Okóbí that Àrèmọ did not.

As weeks went by, I found myself leaning into my combat training. It was the one thing I could control, the one thing that did not make me feel as though I was completely helpless. My progress was slow, but each bruise only invigorated me, leaving me wanting more.

That was what my days became: more, more, *more*. I had possibly sacrificed the chance to ever see my mother again in order to escape a fate of being nothing; I would not allow it to be for naught.

I ran for hours before dawn. My lungs became more efficient, and my legs grew stronger. What Kòlò had told me during our very first run had been true; it never got easier. But I learned its nuances, learned that if I pushed to the top of one hill, I was rewarded in the form of an easy descent so long as I kept going.

In the beginning, Kòlò was at my side, but her trips into Sàngótè became more and more frequent, leaving me alone. Even so, I upheld my promise to her, having my handmaids regularly deliver gifts of aṣọ òkè to her hut. The few times I did happen to run into Kòlò, she thanked me, assuring me that my continued efforts were greatly appreciated.

In my literacy lessons with Gassire, my progress moved at a snail's pace. However, I found joy in the manuscripts that I struggled through because it meant there was still something more for me to learn. I learned that just as with my physical training, my mind was also a muscle that needed consistent challenges to advance.

In my evening music sessions, I collected gossip that, come midnight, I presented to Àrèmọ when we sparred—or, occasionally, when we took a break from our training in order to walk Ajá.

"He becomes restless if he is confined to the stables for too long," Àrèmọ explained one night. "And walking him after dark, when there are fewer people around, makes him less of a hazard to others."

"I understand that," I said. "What I do not understand is why we must ride him."

"It is the best way to connect with him, and he has been wanting to get to know you for a while now."

I looked skeptically at the elephant, who stood next to us outside the stables. Nearby torches illuminated his golden gaze, in which there was not even the slightest hint of interest in me. In fact, now that the stable hands who Ajá had been terrorizing upon our arrival had fled, the elephant seemed quite bored.

"Well," Àrèmọ said after a moment, "at least, I want him to

get to know you. He is kind to those whom he considers a friend."
To Ajá, Àrèmo said sharply, "Up!"

The elephant bent one of his front legs. Àrèmo proffered his
hand to me, and with a sigh I accepted it, allowing him to help
me step onto the bend in Ajá's leg. From there, I lifted myself
onto his neck and straddled the back of his head.

As Àrèmo climbed up behind me, he resumed our earlier
conversation. "In regard to the captain I mentioned to you," he
said, "I am unsure how to proceed at this point. The man is increasingly subverting my orders, and I cannot demote him without offending his family and their allies. I moved his firstborn
son to the front lines in hopes of reeling him back, but he seems
unmoved."

"You're focusing on the wrong son," I said, thinking back to a
conversation I had with the man's senior wife and what she had
confessed to me in her discontent. "His third wife is his favorite,
the mother of his fifth son. That is the son who will inherit his
fortune and thus whom he hopes sees the least combat."

Ajá shifted beneath us, and I added, "Can't we use a saddle
chair?"

"The saddle chair is only for pageantry. You need your feet
hanging behind his ears—pressing on either side of him signals
which direction he should turn. Do not worry, my flower. As I've
told you before, I will never let you fall."

Affirming this, Àrèmo wrapped his arm securely around my
waist and pressed a kiss to my cheek. I rolled my eyes, but I was
smiling.

As he pulled away, he said, "And I know the boy who you
are referring to, but if I recall correctly, he still has several years
before he becomes an official soldier. He was never going to see
combat soon anyways."

"His mother believes he's destined for great things, so why
not help him reach that potential? You've realized how talented
the boy is, and you want him to command his own squad at

the border immediately. To do so at such an age would be an honor—the boy would be elated. His father, however, would likely want to appease you in whatever way he can to prevent such a promotion."

"Very well, I will update you tomorrow," Àrèmọ said, and I could hear the grin in his voice. He put my hands on Ajá's ears, making sure I held them firmly. "We will allow Ajá to wear himself out, then we will review a few more drills before retiring for the night."

I nodded, looking down expectantly at the elephant. When he only continued to shift in place, however, I said, "You have told me how to steer him, but how do I make him go?"

"Ah, that is a very complicated procedure. It has taken me years to master this command, so watch closely." Àrèmọ leaned over me, as close to one of Ajá's ears as he could reach. "Ajá," he said. "Go."

The elephant trumpeted excitedly and launched into a trot. I gasped as I lurched forward, but Àrèmọ, one of his hands still safely around my waist, only laughed. His joy was contagious; I relaxed gradually, growing more at ease with each turn I successfully guided us into.

After Ajá completed several laps around the elephant stables, Àrèmọ and I left him with stable hands before returning to the remote field where he always trained me. I was grateful he was teaching me how to protect myself, but I also learned there was more than one way a woman could find strength. Being betrothed to the Aláàfin did not just grant me an easier life, as I had thought it would. I was placed right next to the Aláàfin's power, so close that, sometimes, I could touch it. The gap was bridged by the rumors and gossip I collected, and each time I made it across, I felt a thrill that made me want more.

Other times, however, the gossip I had gathered was no more than entertainment that we laughed about. I counted these nights no less successful; I liked Àrèmọ's laugh. It was the very

first gift he had ever given me, one of the few things from my
past life that I was grateful to keep. If I did not have my mother,
at least in the meantime, I had him.

Wet season returned, repopulating the skies with perpetual
storm clouds. It was on one such night, when a downpour threatened to spill from above, that the inhabitants of the royal city
gathered outside. Not only was this perfect weather for them,
but also their Aláàfin was returning, and they were determined
to greet him.

There were so many people crowded in front of the great
stone gate that I had to stand on an upturned crate to see. I need
not have bothered; the moment the gate creaked open, there
was Àrèmọ, looming over everyone from Ajá's broad back. The
elephant blended into the night like a large shadow with flashing
yellow eyes.

Cheers erupted as the Aláàfin strolled forth, surrounded by
his soldiers. They had just returned victorious from east of the
Niger, where they had taken the city of Gao from the Songhai.
The city was a trading center like Timbuktu, though not quite
as powerful.

Àrèmọ dismounted, and as he passed his steed to stable
hands, Ajá became restless—I was sure that the beast was only
settled in the presence of the Aláàfin. But Àrèmọ took no notice;
he brushed off the throngs of nobles flocking around him until,
at last, he found me. A smile broke over his face, rejuvenating his
tired features.

"The light of my life," he greeted. "Thank you for guiding me
back home."

I smiled as he pulled me into an embrace. Petrichor danced
around my senses, a smell that I was sure had nothing to do with
the impending rain. The scent was a comfort I had not known I
missed until now that I had it back.

Musicians appeared, and slaves arranged torches into a circle to form a makeshift dance floor, and the Aláàfin's welcome soon turned into a party. As Àrẹ̀mọ went to make rounds, I noticed Rótìmí sitting on the edge of the field, somewhat removed from the revelers. I headed toward him; he and I did not have a friendship, per say, but ever since the party in which Kiigba had been killed, his caustic attitude toward me had faded.

As I sat next to him, I said, "You must join the celebration, Rótìmí. You have yet to show me your vaunted dance skills."

Rótìmí's lips twisted into a wry smile. "I apologize, my lady, but I must once again postpone such an exhibit. At the moment, I am too preoccupied with thoughts of my second-in-command."

He tried to keep his tone light, but there was a heaviness weighing him down. My smile faded. "Did he . . . ?" I began, then stopped, unsure how to ask.

Rótìmí turned to me quickly, chuckling. "Oh, no. No, he's not dead, Ṣàngó yọ mí. That would be my greatest fear—that is, because he keeps Wúràkẹ́mí afloat." He added the last part so swiftly the words ran into each other.

A pause.

He cleared his throat and explained, "It has simply been a while since I last heard from him. I am concerned some situation has arisen."

"Nothing he cannot handle, I am sure," I said. "From what I remember about Captain Ìlérí, he is an intelligent man."

Rótìmí's expression softened, but he turned away before his face could fully melt into a smile. "Oh, look," he said. "It would seem the Aláàfin seeks once more to impress his bride."

It was a clunky attempt at a subject change, but I allowed it all the same. Rótìmí gestured across the field, where Àrẹ̀mọ stood with a few soldiers. When my eyes met his, he grinned before turning back to them. He held out his hand, and a man gave him a longbow and an arrow.

Rótìmí and I exchanged looks of exasperation, but I perked up in spite of myself, excited to see Àrẹ̀mọ excited. More men had gathered behind the Aláàfin, watching as he nocked an arrow. Ahead of him, a guard tossed a mango into the air. It flashed red and green before it was whisked forward by the arrow and pinned to a tree.

As cheers rose around him, Àrèmọ looked toward the center of the field. I followed his gaze to see General Ọmóṣẹwà dancing with one of his wives. Because of his vocal opposition to my marriage with Àrèmọ the first day I arrived, I did not like him. However, it was much harder to remember that as I watched him. His reddish-brown skin, complemented by a deep plum agbádá, shined from scented oils, and his hazel eyes were more green than brown today, like an oasis blossoming in the middle of the Sahara. There was something unreal about Ọmóṣẹwà's beauty; he was a perfection I had never seen from either a man or a woman. Even now, I noticed the gazes of noblemen and women alike lingering on him.

"Ọmóṣẹwà," Àrèmọ called.

Ọmóṣẹwà looked over his shoulder. "No."

"Then I've won by default."

A sliver of amusement cracked through Ọmóṣẹwà's irritation. His wife pulled him toward her, clearly wanting to hold him for as long as possible, but he merely gave her a kiss before walking to Àrèmọ.

"That," he said, "is the only way you could ever win."

A guard, blushing slightly, gave Ọmóṣẹwà a longbow and arrow. Ọmóṣẹwà nocked the arrow, but as another man prepared to toss a mango, Ọmóṣẹwà said, "No. My target is already there."

Spectators exchanged looks of confusion. Ọmóṣẹwà took careful aim before loosing his arrow. It flew through the air and embedded itself into the tree, near the pinned mango. For a moment, I thought the general's target had been the mango and thus his miss was even more embarrassing because it was static.

That was, until a soldier jogged to the wall, inspected the arrow, then announced, "You've killed a fly, sir."

The men roared their praise, even louder than they had for

Àrèmọ. Ọmóṣẹwà remained unmoved. In a bored voice, he said, "It's not dead."

Amazement glazed the guard's face as he looked at the arrow once more. "No—Ṣàngó yọ mí, it's alive! You pinned it by its *wing*."

The entire yard burst into applause. Ọmóṣẹwà flicked a hand in lazy acknowledgement before walking away, presumably back to his wives. I waited for Àrèmọ to do the same, to approach me so I could tell him that, although he lost, I admired his effort. However, Àrèmọ seemed to have forgotten all about impressing me; a glint shone in his black eyes as he lifted his bow, determined to rise to this new challenge.

Disappointed, I turned to continue my conversation with Rótìmí—when Ọmóṣẹwà dropped onto the grass beside us.

"You're sitting with the witch?" Ọmóṣẹwà asked, eating chin chin from his hand. "My friend, you need a wife."

Rótìmí blinked a few times, clearing his throat. I understood how he felt; seeing Ọmóṣẹwà from afar was very different from having him suddenly appear so close. It gave one little time to prepare.

"I am too busy for marriage," Rótìmí said when he had caught his breath.

Ọmóṣẹwà laughed. The sound in itself was a harmony. "I admire your dedication. The dutiful general committed to his work—especially to training soldiers. I've seen you leaving the barracks very late at night. If I didn't know better, I'd think you were looking to replace your second-in-command."

Rótìmí smiled his vague smile. "It is fortunate, then, that you do know better. Although I wonder how it is that you think you have seen me leaving the barracks so late were you not there yourself."

Ọmóṣẹwà's hand, halfway to his open mouth, froze. The two men stared at each other—Ọmóṣẹwà's large, soft eyes locked onto Rótìmí's sharp, sarcastic gaze—before Ọmóṣẹwà laughed.

"I admit, I am fairly committed to my work as well," Ọmóṣẹwà said. "That is why I am so grateful for my wives and children. Because no matter how strenuous my days may be, ultimately, it is their affection that I return to. That is the important part."

Rótìmí's patience had worn so thin that his irritation showed through. "How honorable of you, to be so faithful to your family. I must admit, your declaration of love is simply too much for my cold bachelor heart to take. So forgive me, but for my health, I must remove myself from this conversation."

With a courteous dip of his head, Rótìmí rose to his feet. As he walked away, Ọmóṣẹwà sighed. "I often forget how sensitive Rótìmí is. He is good at pretending otherwise." There was a pause, then Ọmóṣẹwà said, "Do you not want to talk to me either?"

My heart stalled when I saw that he was looking at me. "We've never talked before," I said, dazed. *Not since you called me a witch and advocated for my removal*, I added silently.

"We can start." Ọmóṣẹwà reached over and stilled my hand; I had not even noticed I had been fiddling with my bangles. "And if it's too loud for you here, we can find somewhere quieter to speak."

I met his gaze in wonder, in confusion. Was this not the man who had hated me the moment he had met me?

I should have pulled away. However, this was not like Kiigba's attack; Ọmóṣẹwà's touch was impossibly gentle, as gossamer as a cool breeze and almost making me shiver. I was being given a choice, one that I was tempted to make. And yet—

"But Àrèmọ," I whispered, glancing across the yard. "I don't know if . . ."

Whatever I had been about to say was singed from my mind as I turned back to Ọmóṣẹwà. His tender expression had morphed into a burning anger.

"What does the Aláàfin have to do with this?" he hissed. "Did you mention him to make me jealous, as though I want you? As though anyone would want a witch?"

His anger infected me. "It was you who approached me—*ah*."

My protest broke into a cry as Ọmóṣẹ̀wà twisted my hand painfully.

Once more, I glanced across the yard. Àrẹ̀mọ was too absorbed in impressing his men to notice my predicament. My anger quickly turned to fear as Ọmóṣẹ̀wà's face grew murderous. But there were traces of something else amidst his rage—was that shame?

"It was you," he said sotto voce, "whose spell almost robbed me of my sense. But you see that fly?" His gaze did not leave my own as he jerked his head to the tree across the yard. "The moment that I get the chance, I will do the same to you, putting an end to your witchcraft. This I promise."

11

The party was still going when Àrèmọ and I slipped away for my training session. As soon as we were alone, I told him of Ọmóṣẹwà's promise.

"He did not mean it, my flower," Àrèmọ assured me, rubbing my back. "Ọmóṣẹwà has an unfortunate temper, but he is an extraordinary general. He would not do anything to put his position at risk."

I felt silly as I realized I had overreacted. Àrèmọ had to be right—he understood his general better than I did. I nodded, and as we proceeded with my training session, I put Ọmóṣẹwà's declaration behind me.

But when I went to sleep that night, I revisited my first garden party at the royal city in my dreams. It was not the first time I had dreamt of Kiigba's execution, but this time was the most vivid. So vivid that I could feel the weight of Kiigba's head bumping to a stop against my feet; that I could see its wide eyes, bloodstained and blank.

I awoke from the nightmare with a start. It was not yet dawn, and although my training had gone late into the night, I rose from my bed, deciding to pick up where we had left off. This early in the morning, the grounds of the royal city were mostly empty. Only my guards bore witness to my self-training, but I did not worry about them taking note of me; without my training stick, the movements looked similar to exercise.

I practiced outside the women's compound, feeling calmer with each motion. It was what I would have done to Kiigba had I known then what I know now; it was what I would do to Ọmọṣẹwà or any other man who ever tried to hurt me again.

A slave turned onto a nearby path, pulling a wheelbarrow behind him. I had been in the middle of a drill, but I quickly lunged to appear as though I had been stretching. "Good morning," I said to the slave as he walked by.

He paused to prostrate, and I saw that his wheelbarrow was full of various roots, bark, and flowers. At the same time, I was struck by a medley of heavenly fragrances. "Oh," I said, "those smell lovely."

He beamed. "I am glad you think so, my lady. They are going to be rendered into oils for your wedding."

"My wedding?" I asked, confused; I had not heard anything about this.

"Yes, the Aláàfin has instructed us to acquire every scent we can find. He wants to ensure that you have a wide variety of fragrances from which to select your favorite."

He plainly expected me to be pleased with this information, but when I did not return his smile, his own faltered. "Excuse me, please," I said, turning around.

I marched through the women's compound until I arrived at my hut. My guards repositioned themselves outside as I pushed open my door to see him: the all-powerful Aláàfin and Commander of Death sprawled on a makeshift bed of cushions, snoring softly in his peaceful slumber.

When our training sessions ran especially long and the both of us were too tired to care about optics, Àrèmọ spent the night here. Although men were not allowed in the women's compound, no one was going to oppose the Aláàfin.

I closed the door behind me loudly enough to wake him. He peered at me sleepily as I stood over him, my arms folded across my chest.

"Why was I just told that fragrances are being prepared for our wedding?" I asked.

He shut his eyes and pinched the bridge of his nose, as though he could squeeze the sleep from his system. "I was in the middle of a wonderful dream," he sighed. "There was the most beautiful girl I had ever seen. She looked like you."

"You promised we would not marry until I was ready."

"She looked exactly like you, actually. Same face, same height, same braids." One of his eyes opened and squinted up at me. "Yet you cannot be her, because she only ever smiled at me. But you, imposter, look like you want to step on me."

"Àrẹ̀mọ."

With a large yawn, he sat up, stretching his arms over his head. His blanket pooled around his hips, and though I knew he wore trousers, my eyes unwillingly darted down to his bare torso.

"I am merely planning for the future," Àrẹ̀mọ said. He wrapped his arms around my legs and rested his chin on my thigh, peering up at me. "No date has been scheduled for the wedding. That decision is still yours to make."

Some of the tension left my shoulders, but not all. "But not even preparations should begin yet," I said, moving a braid out of his face. I hated when they came loose from his bun, but he never seemed to care. "I don't want any aspect of our union to proceed without my mother here."

"Yes, so you've said, my flower, but with the blacksmith strikes laying waste to Yorùbáland's reserves, it's becoming clear this is a calculated movement. They do not want to be found, and your mother is likely one of them. It may be best to start looking forward—like to our wedding, for example."

Panic pricked at my heart. "You're speaking as though we'll never find her," I said. *And as though you've given up trying to do so*, I thought to myself.

"It's a possibility that you may want to start considering," he said slowly. "It could be that she has made her choice, just as you made yours. You do still choose this life, do you not?"

"Yes, of course, but—"

"Then why not take it? You can always reunite with your mother after you've been married."

I shook my head. "No. I won't be able to."

"Why not?"

"Because—" I began, but broke off in my frustration.

Because I know you, I finished silently. In my time at the royal city, if I had learned one thing, it was that Àrèmọ could not resist a challenge. Right now, the thing he most wanted to win was me. To do so, the one condition he had to meet was finding my mother; that was why he had been so dedicated to her search. But if I were to marry him before she was found, he would move on to the next challenge that benefitted him, any thoughts of finding her forgotten. It was true that this was what I had always wanted, but not at the cost of losing my mother.

Àrèmọ gazed up at me questioningly. "You've adjusted so well," he said gently. "Maybe you should secure your place here before it goes away."

I raised a brow. "And where is it going?" I asked, pushing him away. "I did not realize your love for me had a time limit."

I turned, but Àrèmọ tugged the hem of my wrapper, preventing me from leaving. "That's not what I meant," he said quickly. "I just love you, and I want to finally prove it."

The placation only irritated me. I already knew what Àrèmọ wanted; my days were spent fulfilling his wants—exercising to bear his future children, learning so he would not have a simple wife, gossiping so he could stay one step ahead of his nobles. I was here in the royal city, after being kidnapped, because it was what he had *wanted*. But I was a noblewoman now, no longer a witch; shouldn't what I wanted have mattered too?

"Right," I said, "because you're the only one allowed to have what you want."

Àrèmọ frowned. "Òdòdó—"

"No, it's true—why wouldn't it be? You're the Aláàfin." I tugged my wrapper out of his grip, and as I walked backwards

to the door, I continued, "We all live to serve you. I had forgotten that for a moment, but don't worry, my king. I will not forget
again."

With a mock bow, I spun and exited my hut.

In Yorùbáland, copper and bronze were known as the hue that
brought down the thunder. Looking at the Aláàfin's personal
chambers, it was evident why.

It was the largest building in the royal city, and it was made
entirely of bronze. The red gold glimmered violently, boldly
challenging the sun. And, from certain angles, the house was
the one winning.

A field stretched from the front of the house to a gate of the royal
city. Its grass was green save for the center, where the shape of the
Aláàfin's three-headed elephant emblem was dyed in bronze. It
was here that the Aláàfin held court once a week, listening to
petitions and grievances.

When the people of Ṣàngótẹ̀ entered the gates, they were immediately greeted by the sight of dozens of soldiers along the
entrance. Each soldier held the jewel-encrusted leash of a pure-
bred dog, and each dog wore a gold or silver collar adorned with
knobs. The citizen would walk forward, as close to the Aláàfin's house as their courage allowed, then fall to their knees and
sprinkle dust on their heads—a necessary prelude before they
dared address their king.

The Aláàfin listened from his carpeted front porch. Leading
up to him was a wide staircase that was flanked by two massive
ivory tusks, which curved upwards and met high above his head.
The cascading beads of the Aláàfin's crown were sprawled over
the layers upon layers of colorful robes cocooning him, leaving
only his bejeweled hands visible, his skin as bronze as the throne
on which he sat.

Standing in a line behind him were ten stoic pages holding
golden shields and swords. The royal griot stood to his right,

announcing the Aláàfin's decisions in his baritone voice. Below
the Aláàfin, on the steps to his right, sat his generals and the sons
of subordinate kings. They wore splendid garments doused with
gold, and jewels were twined in their hair.

Had Kòlò been here, she would have sat on the left side of the
steps, below the Aláàfin and above the other noblewomen. But
once again, she was attending to unknown matters in Sàngótè,
leaving me to sit in her place. The sun beat down incessantly on
the enormous white gèlè wrapped around my head. Keeping my
chin raised against its weight, I watched from over the top of
the other women's gèlès as Aláràá people sought various types
of justice.

A bride was sentenced to death because it had been discovered that she was not a virgin. A craftsman requested more time
to find the funds to pay his taxes because his ivory figurines had
not been selling well recently. A tearful widow with no sons in-
herited her late husband's property and wealth.

Many grievances were related to the blacksmith strikes.
Farmers lamented that they did not have the necessary hoes
and sickles to work their land. Rich men complained of the dif-
ficulty in finding jewelry for their wives and daughters. Soldiers
reminded us that they were short on weapons. There were even
entertainers concerned about the dwindling supply of musical
instruments.

It was two men's turn to speak. As they scooped dirt on their
heads, Gassire's booming voice once again launched into the
same introduction. "Ọba kìí pòkorin. You are in the presence
of Àrèmọ Tèmítópé Ológun Babátúndé Gbekude, Aláàfin of
Yorùbáland, King of Sàngótè, Leader of the Aláràá, Son of
Àgò, Descendant of Sàngó. In his reign, he has conquered the
two great cities Wúràkémi and Ìlódè; he has brought a dozen
villages and towns under the control of Yorùbáland; he has
put an end to the centuries-long war between Sàngótè and
Òyó . . ."

Under the cover of Gassire reciting Àrèmọ's long list of

achievements from memory, an almost imperceptible hiss
sounded behind me. "Òdòdó."

There must have been at least one hundred cases that had been
presented thus far, and between each one, I had heard Àrèmọ's
whispered call. And every time, I had done what I did now:
clutched my shawl and continued staring straight ahead, determined to ignore him.

But he was just as determined to get my attention. "Òdòdó,"
he whispered again, more insistent.

A sigh leaked from my nose, the sound of the last of my patience
leaving me. "There are enough mosquitoes buzzing in my ear," I
said out of the corner of my mouth. "Let them do their job, and
you do yours."

"How am I supposed to focus when all I can think about is
you being upset with me?"

"If I distract you so much, you should not have made me come."

"I'd have been more distracted without you." He paused.
"Will you at least look me in the eye?"

Reluctantly, I turned my head, but I only made it as far as seeing the golden sandals peeking from beneath his colorful robes
before I faced forward again.

"How can I look at your eyes when I am only level with your
feet?" I asked.

Gassire concluded Àrèmọ's achievements. In the absence of
his voice, the air seemed to deflate. Out on the field, the two
men rose.

"My king, I seek to marry this man's daughter," the younger
man said, gesturing to the older. "He previously agreed to the
merging of our families, but now he has suddenly reneged on his
promise."

The older man kissed his teeth. "Eh? There is no 'suddenly'
about it. My king, this man's family owns a large plot of land along
the Niger. Such a wealthy man wants to marry my daughter?
Fine, take her! That is what I said. You know how my enthusiasm
was repaid?"

He clapped his hands together and slowly slid them away from each other, as though wiping something disgusting from them. "Ten cows."

A murmur rippled through the nobles on the steps. The younger man shifted from one foot to the other. "I know many families who would be satisfied with that bride price," he argued.

"Many families are poor, and their daughters are ugly," the older man said bluntly. "Neither of these apply to me. My daughter has hopeful suitors lining up outside our door, and my family runs a lucrative textile shop. In the middle of the city, might I add. What are we to do with ten cows? Teach them how to thread string between their hooves?"

"I believe you have wives, my king," the younger man said loudly. "I hope then you can relate to how fulfilling it is to find the perfect bride, and that is what this woman is. That is why I am insulted by her father's behest that I give something more, because my love for her transcends any material boundaries. So, my king, we would be most grateful if you offered your wisdom regarding how we should navigate this situation."

"Yes, help this man see past his stinginess," the old man said, folding his arms across his chest. Under his breath, he muttered, "Useless man."

The yard fell silent as the Aláàfin deliberated. Behind me, I heard a swishing of robes and a clack of bangles as Àrèmọ conversed with Gassire, too faint for me to hear.

"The Aláàfin has reached a decision," Gassire announced. He paused, the move of a master speaker that caused the two men to stand straighter in anticipation.

"The one thing you both agree on is that the bride is valuable indeed," Gassire continued after a moment. "As such, you are to put her on a scale and fill the other side with gold until the scale is balanced. That is to be the minimum bride price, for a highly prized woman is worth her weight in gold."

The younger man's head shot toward the heavens, his hands covering his face. The older man laughed with glee. They bowed and made their exit, the older walking with a lively spring and the younger dragging behind.

As the next citizen came to make his case, I could not help but look over my shoulder at Àrẹ̀mọ. And even with the beads covering his face, I knew he was looking at me too.

When court finally concluded at sunset, I returned to the women's compound. Just as I reached my hut, a commotion behind me made me turn around.

Ten slaves were entering the women's compound, each holding a pile of gold ornaments and figurines. To my surprise, they all headed to my hut, forcing me to step aside as they marched inside. I did not know how to react until a final person entered the women's compound: Àrẹ̀mọ.

His procession had drawn the attention of the other noble-women nearby. My head held high, I received him with a neutral expression, trying to make it seem as though I had expected this for the curious stares. But upon closing my door behind us, I let my confusion show. I had become familiar with receiving gifts from him—he brought me something new practically every other day—but this was excessive, even for him.

Àrẹ̀mọ explained, "I once told you my soul is intertwined with yours, Òdòdó. That is still true. And no matter how many lives it wears, every version of me will search and find you. I apologize if I implied that my love for you is constrained by something as flimsy as time. If having your mother here will make you happy, then I will redouble my efforts to find her."

A tension I had carried all day eased at his promise. "Thank you, Àrẹ̀mọ. And I'm also sorry for what I said earlier . . ."

I trailed off as I noticed two child slaves waiting patiently nearby. Àrẹ̀mọ followed my gaze. "I also," he said with a smile, "bring you two new attendants."

The two children stood with their hands clasped behind their backs. They were half my height and looked around half my age.

Their skin was even darker than mine, so black that they were nearly blue—and they also looked exactly alike. Same large dark eyes, same bald heads, same tiny builds.

My eyes widened. "Are they—?"

"Twins," Àrèmọ whispered. As if affirming this, the children smiled in unison. "I had to pay four times the price for them as any other slave. Each."

I could only imagine; twins were highly championed in Yorùbáland. It was a symbol of great fortune for a family to be blessed with them. The gift of them was even more valuable than the gold he brought, a rare luxury that reminded me just how privileged I had become now that I was the bride of the Aláàfin.

I hugged him, and, laughing, he wrapped his arms around me in turn. "Thank you, Àrèmọ."

"Of course." After a moment he added, "But you should know, in exchange for all this, I do require something in return."

I pulled back to look at him curiously. "What is it?"

He grinned and gestured to the twins. Stepping forward, they brought their hands from behind their back, revealing the sheets of bronze that they each held.

"The silver flower you gifted me is not enough," Àrèmọ said. "I need more, an entire bouquet of your work."

In my surprise, I laughed. "Deal."

12

The next day, Àrèmọ embarked on a journey to the edge of the Sahara.

There, he had arranged a meeting with northern traders who sold well-bred Arabians. Not trusting anyone else to inspect the horses for him, he had personally gone to see if they were worthy enough for his calvary. During his travels, he promised to check in with as many search parties as his path crossed, all of whom were groups he had dispatched throughout Yorùbáland to find Okóbí.

While he was gone, I decided to make the bouquet I had promised him. Àrèmọ had made it clear that he did not want me to do anything related to blacksmithing, but he did not seem to realize that such an order meant I should not be crafting the flowers he requested. It seemed that, to some extent, he subconsciously believed that blacksmiths truly were witches who could bend the Earth to their will. But in reality, I needed knives to cut the flowers' shapes, fire to combine the pieces, a hammer or pliers to shape the metal. Nonetheless, there was no need to make him face reality. I would simply make the flowers while he was away; if he saw only the final product and none of the process, he could continue believing that such flowers were crafted from metal and magic.

It was not hard to go to the forges unnoticed; they were in a remote part of the royal city, and with the blacksmiths having long abandoned their posts, there was no one around save for my guards, my handmaids, and the twins. After instructing the latter two groups how they could assist, I began crafting the flowers, grateful to have so many helping hands.

Unfortunately, my handmaids and the twins did not take well to each other. My handmaids, so sociable as they worked, were unsure of how to approach children who were so silent.

"Would you like to help me bellow the air, Táíwò?" a handmaid asked one day.

The twin made a sour face. "I'm not Táíwò. *She's* Táíwò."

"And he's Kẹ́hìndé," the other said, walking up to the first twin.

"Is something wrong with your eyes, auntie? Why can't you see?"

I looked at them in surprise; I had not realized one was a boy and one was a girl. Their adolescent bodies and voices made them entirely identical. Although, upon reflection, I was unsure if I had previously thought they were both girls or both boys.

When my handmaid saw I was watching, she forced a smile. "That's right, how absentminded of me. Then you who wears the brown tunic is Kẹ́hìndé," she said, pointing to the twin who had first spoken, "and the twin in gray is Táíwò?"

"No! I am Táíwò," said the twin in brown.

"And I am Kẹ́hìndé!" said the twin in gray.

The poor woman looked completely lost. "Eh? But you just said—?"

"I am Táíwò, and you are Kẹ́hìndé?" the twins asked in unison, turning to each other with identical expressions of confusion. "You are Táíwò, and I am Kẹ́hìndé? Táíwò is Kẹ́hìndé? I am you?"

Through gritted teeth, my handmaid remarked, "My, it seems you've even confused yourselves because you look so alike."

One twin thrust a hand out, revealing a jumping spider. "And you look like this bug, auntie."

The spider leapt to the handmaid, who yelped and jumped back. I turned away quickly; I did not want my handmaids to see me laughing.

The next day, when my handmaids dragged their feet to

return to the forges, I allowed them to stay behind, taking only the twins with me. The difference was stark; the twins did not flock around me, nor did they jabber away. I enjoyed the pampering of my handmaids, but I realized I had forgotten how nice it was to be able to stretch out on my own.

I sat next to a charcoal fire, my legs tucked to one side of me as I worked. The motions, as indelibly etched into my brain as the scars on my arms, came to me so naturally that, as I crafted the flowers, I fell into the daffodil's song for the first time in months.

> *"You listen to her tale*
> *One her teacher always told*
> *Of roads his son walked*
> *Roads paved with petals of gold*
> *See them bloom, see them shine*
> *See this garden become a sky*
> *With a thousand tiny suns*
> *It's no lie, it's no lie*
> *Light the world through the night*
> *Keep this glow inside your heart*
> *Flowers wilt, lands dwindle*
> *But survival is in the art."*

I looked up and nearly dropped my flower in surprise when I saw the twins standing over me. Up until now, they had kept their distance, shifting with the shadows as the sun changed positions. As I willed my pulse to regulate, I looked at them expectantly. In return, they only stared.

"Hello?" I tried to greet them, though it came out more like a question. It occurred to me that babies cried out of hunger. Had these twins been fed? Did they expect me to feed them?

The twins looked at each other, seemed to reach an agreement, then looked back at me. "We like your voice."

"Oh," I said, relieved; I would not have known how to feed children. "Okay. Thank you."

I adjusted my grip on the flower. The twins stayed where they were. I considered going back to work, but I had a nagging feeling that as the older one it was my responsibility to fill the silence.

"Thank you for all your help so far," I said.

"You're welcome."

A pause.

"My name is Òdòdó," I tried again.

"We know."

"Right." Another pause. "Well . . ."

With a slight shake of my head, I returned my attention to the flower. That interaction should be sufficient; it was certainly more than enough for me.

Indeed, they seemed satisfied with it—afterwards, they were constantly at my side. But unlike my handmaids, their treatment was less reverence and more camaraderie, as though they were the ones who had deemed me worthy of their attention.

The twins began talking so much I could no longer imagine a time when they had been silent. "Bàbá knew the raiders would target our village next," one told me one day. They both sat on a table, swinging their legs as they watched me create the flowers.

The other nodded in agreement. "Our village was poor, but it had a valuable location—"

"Right next to the Niger, a section shallow enough to cross."

"—so the Aláàfin's soldiers wanted to turn our home into a base they could use as they ventured east."

"Bàbá rallied the men to fight. He made the women and children leave, but we snuck away from our mother. We wanted to help."

"Except it was hard, trying to find our way back through the jungle—"

"A snake almost bit me!"

"—and by the time we made it home, the Aláàfin's men had already captured our village. Our huts had been destroyed—"

"There was rubble everywhere. It really, really hurt to walk on."

"—and most of our village's men lay on the ground—"

"We found Bàbá first. He was still holding his machete, because that's how brave men die."

"—and nothing was left."

"The soldiers found us soon after we arrived—"

"We didn't try to run. Where would we go?"

"—but they didn't kill us. They sold us at a trading post, and we've been taken all over Yorùbáland ever since. That was three years ago."

My heart ached for the twins. To my amazement, however, they were not sad. As they went on to recount the towns and cities in which they had labored, they did so with a clinical approach. They knew how to visit the past without getting trapped in its clutches, a skill as impressive as it was tragic to have already learned at their young age.

With each story the twins told me, they offered a piece of themselves. In return, I offered myself in the form of singing the daffodil's song every time they asked. They requested it multiple times a day, but it was the only thing they ever asked of me, so I obliged.

Then, just over a week after I had begun creating the flowers, the twins asked me a different question. "Are you finished?"

I did not respond right away. The twins came up on either side of me to admire my handiwork. Laid out on the table in front of us were a dozen daffodils, each glimmering a pinkish bronze in the light of the sunset.

One twin impatiently tugged on my arm as the other prompted, "Òdòdó."

"Yes," I answered. "They're done."

Soon after finishing the bouquet, I realized Àrèmọ's absence gave me the perfect opportunity to do what I had been meaning to do for weeks: talk to Dígí.

The question of how to sneak away from my guards was answered by my new friendship with the twins. At my request,

they positioned themselves in the middle of the women's compound and put on an acrobatic show—or at least they attempted
to. Their humorous efforts were in full view of my hut and the
guards in front of it. The two men regarded the twins with
amusement, along with a dozen noblewomen who had gathered
to watch. I joined the audience for some time, then, when I was
sure everyone was thoroughly distracted, I slipped away.

This morning, I had asked Ìgbín to dress me in a plain brown
wrapper and headscarf. I hoped that an unassuming appearance decreased my chances of being noticed during my trip into
Ṣàngótẹ̀—more so while I left the royal city since, once I was
in the capital, I doubted anyone would be able to recognize me
after only having seen my face once, during the hectic parade
following my arrival.

Nevertheless, if I was recognized on my way out of the royal
city, I was prepared to use the excuse that I was helping Kòlò. I
had seen a cart outside her hut earlier today, which I recognized
as the one that carried her gifts out of the royal city to be delivered. To my relief, when I passed by her hut now, the cart was
still there, loaded with the aṣọ òkè I helped her obtain. I lifted
one bundle of the folded fabrics from the cart. A grunt escaped
me; it was heavier than I thought it would be. Sticking to the
perimeter of the women's compound, far from the twins' performance, I made my escape.

It was an overcast but dry day; sunlight was sieved through
the clouds into weak, gray beams. Up ahead, I saw the large
stone gates of the west entrance propped halfway open, allowing a steady flow of patrols and slaves to move in and out of the
royal city, along with the occasional noble and their retinue. The
traffic was monitored by guards on the ground, and by bowmen
standing high atop the wall.

There was a group of slave women leaving the royal city to
complete errands. I hurried to catch up to them, getting close
enough so that an observer would think I was part of their
group, but not so close that I caught their attention. My arms

strained as I lifted the heavy fabrics so that the top of the stack partially covered my face. The guards at the gate did not spare me a glance as I passed by them.

With the royal city being at the center of the capital, exiting from the west gate put me in the western part of Ṣàngótẹ̀. The streets hummed with life. Women walked around carrying clay pots or woven baskets on their heads. Shopkeepers sat at the entrance of their shops, conversing with one another from across the street or inviting passersby to come inside. Children ran around playing pranks on patrolling soldiers. The good-natured men laughed, while the more irritated ones chased the children away. Music and conversation simultaneously assaulted my ears so that I only registered a single continuous buzz.

The past few months, my trips into the capital had been few and far between, limited to attending the parties of nobles. Even then, I hardly saw anything of Ṣàngótẹ̀, since I was carried in a palanquin amidst a large retinue. It felt strange walking down the red-dust covered roads alone, feeling the firm stone beneath my sandals. The royal city, aptly named, was like a small city in itself; I had no reason to go beyond its great walls, not when it had everything I needed—or if it did not, it had someone tasked with getting it for me. I could spend the rest of my life without ever stepping outside into the world again. It was a thought I had had before, and lounging under the shade of a tree, being fanned by my handmaids, the idea had sounded appealing. But now, walking among the people of Ṣàngótẹ̀, feeling them moving around but not orbiting me, I realized how strange my isolation was.

Because Dígí had told me she would be staying in the ceramics shop closest to the western gates of the royal city, I stopped at the first ceramics shop I came across, which was marked by clay pots positioned outside it. Like the buildings around it, the mud-brick structure had a domed roof and no door. On either side of its open archway was a window edged with gold.

Immediately upon stepping inside, a dense, earthy smell

pressed against me. Pots and vases were scattered across the shop's floor. They were of various shapes and sizes; the only commonality among them was the three-headed elephant symbol of the Aláàfin painted on almost all of them.

There was only one person inside the shop, an old, wizened woman. She sat against the back wall, on which hung a long woven rug spanning from the ceiling to the floor. A round pot with a wide inverted lip sat before her, and with a sharp comb, she carved textured waves into it.

She did not look up from her work when I entered, only said in a soft voice, "You are welcome, my dear. Come look at my work, tell me what you want to buy."

I set the fabrics onto the floor with a dull thud. "Good afternoon, ma," I said, respectfully dipping my head and bending my knees before I approached her. "I am not here to buy anything."

At last, the woman looked up to cast me a flat stare, plainly waiting for me to tell her what business I sought here if it not her own business. I hesitated; I had no way of confirming if this was the correct shopkeeper. If she was not, and she learned that I was looking for the hiding place of blacksmiths, she might think I was aiding the strikes and alert the authorities. I would be taken into custody and brought before the Aláàfin. Then Àrèmọ would know that I had been trying to reach the blacksmiths, even after his request that I leave behind my past life—which seemed even worse a fate than if I had been jailed for my actions.

But it was a risk I had to take. I did not know when else I would be able to get away from the royal city, and besides, I was sure I could move faster than the shopkeeper if needed.

"My sister said she would be staying here," I said at last. "Her name is Alálè Dígíọlá."

The woman's eyes fell to my arms, just now noticing my scars. Much to my relief, she nodded, then moved her pot aside and heaved herself to her feet. "Go and see if anyone is near," she told me.

I moved to a window and peered outside. None of the passersby showed any indication they were coming to the ceramics shop, and there were no soldiers in sight. I looked back to the woman and shook my head. Upon my confirmation, she swept the rug that had been hanging behind her to one side. To my surprise, it did not simply decorate the wall; it had covered a second archway, which led behind the shop.

She waved me through the archway, letting the rug fall back into place behind me the moment I was through. I emerged into a small yard enclosed by a short mud fence. It was bordered by the backs of surrounding buildings, which provided the yard with complete privacy. Three women were present. One sat shaping wet clay into pots, while another rested in the shade of a blanket draped over a corner of the yard to create a makeshift pavilion. The third woman was Dígí.

"Òdòdó, welcome," she said. Although she was as unsmiling as always, her voice was warm, and she came up to pull me into an embrace.

As we parted, I looked around. Pots were scattered across the yard, but unlike the ones for sale inside the shop, the ones here were in use. There were pots that held drinking water and pots that held butters for the skin and hair; pots that held foods such as garri and grains of rice, and one pot, positioned in a far corner, that had a pungent smell coming from it.

As I took in my surroundings, my concern must have been evident, because Dígí said, "Living here has been a vast improvement for us. We have been helping the shopkeeper make pots, to thank her for providing us with refuge, but the work is not nearly as strenuous as blacksmithing. Nor is she as abusive as the nobles and soldiers we used to provide for."

I glanced at the other two women, who dipped their heads to me in greeting. "Where are the others?" I asked.

"Gone. Of the royal city's blacksmiths, it is only us three who chose to stay in Șàngótẹ̀. Some of the others have ventured eastward, in hopes that they will be received with more compassion outside of Yorùbáland. Most, though, have gone to join our sisters. Sticking together is how we give ourselves a fighting chance."

As she spoke, the other two women nodded in agreement. It reminded me of when I first greeted the royal city's blacksmiths at their forges, and it was Dígí who had received me and spoken for the guild. Because I had been the youngest blacksmith in my own guild in Timbuktu, I had often been ignored by my aunties. But the opposite seemed to be true for Dígí; I suspected she was the head of her guild, just as my mother had been the head of my own. She certainly seemed like a capable leader.

"You mean the strikes," I said. "You sound as though you were prepared for them to begin. You even warned me about them at that party in the garden."

When she said nothing, I hesitated, then I asked, "Dígí, did you begin the strikes?"

Her dark eyes glittered. "I did not begin the strikes. *You* did."

"Me?" I echoed, shocked. "I knew nothing about them."

"No, but every blacksmith in Yorùbáland knew about you. We had heard your story, how you left your forge, something none of us ever thought was possible. You were able to rise above your station and leave behind the dismal life of a witch. Your story rippled throughout Yorùbáland and inspired countless blacksmiths to do the same."

Dígí spoke faster and faster as she went on, so much passion spilling from her words that she clearly expected it to soak into me. However, as she spoke, my heart sunk. Living at the right-hand side of the Aláàfin, I had seen how the blacksmith strikes slowly depleted Yorùbáland of its tools and weapons. The same movement that had empowered Dígí was a crushing burden to Àrèmọ. How would he feel if he learned that the cause of so much distress was me, just as he had begun to not only trust but also respect me?

But—something did not quite make sense about what Dígí told me. How could I have inspired the blacksmiths to walk away from their forges? I did not walk away from my forge—I was *kidnapped*. My story was hardly the inspiration Dígí made it out to be. Nor was it unique; although rare, blacksmiths had, in the past, escaped their fate by being chosen for marriage. Although, I supposed my engagement would be the most prolific case to have ever happened.

However, for all my confusion and dread about my apparent role in the blacksmith strikes, one thought still eclipsed any other in my mind. "Dígí, I need to find my mother," I said.

The shift in topic seemed to catch Dígí off guard. "Your mother?"

"She is a blacksmith—or, she was. We were both part of the guild in Timbuktu, which is no longer there. Since coming to the royal city, I have been trying to find her, and I think the blacksmith strikes have been preventing me from doing so."

"Perhaps she is part of the strikes," Dígí said slowly. "Are you not glad about the work she could be doing?"

"She is not part of the strikes," I said. I was certain of it; I still remembered my mother's disapproval when my aunties complained about our living conditions. Life as a blacksmith was difficult enough, and as such, my mother always preferred to avoid potentially creating any further trouble.

I continued, "I just need to be reunited with her. That is what I came to ask of you today—you said blacksmiths throughout Yorùbáland are congregating. They must have a means of communication. Can you use your network to see if you can find her? Once I know, I can bring her to live with me in the royal city."

Behind Dígí, the other two women present exchanged a look that I could not quite discern. Dígí's expression did not change, nor did her gaze leave my own. She looked up at me closely, her large eyes revealing nothing but my own reflection.

After a moment, Dígí said, "If that is your only wish, then I will see what I can do to locate her."

Relief flooded through me. "Thank you," I said. "I need to go, but I very much appreciate this."

"Of course. Alálẹ̀ must help each other."

I dipped my head in farewell then reentered the ceramics shop. The shopkeeper stood next to the back entrance, and as soon as I walked through it, she repositioned the rug over the archway. As she sat to resume working on a pot, I thanked her, then I lifted the stack of aṣọ òkè fabrics I had brought and exited the shop.

I needed to return to the royal city before my guards noticed I was missing and my absence caused a panic. I tried to hurry, weaving through the crowded streets, but the aṣọ òkè weighed me down. The longer I carried them, the heavier they grew, my arms cramping as I struggled to keep them lifted. Sweat ran down my face, dripping salt into my mouth and stinging my eyes. It was likely this obstructed vision, combined with my fatigue, that caused my foot to catch in my next step, pitching me forward.

I slammed onto the ground, and the aṣọ òkè slipped from my grasp, crashing onto the road. They unfurled from their tightly folded stack, falling around me. Murmurs of sympathy sounded from the people around me, but the most help anyone offered was giving me a wide berth.

Embarrassed and slightly disoriented though I was, I was also somewhat relieved that I had succeeded in looking so unimportant that not even my fall had drawn much attention. I began gathering the aṣọ òkè. As I lifted a vibrant yellow fabric, several items fell from the center of it, onto the ground with soft *clangs*.

Curious, I reached to pick one up, only to pull back with a pained gasp—they were much sharper than I had expected. I looked from the thin trail of blood forming on my right palm to the metal objects. Much more carefully, I grasped one and lifted it. Flat and made of iron, it was shaped like a leaf, ending in a long, sharp point.

Having created them my entire life, I instinctively recognized the object as a spearhead. Even so, I could not quite process what I held; it just did not make sense for spearheads to be folded into these fabrics.

I sifted through the other aṣọ òkè. It was no wonder they had been so heavy—out of the remaining three fabrics, two more had spearheads folded within them. I was left staring at fifteen spearheads, most iron, all very real and dangerous. How had these weapons gotten mixed into Kọ̀lọ̀'s present for her family?

The sound of wheels rolling over the road startled me out of my shock. A man walked by me, pulling a cart behind him, and as he passed, he cast me an irritated look. Realizing that I still sat in the middle of the road, I quickly stood, the ache in my knees nothing to the pounding of my heart. I kicked one of the fabrics onto the spearheads, and looking around to ensure no one was paying attention to me, I hurried down the street, leaving both the aṣọ òkè and the spearheads behind.

As I turned down another street, I forced myself to walk at a normal pace, because there was still no technical reason for my fear. Even so, my unease did not subside until the royal city's western gate came into view up ahead. Evening was approaching, but because the sun had never made an appearance, sunset was marked by the day gradually moving from a light to a darker and darker gray. My breath still sporadic, I forced myself to focus on how I would reenter the royal city. Fortunately, the gate was still open for today, but there were less people moving through it than there had been earlier. Although, even if there had been another group of women for me to blend into, I doubt it would have worked again—no doubt the guards were stricter about who entered the royal city than who left it.

I concluded I had no choice but to simply walk inside. It had been more important I was not stopped leaving the royal city, which likely would have put a stop to my trip altogether. But coming back inside, I could present the guards at the gate with any number of excuses; they could not refuse the bride of the Aláàfin, nor would they want to irritate me. It was my personal guards who would be a larger obstacle, but even then, so long as I could get near the women's compound before they spotted me, I was sure I could convince them I had been nearby and get them to shrug off their oversight.

As I approached the gates, my first hunch was proven better than right; the guards standing outside the gate recognized me, and they bowed me through without a single question.

But as I turned down a path in the royal city, my hope vanished; huddled by a tree near the gates was a group of soldiers, among whom I recognized my two guards. And standing at the center of them was Mama Aláàfin.

She had been speaking sternly to the men, but her amber eyes found me almost immediately, and she paused. "There she is," she said.

She pushed the man in front of her aside and strode up to me, her long silver dress making her seem like a creeping storm cloud. The soldiers followed behind her.

"Where have you been?" she demanded. "I came by your hut, only to find that you were gone. Your guards hadn't the slightest clue when you had parted from them. We were about to conduct a search of the entire royal city—and yet it seems that you weren't even here."

"You came to see me?" I asked, addressing the part that most alarmed me.

Mama Aláàfin's eyes narrowed. "You have been absent from your music sessions for the past few days. Of course, upon entering your hut and seeing the flowers on the rug, I learned what has been keeping you so preoccupied—a hobby from your days as a witch. And now you're sneaking around Ṣàngótè. I wonder what my son will think of such behavior when I tell him of it upon his return."

She clearly meant to scare me—and it worked. The flowers, requested by Àrèmọ, would be no issue, but my trip into Ṣàngótè would be harder to explain. My story of helping Kọ̀lọ̀ would not work with Àrèmọ, who would undoubtedly ask specific questions about the delivery. Not to mention, my decision to slip away from my guards would only water the small seed of suspicion he already had toward me, especially if Mama Aláàfin made it sound like I was doing something related to blacksmithing—in which case she would be correct.

Mama Aláàfin watched me with a smug smile, plainly aware of my train of thought. She opened her mouth, perhaps to gloat, but before she could speak, a voice came from behind me.

"Òdòdó!"

I turned to see Kòlò coming up to us, having just returned to the royal city through the gates. "Òdòdó, I am sorry for wandering off," she said as she reached us. "One of the vendors' necklaces caught my attention, but afterward I couldn't find you." She looked around, her eyes widening as though just now noticing Mama Aláàfin and the soldiers. "Is there a problem?"

Mama Aláàfin was clearly irritated. "We have been searching for Òdòdó," she said. "Are you saying you were with her?"

"Yes, she and I went to the market today. We thought it would be more fun if we could go without any fanfare, so we slipped away. We did not mean to be gone for so long—I hope we haven't caused any inconvenience."

Kòlò responded to Mama Aláàfin, but as she spoke, she had been looking at the soldiers, offering each of them a sweet, apologetic smile. In turn, they gave her a forgiving nod, some even offering a small smile in return.

Only Mama Aláàfin remained suspicious. She glared at me, and I quickly took up the role Kòlò had presented to me. "I am glad you were able to find your way back safely by yourself," I said to Kòlò. "I was worried."

"It has been a stressful day for the both of us. Perhaps we should retire early." Kòlò turned to Mama Aláàfin. "That is, if there is nothing else you need, ma?"

Mama Aláàfin chewed her tongue, looking between Kòlò and I. Then, though it seemed to pain her to do so, she stepped aside. Kòlò and I dipped our heads politely before walking away, my guards following a distance behind us.

Once we were far enough away from Mama Aláàfin, I said to
Kòlò in a low voice, "Thank you."

"It is the least I can do, considering all you have done for me,"
Kòlò said. "Your gifts have been most appreciated. And now,
they are no longer needed. Thanks to you, I have been able to
provide for my family more than ever before. I am sure they are
thoroughly spoiled, and anyways, I am leaving tomorrow to visit
friends in the Gilded District of Ṣàngótẹ̀, so I will not be around
to prepare more gifts for the next week. Thank you for all your
help, sweet flower."

She placed her hand on my shoulder to kiss my cheek, and I
felt the last of my anxiety fade—both in regard to my encounter
with Mama Aláàfin and the spearheads I had found folded in
the aṣọ òkè. Of course Kòlò had not intended for the spearheads
to be packaged with those fabrics; I could not imagine someone
as kind as her going anywhere near weapons. It had to have been
the mistake of whatever slave had loaded the delivery cart.

"It was my pleasure to help you," I said, turning to her. "And
if you ever need anything else . . ."

I trailed off as I looked closely at her for the first time, my
smile fading. She was still as beautiful as when I had first arrived
at the royal city, but there was a gray tinge to the skin beneath
her eyes. Curls escaped her bantu knots, as though she no longer
dedicated time to their perfection, and her clothes were rum-
pled. I wondered when she had last slept.

"You seem different," I said. I considered asking why she had
left the royal city alone, if it was related to her appearance, but
because she had not asked me, I felt obliged to allow her the
same courtesy. So, instead I asked, "Are you okay?"

Kòlò looked at me in surprise. Then, she smiled. "I could ask
you the same question."

Taking my wrist, she held up my right hand. My palm was
now stained with dried blood, having spread from the thin cut
going across it.

"What happened?" she asked.

My heart jumped. "Oh—I must have cut myself. I didn't even notice," I lied. There was no reason to concern her about the spearheads that had almost been delivered with her gifts. And it was not difficult to sound surprised—given everything that had happened, I had all but forgotten about the cut.

Kòlò inspected the wound closely. Then, she clicked her tongue softly. "You should be more careful. I don't want you to get hurt." She looked up at me. "Shall I fetch the royal babaláwo to tend to the wound?"

"Sure," I said. "Thank you."

Kòlò nodded and, after giving my wrist a final reassuring squeeze, turned onto another path. As I continued down my own path, I passed a few slaves lighting the torches throughout the royal city to counter the falling darkness.

It was only when I reached the entrance to the women's compound that I realized Kòlò had never answered my question.

13

When Àrèmọ returned to the royal city, he gifted me a necklace he had picked up during his travels. It was made of beads that were smaller ivory versions of the bouquet of bronze flowers I gifted him in return, as promised.

There were still no developments in his search for my mother, nor was he any closer to understanding the blacksmith strikes. I consoled myself with the knowledge that Dígí was also helping me search for her. Although, thinking of my visit to the potter also made me feel guilty; learning that I was the one who inspired Yorùbáland's blacksmiths to strike made me slightly more informed about the situation than Àrèmọ. But there was no point in telling him. It would provide him with more questions than answers, and those questions could endanger my place as his bride.

The night following Àrèmọ's return, he came to fetch me for my training. However, we did not practice for long before he led me off our field and through the royal city. Heavy black clouds obscured the sky, and at first, I thought that was the reason my training was being cut short tonight. But as we embarked on a path that took us further from the women's compound, I finally asked, "Where are you taking me?"

"Patience, my flower," Àrèmọ hummed, his hands behind his back. "By the way, is there anything I should be aware of before I meet with the generals in the morning?"

I shook my head, knowing this was his way of inquiring about useful gossip I might have heard. "I've been making the flowers, so I have not been able to attend music sessions. I'll catch up on what I've missed tomorrow." I paused, processing his question. "You're meeting with the generals? Is something wrong?"

"No more than usual. I speak with my generals most mornings. Just a brief meeting to discuss various affairs across Yorùbáland."

"Can I come?"

My pulse accelerated; the question felt dangerous. I found myself holding my breath for his answer, ready to immediately apologize for such a suggestion if need be.

But Àrèmọ merely shrugged. "I doubt you will find much entertainment there, but sure, you are welcome to watch if you'd like—ah, here we are."

We had just turned onto a path occupied by a handful of sentries. As Àrèmọ strolled up to them, they snapped into a salute, looking like wooden statues in the torchlight. Àrèmọ clapped his hand on one man's shoulder.

"You, stay," Àrèmọ said. "The rest of you continue on."

"Yes, sir!"

As the group marched past us, Àrèmọ said to the man whom he had singled out, "The love of my life is going to kick you to the ground."

"Understood!" the soldier responded. Then wariness filled his eyes, as though his instinct to obey the Aláàfin had preceded him actually processing the command.

Àrèmọ beckoned me toward the soldier. Still unsure what it was that Àrèmọ meant to teach me, I walked up to the man. Although I was the same height as him, he determinedly kept his gaze above my head, a bead of sweat running down his face.

I glanced at Àrèmọ, but when he only offered an encouraging smile, I turned back to the soldier. I brought my leg around, putting all my strength behind the sweeping motion I had seen Àrèmọ use to knock men off their feet countless times before.

My foot met the side of the soldier's thigh—and glanced off

harmlessly. Pain shot up my ankle, but the soldier remained as still as ever. He had not even winced.

As I gripped my ankle, the soldier looked between Àrẹ̀mọ and me. Then, much too late, he lowered himself onto the ground, sitting with his hands behind him as though he had fallen.

"Well done, my lady," he said.

"Àrẹ̀mọ," I snapped, whirling around in pain and embarrassment.

He walked up to us, his face carefully angled so that the darkness did not allow me to discern his expression. "Stand, soldier, and stay here for a moment."

The man did as he was told. Àrẹ̀mọ wrapped his arm around my shoulders, and as he led me away, he said, "Defeating an opponent has little to do with their own shortcomings. It is all about the advantages you possess. Because you are a woman, strength is not one of them—don't look at me like that, my flower, we have just seen it is true—which means that your attacks must utilize precision rather than force."

With his other hand, Àrẹ̀mọ placed his finger on the center of my torso. "It does not matter how much bigger or stronger your opponent is; he still needs to breathe. Take that away from him. She's trying again."

He said the last part louder, and I realized we had circled back to the waiting soldier. Àrẹ̀mọ removed his arm from around my shoulders, leaving me to walk up to the soldier alone. The man looked much calmer, perhaps prepared to act more convincing this time.

I did not have much faith in my kick either, but I had to try. Instead of stretching my foot to the side as before, I bent my leg in front of me and, focusing on the spot where Àrẹ̀mọ had showed me, slammed my foot into the man's chest.

Immediately, he doubled over and fell to the ground, clutching his abdomen. His frantic gasps for air were much too desperate to be faked.

After a moment, I snapped out of my shock. "I'm so sorry, I didn't think that would work—*Àrèmọ, it's not funny,*" I hissed over my shoulder, but he was laughing too hard to hear.

I rushed to help the soldier to his feet. As the man muttered congratulations, I looked over my shoulder. Àrèmọ grinned, his eyes twinkling. Although I felt bad for the soldier, triumph warmed my chest.

A drop of water landed on my cheek. I gave a small yelp as the drop was followed by several more and it began to rain. Taking my hand, Àrèmọ led me as we ran through the royal city. By the time we reached a palm tree, we were gasping and soaking wet.

Àrèmọ pulled me close to him, fitting us both beneath the shelter of the tree's leaves. "I apologize, my flower. I should have been paying more attention to the weather."

"I don't mind waiting it out," I assured him.

A braid had come loose from his bun, though he had not seemed to notice. I pushed it out of his face for him, and I saw a small scar on his jaw. "This is new," I remarked, trailing my hand over the scar.

He put his hand over my own. "Is it? I must have earned it the last time I ventured east. But I am sure I returned my opponent's ambition to him tenfold."

"I don't doubt it," I said with a chuckle. His words brought to mind the stories that the twins had told me, and my smile faded. "Is there a reason you continue to push Yorùbáland east?"

"I want to give her another ocean."

"Why?"

"Have you even been to the ocean?"

I shook my head no, and he said, "I know, because if you had, you would not have asked such a question. You would have already breathed refreshing seaside air and seen how the sea glistens when the sun dissolves into it. You would have already lounged in the shade of silk-cotton trees and watched naked children play in the water—and you would have already imagined our children to be among them, as I have."

Although I doubted anything would have justified the violence the twins and so many others had faced, Àrèmọ's reason
for expansion was particularly lacking in substance. Nothing
more than selfish desire drove him eastward. To some degree, I
acknowledged that a different person—perhaps most people—
would have been horrified at such an admission.

But to have conquered so many lands and to have garnered
such a fearsome reputation simply because he wanted to, simply
because he *could* . . . The idea fascinated me.

Above, a break appeared in the clouds, and the full moon
peaked through. As the pale light broke over us, I suddenly realized how close we were, my front against his.

We had been this close before, of course, when he was fixing
my stance, or pinning me to steal yet another win. But this time,
he was neither the teacher nor the victor. Àrèmọ seemed to have
realized it too; he cupped my face, his tender touch made of
rough callouses.

He moved with an uncharacteristic hesitancy, a question
shining in his black eyes. I pressed the answer against his lips.

He pulled me closer, molding my body into his own. The kiss
did not make my heart flutter or frantic; instead, I relaxed. It
tasted sweet, as dulcet as the music I played with the other noblewomen while lounging in our field. It was as gentle as the people
who regularly attended to me, and it was as warm as the sun that
I was no longer subjected to all day. The kiss tasted like reassur-
ance, security.

The kiss tasted like power.

14

I had never seen Ìgbín so frazzled.

Granted, frazzled for her entailed a slight fumble. But still, it was concerning. She was collecting my measurements—which today was only going fast instead of very fast—when her patience expired. She turned to the twins, who sprinted up and down the length of my hut.

"Children," she said. "Perhaps you should sit."

The suggestion lost any semblance of choice the way Ìgbín said it. The twins dropped to the floor, falling into the same cross-legged position.

With a small sigh, she returned to measuring me. "I know they are twins and a gift from the Aláàfin, my lady, but are they becoming a nuisance?"

"Oh, no, I find them rather charming," I said, a smile tugging at my lips as I watched the twins pull impolite faces at her back.

A noise came from Ìgbín's nose, a mixture of amusement and exasperation. As I watched her take a final measurement around my leg, a thought occurred to me.

"You know," I said, "I just realized that you've taken my measurements every single morning since I arrived."

"Well, I make you clothes every day, my lady. Even if they look the same, they are always new." She gestured to my black bandeau and baggy knee-length trousers, an outfit I wore every once in a while. I had been inspired by Kòlò to try it, and I had found she was right—trousers were a great deal more practical than wrappers, especially for my training with Àrẹ̀mọ.

"But you use new measurements every time?" I asked, shocked.

"Yes. It does not make any sense to sew tomorrow's dress with yesterday's measurements. One day can bring a lot of change."

"Do you mean to say I become bigger each day?"

"No, of course not, my lady."

"I was joking," I said, waving a hand dismissively. I had never been very good at jokes. "I know you meant no offense."

"Of course, my lady."

Her tone was steady, but her eyes darted to my dueling stick, which peaked out from under my bed. I had no doubt that Ìgbín knew of my training with Àrẹ̀mọ, and I also had no doubt that she would not say anything. As a royal tailor, she was privy to many hidden aspects of noblewomen's lives, and she was likely still alive because she knew when and when not to speak.

Ìgbín left as soon as she was done dressing me. She always left so abruptly, but today it felt personal. However, I could not focus on the slight for long; my stomach was turning over in dread and excitement. Instead of going for a run this morning, I would be joining Àrẹ̀mọ's meeting with his generals. He had said it would be dull, but I did not quite believe that; I expected it to be like Gassire's lessons and the noblewomen's gossip, but better.

Once outside the women's compound, I entered my palanquin and was carried to the Aláàfin's chambers. It was as grand on the inside as it was from the outside. Animal pelts, leather shields, and weapons hung on the bronze walls. Vibrant rugs covered the floor of the foyer, and complex bronze statues were placed around the room. Of the arched doors lining the room, the one nearest to the entrance led to the war room.

I was first to arrive; at the center of the spacious room were seven empty chairs positioned around a large rectangular table with a beige, green, and blue surface. I had seen enough maps of Yorùbáland and its surroundings in my studies to know that this was one made physical; there were bumps to signify hills and mountains, and concave points to mark valleys.

My eyes locked onto Timbuktu. It had become instinct that my former home was the first thing I looked for on maps, as though they could bring me closer. But maps were immune to time, and I knew Timbuktu had changed. Once more, I thought of my mother. I had adjusted well to life in the royal city, but I knew I would never fully enjoy it without her here. I had to believe that between Àrẹ̀mọ and Dígí, she would be found soon.

Wooden blocks were clustered throughout the table. Cities had the most, but there were also a good amount along the borders. The blocks represented units of soldiers, I realized. This was not simply a map of Yorùbáland—it was a diagram of its deployments.

I walked around the table in wonder, running a hand over its edge. The polished wood seemed to hum under my touch, as though I tuned an instrument.

I reached the chair at the head of the table. The seat of the Aláàfin, the mouthpiece that breathed into existence Yorùbáland's next song, whether one of glory or defeat. I took a breath, and then, I sat.

I had imagined that when I sat, the chair would grow up higher and higher until I became dizzy. Or that it would widen across the entire room, leaving me no chance of filling it in. I thought that I would have felt *something*, yet I sat in this chair as easily as any other. I felt nothing—and that, was everything.

The door swung open, yanking me out of my reverie. Men poured inside—guards, pages, and lastly, the generals. There was enough space that even after several guards took their positions at the room's perimeter, and one page stood behind each seat, the room became full but not crowded. Voices overlapped and chairs scraped the floor as the generals took their seats.

I looked at them with barely concealed amazement; I had studied and watched them from afar for so long. They were the most powerful men in Yorùbáland, the most skilled soldiers and strategists our army had to offer. And now, they were sitting at the same table as me.

They seemed to be in the middle of an argument. "Careful, Rótìmí. Your notions are beginning to infect other nobles,"
warned a large, dark man whom I recognized as Balógun, the
general of Koumbi Saleh. His city had once been the capital of
the kingdom of Wagadu, but ever since the Aláràá captured it
around two hundred years ago, its significance now came from
its ability to provide Yorùbáland with grain.

"The thing about common sense is that it's quite contagious,"
Rótìmí replied lightly. His gold trimmed tunic and braids glittered as he took his seat.

"Perhaps it is not just common sense," reflected a very old
man who poured into his seat like jelly badly imitating a human.
"With six being Ṣàngó's divine number, it could be said that the
current number of major cities reflects Ṣàngó's will."

The man's dialect was so thick and unfamiliar that I had to
strain to make out his words; it was almost as though he spoke
an entirely different language. It was a southern dialect, I
realized—he must have been Àjàyí, general to the sacred city Ilé-
Ifẹ̀. His role was largely ornamental; because his city was the site
where the òrìṣàs had created the first human beings, Ṣàngótẹ̀ had
not imposed its militaristic ways onto it. His city had only elected
a general in order to fill their spot at the Aláàfin's table.

Ọmóṣẹwà glided into the room, the early light sparkling on
his maroon chest. His eyes were a smooth light brown today, in
which the sun crystalized. My breath caught in my throat. It did
not matter how frequently I laid eyes on him; his beauty caught
me off guard every time.

"Is four not also one of Ṣàngó's divine numbers?" Ọmóṣẹwà's
silk voice caressed the room. "Yet no one complained when
Yorùbáland expanded beyond four cities."

General Ẹ̀míọlá of the city Ayédùn—known as the City of
Spices—sat on Ọmóṣẹwà's right. Like several other men present,
Ẹ̀míọlá unconsciously leaned into Ọmóṣẹwà as he agreed, "That's
right. Most are too busy reveling in the surplus of resources."

"Resources brought by expansion," emphasized Yẹ̀kínì,

the general of Ògúndélé. Tall and muscular, Yèkíní looked as
though he himself was extracted from the acclaimed iron mines
of his city. Yet as Ọmọ́ṣẹwà waved an acknowledging hand at
Yèkíní, the latter quickly averted his steel gaze, and his gray-
brown cheeks tinged with a faint blush.

Àrẹ̀mọ was last to enter. Every page, guard, and general alike
straightened, like flowers reaching for the sun, as their Aláàfin
strolled to the head of the table. His axes hung at his sides,
their bronze heads shining as brightly as the gold woven in his
braids.

"Hence we will continue to expand," he declared. As Àrẹ̀mọ
reached the head of the table, he swept me up and sat where I
had, placing me on one of his legs. "Because the only will of
Ṣàngó," Àrẹ̀mọ continued without pause, "is for Yorùbáland to
prosper, whether she controls one city or one hundred."

My smooth displacement disgruntled me, but all the same, I
settled onto Àrẹ̀mọ's lap, crossing my legs and resting an arm on
his shoulders.

"You presume that having one hundred cities is the same as
being in control of them," Rótìmí said. "My king, Yorùbáland
is prosperous right now. The army is undefeated, the people are
content. Perhaps it is time to shift our focus away from expansion
and instead to maintaining what we do have—"

Àrẹ̀mọ slammed a hand onto the table. The crunch of his
rings against wood struck the room with a harsh silence. The
men looked the same way I felt—startled but knowing better
than to flinch.

"You bring me this tired proposal every other day, Rótìmí,"
Àrẹ̀mọ said, returning his arm to my waist. "It is enough. Abeg,
let us finish this daydreaming and begin."

A muscle in Rótìmí's jaw twitched, but he said nothing more.
Àjàyí cleared his throat. "Perhaps we can start with the growing
ivory troubles, my king," he rasped.

"Ah, yes. Something sensible."

Àrẹ̀mọ waved a hand, and the old man proceeded, "In the

past week alone, scouts have raided ten new illegal storehouses of ivory throughout Ṣàngótẹ̀. According to my contacts, situations like this are beginning to arise all over Yorùbáland."

"Ọmóṣẹwà, where is this surge in ivory coming from?" Àrẹ̀mọ asked.

"The Ẹgbẹ́-Ọdẹ pride ourselves on being the only clan skilled enough to hunt elephants," Ọmóṣẹwà responded. His voice was incredibly soft, which, I had come to learn, meant that he was incredibly angry.

He kept his gaze down, prodding his hunting knife at a wooden block located in the Timbuktu area of the map as he continued, "The king of Ìlódẹ undergoes the strictest measures to monitor who hunts on the Savanna. He oversees each and every piece of ivory that enters Yorùbáland's market, and he has affirmed that there have been no major increases in the number of elephants being hunted."

"Ah. In other words, you don't know," Àrẹ̀mọ summarized.

Ọmóṣẹwà stabbed a wooden block.

"In any case," Àrẹ̀mọ continued, "we will simply have to keep an eye on this situation for the time being, just as we are the blacksmith strikes." He beckoned a page forward, who deposited a handful of wooden blocks on the edge of the table, at the Sahara. "Our first priority is this. My contacts among the desert nomads have notified me of a Portuguese army that is preparing to march southwards. It would seem their intentions include overpowering me and taking control of Yorùbáland."

My eyes widened as the page arranged the wooden blocks into invaders. I looked around at the generals, and my surprise only grew at their irritated but otherwise untroubled expressions, as though this was nothing more than a minor inconvenience.

"So we deal with them before they successfully cross the Sahara," Yẹ̀kínì said gruffly. "A few hundred men usually suffices, yes?"

"Usually, northerners only send a small company to test the waters," Àrẹ̀mọ replied. "But it seems their failed excursions have only increased their confidence, because this time I am told they are around fifteen thousand men strong."

A weighted silence fell after his words.

After a moment, Rótìmí said, "This threat may very well be formidable enough to require our full attention. We'll have to put a pause on expansion east of the Niger."

Balógun scoffed. "Don't sound so excited, Rótìmí."

"Excuse me," I said. "You said you've dealt with potential invaders in the past?"

As one, the men's gazes snapped to me. Even Ọmọ́ṣẹwà looked up from mutilating Timbuktu's wooden blocks. Their faces were a cross of surprise and repulsion, as though they had not noticed I was here, and they resented me for having informed them.

Balógun said, "In terms of how we should proceed—"

"My bride," Àrẹ̀mọ interrupted, "asked a question. She's curious. Humor her."

He leaned into me, plainly planning to kiss my cheek. But before he could, I stood and walked to the Sahara section of the table. I saw no need to give the generals a reason to take me less seriously than they clearly already did.

"Well, to answer your question, my lady, we have invaders show up every few years," Àjàyí said, exchanging an exasperated expression with Yẹ̀kínì, much like two parents would when explaining something rudimentary to a child. "Other peoples see our abundance of resources, and they decide trading is not enough. They decide they want this land for themselves."

"Yes-o. The land where gold grows like carrots," General Ẹmíọlá added dryly. Chuckles went around the room, as though this was a phrase they had heard one too many times.

I picked up a wooden block and turned it over as I thought. It was not just gold Yorùbáland had to offer; we had fabrics, spices, skins—skins like that silly orange one Àrẹ̀mọ had gifted me when I first arrived at the royal city. Except that skin was clearly foreign; if an animal like that lived here, it would only succumb to the heat faster—

"I've just thought of something," I said suddenly.

The men stared at me expectantly. I set the block down and, looking around the table, I announced, "My tailor takes new measurements for me every day—"

An eruption of laughter cut me off.

Over the din, Àrèmọ said, "Thank you for sharing, my flower, but we should return to our discussion."

He beckoned to me, inviting me to sit with him again. Shame struck me, so heavy and abrupt that I almost allowed myself to fall back into Àrèmọ's arms. But I held my ground; I had something to say, and I wanted to say it.

Àrèmọ must have noticed I was upset, because he smiled. "Let her speak," he said.

The laughter ceased almost immediately. I cleared my throat, willing the shakiness from my voice. "Each time armies march from the north, they suffer defeat at our hands. Yet, they continue to come back. Why?" I asked, feeling a little too much like Gassire. "Because you've handled every battle the same, giving them the chance to adjust their approach. And now that you've shown them what to expect, they are confident they've learned how to seize victory."

As I spoke, the amusement on the general's faces faded. Some even looked thoughtful now.

Èmíọlá was among them. "Fine," he said, stroking his long curly beard. "Let us say for a moment that, in our confidence, we have indeed become dangerously repetitive in our dealing of these threats. What, then, do you propose we do this time?"

"Nothing."

The generals did not say anything, but their looks were loud enough that I continued in a slightly raised voice, "Not even the nomads, knowledgeable though they are of the Sahara, would travel in such large numbers. The fact the Portuguese think they can march across the Sahara is proof enough they are ignorant to its brutality."

I thought back to my kidnapping, its brief intermission in the middle of the Sahara. In my mind's eye, flat expanses of sand stretched endlessly before me as I continued, "You do not need to send many soldiers to meet them—just a small unit. Have them strike sporadically and retreat quickly. The invaders will think we have come to meet them, just as we always do, and they will make their camp deep in the desert, where there is no water or shelter. We do not need to defeat the army, only stall them. The desert will do the rest."

Àjàyí hummed thoughtfully. "That could work," he said, and my spirits soared as Rótìmí and Balógun nodded their assent. The remaining three generals—Èmíọlá, Yèkíni, and Ọmóṣẹwà—did not recognize my proposal, but they did not protest it either.

"Then we are all in agreement with the course of action suggested by my bride?" Àrẹ̀mọ asked.

The shift in the room was immediate; as soon as he spoke, the generals' attention turned from me to him. Dread, sudden and heavy, dropped onto my stomach, a feeling I could not fully explain.

That was, not until Yèkíni said, "Yes, for your brilliance has clearly rubbed off on your bride. Well done, my king."

The others chimed in to praise Àrẹ̀mọ, especially the men who had been reluctant to acknowledge me. My insides twisted, as though I was slowly shrinking. Only Rótìmí's attention remained on me, a faint smile flickering on his face. I dropped my gaze, unable to meet his ridicule.

As the generals began formulating a plan, I remained in front of the room, frozen like a fool. But it did not matter; once again, the men could not see me. Not when Àrẹ̀mọ had just confirmed that my only place here was as his bride. My existence, like my ideas, were merely an extension of him.

Eventually, Àrẹ̀mọ said, "I must prepare to hold court. We'll continue this discussion tomorrow."

The generals stood from the table and bowed. Ọmọ́ṣẹwà's shoulder rammed into mine as he left. Otherwise, the men walked around me, though it felt as though they walked through me.

"I hope to hear your thoughts more often, my lady," a quiet voice said in my ear. I turned and was surprised to see Rótìmí. But before I could react, he walked past me, out of the room.

As the door closed behind the last man, Àrẹ̀mọ walked up to me. "Òdòdó," he said, taking my hands in his own. "You must marry me."

Marriage. He said it as though that was my reward for my contribution, yet in this moment, it felt like a punishment. Each impressive decision Àrẹ̀mọ made solidified his legacy as one of Yorùbáland's greatest Aláàfins. But no matter what I did, if I were to be remembered at all, it would only be as his wife.

The thought carried with it a sudden surge of resentment. "Of course I will marry you one day, but you did not need to remind the generals of that by calling me your bride," I said.

Àrẹ̀mọ laughed, only inflaming my irritation. "But you are my bride. And anyways, what does that matter? The important thing is Yorùbáland remains secure."

"Yes, because of me. But your generals acted like I could have never thought of that plan myself, as though I haven't been advising you for the past season." A thought occurred to me, and I went on, "But they don't know I've been advising you for the past season, do they? Because you haven't told them. They don't know how much information I collect for you. They think you've been ruling alone—"

"But, Òdòdó," Àrẹ̀mọ interrupted softly, "I do rule alone, do I not? Can the throne of the Aláàfin seat more than one man at a time?"

His face was impassive, but there was that troublesome glint in his eyes. The one that if it had shone on the horizon, fishermen would rush back to the shore.

My irritation quickly turned into panic; I had gone too far. I had become so comfortable with him that, at times, I forgot he was the Aláàfin. Who was I to question his authority?

I should have apologized—and yet, although the generals had praised Àrèmọ for my idea, the moment before they had listened to me. Just me. No matter how briefly, I had held a place at a table with the most powerful men in Yorùbáland. I could not bring myself to fully let go. Not even for Àrèmọ.

The door swung open, freeing me from having to respond. A boy rushed inside. He looked barely older than the twins, yet as he prostrated before us, I noticed a curved blade strapped to his waist.

"Forgive the intrusion, my king," he panted. "My unit has received word that there's a riot in the capital. It's the slaves, sir—there's hundreds of them. The city guard is near overwhelmed. They're not sure how much longer they can secure the Gilded District—"

"It's happening in the Gilded District?" I asked, alarmed. The boy nodded, and I took Àrèmọ's arm. "Àrèmọ, that's where Kọ̀lọ̀ is."

The edge in Àrèmọ's eyes softened. "It'll be okay, my flower," he said, rubbing my hand.

His consolation only annoyed me—he should have been worried about Kọ̀lọ̀, not worried about my worry. "I know," I said, "because you will save her. She's your wife." When Àrèmọ still looked far too untroubled for my liking, I added, "And she's the princess of Ọ̀yọ́. How would our ties with them suffer if something bad happened to her?"

That, at last, had an effect. "Why are you the one telling me this?" Àrèmọ demanded of the boy. "Where are the senior trainees?"

"That's the thing, sir—the upper age division departed from the royal city last night to bolster the push east of the Niger."

Àrèmọ cursed. "Their crowning. Of all the times they could have been taken on a rite of passage battle . . ." He paced the length of the room, running a hand through his braids as though to extract an idea from his head. "Then the soldiers aged twenty-five to twenty-nine are gone?"

"And the division below that one."

"Which leaves the oldest remaining division as . . . ?"

"Mine—twelve to sixteen."

Àrèmọ paced one more lap before coming to a halt. "Then your division will have to do. What is your name?"

"Bámidélé, sir."

"Bámidélé, summon Generals Ọmóṣẹwà, Rótìmí, and Balógun."

Bámidélé's eyes widened. "They're going to lead us?"

"And I will join you," Àrèmọ said.

At this point, the boy's bulging eyes were in danger of falling out of his head.

"It is my wife they have endangered," Àrèmọ declared. "They have made the attack personal, so I will personally respond. Ready your comrades immediately."

For someone who had been told he would be marching into battle with little preparation, Bámidélé looked rather excited; his dark eyes shone at the prospect of fighting alongside the Aláàfin. He nodded and ran out of the room.

Before I could think better of it, I said, "I'm coming too."

Àrèmọ raised a brow. "My flower, this is battle," he said slowly, as though I did not comprehend the concept. "Real battle. Not just sparring."

I hesitated, though not out of doubt. During my time at the royal city, I had had the good-natured Aláàfin doting over me by day and the patient Àrèmọ teaching me at night. But just a moment ago, I glimpsed someone who I never thought I would have to personally meet: the Commander of Death. I did not want to risk invoking that side of Àrèmọ again.

But then I remembered how Kòlò had embraced me the moment we had met, how kind she had been despite how much her husband fawned over me, even at the cost of neglecting her. If there was a chance I could repay her for her companionship, I had to take it.

"Please, Àrèmọ. Kọ̀lọ̀ is my friend. This is personal to me too."

My heart pounded as he looked at me, his expression overcast. For a moment, I feared his temper would break through again.

Then, to my relief, he said, "You stay close to me, and the moment it seems as though you could get hurt, you run."

I nodded vigorously. He looked at me a moment longer before sighing. "I will get you a weapon. We leave within the hour."

15

The Gilded District was in the southwest part of Ṣàngótẹ̀. It was the capital's wealthiest neighborhood. Glimmering gates guarded the sprawling compounds of Aláràá aristocrats, and the trunks of palm trees were wound in spiraling gold. The entire district seemed to glow as bright as the blue sky that arced over it.

The Gilded District was especially radiant today, as it was on fire.

Thick smoke obscured the area. A cacophony of clashing metal and screams came from beyond the entrance gates, marking the battleground that the district had been reduced to. The perimeter seemed secure; soldiers stood along the gates, charged with containing the chaos within.

Groups of men stationed outside broke their huddles to watch our approach. Àrẹ̀mọ, who was at the head of our formation, leapt from his horse. My dismount was much less smooth; the long ride from the royal city to the edge of Ṣàngótẹ̀ had been my first time on a horse, and with my legs aching and my hands cramped from gripping the reigns for dear life, I hoped it was also my last time. I would have sooner marched on foot with the hundreds of soldiers who had followed behind us.

I did not know if it was Àrẹ̀mọ's confident gait or the dual axes hanging from his belt that gave his identity away, but as he walked up to the men, they snapped into salutes.

"Report," he demanded.

A man with his arm in a sling immediately stepped forward.

"Around dawn, the city guard received complaints from nobles who were having issues with their slaves. I had a few soldiers go in, make a light example out of one, and we thought that was the worst of it. Later, we realized while that was occurring, other slaves scoured the district, recruiting more to their cause. By the time we realized the full extent of the situation, it had escalated into a full-on revolt."

"And my people?" Àrẹ̀mọ prompted. "Where is my wife?"

"Er—well, I admit, I cannot answer that with complete conviction. But," he stammered hastily as Àrẹ̀mọ took a menacing step forward, "as far as we know, we successfully evacuated all the nobles who were present at the time. The only thing left now is to put down the rebels."

"I've never seen anything like it, my king," another man added. A cloth was tied across his face, covering the eye with his Alárààá tribal mark. "The slaves were as organized as soldiers going to war, and more bloodthirsty too. We've managed to keep the situation from spreading to other parts of the capital, but the city guard was unprepared for a disturbance of this severity. We do not even have enough weapons for all our men. I'm not sure how much longer we could have resisted had you not arrived."

Looking around, I realized the city guard was not just out here as scouts—they were also patients. Makeshift triages were dispersed throughout the grounds. Soldiers' bloody wounds were attended to by men who were hardly in any better of a condition themselves.

"How could slaves have caused this much damage?" Ọmọ́ṣẹwà asked angrily.

I saw the same question reflected on Rótìmí's and Balógun's faces. They took this personally. I could understand why; although many slaves were former soldiers, when a regiment was captured, its men were scattered throughout Yorùbáland. That dispersion of clans helped prevent insurgences such as this one. It seemed that not only had the slaves in the Gilded Distrct overcome their differences enough to organize a revolt, but they had done so right under the generals' noses.

None looked more furious than Àrèmọ, but he shook his head. "A question for a later time. What we need to focus on now is cutting them down."

"Excuse me, my king," a shaky voice said behind us. "Might there be a better way to end this? Can't we try to negotiate?"

It was Bámidélé. When he had been told he was marching into battle, the boy had been elated, but that earlier excitement had since evaporated. He was not the only one; anxiety twitched through the division of soldiers. They had done well with the long march, as I was sure they had undergone much worse training, but still, they were just boys. What was worse, only half of them held spears. The city guard were not the only ones with an insufficient number of weapons; the blacksmith strikes had diminished the royal city's weapons store as well. Of what was left, most had been taken by the more experienced units for their crowning battle.

Seeing the boys' nervousness and inadequacies, I was reminded of the quickness of my own heart and the dryness of my throat. I had thought these soldiers would be enough, that this uprising would be a simple inconvenience, but it was becoming increasingly apparent that this was as serious as a battle on the front lines. Really, the only seasoned soldiers here were Àrèmọ and the three generals he brought with him. How were novices supposed to crush such a threat—how was I?

I had been so worried about Kọ̀lọ̀ that I had not even stopped to think about whether or not I could actually save her. I could tell that the generals were confused about why I had accompanied them with an iron machete strapped to my waist; they did not expect me to fight. Maybe I did not have to; maybe it was not too late for me to turn back, or at least stay out here to tend to the wounded.

I turned to Àrèmọ to suggest as much, but seeing him made

me pause. He was stoic, an immovable rock in a sea of doubt and despair.

He cleared his throat. "*Attention*."

The single word whipped through the air, stilling the soldiers immediately as all eyes snapped to him. Even the city guard fell into a salute, and on either side of me, Rótìmí, Ọmóṣẹwà, and Balógun tensed.

"Some of you understandably have reservations about stepping beyond those gates," he said.

With the noise of combat still leaking from the Gilded District, it was by no means quiet, but a kind of hush had fallen over the ranks.

"None of you are full-fledged soldiers," Àrèmọ continued, clasping his hands behind his back, "but what I am asking you to do here today will advance all your timelines. It is not fair, I know. That is why, for those of you who are frightened, you may walk away now if you wish."

I stared in shock. Murmurs broke out among the soldiers. A number of them looked as though they wanted to leave, but no one moved, probably as unsure as I was whether this was some sort of trick.

"Additionally," Àrèmọ continued, "for those of you who wish for your families to also live in fear, please walk away as well."

The soldiers fell silent.

"'Negotiating' will not put an end to these slave revolts." Àrèmọ now slowly walked up and down the front of the soldier block. "It will only teach other slaves their freedom can be won through violence. It will be the beginning of a civil war that you bequeath onto everyone, including your sisters, your mothers, your future wives. All because this single attempt was not immediately and effectively crushed.

"And if that is beyond your concern, then by all means, leave. This battle is not to be fought by the selfish. It will make history, and its heroes will be the youngest the griots will ever praise. If there is a fixed amount of glory to be had from this battle, then it will be distributed among the soldiers who saw this victory through."

The blazing light of the sun cast a fiery glow on what were now rows of determined statues. Spines straightened, and a picture of resilience was carved into each young face. I looked in amazement at the division standing before me; they were no longer scared little boys. Àrèmọ had turned them into soldiers.

He stopped pacing and faced forward. "Bowmen, under General Ọmọ́ṣẹwà's command, you will find high ground and cover your comrades from above. The infantry under General Rótìmí will reinforce the city guard around the Gilded District, ensuring the battle does not leave its borders. Once Ọmọ́ṣẹwà and Rótìmí are in position, General Balógun's men will be the first wave of soldiers to join the fighting. The second wave will be led by me."

Àrèmọ scanned his soldiers. It was as though he met each eye. "It does not matter how underquipped we may be. However few weapons we have, the slaves will have even less. Nor does it matter how organized they were. These slaves have chosen to turn against the Aláràà, and in that step alone, they have chosen defeat."

A cry pulsed through the soldiers. Next to me, Ọmọ́ṣẹwà removed his longbow from across his chest, raising a fist as he jogged to the district entrance. The bowmen parted from the rest and followed him. Rótìmí and Balógun made similar gestures, summoning then leading their men to their positions until the only soldiers who remained were the quarter under Àrèmọ's command.

"Stay alert," Àrèmọ said. "When I give the signal, we move in."

With that, the soldiers gathered in clusters, conversing among themselves. I noticed Bámidélé practicing with his spear, a new confidence in his movements.

A confidence that I still seemed to lack; if my jaw clenched any tighter, my teeth would grind into dust. The only thing Àrèmọ's speech had done for me was make all of this real.

Àrẹ̀mọ turned around, and his eyes found me. As he approached, I commented, "For all the techniques you taught me, you never taught me how to be fearless."

I had meant for it to be a joke, but my voice wavered.

He shrugged. "I can only teach you what I know."

"I meant that I didn't think I would be this scared," I clarified, tucking one of his braids behind his ears. They always came loose from his bun. He never noticed. "I did not even consider that fear would be a thing. Not that you've ever known it—you're calm. Even when everyone else panics, even when we've underestimated the situation, you remain calm—"

"Òdòdó."

In the sunlight, his eyes had become countless layers of dark, dark brown. I took a shaky breath.

"Tell me the secret," I said. I hated how small my voice sounded. "How are you not frightened?"

Àrẹ̀mọ took my hand and put it to his chest, his skin warm to the touch. A rapid pulse raced beneath my palm, as though his heart sprinted across his chest.

"I am leading boys into battle, too many of whom are unarmed, and I am endangering you, the woman I love," he said softly. "I'm terrified."

I looked up at him in surprise. His face was the same tranquil mask he had worn for the soldiers, as smooth as still water. But now, he had pulled me beneath the surface with him. It was strangely comforting, knowing I was not drowning alone. Two was too many to be an accident; if there were us two, then maybe we were meant to be under. If I had him with me, then maybe I did not need air anyways.

Àrẹ̀mọ squeezed my hand before releasing it and walking around me. I turned to see a boy running up to us, who I recognized as a soldier under General Balógun. He was covered in sweat and soot, and there was a nasty gash across his chest, but it did not seem to slow him down.

"My king," he panted, "the slaves have not surrendered, but they are losing momentum."

"Then we will deal the final blow," Àrẹ̀mọ replied. The boy nodded, admiration lighting his darkened face.

Àrẹ̀mọ extracted his axes from their holsters as he turned to his soldiers. He did not need to call for attention; they had seen the messenger, and there was already an electrified charge among them.

"On me," Àrẹ̀mọ yelled, raising an ax. The soldiers yelled back their approval.

As they jogged into a formation, Àrẹ̀mọ turned to me. "It's okay if you've changed your mind, my flower, but I need to know now. Will you stay here? Or are you with me?"

His eyes asked a different question—*Will you dive in?*

I took a deep breath, partly just to see if I could.

"With you," I replied, "yes."

16

It was as though night had fallen early; the sky was a continuous gray cloud of smoke, preventing the sun from breaking through. The streets of the Gilded District were instead lit by blazing wooden roofs, which collapsed into mud buildings with slow, aching groans.

General Balógun had cornered the insurgents at the end of a street, forcing them to take refuge in a damaged manor. Being surrounded only made them more desperate; in their attempt to hold their makeshift headquarters, the entire street leading up to them had been reduced to chaos. Men were engaged in battle on all sides of me. Screams and the clang of their weapons shrieked in my ears, and the heat of bodies smothered me. I could not think clearly; I could hardly even see. The world had become a dizzying blur, and it was all I could do to remain upright.

A spear sliced at my forearm. Bright red rivulets of blood ran down my arm, causing me to yelp, more in surprise than pain.

"Òdòdó!" Àrèmọ's voice came from somewhere within the tumult.

I turned just in time to see him strike down the man whose spear had grazed me. Àrèmọ clutched both of my shoulders. "Òdòdó, this is just another one of our training sessions. We will simply go through our drills, together."

His eyes were as smooth and pitch black as ever, impenetrable by the light of the firestorm roaring around us. "Our drills," I echoed, a cool relief coming over me as I latched onto the solid plan. "Right."

That was all I had time to say—in the next moment, four slaves appeared, surrounding us. Despite Àrèmọ's assurance that the lack of weapons would be mutual on both sides, all four men held a spear. There was something odd about their weapons, but before I could figure it out, Àrèmọ pulled me into him, my back against his. His presence was like an anchor; the noise faded, and my next moves became clear.

The men pounced, launching us into a sequence of striking and dodging. I had fretted that true battle would be much different from training, but the motions came as naturally as falling into an old melody I used to hum. There was no time to think, no time to feel the shallow wounds on my arms. The only thing I could make out clearly was Àrèmọ's warmth pressed behind me. We fought without needing to say anything; he took aim, and I struck. He turned, and I was already facing a new direction. I was his third arm, his third blade. A shadow molded to extend his reach.

As the last man fell, a shriek cut through the turmoil, one different than the yells around me. Despite the baking heat, a chill ran down the back of my neck. I looked around wildly, but there was nothing except flashing weapons among swarming bodies.

Another man was running straight toward me. The muscles in my legs screamed as I sank into a crouch, but as he got closer, I saw that he was only a boy. He was one of ours.

"Àrèmọ," I yelled, elbowing him.

Àrèmọ glanced over his shoulder. When he saw the boy, he jogged to the side of the road, where it was safer to talk.

In the cover of an alley, the boy reported, "General Balógun managed to pry information from the slaves who have surrendered. They have confirmed that the bulk of the remaining slaves are in that manor at the end of the street, so if we can get inside—"

"—then this will be over," Àrèmọ finished with an approving nod.

"There's too much activity in the front," I noted, peering

out of the alley and down the street, where the battle raged on. "How do we get inside?"

"One of General Ọmóṣẹwà's scouts located an unguarded window on the side of the house, second story."

"That'll do," Àrẹ̀mọ said. "Find Balógun. Instruct him to send three of his fastest men through that window to open the doors for the rest of us."

"Understood!"

The boy ran off to carry out his orders. Àrẹ̀mọ and I made to follow him out of the alley, but an earsplitting scream stopped me in my tracks. It was the same as the one I had heard before, but this time it was closer.

And this time, I realized why it had caught my attention so effectively—it was the scream of a woman.

"Òdòdó," Àrẹ̀mọ prompted. He was looking back at me, one foot out of the alley.

He had plainly not heard the scream. For a moment, I wondered if I had imagined it, but I knew I could not have; its terror was very real. I suddenly remembered the city guard's uncertainty of whether they had successfully saved every noble—of whether they had saved Kòlò.

"You go," I told him. "I'm going to find Kòlò."

"We'll go together."

Àrẹ̀mọ stepped toward me, but I stopped him with a hand to his chest. "You're needed elsewhere." When he did not budge, I urged, "Hurry, they're waiting for your leadership to end this. I'll stay out of the thick of the battle until I find my friend. Then we'll make our way back to you."

His jaw clenched; it was clear he did not want to leave me. But out on the street, the noise was growing worse. Àrẹ̀mọ took my hand and pressed it to his mouth.

"I will see you soon," he said fiercely, as though the veracity of his words depended on their intensity.

He held on just a moment more before releasing me and

jogging back to his men. I ran deeper into the alley, hoping its shadow would mask me as I traced the scream to its origin.

I turned a corner, bringing me to the back of the compounds—and I nearly ran into a man. He held a spear, but he did not have a shield like the Aláràá soldiers did; he was not even wearing any shoes. He was not on my side. Luckily, my sudden appearance had shocked him more than his had me. I reacted first.

The man ducked just in time to avoid my machete. He shoved his elbow into my stomach. My back slammed into a nearby wall that enclosed a compound. There was a flash of silver. I dropped to the ground. His spear struck the wall where I had been.

The spear embedded deeply between two stones. I quickly took advantage of his careless force; as he struggled to free his weapon, I jumped to my feet and swung my machete, severing his arm from his body. I had heard wounded animals scream with less anguish than the man did. Before his cries could draw unwanted attention, I swung again.

My machete struck his chest with a force that rattled my arm. He collapsed, gasped greatly twice, then fell silent. I placed a steadying foot on his torso, and as I extracted my machete with a sickening squelch, the full extent of what I had done hit me.

I had killed him. I might have killed when I was fighting earlier, but it had been too hectic to assess the fatality of my blows. I had never even killed a chicken for dinner. Yet here I was, alive and standing over a corpse.

A yell sounded. I whirled around as another man leapt from the shadows, his spear raised. But before I could react, air whizzed past my ear, and an arrow flew into the man's eye.

The man stumbled back, shocked, when another arrow pierced his neck. Blood sprouted from his throat, and with a horrible gurgling sound, he dropped to the ground, dead.

Breathing hard, I turned to my rescuer: a bowman standing atop the wall. "Thank you—"

My gratitude shriveled in the back of my throat as the bowman stepped forth from the shadows. The light of the house burning behind him melded with his eyes so that his gaze jumped and flickered like green fire. It was not just any bowman who had saved me; it was Ọmóṣẹwà—and he now aimed an arrow at me.

"When Ìlódẹ came under Ṣàngótẹ̀'s rule," he said, his satin voice barely audible, "and my people were turned from hunters to soldiers, I was made general because I was the best bowman of the Ẹgbẹ́-Ọdẹ, my king's personal hunter. As it turns out, my skillset translated quite nicely. Shooting men, shooting animals—it's all the same."

I swallowed hard. "It's enough. You've had your fun."

Ọmóṣẹwà chuckled, a melodic, haunting sound. "There is nothing fun about this. On the contrary, I take my promises very seriously."

I did not need to ask what he referred to. Even weeks later, the fly he had pinned to a tree was vivid in my memory, as well as his promise to do the same to me. And the worst part was, even now with all my training and with a weapon in my hands, I was still powerless to stop him.

I moved to take a step forward, but when I heard the creak of Ọmóṣẹwà's bow being wound tighter, I thought better of it. "Please," I whispered. "You can't do this."

"Of course I can. I have not missed a target in thirty years. No matter how small, no matter how fast." He adjusted his aim. "I do not know what spell you cast to become so skilled on the battlefield, but my arrow will pierce through it. I could kill you right now and blame it on the slaves. No one would be any the wiser."

I braced myself. Whether to run, to dodge, to be shot, I did not know—and I did not find out. Screams sounded once more; they were coming from the burning house behind Ọmóṣẹwà. Now that I was closer, I heard multiple women, all crying for help.

"What—?" Ọmóṣẹwà glanced over his shoulder.

I launched forward, sprinting to the wall and jumping as high as I could. My left hand just barely reached the top; my fingernails scraped to dust against the rough stone as I desperately tried to keep myself from falling. With my right hand, I swung my machete above me wildly.

Ọmọ́sẹ̀wà returned his attention to me too late; before he could adjust his aim, my machete struck his leg. It was a weak swing, but it surprised him enough that he lost his balance. He fell over the other side of the wall, taking my machete with him.

I hauled myself over. Ọmọ́sẹ̀wà sat on the ground, gripping a long, shallow gash on his thigh. But once I landed near him, he leapt to his feet and charged toward me.

Ọmọ́sẹ̀wà's specialty was the bow and arrow, but I had no doubt the general was still more skilled than me in hand-to-hand combat. He was certainly stronger, even with his wound. If there was one thing I had learned while training with Àrèmọ, when fighting with a man, the best way I could better my chances of winning was by lowering his own.

I slammed my foot into Ọmọ́sẹ̀wà's chest. With a large gasp, he fell to the ground. But no sooner had he landed than he began crawling to his bow a few paces away.

"*No*," I groaned in frustration, leaping onto him.

My vision was reduced to sky then grass then sky again as we rolled, my yells tangling with his own. I managed to snake my arm behind him and extract an arrow from his quiver. In the next revolution, I pinned his shoulders to the ground with my knees and held the arrowhead to his neck.

"Ọmọ́sẹ̀wà, stop—listen!" I hissed, struggling to keep him on the ground. "Please, for one moment stop and just *listen*."

I pressed the arrowhead into his neck, drawing drops of blood and forcing him to still. I knew he had heard it when his anger shifted to alarm.

"You hear those women?" I asked. "I believe Kọ̀lọ̀ is one of them. I might be a witch, but surely you acknowledge that the princess is a wife worthy of the Aláàfin. So, what will it be—use your time to kill me, or to save Kòlò from certain death?"

Omóṣẹwà glared. I did not have time to wait for him to swallow his pride and respond; the house was burning.

I jumped to my feet and, ducking to grab my machete, sprinted to the house. Inside, trails of flame trickled down the walls, setting priceless rugs and furniture aflame. The mud walls slowed the fire, but judging from the groans, the wooden foundation could not hold for much longer.

"Hello?" I yelled, using the crook of my arm to shield my face from the smoke as I searched the scorching rooms. "Is someone in here?"

Over the crackling flames, I just barely heard the frightened responses.

"Upstairs!"

Stairs. I ran back to the entrance room. Omóṣẹwà stood there, as glowing as the fire encasing us, and his eyes just as destructive. Wordlessly, he jerked his chin to an archway and ran through it.

Dodging flaming furniture, I followed him up a spiraling staircase. The fire was worse up here; it must have been set at the wooden roof and was working its way down. Dark grains of smoke stung my eyes and nose as we raced down the hallway.

"Where are you?" I shouted as Omóṣẹwà yelled, "Kòlò!"

"Here—we're in here!"

It came from the end of the hall. Omóṣẹwà and I dashed to the very last room. I reached for the knob and immediately recoiled. My palm was raw, the top layer of skin burned off.

"Move."

I had barely leapt aside when Omóṣẹwà's foot smashed into the door. The door caved in with a great creak, bringing with it a shower of dust.

"The roof is unstable enough," I said, coughing. "That kick could have brought it all down."

"But it didn't."

He charged inside, leaving me little choice but to follow. The fire had only just started to infiltrate the room, beginning with the wall to our left. Opposite it sat a dozen women clutching each other in fear—all except one, who stood at the window.

"Òdòdó," Kòlò said in surprise as she turned to me. Her bright blouse and trousers were smeared in grime, and her inflamed tribal mark was further reddened by the firelight glowing on her face. Otherwise, though, she appeared unharmed.

I looked around the room, as shocked as she was. I had thought Kòlò being left behind was a gross oversight, one I would have never expected to be repeated ten times over. Were these not noblewomen? How could the city guard not have made evacuating them a priority?

Boom.

A deafening bellow reverberated through my bones, clacking my teeth and jerking me forward. The women screamed as parts of the ceiling fell. Cracks snaked up the walls, gradually widening with sickening crunches.

"The house is about to collapse from the fire!" I yelled, but even as I said it, I knew that was not quite true. It could not have been the fire alone rupturing the walls and shaking the floor beneath my feet. But there was no time to investigate; if we stayed here a moment longer, we would be crushed. "We have to get out now!"

The women rose, but they moved too slow; they shook in fear, and the shuddering house did not help. I ran to them, herding them like cows toward Ọmóṣẹwà, who ushered them out the fractured doorway.

When the last woman was out, Ọmóṣẹwà said, "We need to go."

"Kòlò!" I shouted.

She had not moved. She did not even look away from the window as she said, "I should not have come."

Her tone was airy, as though the building was not crumbling

around us. She was in shock, I assumed, but we simply did not have time for her absentmindedness.

I grabbed her wrist and pulled her out of the room. The house moaned. I could feel the floor buckling beneath my feet, as though each step I took would be the one that would not hold. It was like the whole structure was violently imploding. *What was going on?*

Ahead, Ọmóṣẹwà guided the women down the spiral staircase. Kòlò and I had nearly reached the landing when the house gave a mighty wail. In the same instant, Kòlò twisted her hand so that she was the one grabbing me. I was yanked back, and I fell hard enough that there was a painful *pop* in my wrist as my hand slammed into the ground. A large chunk of the roof dropped right where I had been a moment before, a flaming barrier separating Kòlò and I from Ọmóṣẹwà and the stairs.

Ọmóṣẹwà ran forward, but Kòlò shouted, "No, go! We'll find another way!"

The floor groaned, and the roof rained down. With a grim nod, Ọmóṣẹwà rushed down the staircase behind the women. Kòlò hauled me to my feet and pulled me back down the hall.

"Worry not, little flower," she called; she seemed to have snapped out of her daze. "I know how to get us out. I hadn't even realized you were here."

"I arrived with the other soldiers," I yelled through gritted teeth; her tugging on my hand worsened the throb in my wrist.

"The Aláàfin brought you with him? Why?"

"I begged him to let me come, but he's been training me, so—"

Kòlò came to a halt so suddenly that I nearly ran into her. She whirled around, her eyes wide. "Training? Like an Ahosi woman warrior?"

"Yes, I suppose—" The wall next to us exploded, and the roof slanted precariously inwards. Desperation crept into my voice as I prompted, "Kòlò, you said you knew a way out."

"Yes," she said absently, eyeing the machete in my hand as if just realizing I had it. Then her eyes snapped to mine, and she repeated more firmly, "Yes. Here."

I followed her inside the room from earlier, weaving through flaming furniture and splintering holes in the floor. "We'll take the window out," she said. "I had been about to do so anyways—and tell the other women to come with me, of course—but I hesitated because I was unsure of what fate I would meet on the ground."

"We managed to drive all the slaves back to the end of one street," I said. "Àrèmọ is readying the other soldiers to storm a house they've taken refuge in. The fight should have been over by now, but the slaves were better equipped than anyone expected." As an afterthought, I added, "Most have new spears, which is surprising. With soldiers being short on weapons, it's a wonder that slaves managed to get their hands on any at all."

The four who had surrounded me earlier flashed across my mind, and I suddenly realized what had been so strange about their spears that I had not been able to pinpoint before. "Wait—I've seen those spearheads. I think—they look like the ones that I once found folded into fabrics . . . in the aṣọ òkè you have been sending out as gifts . . ."

Kòlò had been climbing onto the windowsill, but now she paused and turned to me. The fire flickered across her golden-brown face, warping her gaze.

"Kòlò?" I asked uncertainly.

"Forgive me," she said softly, rising from the sill and walking toward me. "It's easier for me this way."

Before I could question her, she punched me in the jaw.

There was a surprising amount of force behind her fist, and I fell backwards. Airborne, free. Time seemed to slow to a stop—then wind back.

Before my eyes, I saw a memory from a few months ago, a day when Mama Aláàfin had taken me and Kòlò to a gathering. The most exciting part had been the food; standing at the buffet table, I feared that I would keel over in boredom. Then Kòlò slid next to me, her eyes alight with mischief. The next thing I knew, we were running through the streets of Ṣàngótẹ̀, breathless and giggling and each clutching a handful of pilfered meat pies.

As we settled onto a sidewalk to enjoy our spoils, two city guards approached us. I panicked, not wanting to be taken back to Mama Aláàfin's disapproval. But Kọ̀lọ̀ merely told me, "Smile on my signal."

The men questioned us, and Kọ̀lọ̀ spun a story about us being the daughters of a local cook, and we were helping him sell his wares, and would they like to try one, free of charge? I could tell the men were not entirely convinced. Kọ̀lọ̀ could too; she elbowed me. Taking my cue, I offered the men a meat pie and a large smile. The last of their wariness evaporated as they accepted the food and, after thanking us, went on their way.

"How did you know that would work?" I asked.

"On a girl like you, a smile goes a long way." Kọ̀lọ̀ laughed at my amazement, adding, "You don't know how to use it yet, but lucky for you, you have me."

I hit the floor. Hard. The beloved memory shattered, and reality rushed back to me all at once.

My head spinning, I looked up in time to see Kọ̀lọ̀, my first and former friend, jump from the window like a bird taking flight. I scrambled to rise, my injuries weighing me down.

Just as I reached the window, the house gave a final roar and, at last, collapsed, sucking me down into its fiery abyss.

17

It was dark, both around and within me. It felt like a chill settling onto my skin, but I did not take cold. It felt like my stomach was completely empty, but I was not hungry.

It felt like peace.

I was moving, I realized. I walked forward, but to where, I could not tell. The only thing I knew was that so long as I kept moving, everything and every thing would be okay.

There appeared a ground beneath my feet, soft at first, then firmer as I went on. A few steps more and I could see. I continued walking. Up ahead, there came to be a long wooden table that stretched endlessly in either direction. Only three people sat at it, but they seemed to take it up in its entirety.

They were the most beautiful beings I had ever seen. They were blacker than the night, yet they shone as bright as the sun and radiated as much warmth. The elegance with which they sat made me think thrones had been created just to accommodate them, and the majesty with which they ate made me think feasts had been invented just to feed them. Had they not been so wholly perfect, they could have been human.

"One has gone astray."

The voice came from everywhere and nowhere; it was possible it had not even spoken, yet I heard it. The three diners had always been able to see me, this I knew, but now with those words, they were looking at me. Their gazes were kindling to my mind, striking a small, clarifying flame that stopped me in my tracks. I was not supposed to be here.

"Go deal with your pupil," a man rumbled like a roll of thunder.

"You dey pick her out," replied a man with a voice as hard as iron. "You go deal with her."

Ṣàngó and Ògún. The knowledge was intrinsic, their faces a sight so familiar that not even blindness could rob me of it.

"Both of you go, and stop disturbing me," the third diner, a woman, susurrated.

I gasped. The woman's form shifted before me, a tumult of churning and twisting. She was a windstorm with stunning eyes. She was beautiful; she was terrible.

She was Ọya.

I dropped my gaze. Immediately, I felt a chilling relief. Had I looked at her a moment longer, I was sure I would have been swept away.

Neither Ṣàngó nor Ògún argued with Ọya, a wisdom they had probably learned from their individual times being married to her. As they descended from the table, the air seemed to mold and shift, as though jumping out of the way for them.

The two of them looked down at me for a moment before Ṣàngó laughed. "My friend," he said to Ògún, "this one dey resemble you."

"Eh? Shine your eye well well. I no look like humans."

"I always think you look like Obàtálá. Did he not make humans like himself?"

"He get drunk on the job. It shows."

"This one no be too bad. So I give her to my descendant—this man, all he did was pray for wife."

"Heh. Imagine."

"Imagine! Every day, every day he pray, 'Can you hear me?' Of course I hear! Let me be. Giving me headache."

"Yes-o. They pray too much. Let me rest now."

"But me that is kind, I go show my descendant how to find good wife. This man, he run my city well. I no know how. Guiding herd of asses easier than guiding him."

"Might as well have your city's ruler be an ass."

"Is that not what I have been doing?"

The òrìṣàs laughed. I realized I could not breathe. It had been gradual, as though the air was souring, curdling into lumps that plopped into my lungs. I tried to cough them up, but the more I coughed, the more bitter air I took in and the harder my body convulsed.

Ṣàngó and Ògún paused in their laughter to watch my coughing fit. In unison, they looked at each other, at me, then back at each other. Then they broke into laughter once more, the sound pulsing through the ground and shaking the sky.

"She has been here too long," Ọya's voice drifted around us. "Olódùmarè is unhappy."

Ṣàngó sighed. "Very well. Safe journey, Alálẹ̀ Òdòdó."

The name sparked my memory, and I suddenly remembered that it was *my* name. Scenes surfaced in my head—a slave revolt; running into a burning building; Kòlò abandoning me as the world imploded. Grief set my heart and nerves ablaze. I remembered fear. I remembered pain. I did not want to go back; I could not take it.

"No," I croaked, the word like a knife slicing across my throat. "Let me stay here. Why must I go back to life?"

Ṣàngó and Ògún laughed.

"Does the arrow fly through the air to its quiver?" Ṣàngó asked. "Does the ocean run up into its rivers?"

I could make neither head nor tail of his questions. The two òrìṣàs, still laughing, turned away, back to their infinite feast. I stretched an arm out. "Wait—"

My eyes shot open. The world was on fire. Blinding reds, oranges, and yellows ate at the ruins encasing me. Not too far above, splintered wood and mud were on the precipice of caving in.

My left hand, stretched out to my side across the rubble, still clutched my machete. Every muscle in my body screamed as I slowly sat up. Blistering heat pressed onto me.

There was an opening to my right, just large enough to slip through. I crawled on my hands and knees, wincing at jagged edges jutting into my skin, toward the sliver of an escape. I was going to make it. I would climb out and find Àrèmọ, and this would all be nothing more than a bad memory—

A wooden plank beneath my hand snapped as soon as I put my weight on it. I lurched forward, and the entire thing gave away. I fell deeper into the wreckage, sliding and snagging against the walls until I hit dirt, my head snapping back onto the ground.

A clang told me the machete fell somewhere nearby. Through blackness spotting my vision, I saw an enormous slab of the wall plummeting toward me. Vaguely, I acknowledged that I should move, but my head was floating, and my body weighed too much. I watched as the slab dropped next to me—directly onto my right hand.

The popping and groaning of the crumbling house dwindled as a buzz overcame my mind. I turned my head, staring at the slab. Beneath it, splattered blood slowly seeped into the ground. It looked like a giant bug had been squashed. Not my hand. That could not be my hand.

My other hand found its way to the slab and gingerly touched it. Then nudged it. Then pulled and pushed and clawed at it with what little strength I had left. It did not budge.

Panic welled in my chest, and with it, pain hammered down on me. In a fit of desperation, I brought my feet up, kicking at the slab from whatever odd angle I could manage. It did not budge.

A flaming piece of wood fell onto my leg. With a sharp hiss, I quickly shook it off before it could finish burning through my trousers. I looked up—in the crack I had fallen through, I saw that the fire was quickly consuming what was left of the house. Even if I could free myself, the only thing waiting for me above was a fiery death. That was, if the entire wreckage did not bury me first.

Tears slid down my face and mingled with the bloody grime on my tongue. I abandoned my futile attempt and laid back down. As I stared up at the burning structure, I thought of the vision I had just witnessed. It would seem as though Ṣàngó had pushed me out for no reason; I would be returning there anyway. The pain would soon be over.

There sounded a large clap of thunder. I shifted as much as I could until I was directly under a gap that opened out to the sky. A drop of water, cold and quick, splashed onto my face, followed by another and another. Before long, there was a steady drip of water going. If the water was soaking through to all the way down here, it must have been raining very hard. Hard enough to put out the fire.

With a pain worse than my crushed hand, worse than my burns and wounds, and worse than Kòlò's betrayal, I realized I would live.

Thunder rolled across the sky once more. It sounded like Ṣàngó's laughter.

I laughed with him. My throat felt like it was peeling as the sound was scraped from it, and my body convulsed with the effort. The laughter quickly became too painful, and it turned into sobs—but the pain, the pain was still there. I could neither laugh nor cry it away.

So, I embraced it. I screamed. I screamed until I could not breathe. I screamed until doing so became more painful than my injuries, and then I screamed louder.

I screamed until I could no longer distinguish myself from the storm.

The heat of the sun pressed against my face, but I did not open my eyes. Fatigue permeated every fiber of my being; all I wanted to do was sleep, and stay asleep.

Since the fire died, the only sound in this wretched tomb had been my ragged breathing. But now, I heard the distant sound of hooves. It grew closer, accompanied by voices. I did not know if they were soldiers or slaves, nor did I know which side had emerged victorious from the uprising. What I did know was that if I laid unmoving, as I did now, I could almost forget about the pain coiled tightly around me.

"How does the ground just collapse like this?"

"It happens, especially during rainy season. It's just bad luck there was a house on it."

"Well, better it happens to a rich man's house than my own. Ṣàngó yọ mí."

There were more hoofbeats. In a more formal tone, one of the voices asked, "Is this the house, my lady?"

"Yes."

My eyes flew open. That action, small as it was, sent a shock-wave of pain through my body. The sudden sunlight made my head spin. In my anger, I hardly noticed.

"My poor sweet flower," I heard Kọ̀lọ̀ croon. "All I can think of is the fear she must have felt as the building fell into the ground."

Grief cracked her voice. Even I almost felt pity for her—a fact that only inflamed my anger. It seared through my veins, my pulse pumping it through my body until rage filled me completely.

For the first time in hours, I tried to get up, pushing at the wall on my hand. I ran into a burning building for that woman, and she left me to die. No, she *pushed* me into Death's open arms. I should have let her die. I would rectify my mistake. I would kill her—

"She's not dead."

The new voice broke the murderous spell that had come over me, freezing me in place. A new pain rose in me, not from anger or injury; it was an ache.

"Àrèmọ," Kọ̀lọ̀ said, "look at this. How could anyone survive?"

"No. Somewhere down there, she's alive. And I'm going to find her."

"Àrèmọ, don't—"

"It could still be unstable, my king—"

Through the overlapping voices came a sound like rocks tumbling down a slope, followed by a solid thump. As Àrèmọ walked around the wreckage above, I felt a glimmer of hope. I wanted to call out, but my voice was lost deep within me, buried under the layers of ash I had inhaled.

It was no matter; he would find me. I was sure of it. He would not leave until he did. If there was one person I could still trust, it was him.

"Over here," a voice said suddenly, one that was nearer than the others—some soldiers seemed to have followed Àrèmọ down.

Footsteps grew rapid, sending showers of ash down onto me—they were running. They must have spotted me through some crevice. My heart lightened; they were going to find me.

The footsteps stopped. A large thud sounded, as though someone had dropped to their knees. Silence roared in my ears. Were they here? Why did I not see them?

"Are you sure . . . ?" a man's voice trailed off uncertainly.

"The body is charred, but it's still clearly a woman," Kòlò said.

A body? One of the noblewomen must not have made it out in time, or it was a female slave. I did not know, nor did I care; it was not me.

"*I'm right here!*" I screamed.

"It can't be her," Àrèmọ protested, but his voice was frighteningly hollow, as though he had been emptied of everything that made him. "Had I known that a mere slave revolt would result in this . . . And I trained her myself . . ."

"Death's cruelty is in his generosity, husband," Kòlò said softly. "He does not discriminate in his victims."

"*I'm right here! I'm right here!*" I screamed over and over—or did I? But if I was not screaming, why, then, did the words ring so loudly in my ears? Why, then, did they hurt so much?

"We must start back to the royal city," Kòlò said. "It is a long ride."

How could I have ever thought her voice to be musical? Each word she uttered now scraped against my mind like fingernails dragged over rugged brick.

There was heavy silence. Then, Àrèmọ said, "Have a wagon prepared for her."

I listened as the soldiers loaded the corpse onto the wagon. I listened to Àrèmọ's quiet sobs and Kọ̀lọ̀'s soothing words, quickly halted when the soldiers called for them. I listened as they mounted their horses and as the hoofbeats grew faint.

I closed my eyes. I wanted to cry, but I was too dehydrated for the tears to come.

Kọ̀lọ̀ had called Death cruel. I did not see why; Death seemed like he would be kind. If only I could meet him.

As sunbeams filled then drained from my tomb, a sugary smell drifted through the blood and ash. It was Death, lurking just out of reach. I imagined him taking me in his cool embrace, his sweet scent easing my passage, like eating honey after taking medicine. I listened for Death's call, but instead the daffodil's song played in my mind.

> *"You listen to her tale*
> *One her teacher always told*
> *Of roads his son walked*
> *Roads paved with petals of gold*
> *See them bloom, see them shine*
> *See this garden become a sky*
> *With a thousand tiny suns*
> *It's no lie, it's no lie*
> *Light the world through the night*
> *Keep this glow inside your heart*
> *Flowers wilt, lands dwindle*
> *But survival is in the art."*

The song that vanquished Death. How it mocked me now.

No, Death himself was not cruel. What was cruel was when he stayed away.

One day passed. Or one hour, or one eternity. I did not know.

Get up, a small voice said, too harsh to be gentle Death. *Keep going.*

No, I told it. Let me lie here. It hurt. Everything hurt.

It hurts to keep moving, but it hurts more to stop.

This time, the voice sounded like Kòlò. That wretched woman. It was her who pushed me to the edge of death; what gave her the right to be the one to pull me back as well?

Then I remembered Àrèmọ and his embrace and his laughter. And I propped myself up with my good hand. My mind rolled this way and that; my vision doubled. Tripled. The shadows around me grew. I shut my eyes tightly.

Keep going.

But the wall slab—it was still on my hand. It would not move.

It'll break.

I strained until my other hand wrapped around the hilt of my machete. Slowly, I dragged it toward me and lifted it.

It barely rose off the ground when my strength gave out completely. The machete dropped, its flat side landing on my trapped arm. I adjusted my grip and tried again. My arm shook violently. With as much force as I could muster, I struck the slab.

A dent appeared. My eyes widened; I had not dared to allow myself to hope. But this time, when I lifted the machete, it was with a more confident grip. I did not need to break the entire slab; just chip off the edge, then I could slide my hand out.

I took aim and brought the machete down once more.

My hand slipped. The blade skidded off the wall edge and embedded into my flesh. I flinched—then realized it did not hurt.

The swollen wrist deflated as air that had built up under my skin escaped with a quiet hiss. I pressed the machete deeper into my wrist. Much later than I should have, I felt pain. I realized it was the first time I had felt pain in this hand since it had been crushed.

Keep going.

When I was young, I had talked constantly. It must have driven my mother mad, because one day she told me that if I continued speaking so much, all the àṣẹ in my body would leak from my mouth, draining me of my soul.

I tore a strip of cloth from my tattered trousers and tied it around my arm with my one hand and my teeth. If àṣẹ could leak from my mouth, it would surely flow out of me now.

I positioned the machete above my wrist. It was just another blow, I told myself. I had been burned, battered, and buried. I had been delivered to Death and turned away. This could not hurt any worse.

I brought the machete down.

Anguish rang sharply in my ears, beating against the inside of my head.

Black and purple spots popped across my vision.

I shakily raised the stump that used to be my hand.

A tangle of severed veins and blood and bone and blood and rotted tissue and blood—*there was too much blood*.

I hunched over. My entire body shook with violent heaves. They produced nothing but stinging bile.

My arm throbbed; my head swam.

And that *smell*.

I tried to turn away from it, but it clung to my nose.

Clearly, Death with his sugared scent was nowhere near.

I had no choice but to keep going.

The world was gray when at last I crawled out of the wreckage.

There was a filthy cloth wrapped around my arm, soaked with blood. I did not remember donning it. The entirety of my right trouser was torn away. Blood ran free down my bare leg.

Dirt towered all around me. It was as though the Earth had opened and swallowed the house whole, and me with it.

Keep going.

I began climbing.

The entire street was a glamorous wasteland. Walkways and gilded gates were stained with blood. Aside from the occasional corpse, the Gilded District was abandoned.

Voices.

Coming from outside the entrance gate. I latched onto the sound, using it like a rope to haul myself in the right direction.

There were men.

In the darkness, I could not see them; only their torches moving between rows of corpses. There were horses, each attached to a cart. The men loaded dead bodies on them.

I stumbled onto the nearest wagon right before my legs gave out. The air reeked of rotting flesh, but I had grown accustomed to the stench.

The warm wood felt cool beneath my feverish skin. Footsteps approached. A corpse landed beside me with a thud that shook the whole wagon.

It rolled with the momentum and came to a stop on its side, facing me. The carrier passed by, the firelight of his torch flashing across the corpse's face and illuminating its features.

The corpse was Bámidélé.

His wide eyes were half-open; his mouth sagged. His final expression was one of fear. Regret. Flies buzzed around a gash on his cheek.

I recalled the boy's excitement. That warmth would never again cross his young face. He had spent the entirety of his short life training to become a soldier, only to die in his first battle.

From somewhere within, I found the strength to reach out and close his eyes.

The wagon came to a halt.

I pried my eyes open. The sun stared down at me mockingly. Around me, mud-brick buildings stretched up to the blue sky. Many of the corpses in the wagon were now gone, including that of Bámidélé. I, cruelly, was still here.

My skin slowly unstuck from the wooden planks as I rose. Ahead, a man walked up to a house, pulling a shrouded body in a wheelbarrow behind him. He knocked on the door, and an older woman answered. When she saw what he carried, she fell to her knees with a wail.

I slid off the wagon. Dizziness threatened to pull me down, but my knees did not buckle. I began walking in the opposite direction of the man; I did not want his help. I could not trust him. I could not trust anyone.

I staggered aimlessly down streets, turning at random lest I was being followed. However, the streets were eerily empty.

Where were the thousands of Aláràá who lived in the capital? Was I dead after all?

No, there was too much pain for this to be death. Each step felt like it would be my last. My chest heaved with the effort of dragging one leaden foot in front of the other.

And there. That sound.

Another reason why this could not be death—there was drumming.

The three-headed elephant emblem etched into the great walls of the royal city came into view. Suddenly, an enormous, brilliant cloth flashed before my eyes.

It was so bright of a yellow I was sure it was a piece of the sun itself. It spun through the air seemingly on its own, but as it moved, I saw that a figure was behind it, trailed by a band of drummers.

Using a hole in the center of the cloth, the figure twirled it like a baton before ducking their head through the hole. The cloth fluttered down onto them and stacked atop the countless layers of vivid draperies that covered them from head to toe.

The area in front of the royal city swarmed with thousands of people. Scattered among them, also trailed by drummers, were numerous figures. Each were clad in every color imaginable and were spinning more onto themselves. Their elaborate attires brushed the ground and masked their faces.

Egúngún.

Masquerade.

This was a festival. All around danced colorful egúngún spirits, embodying the bond between the living and the dead. Egúngún came out on various occasions, such as the death of an important person, and the festivities could go on for days.

A very important person must have died, for it seemed as though every citizen of Ṣàngótẹ̀ was present. There were entertainers juggling and dancing; there were scores of foods cooked by chefs.

People jumped aside as I trudged forward. Children burst into tears. Soldiers reached for their weapons but did not pounce, on the defensive rather than offensive.

One word circulated around me. Whispered at first, then louder, until it seemed to hover over the entire area. Each beat of the musicians drummed it into a tangible existence.

Witch.

I kept moving. I had to. As I parted the crowd like a knife slicing through overripe fruit, I spotted people gathered around a platform. On it kneeled four women. Their heads were bowed as they whispered prayers into their hands or else sobbed silently.

I knew them. They were my handmaids.

Behind them stood two men. One was a soldier, a machete ready at his side, and the other man—I knew him too. Gassire. It was Gassire. He was speaking.

"—a woman warrior who rivaled the Ahosi of Dahomey. She fought valiantly for the Aláàfin, offering her life to vanquish his foes. As she makes her transition, let the slaves who served her in this world now do the same in the next."

As the soldier raised his machete to the first woman's neck, Gassire scanned the crowd. His eyes passed over me then instantly darted back, widening with horror and disbelief.

"*Wait.*" He spoke so firmly that the soldier's swinging machete froze a breath away from the woman's neck, as though it had run into the word.

Gassire stepped forward. "Òdòdó?"

He said this without his previous bravado, breaking the web of grandeur he had been spinning. The word brought me to a halt.

But it was not just a word, I realized. It was my name.

The audience followed Gassire's gaze. There were gasps, and screams, probably, but I could no longer hear anything. A white noise clogged my ears. It dawned on me which life all these people had gathered to celebrate: mine.

I had walked into my own funeral.

The last of my energy dissolved as the full extent of my injuries rushed toward me. My head swam; my heart raced. Everything grew dark.

18

I t became impossible to discern reality from the workings of my mind.

As I was carried into the royal city, the sun slowly transformed into a daffodil. More sprouted next to it, populating the sky until daffodils overflowed down onto the world around me. I lay among them, but when I looked closer, I realized what I had thought were yellow flowers were actually flames. Fire blazed around me, searing my eyes as it burned brighter and brighter.

The world went black. From the darkness, a man's face emerged above me. The white dots peppered over his skin marked him as the royal babaláwo.

"Will she live?" Mama Aláàfin's voice drifted toward me from somewhere in the void.

"I am not sure." The royal babaláwo's lips did not move, but I knew the response came from him. *"Normally, I would say no, for I have seen soldiers in much better condition die much sooner. But if she has already made it this far . . ."*

Mama Aláàfin kissed her teeth. *"I do not know why my son has allowed this witch to cause him so much grief. Whether she lives or dies, he needs to do away with her. Or I will do it for him."*

I began to itch, right beneath the surface of my skin. As the feeling intensified, a droning sound grew louder. It clogged my ears and every space in my body, preventing me from moving even as it felt like thousands of insects crawled around inside me.

Still floating above me, the royal babaláwo's face was impassive.

Then it was smiling. There had been no transition between the two expressions.

"*Hush*," he said, and the word came like a wave, washing away the sound and tingling, as well as him. His face smeared across the darkness in all directions. As he faded, his white dots remained. They glowed brightly in his absence, set against the darkness like stars in the night sky.

I blinked, and Dígí stood over me. Instead of her blacksmith cloak, she wore a wrapper similar to what I had seen my hand-maids wear.

"*Please don't die, Òdòdó*," Dígí said. Even while pleading, she remained expressionless. My face was reflected in her large eyes, like looking into a still pond. They swelled until my reflection completely consumed her face so that when she next spoke, it was my own face telling me, "*We need you to live.*"

It was a lazy day with scarcely a breeze. The heat was so insuffer-able that even Àrèmọ had allowed his soldiers to take the after-noon off—albeit grudgingly, and only after a dozen had fainted.

He and I had escaped from the heat to my hut. I sat on a stool, and Àrèmọ sat between my legs as I braided his hair. Though he wore only a pair of trousers, his chest shone with sweat. It mixed with the water dripping from the half of his long curly hair that was still unbraided.

"It's my turn," he announced.

"Go on then," I said, sectioning his hair with a three-pronged wooden comb. "Ask your question."

"How about this—will you marry me now?"

"You've just asked that question."

"I can't ask it again?"

"No. That's not how the game works."

"I'm not sure I like this game."

I sighed. "Me neither." To Gassire, I asked, "Can you make up a story for us?"

The griot, who sat on a nearby divan, glanced up from his manuscript. "I'm not a storyteller."

"But you've—sorry," I said to Àrèmọ, who had flinched after I pulled his hair a little too hard. "You've told stories before."

"You asked if I could 'make up' a story. A griot does not 'make up' stories. A griot is society's vital vessel through which flows legends, traditions, *histories*." Gassire stood, gathering his manuscripts. "Histories you would learn, my lady, if we could ever begin your lessons. But as you and the Aláàfin seem more concerned with the art of braiding, I'll take my knowledge where it is needed."

With that, he swept out of my hut and slammed the door behind him.

"We've offended my griot," Àrèmọ remarked.

"Yeah."

"We should apologize."

"Yeah."

Neither of us moved. It was very hot. Wading through the humidity took quite some energy.

"Tomorrow," I added.

"Tomorrow," Àrèmọ agreed. With a great yawn, he wrapped his arms around my calf, rested his head on my knee, and said, "Give me a question."

"Hmm," I hummed, reaching into the mental store of riddles I had collected from Timbuktu's travelers. "Okay, I've got one. Close your eyes. Imagine you're in a room with no doors and no windows, and the room is filling up with water. What do you do?"

"There's no doors?"

"And no windows."

"I see."

Silence settled between us. I had finished one and a half braids when, at last, Àrèmọ turned around. A smile that could outshine the sun lit his face, pushing his dimple deep into his right cheek as he answered, "I would simply open my eyes."

Open my eyes.

Open my eyes.

Open your eyes.

I opened my eyes.

Everything was heavy. It was a new day, but above me, there was the same domed ceiling as in my dreamt memory. I was in my hut, in the royal city.

Shapeless curls, soft and damp, floated around my face, cushioning my head. From them drifted a flowery perfume; someone—my handmaids, probably—must have undid my cornrows and washed my hair.

I moved to brush the curls from my face, but my effort fell short—there was no hand. Only a stump, now wrapped in clean bandages smelling strongly of herbs. Moment by moment, the last few days returned to me, and I became aware of the aches and burns littering my body. With a small groan, I turned to my side—and froze. There, sitting in a chair at my bedside, was Kòlò.

She wore a multicolored dress, but the way she sat, she might as well have worn her usual trousers. Leaning back in the chair, her long legs were splayed out in front of her. Her elbow was perched on an armrest, and her mouth rested on her fist. My eyes found hers so quickly that she must have been staring at me this whole time; I wondered how long she had been sitting there, watching me.

Silence stretched between us, neither of us moving. After what seemed like an eternity, Kòlò finally spoke.

"It is possible," she said, removing her hand from her mouth, "that I overreacted."

There was a brief pause. Then Kòlò continued, "But you must understand, I had thought you were an idiot. And I had relied on that belief. So, when you began demonstrating oth-erwise, I—Well, I panicked." With a sigh, she leaned forward, resting her elbows on her knees. "But in retrospect, none of that was needed, was it? What could you have said—that I took from the royal city's weapon stores to supply slaves, and you know I did because you enabled me? No, you actually love that monster. You would have never admitted your treasonous role to Àrẹ̀mọ. So, I am truly sorry I thought I needed to take such extreme measures. But it's alright. Ultimately, no harm has been done."

Her gaze fell to my arm stump. "Oh, right. Except for that." She shrugged. "Do not worry. Not even losing a hand could take away from your beauty. In fact, you remind me of Ọbà. They say she was the first wife of Ṣàngó, but his favorites were Ọya and Ọ̀ṣun. So, to win back his favor, Ọbà cut off her own ear and fed it to him. Quite romantic, the lengths she underwent to prove her dedication to her husband. Although, whenever I was told that story while I was growing up, I always wondered: would he have done the same for her?"

Something screamed a terrible, inhuman shriek. Something lunged at Kọ̀lọ̀, flailing and kicking, causing frightened slaves to rush inside the hut to restrain it. The thing was a person, was me, I realized, but I did not have the capacity to think much else. A cold rage froze my mind on one thing and one thing alone: Kọ̀lọ̀.

I trusted her—I had felt *sorry* for her. And of all people, she tried to kill me twice over; first when she pushed me into a crumbling building and second when she prevented Àrẹ̀mọ from finding me but I would not let her try it a third time I was going to *kill* her—the machete. Where was my machete? No matter; I would use my bare hands, I would—

Vaguely, I heard the door open behind me, and the next thing I knew, the royal babaláwo's scent of palm nuts invaded my senses. There was a slight pressure on the side of my neck. As it grew heavier, my consciousness dimmed until everything around me, including Kọ̀lọ̀'s smirk, faded to black.

19

When I next awoke, I was back in my bed, staring up at the ceiling.

My previous audience had been replaced by Àrẹ̀mọ, who sat on a stool at my bedside. He had never looked so small; his head was bowed, and his shoulders were hunched. With a surprising amount of bitterness, I noticed he was holding one of the bronze flowers I had given him.

"Àrẹ̀mọ."

I said his name so softly that I hardly even heard myself, but his head immediately snapped up.

"You're awake," he gasped. His face sagged with exhaustion, and several braids had escaped from his bun. They hung limply in his face, but he did not seem to notice. He never did.

"Here. Drink." He leaned forward to put a cup of water to my mouth.

When I had drunk my fill, Àrẹ̀mọ put the empty cup aside and said, "I could hardly believe it when I was told you returned." He took my remaining hand in both of his own. "I thought I had lost you."

I stared at my hand enveloped in his. Every part of me ached, but where my skin met his, I burned. Keeping my eyes on our hands, I swallowed hard, but it did nothing to calm the feeling bubbling in the back of my throat.

"Can someone be lost if no one looked for them?" I asked.

"I . . . uncovered the body of a woman—"

"Who was not me."

A heavy pause dropped between us.

"Her features were distorted from the fire. I thought . . ." Àrẹ̀mọ trailed off, perhaps realizing how flimsy his words were.

"I admit," he said after a moment, "I may have formed a conclusion with too much haste. But please understand, it felt like my entire world was slipping away from me. I was desperate to have something concrete to hold on to."

"And desperate to get back to the royal city, I am sure." The frustration bubbling in my throat was beginning to froth over, flooding my eyes, my airway, my heart. "Following the revolt, you only had so much time. And you made your choice what to focus on."

"That's not true, my flower. I would have spent all day looking for you if that's what it would have taken, but—"

"I was right there!" the words exploded from me.

I could not subdue the feeling a moment longer; it seethed in me, pushing me to meet his eyes at last.

"All you had to do was look harder," I whispered, my voice cracking under the strain. "I was right *there*. And you didn't find me."

My supposed death had turned him into glass. Now, with my words, he shattered. His shoulders fell; his black eyes were vacant, clear windows to a rupture within him.

The boiling within me reached a peak so intense that it threatened suffocation. This was anger, I realized; an anger different than what I felt toward Kọ̀lọ̀. A pain that could only be so deep because I allowed it in.

Àrẹ̀mọ had trained me, he had dragged me into this life. He had made me a piece of himself. And just when I was beginning to embrace him, he cut me away.

Perhaps he truly did his best. Perhaps I could not blame him for not finding me.

But I did.

I tore my hand from his grip. Swiping tears from my face, I turned my back to him and shut my eyes tightly. But it did not work; I could still see him—each training session, each gift, each silly declaration of his love.

The afternoon sun gradually caramelized into a final blaze, casting long shadows across the room. I felt myself relaxing, drowsiness setting in. Just as the last of my tension left me, a stool scraped against the floor.

With a jolt, I realized Àrèmọ was still here. He had silently sat beside me for hours. There was a hollowness in my chest; anger was so volatile, deflating as quickly as it swelled. In the space it deserted, I found I had more than just rage. There was the fear I would never see him again, the realization I missed his smile. The desire for him to smile now and pull me into his arms. The hope that maybe, maybe, that smile could mend everything.

I found there were so many other things I had left to say—but I could not find it in myself to say them. Instead, I listened to his footsteps as he exited the room.

Àrèmọ returned the next day, and the day after that.

It seemed that when he was not occupied by training, meetings, or feasts, he was here at my side, talking for hours. Most days, I turned away from him. But some days, when my memory of his face grew stale, and I was curious as to whether there was still a dimple on his cheek, I would look at him. Those were the days when he was the most animated with his stories, which were typically a nonsense compilation of everything from a fond memory of me and him to speculation on the meaning behind an oddly shaped cloud he had seen that day.

Once, he gave me an update about how the situation with the Portuguese invaders had played out.

"Our suggestion worked even better than anyone could have predicted," Àrèmọ said. His eyes shone in the way they always did when there was violence, victory, or both. "The enemy did not even make it halfway across the desert before they were forced to retreat. I have been told there is now an area in the

northern Sahara where desert nomads avoid, for it is littered
with thousands of scorched carcasses. And if it was not the heat
that killed them, it was wild animals and illness. My generals'
praise has been endless—they are truly impressed with us for
coming up with that, my flower."

I had given him my full attention that day. Consequently, that
was also one of the days he stayed the longest.

But aside from Àrèmọ informing me of that success, he did
not mention any other current events. With his life still filled
with royal and military duties, I knew he must have been con-
sciously avoiding telling me of the world beyond the walls of my
hut, as though that would speed my recovery.

I did not think much of this—I could not. That should have
bothered me. It might have. But everything was blurred, and the
world softened. Each day, I merely stared into space. Anything
more took an effort that I found myself indifferent to.

Then came the day when Àrèmọ mentioned Kọ̀lọ̀.

The name sparked my mind. "Kọ̀lọ̀ still lives here?" I interrupted his story. "In the royal city?"

The shock on Àrèmọ's face was evident; I had not spoken to
him since the very first day I awoke. Granted, this was the first
time since then that I had spoken at all.

He quickly recovered from his surprise. "Of course Kọ̀lọ̀ lives
here. Where else would she reside?"

"She should not be here."

"Why is that?"

I frowned; I was not sure. But I could not shake the uneasiness
prodding at me, obscured somewhere within my head's haziness.

"You can't trust her," I said slowly, unraveling the stubborn knot that was my mind. "At the revolt, she did something
strange . . . No, bad. Both. She . . ." An end came loose, and the
rest of the thread subsequently unfurled. "She pushed me," I said
suddenly.

Along with the realization, the memory of Kọ̀lọ̀'s visit to my
bedside also surfaced in my mind. I knew she had been right—I

could not tell Àrẹ̀mọ about the spearheads without implicating myself. Even if I convinced him of the truth, that I was completely unaware of how she was using my gifts, it was possible I would be spared from his wrath, but I would not be spared from his disappointment. His trust in me would never be the same.

Nonetheless, if she was willing to supply a slave revolt, there was no telling what she else she had planned to undermine Àrẹ̀mọ. I needed to warn him about her. I took a deep breath, then I said, "Kọ̀lọ̀ is the reason I was stuck in that house when it collapsed. She made sure I could not get out."

I expected anger to overtake Àrẹ̀mọ. I expected him to jump up, demanding for Kọ̀lọ̀'s detainment.

But he just looked at me. "Why would she do that?" he asked.

"I don't know," I was forced to lie, painfully aware of how it weakened my claim. "But it's true. You need to believe me."

"Òdòdó," Àrẹ̀mọ said, very, very gently, "Kọ̀lọ̀ has told me of those disconcerting moments leading up to the building's collapse. None of the women could have been thinking straight. It was pure chance that decided who made it out and who did not."

"No," I said, though it came out more like a groan. "Àrẹ̀mọ, listen—"

"Have you eaten today, my flower?" Àrẹ̀mọ interrupted. He watched me closely.

"What? I don't know. What does it matter? Are you listening to me?"

"Of course. You really should eat something though. It's essential to your recovery. Where is—Ah, there you are."

He gestured at the door, beckoning to my handmaid, who had just entered the hut. In her hands was a gold tray that held a steaming bowl of ẹ̀gúsí soup and a ball of pounded yam.

"Àrẹ̀mọ," I said, "you must get rid of Kọ̀lọ̀. I have a very bad feeling about her."

"Yes, I understand."

But his tone suggested the words were more so to placate me than to show agreement. He gave me an infuriating smile as he continued, "Though we can discuss that another time. For now, I will leave you to your meal so you may regain your strength."

He kissed my forehead before leaving the room. I knew he had no intention of addressing my claims, probably hoping I would forget about it. But it was not over; far from it. Specks of anger were spattered in my blood. They had been there this whole time, but now they adhered to one another, building in my veins. How could I have forgotten this obstructive feeling, this memory that had almost choked me to death?

My handmaid sat on the side of my bed and dipped a piece of pounded yam into the green and yellow soup. I thought of Àrẹ̀mọ's insistence that I eat; now that I thought of it, I had not eaten today. Although I was hungry, it seemed easier to think.

As my handmaid offered me a piece of the food, an idea occurred to me. "Do you like ẹ̀gúsí?" I asked.

She started, shocked to hear my voice had returned. "Yes, my lady," she said. "It's my favorite."

"Share my meal with me, then."

"Oh, no, my lady. That's not—I did not mean to suggest that."

"I know, that's why I'm inviting you. How long have you been at my side now, and we've never eaten together? Please—it would mean a lot to me."

For good measure, I gave her a small smile. My face strained at the motion.

As much as I disliked Kòlò, her advice about smiling still held true; my handmaid's face softened. She looked at the food, and for a moment, it looked as though she was going to eat with me. Then, her head shot up, as though she had just remembered something.

"I would love to, but I can't," she admitted. "Your food has your medicine."

"Medicine? For my injuries?"

"Yes, and your mind. When you first woke up and had your outburst, the royal babaláwo realized you were ailed by paranoia." My pleasantness seemed to be easing her back into her usual gabbiness. "For your well-being, he advised the Aláàfin to ban visitors from seeing you, and he is also giving you something to help make your mind whole again."

"And if I do not wish to take the medicine anymore?"

My handmaid tensed; my question had come out with a little more force than intended. I quickly forced a laugh.

"A joke," I said, smiling through my anger.

She smiled in relief and offered me a bite. I accepted. Although the food was soft and full of flavor, I chewed slowly, unable to enjoy it. I counted each bite, and after swallowing the fifth, I cleared my throat.

"That's enough. I'm tired. I wish to sleep."

She nodded and stood, moving to pick up the tray, but I held up my hand. "Leave it. I'll eat it when I get hungry later."

With a bow of her head and a bend of her knees, she left my room. I propped myself onto my elbow and stared at the remnant food, my eyes unseeing.

Then, I stuck two fingers down my throat.

The gag was immediate; my food surged back up my throat. I hunched over, catching it in the bowl. When the last of it was gone, I laid back onto the bed. My throat stung, and I was gradually becoming more aware of my aching injuries. But my mind remained clear.

20

E ach day, when the royal babaláwo came to dress my wounds,
he would ask, "What happened at the slave revolt?"

I always answered the same way. "Kòlò pushed me. We
were about to escape through the window when she prevented
me from leaving. Please, you have to believe me—"

But by that point, the royal babaláwo would stand and leave,
shaking his head sadly. Soon after, my handmaids arrived
with food. I tried telling them about Kòlò too, desperate for
someone—anyone—to believe me. But they no longer spoke to
me, only dutifully delivered my food with eyes full of sympathy.
Frustrated and embarrassed, I dismissed them, then I dumped
the tainted food out of my window, in the slim space between
my hut and the short wall that bordered the women's compound
where it could go unnoticed. I left the empty bowls at my bedside, so when my handmaids returned later to retrieve them,
they would think I had eaten.

I knew that my inability to tell the full story weakened its
credibility, but still, I could not understand why no one so much
as considered believing me. I was not a witch; I was still the
Aláàfin's bride. And yet the slaves who had once been so dedicated to serving me now only handled me with infuriating con-
descension. The nobles who had tripped over themselves to win
my favor were nowhere to be found. I was no longer worth their
time. It was as though my status was no longer a watertight assurance—or maybe the cracks had always been there, and only
now that I needed it to hold me did it fail.

Maybe the royal babaláwo was right, and I truly was sick with paranoia. My first few waking moments upon my return to the royal city had been disorientated—perhaps Kòlò sitting at my bedside had been a dream. And, at the revolt, the smoke had made it difficult to see. Maybe she had pushed me by accident. Maybe I had tripped and fallen on my own.

I could no longer believe my own mind. By the time Àrèmo came to see me each day, I was too discouraged to defend myself further. He would only think my condition was worsening, just like everyone else, and so I lay static during his visits. But now that I was fully present, it took everything in me not to fidget as he rambled. I was hungry. Hungry for news of the world beyond this gilded cage. Hungry to confront Kòlò and prove her guilt.

Above all, I was hungry for actual food; I did not know how much longer I could keep up this farce. My stomach cried every time I robbed it of food, and though my head remained full, my hunger was starting to take its toll.

The morning my food had been brought and I could not rise from my bed to dispose of it out the window was when I knew I had to choose: starvation, or being drugged into complacency. Somehow, both options seemed equally fatal.

The day I was faced with that decision was the same day I heard giggles in the back corner of my hut. Weakly, I raised my head, but there was nothing other than statues and plush furniture. However, when the giggles sounded again, I knew I was not alone.

"Táíwò?" I croaked. "Kẹhìndé?"

I managed to push myself into an upright position just as two children jumped out from behind a divan. Identical grins were cracked across their faces. They ran toward me and jumped onto my bed. One threw themself onto me, wrapping their skinny limbs around my waist, while the other slipped behind me and stood with their small hands on my shoulders.

"Òdòdó, we miss you!"

"They won't let us be with you anymore."

"We had to sneak in here just to see you."

"They've given us to a goblin—"

"—who they say is a woman but—"

"—how could a woman be so cruel?"

"And ugly?"

"And demanding?"

"And *ugly*!"

I placed my hand atop a twin's head. "Hush," I said tiredly, for their voices worsened my headache. "We'll be reunited soon. First I need to heal."

"Because of the slave revolt," said one twin. It was not a question; I wondered if everyone in the royal city knew.

"How did you lose your hand?" the other twin asked.

It was not quite the royal babaláwo's question, but I still flinched. But the twins did not push; one merely poked at my arm stump in wonder while the one behind me pulled and released my curls, allowing them to spring back into place.

Eventually, I found the courage to say, "I don't remember well. But I think my friend might have pushed me . . . and that caused me to get hurt."

"Oh. We're sorry, Òdòdó."

It took me a moment to process their genuine response. "You believe me?" I asked.

"Sure."

The simple word seemed to flood every part of me. Suddenly overcome with the feeling I was overflowing, I looked up at the ceiling before I spilled myself.

"It's okay, don't cry!" a twin said, hugging me. "You don't need that friend. You have us. We'll be better friends to you!"

"No, it's not that. I . . ." I began, but I trailed off as an idea occurred to me. "Táíwò, Kẹ́hìndé. As my friends, could you help me with something?"

"With what?"

"Tell my handmaids that, by order of the Aláàfin, you two are replacing them as my attendants." I spoke quickly; I had to tell them before the royal babaláwo or Àrẹ̀mọ came. "Then, when you retrieve my food, do not let anyone put herbs, medicines, or anything strange in it. Say you'll do it yourselves, then bring it to me untouched. Can you do that?"

"Okay," the twins said.

When they slipped off me, however, they paused at my bedside. I waited, but they only stared up at me with their wide black eyes.

"Yes?" I asked.

One elbowed the other. The victim scowled at the culprit before turning back to me. "Is it true?"

My heart jumped. "About my friend?" I asked, my newfound confidence wavering.

But the twins shook their head. "No, about the other thing. About what they say."

Cautiously, I asked, "What do they say?"

"They say that you followed the Aláàfin into battle and died."

"That the Earth swallowed you, but you clawed your way from its bowels."

"You, the woman warrior, made of darkness and anger and beauty."

"You, the warrior witch who burns everything in her path, like the fire in a forge."

"You, who holds death like a kiss."

"So, is it true?"

"We won't tell anyone, we just want to know," one promised. Then, in unison, they asked, "Did you come back from the dead?"

My eyes narrowed. But when the twins' curiosity did not subside, I looked down at my lost hand. Unwittingly, I thought of the house's wreckage—the fire burning all around me; the wall pinning my hand. The memory was so vivid that, even now, I felt the ghost of an injury on a limb I no longer had. I thought of my vision, the òrìṣàs' insatiable appetites and their laughter. And as I did, understanding dawned on me.

"Does the arrow fly through the air to its quiver?" I repeated Ṣàngó's question with so much bitterness the words left a sour taste on my tongue. "Does the ocean run up into its rivers?"

The twins' eyes were vast, dark pools of innocence into which my questions had clearly not submerged. I wondered if that was how I had looked. I wondered if I would ever look that way again.

"No, I did not come back from the dead," I replied at last, dulling the edge in my voice for them. "Because I was never dead."

I had only wished I was.

Fortunately, neither the royal babaláwo nor Àrèmọ took special notice of the twins when they replaced my handmaids. I knew the twins had listened to me because when I ate, my mind remained as full as my stomach mercifully became.

Food was not all they brought; they also brought news. A lowborn woman had received a handsome payment from a noble whom she had never met; though she had met his eldest son once, nine months ago. A well-known merchant had made a show of selling his villa in favor of a quieter life in the countryside, but as soon as his going-away party ended, he had given all his earnings to a debt collector.

Shocked, I asked how they learned such things.

Táíwò shrugged—at least, I thought the twin was Táíwò. I had long abandoned trying to distinguish the two and instead assigned their names based on what felt right. The twins never corrected me, whether because my intuition was never wrong, or because it was of little importance to them.

"We hear it from our friends," answered the twin I chose to be Táíwò.

Kẹ́hìndé nodded. "They tell us while we play."

"They hear it from their parents."

"Adults always have so much to say."

Later that day, as Àrèmọ spoke to me about anything except state affairs, I stared at a spot on the ceiling, ruminating over the unique network to which the twins had access. The twins were slaves, but slaves or not, a pair of twins were enchanting to everyone in Yorùbáland; that must have been why they were allowed to play with the sons and daughters of nobles. I supposed it made sense that highborn children were privy to confidential information, but just as Àrèmọ had never considered the privileges that wives had, I had never considered that children also had ears. That was a fact, I was sure, that would be neglected by most people.

When Àrèmọ left and the twins arrived with my food, I reanimated myself. "I want you two to make friends with as many children in the royal city as you can—especially those of the generals," I said, sitting up in the bed. "Make sure you listen closely when they tell you stories. Then at the end of the day, you may come play with me—if my guards question you, inform them the Aláàfin has decided that I require my attendants throughout the night—and then you can tell me all the stories you heard that day. Okay?"

Their faces lit up, and they nodded eagerly. "We'll get the best stories for you."

And so, what I found wanting in Àrèmọ's visits during the day, I received at night when the twins relayed what they had heard in the households of high-ranking people of the royal city. There was an ongoing increase in the amount of ivory circulating within Yorùbáland. More and more craftsmen found themselves bankrupt as the demand for fine ivory pieces dropped in favor of a growing number of cheaper street vendors.

On the other hand, it seemed like every forge in Yorùbáland had been abandoned. Occasionally, clusters of blacksmiths were discovered hiding in remote villages. They were too valuable to be killed, but they could not be coerced into retaking their posts either—most of the women were unmarried with no family to speak of, so they had nothing to lose. The only thing that could be done was to take them into custody. As Yorùbáland's supply of weapons and tools ran low, the generals were discussing the possibility of outsourcing metalwork from the north with the help of the desert nomads. However, there was still much debate, given that such a trade could signal to the Songhai, the Igbo, the Fulani, and all the other peoples constantly closing in around Yorùbáland that the Aláàfin was losing his strength.

What was more, my participation in the revolt seemed to have elevated me in the eyes of every citizen and soldier in Ṣàngótẹ̀. They now regarded me as a great woman warrior, apparently oblivious to the fact that I had done little more than gotten myself trapped beneath a burning building. Among the Aláàfin and his generals, however, the focus was on a different person. A person who they did not know; they only knew it was too strong a coincidence that the most organized slave revolt they had ever seen had occurred the same day the Aláàfin's competent soldiers were away. The incident was even more suspicious given that, amid a weapon shortage, the slaves had far more spears than was expected—spears that seemed to have been taken straight from the royal city's stores. The generals suspected some of their men lacked loyalty.

I knew it was not just men they should be suspicious of, but a woman as well: Kòlò. I was sure she enabled the revolts to hurt Àrèmọ as revenge for how he neglected her, but without any proof, Àrèmọ had no reason to take my claims seriously. The few times I tried to share my suspicions with him, there was a mollifying insincerity to his response before he asked if I had eaten that day.

No, in order to present my case to Àrèmọ, I required evidence.

However, unleashing the twins onto Kòlò had thus far proved futile. "We can never get close to her," Kẹ́hìndé complained. With him hanging upside down over one of the divans, his frown had turned into a smile. "She has no kids, no one for us to be friends with."

"We've tried to serve her, but she's not like the other rich people," Táíwò pitched in, her voice bouncing up and down as she jumped on the bed. "She knows how to do things by herself."

"We can't clean her hut, because she's already done it."

"She fetches her own meals."

"She even delivers her own messages—"

"Messages?" I asked suddenly, pausing in the middle of practicing a punch.

Each night after Àrèmọ left, I had been doing my training drills. Fighting with one hand proved to be harder than I could have imagined, and I doubted I would ever see combat again, but that was not my goal. Not only was secretly training the only form of exercise I could access, helping me slowly rebuild my stamina, but it was also the one thing I could still control. If I dwelled on my confinement for too long, then I truly would become the madwoman that the royal babaláwo claimed I was.

"What messages?" I prompted.

"Sometimes we're able to join her entourage when she goes into Ṣàngótè. She goes to the same market every time, and while she makes us and the other slaves run errands, she talks to a man. He looks like one of those athletes who run messages between people."

"Whose messages does he bring?" I asked.

"We don't know where he comes from, he's already there when we arrive—"

"—and we don't know where he goes. He's too fast to follow."

My heart leapt; Kòlò's mysterious correspondence could be the key to her ulterior motives. "You must keep trying to get close enough to hear her conversations with that man without them noticing you," I said. "And from now on, tell me what you know about how Kòlò spent her day. I want to know every little thing, right down to what she ate for breakfast."

By that time, the twins had befriended the youngest daughter of General Balógun. Always reluctant to end her playtime with the twins, the girl often insisted they sleep over at her house. As their complete refusal would offend her, likely losing them a valuable source of information, there had to be one twin staying at Balógun's house each night, resulting in them alternating who spent the nights with me.

Curiously enough, the absent twin never needed a recap of the previous night. In fact, they even knew the little jokes and things that simply should have slipped through the cracks of re-layed information.

One night, when I was with Kẹ́hìndé, my curiosity got the better of me. "Do twins share a mind?" I asked.

Kẹ́hìndé looked at me blankly. Then, he broke into a fit of giggles. After a moment, I laughed too, trying to pass the question off as a joke. Clearly, the answer was obvious—even if I did not know what that answer was.

By daylight, I was immobile, a static portrait that Àrẹ̀mọ treated as delicately as a piece of art. By moonlight, I found a source of strength in the twins' daily reports.

And in between day and night, in the fiery light of a furnace-like sunset, I stood at my window. Some days—lately more often than not—a song would flow through a nearby field, on the other side of the short wall bordering the women's compound. The song was so full of sorrow that palm trees would bend in their suffering; so full of sadness that the humidity swelled into tears the world wept.

Rótìmí would amble by with a talking drum, the epicenter of a mournful tremor in the earth. When I played the talking drum, it was as a musician did to an instrument. But Rótìmí, he recruited the drum as a companion. He poured his anguish into the instrument in such a way that it did not just talk; it wailed with him.

The first time I heard him, I had thought the nearby guards would make fun of him, that they would judge this display of vulnerability coming from such a powerful man.

But as he passed, the guards only bowed their heads sol-emnly. There was simply no way to mock a man in that much worldly pain. A man who yearned for his lost beloved like the sun yearned to shine. A man who made others miss a person they never even had.

There was nothing to do but grieve for a man like that.

Each time he sang, Rótìmí sowed seeds of misery in his wake. Time seemed to stop in its tracks, the sun clinging to the sky just to see those seeds sprout. They never did. And when day sank away in disappointment, I did not think the gray of dusk was ever as bleak as in those moments.

Only then did I turn away from my window and, wiping tears from my face, return to my bed.

21

By the time the moon had undergone a complete cycle, my injuries were mostly healed. However, the royal babaláwo still considered me too mentally unfit to leave my hut.

Although I knew what I needed to do, I could not immediately bring myself to do it. But with each passing day, I began to fear that if I remained in recovery for much longer, I would be thought incurable and no longer eligible to marry the Aláàfin.

It took two days for me to smother my contempt. By the time the royal babaláwo came to check on me in the morning, I felt as though a part of me had been suffocated.

He bowed shallowly, and, without preamble, he asked, "What happened at the slave revolt?"

I swallowed the last of the frustration threatening to choke me. Then, I said, "Kòlò and I were fleeing from a burning building when I tripped, and it collapsed before I could escape. I realize now that it was ridiculous of me to suggest otherwise."

I spoke slowly, reminding myself it was a lie between each word. Even so, it felt like a piece of me had been ripped away.

To the royal babaláwo, however, this admission apparently made me whole. With an approving nod, he decided that, at last, I was well enough to return to my normal activities.

I doubted things would ever be "normal" again. Yet as my chattering handmaids poured into my room, it was as though nothing had changed.

"You've healed well, my lady!"

"And this is the woman who charged into battle-o."

"Where? You mean this pretty face has the heart of a lion?"

"Yes-o, you've recovered well, my lady. Well done, well done."

When I had imagined myself returning to my routine, I had thought having my handmaids' adoration once more would bring me joy. Instead, I felt irritated. I would not soon forget how these women had patronized my pleading with appeasing words and pitying gazes, as though my voice was meant to be quelled rather than heard. It was only now that a man had pronounced my worthiness that they suddenly remembered their responsibility to serve me. It was a restoration of power I could not fully enjoy, not if it could be taken away so easily by circumstances out of my control.

The knowledge hovered over me like a dark cloud as the women sat me on a low stool in front of my mirror. They began working on my hair, which after being unbraided for so long in this humidity had become a large black sphere around my head. After dousing the curls in sweet and nutty oils, a cornrow was braided down the center of my head, and more stemmed horizontally from it, parallel to my hairline. The rows spanned from the very front to the very back of my head.

As they added columns of wooden beads onto the ends of the braids, Ìgbín swept into my room. With precise movements and an equally precise greeting, she clothed me in a vibrant red wrapper. But clothes were not the only thing she had for me—she also brought a golden hand.

"The Aláàfin had it custom made for you," she explained as she clasped the cold metal to my arm stump. "He had intended to force one of the found blacksmiths in Ṣàngótẹ́'s custody to make it, but when told that it was for you, the woman forged it willingly."

The reminder of how many blacksmiths looked up to me was uncomfortable, particularly because I knew that admiration was what had caused the strikes. However, my unease was quickly forgotten as I beheld the golden hand; it was so similar to my lost limb that it was somewhat disconcerting when it did not respond to my will, merely frozen in a slightly cupped state. The solid gold was heavy and shone against the darkness of my skin. Carvings of tiny flowers were etched into the metal wrist, and vines looped elegantly over the knuckles and fingers.

Before Ìgbín slipped away, she informed me that the Aláàfin requested my audience. I was taken by palanquin to the Aláà-fin's chambers. Àrẹ̀mọ sat hunched over the table in the war room. He arranged and rearranged wooden blocks on the map, and his eyes moved rapidly, as though he could see each battle playing out before him. I wondered if he had been here all night; his braids fell freely around his face, and his plain attire lacked his usual glamorous accessories, save for his shining rings.

When he noticed my arrival, he straightened immediately, a smile cracking across his face. "Òdòdó." He said my name as a soldier declared victory. Gesturing to my new hand, he re-marked, "I see that you received my present."

I had hardly walked up to him when he pulled me into his lap. His excitement sent an ache through me. Sitting together like this was an arrangement we had fallen into countless times before, but this time, the fit was not as harmonious.

Àrẹ̀mọ noticed the discordance in our touch as well. "You are still upset with me?"

In the corner of my eye, I saw him tilt his face to better look at mine. I determinedly kept my gaze forward. Now that I did not need to take the royal babaláwo's medicine each day, I could no longer pretend as though my mind was addled. And he could no longer pretend as though I was happy to see him.

"I do not know what to say," I replied honestly. I teetered between anger and forgiveness; between pushing him away for abandoning me or pulling him closer, grateful I had the chance to do so again.

"Tell me the truth," he said. "Tell me this is all my fault. Tell me how much I've disappointed you, how I failed to protect you when you needed it most."

He pressed his forehead to my cheek. The small touch was laced with vertigo, stealing my breath from me.

"And then tell me you forgive me," he continued. "Please. You are the bones that make up my spine. I cannot be without you. Do not turn away from me, and I promise I will never again give you a reason to doubt me. No matter how much time it may take, no matter what I'd be risking, I promise my love for you will always come first."

I closed my eyes. It was a long, long way down. If I refused to look, I could almost convince myself that this dizzying sensation was flying, not falling. Almost.

"My king," a rasp came.

Rótìmí marched into the room. He looked nothing like his normally composed self. He had allowed his short braids to become fuzzy with escaped curls, and his tunic billowed around him, as though he had lost a great amount of weight in a short amount of time. There was something more, though, that was missing that I could not quite put my finger on.

Àrèmọ sighed heavily before pulling away from me. "Abeg, why must you disturb my happiness?"

"I once again request your permission to conduct a rescue mission from the salt mines of Taghaza."

"And I once again must deny your request," Àrèmọ said tiredly.

"A rescue?" I asked. "Of whom?"

"My second-in-command, Captain Ìlérí, has been wrongly captured by desert nomads while traveling along the outskirts of the Sahara," Rótìmí answered promptly, as though he had summoned the words many times. "At the time that they found him, the nomads were escorting a group of criminals. My second and his squad were not native to the area, so they were mistaken as escaped prisoners. I have received confirmation he has been sold into slavery at Taghaza.

"He has been exposed to those brutal conditions for weeks now. Even with the influence of Wúràkẹ́mi's king, by the time this misunderstanding can be formally cleared, it is unlikely that he will have much life left in him. The only solution is facilitating his escape. I already have the men. All you need to do is give me the go ahead. I am certain that I can get in and get him out before anyone notices I was ever there."

"I trust you are more than capable of carrying out a jailbreak, but that is not the problem," Àrèmọ said. "Taghaza is outside of my jurisdiction. I have no control over who goes or comes from its mines. For the sake of the salt trade, it would be unwise to make the desert nomads think I am overstepping my bounds. You are a smart man. I know you understand that."

From the lines under Rótìmí's eyes, it was clear that he indeed understood this. But from the set of his jaw, it was also clear he did not care.

When Rótìmí did not back down, Àrèmọ scoffed. "You would truly have me risk Yorùbáland's crucial alliance with Taghaza for the sake of one man?"

"I would." No hesitation. No waver.

Àrèmọ threw his head back in laughter. "Rótìmí, I tell you this as your friend. There are hundreds of competent Òòrùn soldiers—many of whom come from better families than your current second-in-command, I believe. Promote one of them, promote them all. Your current second is as good as dead. Move on."

Very slowly, Rótìmí closed his eyes, and he pinched the bridge of his nose. It was a gesture more potent, more shocking, than tears.

It was then I realized what was so off-putting about Rótìmí: his smile. Or rather, the lack thereof. For once, there was no caustic humor underlying his expression. He did not laugh at the world in secret. Pain had dragged him down to the rest of us, ejected him from whatever unearthly bubble he had constructed around himself, like the sky discarding a burning star.

The song he played each sunset drifted through my mind. Just the memory of its sorrow was enough to twist my heart. This was the reason for it, then; it was the capture of Captain Ìlérí that was the source of so much grief.

"Àrèmọ," I said, placing my hand on his, "what would you do if I was trapped in Taghaza?"

"I fail to see the relevance of that situation to this one."

I glanced at Rótìmí. He was looking at me with narrowed eyes, but he did not interrupt.

"I imagine," I said, "that a general's bond with his second-in-command can be as cherished as the one with his wife. And if I had been captured, would you simply move on?"

"Of course not," Àrèmọ replied at once.

I tilted my head to one side. Àrèmọ held my gaze for a moment, considering my words. Then, he turned to Rótìmí.

"One month," he said. "That's the longest I will wait for your return before I choose an Òòrùn captain to replace you as Wúràkẹ́mi's general and representative."

Relief burst from Rótìmí with so much force that he hunched over. "Thank you," he gasped. "Thank you, my king. Thank you."

He addressed Àrèmọ, but his eyes were on me. I gave him a small nod. With another round of gratitude, Rótìmí bowed before all but running from the room.

As the door shut behind him, Àrèmọ said to me, "You referred to yourself as my wife just then. But you have not yet allowed me to marry you."

I sighed. "My mother—"

"—has not been found, and you require her blessing," Àrèmọ finished. "That is your stipulation, I know. But Òdòdó, I almost lost you before I ever truly had you. I do not want to take that risk again. Say you'll be my wife, prove you love me, and I promise I will always protect you."

Had you, Àrèmọ had said. Was that what it meant to be his wife, to be had by him? It was true I had wanted to reunite with my mother before getting married, but admittedly, I had also begun to have doubts about my union with Àrèmọ. To be his to protect was to be his to confine in a hut for weeks, to declare unwell and strip of respectability at a moment's notice. To be his to protect, it seemed to me, was to be owned by him.

"I've only just finished recovering," I said at last, detangling myself from Àrẹ̀mọ's embrace. "I am too winded to make such a decision right now. Let me think about it."

I stood, and I had just reached the door when, behind me, Àrẹ̀mọ said quietly, "I loved you before I met you, and since you came into my life, my love for you has only grown. After all this time, you don't feel even a fraction of the same?"

I paused, my hand on the door handle. Then, without looking back, I exited.

As I walked through the Aláàfin's chambers, Àrẹ̀mọ's question replayed in my mind. *You don't feel the same?*

Prior to the revolt, I had come to trust Àrẹ̀mọ, and even now, I was inclined to try rebuilding that trust once more. Since the day we met, I had never shied away from him because he had never truly felt like a stranger. I did not know if that was love. Stories made love sound like going on an adventure. But him, he felt more like coming home.

Still, although his hurt pained me, I did not think it was completely fair. It was easy for Àrẹ̀mọ to love me; it cost him nothing. However, it seemed that I was expected to love him by giving myself to him. I had already given him my hand; how much more of me must I give? What would I have left?

I could not refuse Àrẹ̀mọ's proposal, as doing so would mean returning to being a blacksmith. However, I was not ready to become his wife; not yet. There had to be another way to prove how deeply I cared for him.

I had just reached the entrance to the Aláàfin's chamber when the front door swung open. I was forced to stand aside as a group of men entered, headed toward the war room. The only man I recognized was Ọmọ́sẹ̀wà. Engaged in conversation, it was only after he had stepped inside the room and moved to shut the door that he noticed me. His hazel eyes met mine, but before either of us could react, the door closed between us.

22

Because Ọmóṣẹwà had gone to the war room without any of the other generals, I surmised he was not there for a routine meeting. Most likely, he was there because Àrẹ̀mọ sought to resolve the mysterious surge of ivory flooding the market, an issue I knew was a large concern among nobles and merchants, thanks to the twins. The men around Ọmóṣẹwà were likely from Ìlódẹ, there to discuss how the City of Hunters had been losing control over the ivory trade for the past few months.

I knew Àrẹ̀mọ was becoming impatient with me about our marriage. I did not want to believe his impatience would turn to indifference, or worse, but after speaking with him, it was not a chance I wanted to take. If I was not going to accept his proposal, I needed to do something else to prove that I cared for him—and the ivory troubles presented the perfect opportunity.

Àrẹ̀mọ no longer spoke to me about his meetings, so I turned to my music sessions and my gatherings with the other noble-women, probing them for anything they knew of the ivory situation. What I could not get from them, I received from the twins, who obtained information from the highborn children of the royal city.

Over the next few days, I collected stories, rumors, and conversations. The Ẹgbẹ́-Ọdẹ was the only clan of the Yorùbá tribe skilled enough to bring down elephants, and they closely monitored the Savanna around their city for any ambitious outsiders. Thus, the generals' leading theory was that the influx of ivory stemmed from rogue Ẹgbẹ́-Ọdẹ hunters who used their previous affiliation to hunt undetected. And yet, there did not seem to be any significant change to the elephant population on the Savanna.

An entirely different theory occurred to me. I had my hand-maids bring me as many of the royal city's ivory figurines as they could find, and I also had them buy figurines from several of the many new street vendors popping up around Sàngótẹ̀. Examining the street pieces, I could understand why the generals were at a loss for where such seemingly fine pieces were coming from; their craftsmanship rivaled the pieces that had already been in the royal city, which were undoubtedly commissioned at a much higher price.

Nonetheless, my attention was not caught by the ivory figurines' designs, but rather by the quality of the ivory itself. Compared to the royal city's pieces, many more of the street pieces were made from bleached ivory. To the untrained eye, bleached ivory was hardly any different, only visibly manifesting as slight discoloration. But living in Timbuktu, I had seen how ivory merchants were careful to store their wares away from sunlight because they knew bleaching made ivory less durable over time.

Assuming the newer ivory merchants were similarly protective of their supply, the bleaching of the street pieces must have occurred before their ivory was carved into figurines. This likelihood that the new ivory flooding the market had been carelessly left in the sun only strengthened my theory—and yet, the solution I suspected seemed so obvious that I was hesitant to pursue it at first. However, no matter how many ways I tried assembling the information I had collected, I found there was no other way the pieces could fit together.

Perhaps it was not strange the generals had not thought of it first; in my brief encounter with them, I had witnessed how myopic they were. The men could only fathom victory if it was achieved through strength. But as I was quickly learning, power was no less valid when subtle; after all, an ember was never as feared as a flame, yet it burned just as hot.

Still, I could not act on my hunch just yet; Àrèmọ did not trust my word as much as he once did. I forced myself to be patient until the time was right.

The right time arrived two days later, in the form of the arrival of King Làjà of Ìlọ́dẹ. With the ivory situation growing more dire, Àrèmọ had summoned the Ẹgbẹ́-Ọdẹ king to the royal city to discuss a plan of action.

The twins had told me of this the night before he arrived, so I took the necessary measures to slip away from my daily routine in the morning. I was on my way out of the women's compound and had just reached the entrance when a woman rounded the corner ahead of me. My skin prickled, and my throat constricted, as though her cocoa butter scent was poisonous gas.

"Hello, sweet flower," Kòlò greeted me.

Anger boiled within me. The last time I had seen Kòlò, I had leapt at her in a fit of rage. It was only today's bright sunlight and the nosy noblewomen nearby that narrowly prevented me from doing so again.

As if she was aware of my internal struggle, Kòlò gave me an infuriating smile. "I am glad to see you've recovered well. For a moment, I had believed you were lost to us forever."

"Don't worry," I said through gritted teeth. "I'm not going anywhere."

Kòlò's eyebrow quirked, but her tone remained light as she said, "I'm happy to hear that. I'd love to catch up, but as I'm sure you're aware, Àrèmọ has ordered us to stay away from one another. And anyway, I must prepare to visit some friends in Sàngótẹ̀."

She waited expectantly. The air between us was pulled taut with the agitated anticipation of a band stretched too wide. I held her gaze steadily, and in her dark almond eyes, I saw that she, too, was ready to act if the tension snapped.

After a moment, however, I stepped aside. A slight smirk

flickered over her face as she walked past me. Stiffly, I turned
to watch her go. I suppressed the urge to follow her to Ṣàngótẹ̀,
knowing I did not have the time; nor did I have time to set the
twins on her trail. Right now, I needed to focus on King Làjà
and the ivory situation. I would have to prove Kọ̀lọ̀'s guilt later.

Swallowing my frustration, I entered my palanquin. I was
carried to the compound in which King Làjà sojourned, the
yard of which was occupied by two groups of three women. All
were dressed in lavish lace fabrics as they conversed in the shade.
His wives, I presumed; he must have left his more senior wives
in Ìlọ́dẹ and only brought his youngest to parade, because King
Làjà looked less like these women's husband and more like their
grandfather.

The king sat outside the house. One slave held a parasol over
him, and another fanned him with a palm frond. Even so, beads
of sweat ran from his fez cap down his round face, dripping
stains onto the neckline of his bright yellow agbádá. As I approached, he shooed away the girl sitting on his lap—who was
younger than I—and he turned his attention to me.

"Ah, the beautiful Alálẹ̀ Òdòdó," he said in a gravelly voice
that raked across my ears. "The Aláàfin's witch. Come, sit."

I knelt before him. As I rose and settled onto a stool, I said,
"Good afternoon, my king. I am pleased to make your acquaintance, but you should know I am no longer a witch."

King Làjà barked out laughter, his jowls quivering so low that
they nearly brushed his collarbone. "Don't worry, I'm not frightened, my dear. I always say my people are too superstitious.
Witches should be honored, not feared—why, it was a witch who
saved my third son."

"She saved his life?"

"Might as well have. He was born with weak legs, but she
made him braces. Now, he can walk as well as any other man.
So, you see, I am quite fond of witches. And besides, you are not
just any witch, are you?"

He leaned forward. As subtly as possible, I brushed my hand

over my nose to lessen his musk, which was strengthened by the slave's fanning.

"Your reputation precedes you as far as Ìlódè," he continued, his voice lower, quicker. "It is no wonder the Aláàfin treasures you so. I, too, would cherish a witch with the ability to rise from the dead. His own immortal Ahosi."

He peered at me through sunken, bloodshot eyes. Although the only resemblance between this man and Ọmọ́ṣẹwà was the three vertical scars on their right cheeks, I was strongly reminded of the ill-tempered general. However, whereas Ọmọ́ṣẹwà regarded me with an anticipation masked with aggression, his king had an air of obsession about him.

But I had grown weary of these superstitions. It did not matter whether they manifested as fear or as fixation; they all stemmed from the same thing. Men called us witches, they thought us demons, and yet, it was them who wished to possess us.

"What I am to the Aláàfin," I replied simply, "is his future wife."

King Làjà's disappointment was immediate. "I see." He gestured at one of the girls in the yard. "That is my future wife over there. See how quiet she is, how well she keeps to herself?"

"And a lovely bride I am sure she will be, ever dedicated to her king," I said. "That is how I hope to be, to my own husband. Which is why I must confess, I do have an ulterior motive for visiting you today. In truth, I was hoping you could assuage my worries about the Aláàfin leaving for the Savanna tonight."

He raised an eyebrow that got lost in the folds of his forehead. "How do you mean?"

My heart skipped a beat, but I pushed on. "Surely the men who are behind the ivory situation mean the Aláàfin harm. Isn't it too dangerous for him to inspect the Ẹgbẹ́-Ọdẹ army, given that there must be enemies among them?"

"It will be fine," the king replied dismissively.

I exhaled in relief. *So Àrèmọ is planning to leave tonight to inspect the Ẹgbẹ́-Ọdẹ ranks.* I silently filed the confirmation in my mind. I had been unsure, but it was an educated guess; if there was one thing Àrẹ̀mọ hated, it was incompetence. With the ivory situation beginning to spiral out of control, it was clear that King Làjà had been invited here to be questioned by the Aláàfin so that Àrẹ̀mọ could handle this situation himself. Which meant all I needed to do was feed Làjà the information that he would then give to Àrẹ̀mọ.

"One thing that is certain is there cannot be more than a handful of men behind the influx of ivory," the king was saying. "Only the best hunters can kill the number of elephants it takes to have flooded the market like this. The Aláàfin's safety is not at all in question—for each enemy that he may unknowingly come near, he will be surrounded by a hundred more allies."

"Of course. You know better than I," I said. "Although, it's a shame this will all be ending soon."

The king scoffed. "Hardly. If this goes on much longer, our economy runs the risk of destabilization. It has been a massive pain."

"Yes, for the nobles, I am sure. But perhaps it has been a source of inspiration for commoners, to have found their own unique access to a commodity as unattainable as ivory."

"Woman, what are you on about?"

I laughed to mask my frustration; the king was just as shortsighted as the others. It was becoming difficult to push him enough so that he got where he needed to be, but not so much that he noticed he was not getting there on his own.

"Forgive me, I'm rather dense," I said. "My mind has been addled ever since I witnessed a horrific scene the other day. Oh, it was terrible—a pack of strays attacked a lone dog. Ripped the poor thing to pieces. Soon after, birds came to feast on the meat—but in that way, I suppose there was a kind of beauty to the brutality. Those birds were so tiny, I doubt they would have ever been able to get such a nice dinner if the dogs had not done the work for them first."

King Làjà opened his mouth, then paused. Slowly, his furrowed brows came apart, the number of wrinkles in his face lessening. I could almost feel his mind working, sifting through my words. I tilted my head, maintaining a smooth mask of slight curiosity as impatience twisted within me.

"My king?" called a soft voice, breaking our concentration.

I suppressed a groan when I saw Ọmọ́ṣẹwà enter the yard. Clothed in a crisp white tunic and pair of trousers, everything about him looked brand new. A purity which drew the eye against its will; along the yard, King Làjà's wives paused in their conversations to stare as the general strode to the front of the house and prostrated before us.

"I come to escort you to the Aláàfin's chambers." Ọmọ́ṣẹwà spoke to his king, but his eyes were narrowed at me. "He and the other generals are ready to receive you over a meal."

King Làjà still looked thoughtful, but I could no longer urge him on now that Ọmọ́ṣẹwà was here. I could only hope the seed I had planted would take.

"I will get out of your way then, my king," I said, rising from the stool. "I hope I have not bored you too much with my rambling."

"No, no. Not at all . . ." he replied distractedly. His expression shifted, and his eyes sharpened as though something in his vision came into focus. "Actually, you may have been more helpful than you will ever know."

I bent my knees and dipped my head once more, and, ignoring Ọmọ́ṣẹwà's glare, I began making my way through the yard.

Behind me, I heard King Làjà say, "Ọmọ́ṣẹwà, I've just had the oddest idea . . ."

The seed sprouted.

I smiled; this time a true one, for it was all to myself.

I rushed to my hut and called for Ìgbín. She promptly arrived to clothe me in a black bandeau and pair of trousers—an attire I had not worn since the battle that nearly cost me my life. I also asked that she bring me a machete from what remained of the royal city's military supplies, and, as always, she asked no questions as she helped me place the weapon in a sheath on my belt.

After she tied my braids into a low tail, I hurried out of my hut. Outside the women's compound waited my palanquin carriers, but I shrugged them off and walked briskly to the elephant stables. Upon arriving, I was relieved to see that the grand mudbrick buildings were still empty; the generals had not yet come.

They would, though. If King Làjà had truly grasped the meaning I had tried to instill in him, men would meet here before journeying to the Savanna. I settled onto the short wall that divided the sandy stable grounds from the grassy field. All that was left to do was wait.

In the sky above, the sun sank one notch lower. Two notches. I waved away nervous stable hands who asked if I needed anything. I walked along the top of the wall in a test of balance, my arms outstretched on either side of me. Three notches. Four. I watched as Ajá sauntered out of his stall and up to a pile of melons. The elephant looked so innocent as he ate that I had the urge to pet him, but I resisted; although my midnight rides on Ajá with Àrèmọ had made the elephant warm up to me, I was still somewhat wary of him.

It was not until the sunset lit the sky on fire that I heard voices. I unfolded my arms from on top of my face. When I saw ten men approaching, I quickly slid off the wall, where I had been lying down. They were soldiers, clothed in cotton tunics and knee-length breeches, being led by Ọmọ́sẹ̀wà and Àrèmọ.

Ṣàngó yọ mí. I almost muttered the prayer, but the memory of my vision at the wreckage soured my tongue so much that it curled inwards. Ṣàngó had nothing to do with this. It was all me.

When the men saw me, they came to a collective halt, varying degrees of surprise on their chiseled faces.

Ọmọ́sẹ̀wà's shock contorted into anger. "What do you think you're doing?"

"I am helping the Aláàfin prepare for his journey to Ìlódẹ," I replied calmly, my gaze on Àrẹ̀mọ.

"Your playtime as an Ahosi is over. Who told you of this?" Ọmóṣẹwà demanded, then paused, and I knew he was thinking about earlier today. "You witch—what sorcery have you done on my king?"

He stepped forward, but he was stopped by an arm held in front of him—Àrẹ̀mọ's. Ọmóṣẹwà looked indignant, but Àrẹ̀mọ's focus remained on me.

Our gazes were as coupled as a lock and key that sealed away the rest of the world as Àrẹ̀mọ approached me. "You made a fool out of a king," he said, his voice lined with amusement.

"That king," I said, "was making a fool out of you by allowing this to go on for so long. Now, you can solve this matter once and for all. And I will join you, for I know how your people are infatuated with their warrior witch. I cannot fight, but I do not need to—just the sight of me will improve your men's morale."

And improve my reputability, I added silently. Helping Àrẹ̀mọ presented a dual opportunity to also distance myself from my reputation as a madwoman, which was easiest to do by leaning into my other reputation as a woman warrior. Although I was unsure how I felt about the title, especially given that my hand prevented me from ever living up to it, it did not escape me that unlike the esteem I would be given as a wife, the respect I earned as a warrior was entirely my own.

"But most importantly," I added, "I am coming because I want nothing more than to support my future husband. All that you have given me, now it is my turn to give a gift to you."

"It could be dangerous," Àrẹ̀mọ warned, but he was smiling.

"We both know it won't be." I tucked a braid behind his ear; he never noticed when they escaped from his bun. "That is why you will let me join you."

My hand lingered on his cheek. He leaned into it for a moment, almost unconsciously, before glancing over his shoulder. "I am letting her join us," he told his men.

Ọmọ́ṣẹ̀wà looked livid, but the others exchanged looks much less hostile. Some even seemed excited.

Àrẹ̀mọ turned back to me, his black eyes shining. "As I am sure you are aware, we will need Bínú. You may keep him distracted."

I nodded then turned to vault over the wall. I plucked a melon from a pile to give to a stable hand and said, "Lure Bínú out."

His eyes wide, the stable hand nodded before rushing into the first stall. A loud trumpet dragged through the air. A moment later, the boy emerged, walking backwards slowly with the melon outstretched in front of him. Bínú followed soon after. The boy deposited the melon on the ground, and the elderly elephant stepped on it, shattering it. Bínú's trunk curled around a piece and brought it to his mouth.

I moved to Bínú's right side, making sure he could see me. As he ate noisily, I stroked the side of his face. His sagged brown eye watched me, but he allowed my touch. His skin was rough; each ridge and each groove was a memory, a history. They said that elephants lived longer than most people. That meant Bínú was likely the eldest inhabitant of the royal city. There was a stiffness in his joints when he walked, and the smacking noises as he chewed were the result of his mouth being more gum than teeth. The only life left for him was one of pain.

This is a kindness, I told myself firmly. I had to believe that, because as much as I dreaded to harm such a beautiful creature, I needed to be right about this.

I kept Bínú's attention on me, so by the time he noticed that Àrẹ̀mọ, Ọmọ́ṣẹ̀wà, and the other men had come up around him, it was too late. With their weapons, they struck his legs, underside, and the back of his head quickly. Bínú reared back with a furious roar, but before he could swing at anyone, we had all retreated to a safe distance.

Bínú was in no state to attempt another attack; the elephant tried valiantly to remain standing, but he soon collapsed with a feeble trumpet. Blood oozed from his wounds, coloring the sand below him red. The efficiency of the coordinated attack had allowed Bínú the most humane execution possible; he did not struggle for long before he stilled.

Àrẹ̀mọ gave me an approving nod then turned to his men and announced, "Let us see what scavengers our bait attracts."

23

Once night fell, soldiers used bulls to haul Bínú's body out of the royal city and the capital. Thereafter, they deposited his remains deep in the wilderness surrounding Ṣàngótẹ̀ under the cover of darkness.

Àrẹ̀mọ had instructed the men to place the carcass near an area known to be occupied by a pride of lions. The expectation was that the pride would find the carcass in the morning and quickly make a meal out of it.

Meanwhile, the soldiers would set up a hidden camp nearby, keeping watch until scavengers came to collect the tusks of an elephant that had seemingly been hunted and eaten by lions.

In the interim, all that Àrẹ̀mọ, Ọmọ́ṣẹwà, the other soldiers, and I could do was wait. Each day, I checked with Àrẹ̀mọ, and when there were no updates, my impatience mounted. But even as Ọmọ́ṣẹwà snidely insinuated my plan was a failure, I remained undeterred; for the first time in months, Àrẹ̀mọ had trusted me. This had to work.

On the fifth day after Bínú's remains had been set outside the capital, all but one of the soldiers finally returned to the royal city. They reported the trap had taken; a band of scavengers had descended on what was left of the carcass, taking the entirety of it away on a bull-drawn wagon, which they guided from atop horses. One of our soldiers was trailing them on horseback, mapping their route.

It took another eight days for the man to return to the royal city, ready to lead us to the scavengers' base. Because the route

followed along a river, we commissioned a group of nomadic
fishermen for transportation, which significantly reduced our
travel time as compared to if we had ridden horses like the scavengers had. We glided down the watery highway in a long dug-
out canoe, and when night fell, we camped on the riverbanks.

We resumed our journey at dawn. It had been too dark before
for me to see anything, but now I found myself sitting on the edge
of the boat in wonder as the Sahel transformed into the Savanna.
A lifetime of living in the desert did nothing to prepare me.

The river, wide and wandering, glittered in the light of dawn,
its rapids roaring around us. Among the expansive, swaying
grasslands, there were fields of grain, cotton, and other crops
where there was enough water. Massive bull elephants, even
larger than Ajá, roamed the vast land. Lion cubs wrestled with
one another under the protective gaze of the lounging pride.
Herds of antelope frolicked around small villages scattered
through the grasslands.

As we passed a watering hole, I witnessed a giraffe keeping
a lookout as its offspring drank. I had never considered how
giraffes drank, but if I had, I doubted I would have pictured
this—in order for the young giraffes' necks to reach the pond,
their legs were spread so awkwardly wide that they trembled.

It was such an unexpectedly comedic display from an otherwise graceful animal that I could not help myself; I laughed
aloud. When Àrẹ̀mọ saw me laughing, he joined in, and when
his men saw him laughing, they, too, joined us. Soon enough,
the entire boat rocked with laughter. Even Ọmọ́ṣẹwà managed a
smile—or, at least, he did not look as angry as normal.

"I shall return another day to capture a giraffe for my bride!"
Àrẹ̀mọ declared to his cheering men, ignoring my protests.

Dusk had begun to creep in when the time came to disem-
bark from the boat. The man who had tracked the scavengers
led us inland on foot. There was still a day between our location
and Ìlọ́dẹ, and it had been awhile since we last passed a village.
Even the amount of wildlife around us had dwindled to none.

Yet by the time night had completely fallen, we reached the edge of a dry gorge, within which a cluster of tents stood in high elephant grass. Throughout and surrounding the camp were countless stacks of gigantic, gleaming ivory tusks. Elephant carcasses, many of which still had rotten flesh clinging to their bones, were piled on one side of the gorge—no doubt discarded there so the remains from which the scavengers extracted tusks would not be found.

"They must be collecting dead elephants from all over Yorùbáland," I murmured. I was not alone in my fascination; the other soldiers' low voices rustled around me.

It was ironic, I noted, that Yorùbáland's ivory troubles were the result of the City of Hunters losing their monopoly on ivory, yet all this time the heart of the operation had been within their lands. I snuck a glance at Ọmọ́ṣẹwà. The flickering firelight of distant torches illuminated a rage simmering in the air around him.

"As if it's not bad enough that those men are traitors, they're cowards too," he growled. "There is nothing more pathetic than a man who reaps riches he did not fight for."

"You will get your justice very soon, my friend," Àrèmọ replied. His calm voice was a sharp contrast from the fury brewing on his face. I wondered what he was angrier about—that these men were much more unremarkable than they ought to have been, or that he had not realized their operation himself.

Àrèmọ pulled back from the edge of the gorge and indicated for the rest of us to do the same. "From the number of tents and torches, they have between twice and three times the men we do," he said. "We are outnumbered, but they are outmatched. They are unprepared for combat, and something tells me they would not be formidable opponents anyways.

"Regardless, there are to be as few deaths as possible. Despite their crimes, we must acknowledge that these men have operated this camp with extreme efficiency. It would make most sense to allow them to continue their operation, this time for Yorùbáland

instead of against it. I will bring them under the supervision of
Ìlódẹ, and until we secure their compliance, we will take them as
our prisoners and collect their ivory as our own.

"Ọmóṣẹwà," Àrèmọ continued, "have your bowmen ready
around the perimeter. The rest of us will soon follow."

"Understood," Ọmóṣẹwà said. He snapped into a salute before beckoning to two soldiers, who broke off from the group.
Together, they made their way down into the gorge, staying in
the cover of the tall grass.

As the remaining men readied their weapons, Àrèmọ met my
gaze then pointed with his eyes to a spot a short distance away.
As I met him there, he said, "Remember, you are to avoid combat. Wait at the center of the camp, where my men and I can
see you at all times. You won't be waiting long—these are not
disciplined soldiers. Once I will kill their leader, any resistance
the others may put up will melt away."

The mask of the strategic Commander of Death lifted for one
moment, allowing Àrèmọ's soft smile to slip through. "Thank
you for this, my flower. I could not have asked for a more considerate gift."

He pressed a kiss to my own smile before he turned away,
drawing his axes from their holsters. "We're moving in," he announced.

He glanced at me to make sure I was with him, then we
dove into the sea of grass. The other soldiers followed behind
us. Sharp blades of grass scraped my skin as we moved down
the gorge quickly but carefully, knowing that descending from
above gave the camp a chance to spot us before we reached it.

Fortunately, when we at last emerged into the camp, it was
with the element of surprise still on our side. The Aláràá men
rushed in screaming and brandishing weapons, causing the
ivory scavengers to drop what they had been doing—most were
gathering firewood or moving ivory onto carts—and run away.
Àrèmọ had been right; these men could hardly be called soldiers.

Some ran into tents and emerged holding spears, their faces

brave but their stances lacking. Others cleared the tents, fleeing, but any that got too far were crippled by arrows that shot out from the darkness.

It was like running through a flock of birds. The men darted every which way, no order to their fleeing or fighting. I wove through the chaos, making my way to the center of the camp, where Àrèmọ's soldiers collected the criminals. We were easily winning; it looked as though more than half the camp had already been gathered. There was a large cluster of wailing men on their chin and knees, their hands behind their heads.

I had just joined the four Aláràá soldiers standing guard over the captured men when the noise around me diminished. The mass of men parted, and Àrèmọ emerged from them, slowly, for he steered a man in front of him with his axes crossed over the man's neck. Once they reached the center of the camp, Àrèmọ kicked him in the back. He landed on the ground with a pained grunt.

"This is who is in charge?" Àrèmọ asked the captives.

None answered, but they did not need to; the confirmation was in the way they were cowed by the mere sight of this one bloody and bruised.

He raised his head, and his gaze found mine. The tears welled in his brown eyes startled me. He was clearly not dangerous or cruel. His largest offense was choosing to not operate under the control of the Aláàfin, but surely that did not mean he deserved a punishment as extreme as death . . .

Bronze flashed through the air. The camp leader's eyes widened then rolled backwards. He fell to his side with a thud that seemed impossibly loud for his slender frame. Blood poured from his neck, pooling onto the dirt around him.

Àrèmọ breathed heavily, his axes hanging limply from his hands. One dripped with the same blood that was spattered on his face. Suddenly, an inexplicable disgust churned my stomach, so strong that my heart was nearly sucked into it.

But then Àrèmọ looked at me. He met my gaze like there was

no one else around us, like I truly was a gift given to him by the òrìṣàs. He stepped over the man's corpse and pulled me into him, his arms wrapped around my waist.

"Òdòdó," he breathed, and somehow, I heard him even as his men yelled at the captives, rounding them up. "I know you will marry me one day. And until that day, I will never again doubt your love for me."

My revulsion passed as quickly as it had come, replaced by a dizzying triumph that bubbled up and out of me as laughter. The momentary disgust, I decided, was the result of the sudden violence catching me off guard. But for as long as I had known Àrèmọ, there was no reason for me to have been surprised. I knew who he was: the same as me. He waged wars, ravaged entire villages, and killed countless people. And I committed an act equally as violent: I loved him.

24

By the time we returned to the royal city, the tension that had been between Àrèmọ and I was dissolved. His doubts about my loyalty seemed allayed, and, for my part, I was beginning to move on from the slave revolt. Soon, either Àrèmọ or Dígí would find my mother, and then my life in the royal city would be complete.

It did not take long for word of my participation in the ivory raid to spread throughout the royal city. As I had predicted, it was a popular choice; according to the twins, conversation around me moved away from pitying the mad, jealous bride of the Aláàfin and toward marveling at the royal city's warrior witch. The nobles who had vanished during my confinement reappeared once more, offering compliments and invitations to gatherings, if only to have me there as a spectacle.

My new reputation was less welcomed among the noblewomen. During my nightly music sessions, they were polite, but they kept their distance, as though afraid I would pull them into the world of violence. My days of being able to gossip among them were over, but fortunately, I still had the twins.

Even so, it made little difference. Àrèmọ trusted me again, but he no longer sought my advice. I was determined to restore my position as his advisor. So, one afternoon, when Àrèmọ requested to spend the rest of the day with me, I agreed, planning to use the opportunity to show him I could still be useful in determining state affairs.

Outside the women's compound, my palanquin waited for

me, along with its carriers and my guards. There was also one
of my handmaids, and as I approached her, she offered me a cup
of a millet beverage.

"Dry season is nearly upon us, my lady," she explained. "Be
sure you stay hydrated."

I thanked her and reached for the cup, but there was a mis-
connection in the transfer, and the cup spilled onto me.

"I'm so sorry!" she exclaimed.

"It's okay," I said. Normally, I would have been distressed by
the stain on my red wrapper. But since making up with Àrẹ̀mọ
and returning from the ivory raid, I had been in a permanently
good mood.

"No, I must amend this, my lady. Please, allow me to take you
to get a new wrapper—there's a fabric storehouse right there."

She gestured to a small building, two fields over from the
women's compound. I shrugged. "Sure. Thank you."

As we reached the storehouse, my handmaid cast a wary look
at my guards. "They can't come in while I dress you."

"They know that, of course," I said. Indeed, the men were already positioning themselves around the outside of the storehouse.

My handmaid dipped her head apologetically and held open
the door for me. It was a small room with only two tiny windows
in the top corners of a wall, likely to minimize the number of destructive elements—such as rain or insects—that entered. Nevertheless, the space still glowed, illuminated by cloths of every
color and pattern imaginable. The folded fabrics were packed
close together on shelves spanning from the floor to the ceiling.

As I watched my handmaid begin sifting through them, I
remarked, "Maybe it would be better to call on Ìgbín."

"It's okay, I don't want to disturb him. I'll find one suitable for
you in just a moment."

"If you insist." Then, processing her response, I added, "Sorry,
did you say 'him'?"

She gave me a brief smile. "Did I? Apologies, my lady. A slip
of the tongue. I meant no need to bother her."

She continued looking through the fabrics, but her movements were stiffer, as though she felt my sudden interest in her.
I tried to get a closer look at her face. I had never paid much
attention to the women who attended to me, but I was still fairly
sure I had never seen this one before.

"Where are the rest of my handmaids?" I asked.

"They stayed behind. I only wanted to bring you a refreshment."

"I see."

The woman examined the fabrics a moment more before she
turned to me, apparently realizing there was no use in maintaining her act. "Òdòdó, don't call your guards—"

But I had already moved behind her, wrapping my arm
around her neck. "Hush," I said gently as she struggled against
my grip. "I agree, there's no need to make a scene by alerting
my guards. This is between you and me—and Kòlò, I assume.
Correct?"

"What?" she gasped.

"Has Kòlò sent you to kill me, to finish what she could not?
Don't lie. Lying will only make it worse for you."

"I don't know who that is. Please, let me explain—"

"You foolish girl, what are you doing?" a new voice hissed.

It was a whisper, but I startled so badly that I released the
false handmaid, who fell to the ground in a coughing fit. I had
been so intent on unmasking the imposter that I had not noticed
when a new woman stepped into the storehouse.

My heart stilled. She wore the shabby wrapper of a slave—
which was likely how she had come into the royal city unnoticed—
yet she still retained a might that should have been too big for her
small stature to contain.

"Mama," I breathed.

Okóbí strode forward to help the false handmaid to her feet.
As the woman took Okóbí's hand, I noticed, for the first time,
the scars and burns on her arm.

"Let the others know we will join them soon," Okóbí told her.

She nodded, and, with a final anxious glance at me, she left the storehouse. I would have apologized to her, but my senses had narrowed to Okóbí, and the rest of the world faded away. I hugged my mother with such fervor that I practically leapt at her.

Okóbí grunted. "Don't you know that I'm no longer young? You're going to break me."

Yet she too embraced me tightly. It was not the first time I had been hugged in the past few months, but that was what it felt like. No one else's arms could stretch so perfectly around me, holding me without expecting that same support in return. It was a feeling that could only be received from a mother.

Okóbí pulled back and took my face in her hands. She scrutinized my features, her dark eyes tired yet sharp. "Òdòdó, my daughter. I have a plan in place to distract your guards long enough for us to leave the royal city, but it will only work if we go right now."

"Go?" I asked. "Go where?"

"Home, of course."

She took my hand and turned to leave, but I did not move. "Ma, I am already home," I said slowly. "The royal city is my home now."

Okóbí's disbelief quickly turned into anger. "What nonsense is this? You have been stolen and locked away, yet you believe this is your home?"

"I haven't been locked—" I began. Then, remembering the month of my recovery, I said instead, "I have been well taken care of here."

Her eyes swept over me and paused at my right arm, widening in horror. "Then where is your hand?"

I groaned. "You don't understand—"

"No, it seems I am the only one here who does understand this situation! Òdòdó, you *disappeared*. I did not know where you were, or if you were even still alive! It was only months after the strikes began, after constantly receiving misinformation from our other so-called sisters, that I finally found blacksmiths willing to help me. They told me the Aláàfin acquired a witch whose description matched yours. Since then, I have worked tirelessly, avoiding search parties and doing everything in my power to reach you, and you dare stand here and tell me you wish to stay?"

I faltered; she had been *avoiding* the Aláàfin's search parties? All this time, I had been trying to reach her just as hard as she had been trying to reach me, but we had only been working against each other. That, however, was not the most shocking aspect of what she had just said.

"Misinformation?" I repeated. "What do you mean?"

"After you were kidnapped, your aunties and I left Timbuktu to search for you. We roamed Yorùbáland, seeking out as many blacksmith guilds as we could, because they were the only ones willing to hear our plea. Many said they would help me expand my search, and some did, but I was not naïve. I knew most witches left their forges, not to find you, but rather because they were eager to leave behind their sorry lives, just as your aunties had been.

"Then I was put in contact with a witch who claimed to know where you were. But nothing she told me led me any closer to you. Her guild belonged to the royal city, the Aláàfin's home, and perhaps that should have been enough for me to know she had ill intentions—for all I know, she had been working with him."

My heart twisted with something not unlike what I had felt when Kòlò pushed me in that burning building. I knew there was only one blacksmith who had been part of the royal city's guild and who would reach out to my mother: Dígí.

I had asked her to help me locate Okóbí, and she succeeded— yet she had not told me. Worse, she had been keeping us apart. I knew it could not be because she was working with Àrèmọ, as Okóbí suggested; she had proven to be an adamant supporter of the strikes, which directly opposed him. But why, then, would she do this? And how many times would I be betrayed by a person who I thought I could call my friend?

A rustle sounded somewhere above. I looked up in time to see a pale red color flashing across a window—it must have been a bird flying by.

"But none of that matters now," Okóbí said, bringing my attention back to her. "I have, at last, found you. Now I can save you, and we can return to Timbuktu."

"That's not—there's nothing to save me from, ma," I said. "I am going to be his wife. The Aláàfin brought me here because he plans on marrying me."

"So I have heard," Okóbí sneered. "And yet, even after tricking you into eating cowpeas so that you would be forced to stay, and after holding you hostage for a season, he has still been unable to get around to marrying you?"

"Mama—"

"No, enough of this nonsense. The man is a maniac, and I refuse to allow him to continue playing his demented games with you. We are leaving. Now."

Okóbí seized my arm and dragged me to the door. "Wait—" I said, trying to step back, but her grip was viselike. My frustration reached a boiling point, and I snapped, "*Stop!*"

I yanked myself from her with so much force that I stumbled back into the shelves of fabric. "All we have ever done," I said, "is labor over a forge. We slowly kill ourselves to fulfill the needs of a world that detests us. Then the Aláàfin finds me, and he offers me a life in which you reaching old age is not an abstract concept. The *king of kings* finds me, and he offers me a place at his side, where I'd be too high up to ever be looked down upon again. Where anyone would be too scared to even *dare* consider raising a hand against us. And you truly believe I ate those beans unwillingly?"

The words poured out of me, picking up speed until I had been emptied. I was left slightly out of breath, and, for a moment, my panting was the only sound within the storehouse.

Okóbí's expression had become oddly neutral; for once, she did not look at me through narrowed eyes or with bared teeth. It was the gentlest face I had ever seen her wear.

"Do you know who your father is?" she asked.

I blinked, shocked. It was a question I had asked when I was younger, but over time she had beaten the curiosity out of me.

After a moment, I said, "No."

"Neither do I. I never said a word to the man, I only occasionally passed him as I ran errands for my family. But I suppose that was enough for him to think he had a right to me. A right to pull me into an alley one day. A right to hit me until I could no longer scream, until I could not feel anything except his weight bearing down on me—"

"Stop," I said. "Please."

I looked away, as though doing so would shield me from the harsh reality. But Okóbí grasped my chin painfully, forcing me to look at her. She still wore that glazed expression. I realized it was not an absence of emotion but rather the result of an overwhelming anger, too much for her face to capture it all.

"Being a witch is not the curse you think it is," she said. "Living untethered to a man is the kindest fate a woman can meet. I see now I have shielded you from the world too much, for I learned that truth at an age younger than you are now. I will better fulfill my responsibility to teach you, but first, we must return home. You are my daughter—your place is with me."

The horror that had been mounting within me was singed away by a sudden blaze of rage. "Yes, I am your daughter," I spat the words back at her. "And I will be the Aláàfin's wife. And one day, I will be someone's mother. But when will I get to be a person?"

Okóbí's eyes were two sharp pieces of flint. "I know you are a fool, but not even you could think more freedom can be found living in a glass box—and that's what being a powerful man's wife means, Òdòdó. Seeing life, but never being able to truly touch it yourself. Don't think you will ever break through it.

Attempting to walk that path of broken glass will only leave your feet bloody and scarred."

"Does that mean I must let you drag me back to the pathetic life of a witch?" My false hand caught in the minimal sunlight streaming in through the storehouse's small window. As I watched my hand glimmer, I added, "In case you've forgotten, witches have scars too. At least in this life, when I bleed, my scars turn to gold."

For a moment, we stared at one another. Then Okóbí walked to me, and she raised her hand. I fell into a defensive stance. It was instinct, one I did not try to fight. Perhaps if I had found my mother earlier, had known of her disapproval, I would have put an end to my union. Perhaps I would have returned to Timbuktu, disheartened but obedient. But now, I had felt the euphoria of sitting at the table with the generals, of having a say in state affairs. I could not simply walk away, not even for my own mother.

But to my surprise, Okóbí only cupped my face. For the first time, I noticed the gray hairs that now spilled out of her tousled cornrows, and I saw new wrinkles on her face. Her eyes were mournful, as though when she looked at me, she saw something she had lost. I suppressed an inexplicable urge to hug her again, just to prove I was still here.

"My daughter," she said quietly, almost to herself. "See what that man has done to you."

My anger sparked again, brighter than before. Just as the generals had praised Àrèmọ for my ideas, my mother now blamed him for my decisions. She, like everyone else, thought I was incapable of thinking for myself.

"I've made my own choice," I snapped, pushing her hand away. "I'm staying. If you are determined to labor at a forge, then you are free to return to Timbuktu alone."

I turned and walked away. Behind me, Okóbí laughed. It was not an amused sound; it was twisted, like one that would accompany a cruel joke.

"No, I am not," she said. I walked out of the storehouse, the door closing behind me just after Okóbí continued, "At this point, I have as much freedom in living for anything other than you as I did in having you."

25

I stormed away from the storehouse.

On the path ahead, my guards jogged toward me. "Forgive us, my lady. There was a disturbance, we thought—"

I ignored their apologies, pushing past them and hurrying down the path. Whatever distraction Okóbí had implemented to trick them into leaving their posts did not matter; the only thing on my mind was reaching Àrèmọ.

I had been waiting for over a season to find Okóbí, to bring her into the comfort of the royal city, only to discover that my mother never had any intention of trying to better our lives. I could have long secured my place here—but it was no matter. Now that it was clear where my mother stood, I refused to let her waste a moment more of my time.

Guards standing on either side of the entrance to the Aláàfin's chambers held the door open for me. I checked the war room, but Àrèmọ was not there. I found him in the dining room, sitting at the table. A woman stood next to him, whispering into his ear.

"I am ready to be your wife," I announced.

Àrèmọ did not acknowledge my words. With his arms crossed over his chest and his gaze fixed on the far end of the room, he seemed to be listening intently to whatever the woman was telling him.

"Àrèmọ, did you hear me?" I asked impatiently. "I said I want to marry you now, as soon as possible."

The woman at his side straightened and stepped away from him. Her face vaguely shocked me. A moment later, my mind caught up with the feeling, and I recognized her as one of my handmaids, a true one this time. She wore a pale red wrapper—the same color I had seen outside the storehouse window. Suddenly, I realized it had not been a bird flying by that I had seen; it had been her, leaping from the window after sitting on its sill for who knows how long.

And when Àrèmọ finally looked at me, I knew he had been informed of my meeting with my mother.

"You planted a spy among my handmaids," I realized aloud.

"I knew there had to be a reason you were not accepting my proposal," Àrèmọ said. "You still choose your life as a black-smith over me."

"You planted a *spy* among *my* handmaids," I said again, my anger burning hotter with each word.

Àrèmọ stood from the table, walking up to me. "How long have you and your mother been conspiring against me?"

"How long have you been spying on me?" I countered.

I looked back at the woman. She flinched and quickly dropped her gaze. I did not think she had been my handmaid since I arrived at the royal city; it must have been after the revolt, when Àrèmọ's patience with me began to dwindle, that he placed her. At the very least, he had placed her sometime after I had become his advisor; he never would have thought to use a woman as a spy if I had not been the one to teach him women had working minds.

I was yanked out of my rumination when Àrèmọ swiped at a nearby gilded figurine, flinging it across the room. I jumped as it smashed against the wall with a resounding crunch. Fragments crashed to the ground, the intricate artwork now a heap of glittering scraps.

Rage simmered on his face, his eyes a thousand shades of brown that twisted and churned into a black tempest. A sharp terror pierced through me, extinguishing my own anger and leaving me cold with fear.

"Like a fool, I had believed you were only postponing our

wedding so your mother could bear witness to our union," he
snarled. "But this entire time, you were just stalling while your
own mother incited the blacksmith strikes."

The connection between Okóbí's search for me and the
strikes was one I had not made until now, and the realization
tore through me. But I would assess the wound later; right now, I
had to prevent any further, more serious damage.

"I did not know she caused the strikes," I said feebly. "I only
just found out."

"If I had not confronted you, would you have told me?"

My hesitation was all the answer he needed. "How could I
have been so foolish?" Àrèmọ asked, running his hands through
his braids. "My own bride, connected to a traitorous plot that has
nearly bled my kingdom dry. I have killed men for less."

My heart jumped into my throat. "You don't mean that," I
choked, striding up to him and cupping his cheek. "Please. You
don't mean that."

Although his expression remained darkened, the storm in his
eyes subsided. He leaned into my touch, slowly, as if everything
pained him to do so.

"No," he said. "I don't."

Àrèmọ's voice was so quiet that even standing as close as I was
to him, I almost did not hear. A sigh of relief seeped out of me.
I placed my gold hand on his face, holding him with both of my
hands. He did not react. I hesitated, then I leaned in to kiss him.

He stepped back. "Guards," he called.

Always nearby, two men stepped into the dining room. Àrèmọ
told them, "Escort Òdòdó back to her hut."

"Yes, my king," the two men said in unison.

They stepped up to me, but I ignored them. "Why?" I asked
Àrèmọ.

The stare that he leveled at me was so flat that it was scarier
than his anger, and more painful than his disappointment. "Join
her personal guard in keeping her detained," he said to the men,

even while looking at me. "See that no one comes in or out of her hut until further notice."

One of the soldiers placed a hand on my shoulder. I pushed him away, asking Àrèmọ with more urgency, "What are you going to do?"

This time, both soldiers reached for me. The harder I fought their grasps, the tighter their grips became, becoming less a suggestion and more a command.

"Àrèmọ, please. Àrèmọ!" Panic pushed my voice to a yell. But he turned his back on me, allowing the guards to drag me out of his chambers.

It was only once I had been hauled outside and down the stairs of the Aláàfin's chambers that I accepted I would not be winning this particular battle. I pulled myself from the guards' grasps and walked to the women's compound willingly, my head held high as the guards trailed me so that anyone I passed would not realize the prisoner I had become.

But upon entering my hut and having the door closed behind me, I did not take more than two steps before I collapsed onto my colorful rug. I thought back to when I had visited Dígí in Ṣàngótè and she told me I had inspired the blacksmith strikes. Now I know she had only given me a half-truth—really, I had driven my mother to leave her forge, which in turn had inspired other blacksmiths to do the same. Even so, I had been right in thinking that my mother was not involved in the strikes; Okóbí may have sparked them, but it was clear she played no part in them now. Nor did I—and yet I would be the one to suffer the consequences.

Agitated, I stood and began pacing, waiting for Àrèmọ to arrive, whether to tell me he had forgiven me, or to expel me from the royal city. But he never came, and following his orders, my guards made sure I saw no one else either. Not Ìgbín, not my handmaids;

not even the twins managed to sneak inside, though I was sure they would have tried. Days passed, and my only human interaction was when a guard's hand cracked the door open to push through a bucket to relieve myself, or a tray of food and water.

I had not felt so helpless since before coming to live at the royal city. Even following my injury, when I had been confined to my hut, I still had the twins' information to hold onto. But now, there was nothing I could do except wait to learn of Àrẹ̀mọ's intentions. My fate was entirely in his hands.

I hated it.

I alternated between restless slumber and anxious wakefulness, startling at each little sound I heard, prepared for the worst to come from them. The sixth time I awoke, Táíwò's and Kẹ́hìndé's faces hovered above my own. They wore identical expressions of sadness.

"We're so sorry, Òdòdó," said one—Kẹ́hìndé, I decided.

"But you still have us, okay?" Táíwò asked.

"We'll be your friends, at least."

"No matter what."

My heartbeat stuttered. "What are you talking about?" I asked, pushing myself up into a sitting position. "Táíwò, Kẹ́hìndé, what have you heard?"

They looked at each other in a silent, sad exchange that only made me more nervous. A knock sounded at the door, and one of my guards stuck his head into the room.

"If you've delivered her things, get out," he boomed, launching the twins off my bed. "My lady," he added, looking at me, "please get dressed. We will escort you as soon as you're done."

With one last sympathetic look at me, the twins ran out the hut. Confused, I looked around and noticed that a machete now rested on one of the divans. Next to it was a black bandeau and a pair of baggy trousers—my combat attire.

As it was apparent that I would be taken somewhere whether I was ready or not, I donned the clothing. The process was somewhat awkward; this was my first time dressing myself in a while, and with one hand, nonetheless. After lacing up my drawstring with my hand and teeth, I took the machete and opened my door.

Two guards waited outside my hut. "Where are you taking me?" I asked.

They did not answer, only stood with their spears at their side and their solemn gazes trained on me. "What, did they cut off your tongues as well?" I asked impatiently. Nevertheless, I followed them out of my hut and through the women's compound.

The fear that I was being expelled from Ṣàngótẹ̀ was suffocating. Would Àrẹ̀mọ not even say goodbye before he left me to fend for myself with only a machete? And where was everyone? As I was carried in my palanquin from the women's compound, I passed hardly any people. Where were the royal city's nobles and soldiers? What was going on?

By the time I got out of my palanquin, my heart had beat a dent into my chest. It took a moment for me to recognize the building before me; without its great staircase and elephant emblem-stained yard, I almost did not realize this was the back of the Aláàfin chambers.

There was a faint buzz, like a distant crowd. Before I could make sense of it, I was ushered through a wooden door that very nearly blended in with the bronze walls. We walked through a narrow hallway without any windows or torches. Darkness pressed onto me, heavy and humid. I only knew we reached the end of the hallway when one of my guards rapped his fist twice against a door then pushed it open, allowing light to flood in. I stepped inside, and by the time I blinked my vision back, my guards were gone.

The room in which I now stood was strikingly humble, with plain wooden furniture and a simple woven rug in the center. It was as though all opulence had been sucked up by the man at the far end of the room. Standing before open wooden chests, he was covered in layers of colorful clothing, draperies, and looping jewelry.

"Àrèmọ," I said. This must have been his bedroom. It struck me as somewhat odd that I had never been in here when he had spent so much time in my hut. "Please, tell me what's going on."

He took his time fastening one of the many bangles on his wrist and shaking his sleeves over his hand before, at last, acknowledging me.

"As the Aláàfin, sometimes I must put what's best for Yorùbáland above my own desires." Àrèmọ's expression was blank and his words controlled, as though this was a speech he had practiced many times. "And so, for a moment, I doubted how wise it was to marry a woman who propelled the infertility of my kingdom. But I have chosen to love you, Òdòdó, and it is a choice I want to stand by. So, if you can prove your loyalty to me, I will forgive you, and our marriage will proceed."

I looked at my machete, understanding dawning on me. The voices I heard before entering the Aláàfin's chambers, my combat attire—it was starting to make sense. He wanted me to duel an enemy out on the field, in front of everyone, to show the lengths I would go to prove my devotion to him.

My fists clenched, but my palms still tingled, as though I could feel my security slipping through my grasp like grains of sand. I was no longer as capable a fighter as I once was, but it did not matter. I would rather die here, in the royal city, then live the dismal life of a witch.

"Very well, then," I said reluctantly. "Who am I fighting?"

"You will know your enemy once they are brought before you." My hesitation must have shown, because Àrèmọ asked, "Is that an issue?"

I swallowed hard, pushing my fear so far down that I was unsure if I could ever reach it again. "Of course not."

Àrèmọ nodded, then he turned to a long, thin box. From it, he extracted the shimmering conical crown of the Aláàfin. Its beads swayed softly as he donned it, his face disappearing behind the beaded mask.

"It's time."

Àrèmọ turned, leaving me no choice but to follow him out of the room and through the Aláàfin's chambers. My sandals clacked against the polished floor, each step like a steady hammering that sealed my fate.

Two guards stood on either side of the front entrance. One opened the door for us, and immediately, I was engulfed by a cacophony of voices that escalated into screams and cheers as we stepped onto the carpeted porch.

The field in front of the Aláàfin's chambers had been transformed into a green blanket with a thick multicolored border. Up ahead, the massive gates of the royal city were propped wide open, inviting all of Ṣàngótè to sew themselves into the audience that hemmed the field. There were hundreds, if not thousands, of Aláràá—all here to watch me win my duel.

As Àrèmọ took his seat on the bronze throne at the edge of the porch, Gassire rose from where he sat on the topmost step. He looked at Àrèmọ, and Àrèmọ's silence must have answered whatever his question was, for he nodded. I did not miss the grimness in Gassire's eyes as they darted to me before he turned back to the crowd.

Gassire stood next to the Aláàfin and raised his arms. His sleeves billowed, though there was no breeze. Silence tumbled over the crowd, flowing from near to far until everyone had been subdued.

"Ọba kìí pọ̀kọrin." His baritone voice wove around the entire area, the string that threaded us all together. "Gather, gather, come and see. The brave Òdòdó, the woman warrior who put down the slave revolt, who defeated an entire northern army without lifting a finger, comes now to cure us of the plague that has run rampant through our land."

A round of cheers rose from the crowd. My heart pounding and my limbs heavy, I began descending the great bronze steps.

In the center of the field, a wooden pole sprouted up from the ground. Assuming this was some sort of marker for my arena, I approached it as Gassire continued, "For nearly a year now, Yorùbáland has run barren of blacksmiths, and we have all suffered the consequences. Our crops have been without equipment for harvest. Our battles have been without weapons with which to fight. You, the good common people, have been denied basic tools needed for day-to-day life. All because blacksmiths everywhere were laying down their hammers and abandoning us. But, my friends, today I tell you: we will no longer stand for it!"

What does this have to do with the man I'm dueling? I wondered. As the audience made their approval heard, I shielded my eyes from the sun and looked back at Gassire. One of his arms was extended before him, pointing beyond me.

My head—along with everyone else's—turned to the gates of the royal city. The crowd directly in front of the gate parted, making way for two soldiers as they escorted a robed person who had a sack over their head and chains around their wrists.

I waited for them to free the man and exchange his chains for a weapon so that our duel could commence. However, upon reaching the wooden pole in front of me, the soldiers began chaining him to it. I watched in shock; how could I be redeemed by winning against a bound opponent?

"For it is our fearless Òdòdó," Gassire's voice rumbled, "who tracked down the wretched witch responsible for making her sisters release misery onto Yorùbáland. It is our fearless Òdòdó who put aside her past to make you, her people, this promise: *she will revive the life of this land today!*"

Cheers thundered so loudly that I vaguely wondered if Ṣàngó felt threatened. My heart, which had gradually quickened with each word Gassire said, plunged to my feet.

The prisoner, I noticed now that I stood directly in front of them, was short. And they were wide too, with arms more muscular than their legs.

No . . . I silently pleaded. *It can't be. Please . . .*

One soldier stepped forward and grabbed the sack over the prisoner's head.

"Because today," Gassire shouted, "our beautiful Òdòdó will bestow the kiss of Death onto the witch who has put us through all this grief"—The soldier ripped the sack off the prisoner's head—"*the Alálè called Okóbí!*"

The audience's yells filled the air so thoroughly that the sky was on the verge of popping off the Earth. An iron dagger with a gilded hilt was thrust into my grasp. A hand landed on my shoulder, and beads clattered behind me. "After speaking to you that day," Àrèmọ said softly in my ear, "I went looking for your mother. It was not hard to find her—she had not even left the royal city, working among the slaves, likely waiting for another chance to speak to you. She confirmed that she began the strikes, not you, and that you are not affiliated with the blacksmiths. And if that truly is the case, then it will be easy for you to cut this final tie to your past life. Show my people you are loyal to them by killing the villain who has ravaged Yorùbáland."

"No . . ." I whispered, but as hard as I shook my head, I could not shake myself out of this nightmare.

"Do it," Okóbí snapped, startling me.

Rage steamed off her, but there was no hint of surprise or betrayal in her expression. She had vouched for me, even while knowing what it would cost her.

"Mama—"

"I said get it over with!"

Her voice, typically as rigid as steel, was infiltrated by cracks. She glared at me with glossy eyes, and I began trembling so badly that my teeth rattled in my ears. All of this was wrong; I never meant for any of this to happen—

"Or," Àrèmọ said, "are you hesitant to kill your co-conspirator?"

"You have never before appreciated how much I've given up for you—what's one more sacrifice now?" Okóbí shrieked as the crowd grew louder.

"At your request, I searched endlessly for your mother. But were you working with her behind my back this entire time? Have you enabled the strikes that nearly laid waste to my kingdom?"

Cheers and screams assaulted me from every angle. And boos? Was the crowd booing? They were getting restless; they came here for justice, and if they left unfulfilled, this would easily become a riot. Everything was becoming undone.

"What does it matter?" Okóbí yelled. "Isn't this what you wanted?"

"After all that I've done for you, this is how you repay me?" came Àrèmọ's whisper from behind me, just barely audible.

"This is the one thing I can give you—just take it and be grateful!"

"Please, don't break my heart, Òdòdó. Tell me I am wrong about you working with her. *Show* me that I am wrong."

It was too much noise, too much pressure. It was too much, too much, too much—

"Insolent girl—"

Okóbí broke off abruptly, her eyes wide. She coughed, a terrible gurgling sound that splattered blood against my face.

In horror, I looked down to see a dagger embedded in her chest. The dagger's golden hilt was held by a hand. A breath later, I realized that hand was mine.

"No . . ." I breathed, salty tears dripping onto my tongue. "No, no no . . ."

I quickly extracted the dagger, but that only made blood gush out of her chest. Okóbí had gone limp, her head leaning against the pole behind her as she regarded me through half-lidded eyes.

"You'll . . . be okay . . ." she said, more a command than an encouragement.

Okóbí died with a smile on her face, and a tear sliding down her cheek.

My stomach twisted violently. I dropped the dagger as my

hands flew to my mouth, choking on the taste of blood and tears and metal and vomit.

"It is done!" Gassire boomed, and the tumult of the world flooded my senses once more.

I fell to my knees and hit the ground, hard, for there was no one to catch me; Àrẹ̀mọ was already climbing up the steps back to his throne.

"There is nothing our woman warrior will not do for Yorùbáland!" Gassire said. "Rejoice, my friends, for Òdòdó is not yet finished proving her loyalty to the Aláàfin—she is to wed him in two days!"

Applause swelled. The entire world was shaking.

Then, after a moment, I realized it was just me.

26

The bee was fat.

It had clearly eaten very well in its lifetime, but still it sought more nectar. The buzzing bee bobbed up and down, as though its tiny wings strained to combat its girth.

The bee did not question the thousands of vibrant flowers littering the field, which appeared seemingly overnight; it merely reached into a flower's center and extracted sweet nectar as enthusiastically as if this were its very first meal.

The word *flower* drifted over. The bee, ever the glutton, raised its head curiously, swiping the sticky liquid from its mouth. The word seemed to be the only one that the bee was able to distinguish from the droning sound that the humans emitted. With the bee's interest piqued, it lazily launched off the flower to make its way to the humans, where the word came again—

"Òdòdó!"

Two fingers, adorned in rings, snapped in front of my face. With a start, I was wrenched out of my daze. As the bee buzzed to the bouquet near me, I turned my attention away from it to the three noblewomen with whom I sat on a mass of blankets.

They looked at me expectantly. Having nothing to give them, I asked, "Yes?"

"We've asked you twice now, which do you like better?" one woman said. "Hurry, choose so Ìgbín can prepare your fifth outfit change for the wedding tomorrow."

She gestured to two slaves in front of us, each of whom held a large sheet of lace fabric. The first was a striking magenta with light red and pink flowers blooming over it. The other had a beige base and swirling lilac designs, like purple flames consuming sand.

I raised a trembling finger to the first fabric. The slave, believing this to be my pick, nodded and made to leave. But I said, "My mother hated that color."

Okóbí had hated many colors, and many things in general. In my mind's eye, I could see her critiquing the hundreds of decisions that had been made regarding the wedding. She would have said that I was a fool, that I could not even get married correctly, that I should choose a fabric full of color to distract from the emptiness of my head.

For as long as I could remember, Okóbí had hated me as well. In fact, she hated me so much that, ultimately, she had given her life to save me.

My lungs constricted. The world whirled around me, blinding in its vibrance. Although I had been emptying my stomach all day, nausea twisted it once more.

"Excuse me," I mumbled as I rose to my feet.

Two of the dozen soldiers standing guard around us made to follow me, but I waved them away. I staggered through the field, not knowing or caring if I was crushing flowers beneath my sandals, until I at last stumbled off the grass and onto one of the royal city's paths.

I hunched over as my lungs relearned how to function, swallowing large gulps of air. Only when the world stilled was I able to straighten.

Twining my hand around my golden necklace, I looked over my shoulder, back at the scene I had cut myself out of. The noblewomen were still organizing wedding plans, slaves hiking through mountains of flowers to see their wishes through. They had made most of the decisions today; it was clear that I was not needed.

I walked away, turning onto new paths at random without a specific destination in mind. I wanted to get lost, but I had invested too much time in learning my way around the royal city for its winding routes to ever be a maze again. I wanted to disappear, but every slave and soldier I passed bowed to me, and every noble attempted to start a conversation with the acclaimed woman warrior and bride of the Aláàfin.

I had gotten my wish; no one questioned my place here anymore. The royal city and everyone in it were undoubtedly mine. I was not sure if this was what I had wanted, but it was certainly what I had asked for.

A sharp cry pierced through my stupor. I halted, looking around, and noticed a medley of low voices coming from nearby. Curious, I followed it to a palm tree, under which there was a small crowd.

As I approached, people parted for me with solemn nods. Once I reached the front, I saw what everyone was huddled around: the royal babaláwo, who stood next to a handful of women grieving over the body of a fallen soldier.

My mind came to a grinding halt. That face was familiar to me, but now void of any anger or hatred, it took a moment for me to recognize General Ọmọ́ṣẹwà.

He was even more beautiful in death, his body strewn delicately on the ground. A river of blood flowed from a gaping wound in his abdomen, painting the flowers beneath him red. His head lay in the lap of one of his widows while two other women clasped each of his hands. Sunlight fluttered down onto the grieving family, capturing this moment in time as a golden picture of mourning.

Realizing that my mouth was slightly agape, I closed it. Perhaps today was not all bad, then; my mother was gone, but at least Ọmọ́ṣẹwà was not here either.

I took one final look at Ọmọ́ṣẹwà's soft eyes, half-lidded in death. Then, I turned around. From the revolt, I still had reservations toward the òrìṣàs, but, as I made my way through the crowd, I could not help but mutter, "Ṣàngó yọ mí."

"That's a rather callous remark," an amused voice said.

My eyes widened. "General Rótìmí," I said in surprise as he fell into step beside me. "I was unaware you had returned from Taghaza."

The phrase felt odd and clunky on my tongue, like a bad lie. People did not *return* from Taghaza, as though it was a simple trip. Yet here Rótìmí was, a person who had journeyed to the land where men went to die and had lived to tell the tale.

However, the general did not get out unscathed. His gait was uneven, as though he was forced to favor one foot over the other. His arm was wrapped up to his elbow—possibly higher under the sleeve of his tunic. A shadow of stubble covered his jaw, but even darker was the tinge in his gold-flecked eyes. It was like seeing a sun that did not shine.

"I only returned to the royal city last night," Rótìmí said. "Just in time for the highly anticipated wedding, it would seem."

"Ah, yes . . ." I trailed off, unsure what to say.

If Rótìmí found my detachment strange, he did not comment. As I turned onto a new path, he merely turned too, willing to wander with me.

"Well," I tried again, "congratulations on completing your mission. I imagine it could not have been easy."

"Yes, it was quite difficult. So difficult, in fact, that it failed."

I looked at him in shock, and Rótìmí continued, "My men and I were on our way to Taghaza when we received word that a captured Òòrùn squad had escaped from there and was on their way back to my city, Wúràkẹ́mi. We were able to intercept the escaped squad—but my second was not among them. In his efforts to free his men, he had been forced to stay behind.

"We rode full speed to Taghaza. Our infiltration of the salt mines went smoothly. There, the slaves told us that a few un-ruly slaves—including a man who sounded like my second—had been sold to traders from the far north. None of the slaves knew the exact location where he was taken, but what they did tell me was that the sale had occurred hours before my arrival. I had missed him by mere hours. If I had just remained on our initial route, if I had never turned back . . ."

He trailed off. I cast a sidelong glance at him. Despite the tragedy of his words, his tone was casual, as though his mournful song had not nearly made buildings crumble in defeat just weeks prior. He once told me that his second-in-command's death would be his greatest fear. It seemed he had never considered there could be something worse than that death: both him and his second being perfectly alive, but unlikely to ever see each other again. Was this what a man looked like when his greatest fear paled to the brutality of fate? Rótìmí stood tall, his steps light despite his injuries. He walked through this world as though he no longer belonged in it, as though he wanted for nothing, so there was nothing to limit him. He had obligations to neither desire nor hope; not even pain. Anything that could hurt him, he had already undergone.

"Nevertheless," Rótìmí said after a moment, "you have my immense gratitude for giving me the opportunity to try. I am forever indebted to you."

I shrugged uncomfortably. "It was the Aláàfin who gave you permission to go."

"Ah, of course, the Aláàfin and all his wisdom. Then I am grateful he has a woman like you to support his brilliance. He will certainly need all the advice he can get now that he is short of a general."

"Speaking of which," I said, "do you know how Ọmóṣẹwà died?"

"Indeed. Yesterday, when I returned, Ọmóṣẹwà visited my quarters. He prattled on about his disapproval of your upcoming wedding, and he speculated as to how he could put an end to it. I will spare you the details, because the things he said were quite alarming. Could have gotten him in a lot of trouble. So, as his friend, I decided to take him to the nearby wilds and calm him down by doing what he most enjoyed: killing things. But alas, our hunting trip went awry when a crazed warthog gored him.

By the time I brought his body back to the royal city, it was too late."

"I see," I said slowly. "I never knew warthogs could be so aggressive."

"Untold menaces."

"And how did you escape the warthog's wrath?"

"I wonder."

Rótìmí's slightly supercilious smile had returned, but this time, I did not think to be offended by it. This time, we were on the same side of the joke.

"Òdòdó!"

We turned to see a twin—Táíwò—skipping down the path toward us. She crashed into me with enough force to push me a step back as she wrapped her arms around my legs.

"Do you want to hear a story?" she asked.

It was the question the twins asked to let me know they had something important to tell me. "Sure," I said. To Rótìmí, I said, "I should humor her, but truly, thank you for your companionship."

I knew he understood that I was thanking him for more than his company today, and when he bowed, I understood it was not just a polite gesture.

As he walked away, I placed a hand on Táíwò's head. "Where is your brother?" I asked. It was always strange to see them apart; it seemed like something was missing.

She pulled a face. "Playing. We couldn't both come, or else they'd notice we were gone and start whining. Then I wouldn't be able to tell you the story."

"Alright, then. What is your story about?"

Her dark eyes glittered in the sunlight. "Kòlò."

I looked around, making sure none of the passersby had heard her before I took her hand. I led her onto the nearest field, and once we were a decent distance away from the traffic on the stone paths, I squatted beside Táíwò under the shade of a palm tree.

"What have you heard?" I prompted.

"I was running errands at the market when Kọlọ walked by. She didn't even notice when I started following her—she used to be so observant, but it was easy this time, like trailing a sleep-walker! I followed her to a street corner, where a messenger man was. And she told him"—Táíwò altered her voice and manner-isms to match Kọlọ, for her perfect memory could store more than just words—"*Tell the king the east camp has been taken. His loyal soldier has decided to transfer the remaining wares to the western wilds.*"

The excitement within me dulled. This was not evidence of Kọlọ's involvement in the slave revolt.

And yet—wilds? Where had I heard that word before . . . ?

Rótìmí. Had he not just told me that he took Ọmọ́sẹwà to some wilds to hunt? If there was such land near Ṣàngótẹ̀, I was sure, then, that it was especially prominent around Ìlọ́dẹ, City of Hunters. And *east camp*—the ivory camp had been east of Ìlọ́dẹ.

I thought of the man whom Àrẹ̀mọ had killed at the raid. Perhaps he had indeed been the leader . . . of that camp. But of an entire black market?

I opened my mouth, but whatever I had been about to say was completely forgotten as something occurred to me. "Táíwò, can you repeat the last part of the message?"

"*His loyal soldier has decided to transfer the remaining wares to the western wilds.* That part?"

"Yes. Are you sure that is exactly what Kọlọ said?"

Táíwò stomped her foot impatiently. "I know what I heard, Òdòdó."

"I know, I trust you," I said, my calm voice a stark contrast to the racing of my heart.

Táíwò beamed as I kissed her cheek. "Thank you, Táíwò," I said. "You and your brother have done a very good job."

My mind felt the clearest it had been all day as I rose to my feet. Táíwò's eyes followed me up as she asked, "What are you going to do now?"

I gave her a small smile. "The best that I can."

27

What Àrẹ̀mọ did not know about the bronze flowers I made him was that they had half a dozen failed drafts. Some had a stem that came out too thick; others' petals had failed to take the correct shape. They were still recognizable as a flower, but I had not wanted "recognizable." For Àrẹ̀mọ, I wanted perfect.

After my talk with Táíwò, I stopped by my hut and came across one of the flowers with misshapen petals abandoned on a table. Knowing that I likely had a long wait ahead of me, I decided to take the flower with me to work on. Perhaps I had been too critical, too quick to give up on it. After all, perfection was perfection; no matter if it was born, or if it was achieved.

I still had a rounded stone from when I first made the flowers. Holding the daffodil on a table, I used the stone to hammer at its petals, curling them inwards to fix their shape. It had taken a moment to adjust to crafting flowers with a gold hand, but the motions soon came as natural as before, engrained in muscle memory regardless of whether the muscle was there. I had just developed a rhythm when the door opened and in walked Kòlò.

When she spotted me standing at a table against the back wall, she paused. "Why are you in my hut?" she asked.

Applying enough force to slightly curl the flowers' petals inward, but not so much force that I folded the metal in half completely, required careful focus. So, I did not look up as I replied, "To see you, of course."

After a beat, Kòlò closed the door behind her. In my peripheral,

I saw her walk inside, her movements cautious. Yet, when she spoke, her voice was as smooth as ever.

"You have much to do for your wedding," she said. "It may be best for you to leave."

"But I have so looked forward to this moment. Because ever since you left me for dead, I have been anticipating the moment I could finally return the favor—Oops."

My last strike had been too hard; the petal I had been hammering broke off from the flower.

I released the flower and picked up the dagger I brought, which I had pilfered from an unsuspecting soldier on my way here. At last, I looked up at Kọlọ. To her credit, her back remained straight and her chin raised. The only sign of unease was the occasional flick of her brown eyes to my dagger.

"I know you played a role in the slave revolt," I said softly. "I also know you are tied to the recent ivory situation. And I have never been the wisest, but it would take a different kind of fool to not see that the two events are related. You're the traitor the generals fear is among their ranks."

It was not a question. Kọlọ did not treat it like one. With a heavy sigh, she tilted her head and gripped the side of her neck. Her almond eyes shifted to one of the windows, outside which night was quickly falling.

"Well," she said quietly, "I suppose that's it, then."

Kọlọ moved forward. I quickly readied my dagger—but she took no notice. She was not approaching me, as I had thought. She merely walked to her vanity and sat on the stool in front of it.

I watched in disbelief as she began removing her many gold bangles and placing them in a wooden box, one by one. My hand itched around the dagger; this was not how I expected this to go. But I had already made my move; it was Kọlọ's turn now. I would draw on my everlasting patience, I decided, and see what kind of game she was playing.

After a moment, Kọlọ spoke. "I should have vacated the

Gilded District long before the revolt began. Had I not been there, Àrèmọ would not have come, and what were supposed to be unarmed little boys would not have turned into soldiers."

She rubbed the bangle imprints on her now bare wrists thoughtfully before she went on, "But then again, I never would have expected him to know I was in the Gilded District, much less do anything about it. I did not think he cared enough about me."

"He doesn't," I said, emulating her light tone. "I was the one who told him where you were that day, and I urged him to rescue you. You, my friend."

For a moment, I thought I saw something like remorse in Kọ̀lọ̀'s face. But then she laughed, and I knew I had imagined it.

"Of course you did, my sweet flower," she said, turning back to her mirror and removing her beaded collar necklace. "Your arrival was useful at first, because it relieved me of Mama Aláàfin's constant surveillance, since she turned her full discontent on you. It allowed me to move freer and do what I needed to— not to mention, your help was sincerely appreciated in supplying weapons to the slaves. But I am glad you lost the Aláàfin's trust when you did. He was starting to listen to you, and you might have convinced him to revisit the fraying edges his ego would have otherwise overlooked until the whole thing had already unraveled."

As Kọ̀lọ̀ reached for her second earring, her hand brushed her left cheek, and she flinched. I noticed the horizontal scars there were red today. "Your tribal mark is bothering you?" I asked politely.

"Yes, it—"

"—never healed right," we finished together.

She glanced at me in mild interest as I commented, "So you've said. I guess that's what happens when you've had what's supposed to be a lifetime mark for only a few years."

For the first time, Kọ̀lọ̀ faltered; her round earring slipped from her grasp and bounced against the floor once. Twice. Three times. It rolled to a stop.

Kòlò threw her head back in laughter. "I don't care what everyone else says, little flower. You can be quite clever."

"Where is the daughter of King Adéjọlá?"

"Safe in Ọ̀yọ́, where she belongs," Kòlò said. She faced me, resting her chin on her hand with a small chuckle. "As if my king would ever send his princess to marry the enemy."

I frowned. "Ṣàngótẹ̀ has made peace with Ọ̀yọ́."

Anger flashed over Kòlò's face. For a moment, in the torchlight, she looked inhuman; a feral beauty.

"Yes, how kind of the Aláràá to finally stop killing their sister clan. It only took a few centuries of bloodshed," she said bitterly. "Ṣàngótẹ̀ does not get to suddenly grow a conscience and think we will forget their sins. If the Aláràá truly cared about honor, they would free the Ọ̀yọ́ who were taken as slaves during the war. If the Aláràá truly cared about honor, they would have never insulted Ọ̀yọ́ by breaking off to form their own city and install an Aláàfin without our permission in the first place."

Kòlò deflated, as though rage required more energy than she possessed. "But there is no point in telling you all this," she said wearily, turning back to her jewelry box. "These are men's grievances against other men. There is no room in this war for women like you and me. I know I should be upset my mission failed, but I have been alone in this wretched land for nearly three years now. My only grievance is that I never got to go home."

For a moment, my own anger was overshadowed by shock. When had Kòlò's golden skin become so gray? Her frame, once so toned and nimble, was now as gaunt as a beggar's, and creases accumulated on her high forehead. When we met, she had been no more than three years older than me, but these past few months seemed to have accelerated her aging.

I was so focused on her appearance that I hardly noticed when she took a small pouch and emptied it into her mouth. "No!" I said, pushing myself off the wall. But by the time I reached her and knocked it out of her hands, she had already downed most of its contents.

The pouch fell lightly to the floor. I noticed it was embroidered with gold, making it gleam as brightly as the accessories in her jewlery box—that must be where she had stored it. While she had been talking to me, seemingly removing her jewelery, she had really been retrieving this.

From the pouch fell a single reddish-brown seed; the rest had been consumed by Kọ̀lọ̀. She chewed quickly. My heart pounding, I grabbed her face, even though I knew it was too late. "What did you just eat?" I demanded.

"The seeds of castor beans, a highly poisonous plant from the eastern part of the continent," she said, her voice slightly muffled from how I held her face. "Ingesting just five of those seeds is sure to kill you, and, well"—She let out a short, grim laugh— "that was a lot more than five."

She stood, so unsteadily that she was forced to hold her vanity in order to keep her balance. Instinctively, I stepped back, raising my dagger. Kọ̀lọ̀ regarded me with amusement.

"Do you mean to use that on me?" she asked. "The seeds will provide me with a quick death, but it will be very painful. Taking my life with your blade may just do me a favor."

Already, sweat had begun to glaze her forehead, and the arm which supported her on the table shook. I had come here for revenge, but it was clear nothing I could do would bring her more suffering than her own fate.

I stepped aside. Kọ̀lọ̀ laughed lightly, inflaming my anger, but I merely watched as she staggered forward, holding onto whatever was nearest for support, until she at last stumbled onto her bed.

I strode forward, standing over her. "In the message you sent at the market, you called yourself a soldier," I said. "You're an Ahosi warrior, aren't you? How many others are here? What is your king's goal?"

Kọ̀lọ̀, of course, answered none of my questions. "When I die, it will look as though I was taken by a sudden and lethal illness," she said instead, turning on her side so that she faced away from me. "But if you are near when my body is discovered, given our recent history, you may be accused of poisoning me. You should go, little flower."

"That is considerate of you," I said flatly.

"Well, I do care." She glanced over her shoulder, up at me. A small smile appeared on her face, the faintest of lights in her haunted features. "You know," she said softly, "under different circumstances, I think you and I would have been friends."

Kòlò's expression was genuine; she really believed what she just said.

Strangely enough, I found that I agreed. "I think so too," I said honestly.

The realization and its timing were so incredibly unfunny that I could not help but laugh. It started small, a giggle that floated out of me. But slowly, the sound clouded over the room, thundering louder and striking against me with so much force that it felt as though I was breaking. Cracks slowly widened within me, threatening to make me fall apart. I crouched down and clasped my hands over my mouth, as though in a desperate attempt to hold myself together. But the more I tried to muffle myself, the harder I laughed. The fit dragged on for so long that I could not tell if the tears that blurred my vision had been summoned by my laughter, or by the pain it caused.

Eventually, the torrent began to reduce to an irregular trickle of giggles. After what felt like years, I was able to straighten up. On the bed, Kòlò had curled up into a ball. Sweat pooled in the linen sheets around her and her entire body trembled.

"Kòlò," I said.

There was no indication she had heard me. It was possible the poison had rendered her unconscious—but even if she had been awake, why should she respond to my call? I had addressed her as Kòlò, but this woman was not Kòlò. The real Princess Kòlò, daughter of King Adéjọlá, was someone whom I had never met.

The real Princess Kòlò, daughter of King Adéjọlá, sat in her palace in Ọ̀yọ́, her father awaiting an update from his soldier that would never come.

The woman before me was one of the only friends I'd ever had. And in the end, I never even knew her name.

No one was around when I stepped outside. Àrẹ̀mọ's first wife had been right about how little attention he had paid her; she did not seem to have a personal guard as I did. She had not needed one, of course, but he had been unaware of that. It was no wonder she had grown so lonely here.

As I stepped out of the women's compound, my guards exchanged a look. I realized that I was humming the daffodil's song, a dazed smile on my face. I tried to stop, but, in the song's absence, I felt laughter rise within me like vomit, threatening to spew from me once more. And so as I made my way through the royal city, swaying slightly, I continued humming. My guards had no choice but to fall into step behind me.

When we reached the Aláàfin's chambers, my guards stopped at the base of the steps as I climbed them. Two sentries at the top crossed their spears over the front entrance, blocking my way.

"The Aláàfin and his generals are—they're hosting a dinner, my lady . . . and they do not wish to be disturbed . . ." one soldier explained, trying to speak over my humming, but when I made no room for his words, he trailed off.

I stared at the door expectantly, the daffodil's tune filling the silence, occasionally punctuated by a giggle that managed to slip out of me. The soldiers exchanged a nervous glance. Eventually, they returned their spears to their sides, falling back into attention. Nodding, I pushed the door open.

The Aláàfin sat at the head of his great dining table. Generals Yẹ̀kínì, Èmíọlá, and Rótìmí sat on one side of him; Generals Àjàyí and Balógun sat on the other. The rest of the table was occupied by noblemen dressed in colorful agbádás. Splayed on the table before them all was a lavish feast.

As jolly as the men's conversation was, no one heard me at

first. However, as I stood near the entrance, swaying in place, the men began to notice. They would glance at me then away quickly, as though determined to not acknowledge me. But their discomfort was evident in how the volume of the room gradually decreased, until my humming was clearly audible.

Àrèmọ was one of the last men to notice me. "Òdòdó?" he asked, and the rest of the table quieted completely.

I opened my mouth to respond, but as soon as I stopped humming, my laughter gushed forth freely. Àrèmọ glanced around the room—at the generals, nobles, and guards staring at me— then pushed his chair back and stood, unrolling himself to his full height. His sandals clicked against the floor as he walked up to me, stopping so close that I could feel his breath on my face.

"I think I have missed the joke," Àrèmọ said as he watched me, smiling hesitantly, though his brows furrowed with confusion.

I took a deep breath, stifling my laughter to the best of my ability. "There are more scavengers," I managed to say. "They are moving their remaining ivory to the wildlands west of Ìlódẹ. I am certain they are still in transit. If you leave now, you could catch them before they reach their other camp."

Àrèmọ only stared. He did not believe me. I had just discovered the spy who had infiltrated his kingdom, as well as her latest plot, and of *course* he did not believe me. At the realization, my laughter escaped, echoing loudly throughout the silent room. To avoid being toppled by it, I was forced to rest my hand on Àrèmọ's shoulder and my head on the back of my hand.

"Perhaps I should escort you back—" Àrèmọ began.

But I interrupted, "The men whom you arrested at the ivory camp, who you said you would hold prisoner until you're able to reform them into your own workers—are they still in your custody?"

I pulled back to smile up at him. He hesitated, then he said, "Yes."

"Ask them about their second camp located west of the City of

Hunters. Even if they are not yet loyal enough to tell you about it, their reactions will be all the confirmation you need."

Àrẹ̀mọ considered me. I met his stare unwaveringly.

After a moment, he nodded. "I will test your theory after dinner."

He scanned the room. When he turned back to me, an amused smile tugged at the corner of his mouth. "And the end of this dinner might come sooner than expected," he said. "You seem to have frightened my nobles."

"*They* have no reason to be scared." I cupped his face in my good hand. "It is you who I love."

Àrẹ̀mọ blinked; I had never said the words so frankly to him. Then, he grinned. He put his hand on my waist and pulled me into a kiss. I wrapped my arms around his neck, allowing myself to sink deeper and deeper into him.

28

Not only did the prisoners from the raid confirm that there was a second camp collecting ivory, but Àrèmọ was also able to extract from them an exact location. The wedding was postponed while Àrèmọ led a small unit of men to put an end to Yorùbáland's ivory troubles once and for all.

In the meantime, Àrèmọ's first wife had been found dead in her hut. She had been right; it was concluded that she had taken ill, a belief that was supported by the haggard appearance she had developed in the last few months of her life. With Àrèmọ gone, it was Mama Aláàfin who made the decision that the body of his deceased wife should be returned to Ọ̀yọ́, so her burial rites could be performed there.

I was left to go about my days normally. The first three days Àrèmọ was gone, I was calm; I even contributed to the planning for my wedding. On the fourth day, however, doubt began to taint my confidence. The fifth night found me pacing grooves into my floor. Perhaps I should have accompanied Àrèmọ; what if something had gone wrong? What if I had made a mistake sending him into potential danger before first cementing our union? What if—?

The door to my hut burst open. There stood Àrèmọ, his trousers and his axes stained with blood. His hair was the messiest it had ever been, but beneath the grime caked onto his face, he wore a grin so bright that it seared away my uncertainty.

"I love you, Òdòdó," he declared over my laughter, spinning with me in his arms. "And tomorrow, I shall marry you."

The morning of your wedding, you awaken feeling entirely different.

They call you Òdòdó, and to that name you answer, but you would answer to any other name as well. There is no one word big enough to encompass the entirety of your self. You feel as though you have been stretched and pulled, and now, you may wear any time and any space. None fit perfectly, and so they are all yours to choose. Today does not simply arrive; you have chosen to be in this day and in this time. You have chosen to be a bride to the Aláàfin, for it is a wonder unlike anything you will ever experience.

It is countless women, slaves and noblewomen alike, pooling into your room at dawn and sweeping you away to the bathhouse then to a beauty room, like a leaf caught in a river current. It is the sweet oils and perfumes they lovingly massage into your skin and the intricate braiding patterns they install in your hair.

It is the younger women jokingly offering to help you run away and telling you the story of the bride who married a man, who was actually an ogre that gobbled her up. No, that's not right; he is a goblin, like the ones who wreaked havoc in the old times, now returned to antagonize the poor unsuspecting bride. No, no, that's not it at all! He is a demon, of course, and what he actually did is drag the bride down down down below to his dark domain so that she never saw the light of day again.

It is no one being able to agree on the exact details of the story, but you understand anyways. Because no matter how different their versions are, they all have the same roots. Roots that have been here long before you existed, and roots that will remain long after everything else has turned to dust. Cities have risen, and cities have fallen. Entire empires have been sparked from nothing, flamed, then waned. But this story, this story remains. It has seen its culture deliberately stolen and burned. History has tried to kill it, has tried to bury it under the guise of "lost" or "forgotten." But now, you know this story. It is a part of you. Great though the world's animosity may be, the world will never succeed at killing us so long as there are minds and hearts in which our story may live.

So, yes, you understand the stories the women tell, confused and whimsical though they may be. For even if the details of other times or spaces mask the stories' roots, still those roots remain.

Your wedding day is the older women shooing away the younger so that the former can lecture you of your wifely responsibilities. It is being dressed in extravagant aṣọ òkè fabrics that will be the first of many, many outfits you change into today. It is your pampering retinue leading you to an entirely bronze edifice, where what seems like all of Ṣàngótẹ̀ waits to commend their beloved bride. But of all the pairs of adoring eyes, the only ones you notice are those of the Aláàfin.

It is the speech given by the royal griot, and the part of it that is met with the most applause: when you have officially been announced as the new wife of the Aláàfin. It is the cowpeas you eat, and it is the cheers of approval that thunder through the clear, sunny sky.

It is a long procession of gleaming jewels and vivid cloths brought by hundreds of camels. All are gifts from the kings and chiefs of Yorùbáland, determined to outdo one another in their lavish displays of devotion to the Aláàfin—and all lose substantially to Wúràkẹ́mi. The king of the Gold Coast has sent you one hundred colorfully dressed slaves, each carrying an ornamental gold staff. Behind them follows a line of camels carrying glittering gold that stretches for miles, from the border of Ṣàngótẹ̀ all the way to the gates of the royal city.

It is the Aláàfin presenting you with his own, personal gift: a baby giraffe.

It is a feast large enough to keep a small town well-fed for weeks. It is the festivities beginning at one venue, where peacocks strut among dancers under kaleidoscopic moonlight filtering through a multicolored glass ceiling. It is then being deposited at another venue that is illuminated by the spinning light of fire jugglers, where eager artists capture your likeness on the spot and send you on your way with miniature clay statues of yourself. It is the celebration overflowing from one venue to the next, to the next, until it has flooded Ṣàngótẹ̀, and it is being drowned in gold and silver no matter where the festivities land. It is lively music that soars over the entire capital, then falls to its knees to embrace you all as the distant light in the sky blinks on and off, on and off, too dull for the glittering extravaganza to take any notice.

It is the parade of singing and dancing people following behind your elephant steed as you and the Aláàfin are, at last, carried to his chambers. It is every single subject kneeling for their king, but when the doors close, and it is just you and him, it is you who puts their king on his knees.

It is your hand running along each and every one of his scars, drawing out their stories from him like a man confessing his sins. It is him offering himself in libation, and it is the entire world trembling with rapture as the divine is coaxed out from between your thighs. It is the deliverance to his lifelong search for paradise; the scripture that your nails etch into his back; the hymns that he can't help but moan in your ear. He calls you queen; he calls you mercy. He says your name over, and over, and over. A fervent prayer; a man begging for hallowed relief.

Worship has never felt quite like this.

29

I was very warm and very sleepy, and just a little bit drunk, when I awoke from a slumber so deep that I had forgotten I existed.

I blinked blearily out the window, but the moon was up, a large blotch of brightness on the black canvas above. Content that I did not yet have to rise, I turned over in the bed. When my outstretched hand met bedsheets instead of warm skin, however, my eyes opened.

Àrèmọ stood on the other side of the bed. He was already dressed in trousers and was donning a belt with ax holsters. I meant to ask what he was doing, but all I managed was a small groan. It got his attention nonetheless.

"I have some matters to attend to, my flower," he said, reaching across the bed to brush my cheek. "Go to sleep. I will be back when you open your eyes."

He had only just gotten dressed and already a braid hung free from where he had tied his hair. He never noticed when that happened. I wanted to move it from his face, but my hand was much too heavy to lift, and his smile was so soothing . . .

My eyes snapped open. This time, the room was bathed in bright sunlight, and a slight breeze waltzed in through the windows. I did not move immediately, savoring the stillness of the world and the fresh scent of dawn. The world felt new again. It would have been the perfect start to the day, if there had not been one thing missing.

I turned to the side and was met with the sight of an empty

bed. The wool mattress was still indented where Àrẹ̀mọ laid the night before. I pushed myself into a sitting position as slow as I could, but my vision still swam, my head laden from the multi-day festivities.

I frowned, absently rubbing the empty side of the bed with my good hand. Àrẹ̀mọ had told me that he would be back by the time I woke—or had that been a dream? Strangely enough, I was not sure if the distinction mattered; it would seem I expected him to keep his promises regardless of if they had been said by him, or by the image of him that resided in my mind.

I looked around the room, taking note of the mountains of colorful cloths that were strewn haphazardly across the floor. Just as I wondered if I could get into one of them by myself, a knock sounded on the door. In walked Ìgbín, clothes in hand, for neither a change in my sleeping arrangements nor the largest event in Yorùbáland could shake the tailor off the steady course of her routine.

Breakfast was ready on the table when I stepped into the din-ing room, and, I noticed, the meal had only been set for one. As I ate, one of my guards informed me that the Songhai had taken advantage of the distraction that was the Aláàfin's wedding and marched on Gao, attempting to recapture the trading center Yorùbáland had taken from them. While Àrẹ̀mọ and I were getting married, our army had been engaged in brutal combat. Fortunately, the Yorùbá were on the brink of victory, and as such, Àrẹ̀mọ had taken about a hundred men to the frontlines to raise his army's morale. He was so set on making it there in time that instead of taking Ajá, he recruited the quickest stallion as his steed.

The Aláàfin would not be gone long, my guards assured me. Only for the time it took to make that final push to triumph. For all we knew, he could be on his way back to the royal city.

But the sun made its arc through the sky, and Àrẹ̀mọ did not return. Nor did he come back the next day, or the day after that.

It was on the sixth day after my wedding that I was summoned by Mama Aláàfin. She lived in the area of the royal city where noblewomen with children resided. Unlike the women's compound, which was a cluster of huts, this section was a proper neighborhood, with quaint mud houses spaced along a stone path. I could discern Mama Aláàfin's house right away; its garden bloomed with a vibrancy that could only come from being attended to multiple times a day, and the house's wooden door was trimmed with bronze.

When her slave let me inside, I stepped into what was less an entry room and more a lavish warehouse. Every inch of the floor was covered in expertly woven rugs, edges overlapping in the determination to have them all present. A jumble of animal pelts clung to the walls, making the interior look as though it had grown blotchy fur. Countless lacquered tables and velvet divans interlocked across the room like one large puzzle.

It was hard to imagine there had ever been enough space for Àrèmọ to be raised here; the house was filled with what must have been decades of hoarding. It was the result of a woman who had been overindulged, first by her husband and now by her son.

Weaving through the clutter, the slave led me to a room at the far end of the house. A single knock on the door prompted Mama Aláàfin's call from within.

"Come in."

The slave bowed me inside. Opposite me, silk curtains lined the archway to a small patio. Beyond it, the sun melted into the edge of the world, bathing the room in a warm glow.

After several long moments of navigating through a maze of gold and silver statues, I at last reached where Mama Aláàfin sat at a small circular table. She wore a silk robe, and one woman soaked her feet in water that had flower petals floating on its surface. Another woman gently detangled her curls, which fanned around her face in a massive gray mane. I had only seen Mama Aláàfin's hair in beaded and jeweled braids, so I could not help but stare. It was said that beauty faded with age, but hers had held on remarkably well.

As I approached, her eyes opened, and she smiled. "Òdòdó."
She gestured to the empty stool across from her. "Sit, sit."

I did so hesitantly; we had never spent much time together
outside of breakfasts, and even then, she treated me with ill-
concealed contempt.

"Is there something I can do for you, ma?" I asked.

"Must that be why I invited you here? Can't I just want to
have tea with you?"

"Tea—?" I began, but in an instant, a slave appeared next
to the table, setting a cup in front of me and tipping a pot of tea
into it.

"You will forgive me if I prefer something a little stronger,"
Mama Aláàfin said. She held her hand out, and a goblet of palm
wine was deposited into her grasp.

After taking a sip, she said, "I had wondered if my son's attrac-
tion to you was merely a phase, but here you are: Ìyàwó Aláàfin.
Àrèmọ's wife. And since you are now officially my daughter, I
would like for the relationship between you and I to be more
agreeable."

Some of my apprehension faded, but not all. The last time
Mama Aláàfin had been nice to me, I had done something that
nearly invoked Àrèmọ's temper. I knew better than to completely
let down my guard around her. Nevertheless, she had clearly
failed in her mission to dispel me from the royal city. Nothing
she said could hurt me, nor would I allow myself to be tricked by
her words again.

So, cautiously, I said, "I would like that too." I picked up the
cup of tea and took one sip that turned into several as the deli-
ciously spiced drink warmed my stomach.

"You and my son remind me of myself and Àrèmọ's father,"
she remarked dreamily, resting her chin on her hand. "He had
eight wives, you know. I was the youngest."

"Really?" I asked, surprised.

She nodded, her amber eyes glowing, and I was struck by
the odd feeling that came with the realization that elders were

not born at their advanced age. There existed a time when they had been young, growing and seeking wisdom from elders of their own—an entire reality stolen by the greedy hands of time. Mama Aláàfin must have even had her own name, once, in some distant life.

"Not only were the senior wives here first, but most had also already given the Aláàfin strong heirs," Mama Aláàfin continued. "So, you can imagine how jealous they were when I became his favorite—ah, then again, perhaps you don't need to imagine. I am aware of the discord that was between you and Kọ̀lọ̀. I was completely taken aback to hear of her sudden passing. She was so young—I had not even known she was sick."

"It was a shock to everyone. My only consolation is the fact we were able to make amends before she passed." The lie came smoothly, but the next words were harder to say. "We looked past my claims against her concerning the slave revolt. I was distressed and not in my right mind."

Since my recovery, I had forced out different variations of the admission while at gatherings or conversing with other nobles. Although the words still sparked anger within me, I had thought I had enough practice to sound convincing.

But Mama Aláàfin raised a brow. "You have mastered this life well, my dear. Certainly much improved from when you first arrived."

My tea felt uncomfortably warm inside me, but I met Mama Aláàfin's gaze evenly. I made sure I was not the first one to look away.

"I see myself in you," she said after a moment, picking up her goblet. "Beautiful, the favorite wife despite being the youngest. Born to a common family," she added, gesturing to the left side of her face, which was free of the Aláràá tribal mark. "Oh, and, of course, because we were both thought to be witches."

"You were a blacksmith?" I asked, wiping a bead of sweat from my brow.

"There is more than one way to be a witch. I was worse than

a blacksmith—I was barren. I underwent childbirth before Àrèmọ, but within a few months, the child died. It took four failed births for me to realize I was not giving birth to children at all. I had been cursed with an àbíkú."

My eyes widened. My aunties had told me that for the first year of my life, my mother had called me an àbíkú. Or rather, she had hoped that I was one, that I was a spirit who stole into a pregnant woman's womb to be born into a borrowed body I would soon desert. When it became clear that I was not merely a tourist on Earth, Okóbí had become more tolerant of my existence.

I shifted in my seat; I was beginning to feel uncomfortably warm.

"I was convinced it was the senior wives who set the meddlesome spirit onto me," Mama Aláàfin continued, oblivious to my discomfort. "There are ways to deal with àbíkú—rituals done in the dark, only spoken about in hushed voices and never in public. It was dangerous, of course, but I was determined that my fifth birth be successful. Because I knew he would be the heir to Yorùbáland if only I could keep him alive—"

"Excuse me," I gasped suddenly, clutching my stomach. I had tried to ignore it, but my insides felt as though they had been set aflame. "I don't feel well. I have to—"

I had barely risen to my feet when a sharp pain seared through my abdomen, forcing me onto the floor. Faintly, over the pain pulsing through my body, I heard Mama Aláàfin snap her fingers. A slave deposited a bucket in front of me, just in time to catch my vomit. In horror, I saw that it was streaked with blood.

"So, you see," Mama Aláàfin said, her voice distant, "I have sacrificed everything for the Aláàfin, both past and present. I hope, then, you understand why I cannot allow you to ruin all that I have built."

I looked up at her, my head spinning. "You poisoned me," I rasped, my pain so great it left no room to even feel fear.

"Poisoned?" Mama Aláàfin laughed. "Ṣàngó yọ mí, no. I can

only imagine the horrors that the murderer of Àrèmọ's precious bride would face at his own hand. But though he may be blindly devoted to you, even he desires heirs. If you had granted him that, no doubt his love for you would have eclipsed the love he has for his mother. But now, even if I cannot get rid of you, I can make sure you are a forgotten wife."

She sipped wine thoughtfully, watching me writhe on the floor from over the rim of her goblet. "I simply could not let you beguile my son," she said softly, almost to herself. "I just see too much of myself in you."

30

When Mama Aláàfin grew tired of me convulsing on her floor, I was carried back to my hut.

For two days and two sleepless nights, I was confined to the pool of sweat that my bed had become. I twisted until the linen sheets were permanently entangled with my limbs; I dug my fingers so deep into the wooden headrest that it splintered my skin.

My insides compressed into a tight ball. Nothing alleviated the pain. I could not take it anymore; I should have been dead already. *Please* let me die.

Then, on the third day, there was peace.

A low and constant buzz filled my ears, as though a great sound had been ripped away. Disoriented, I pushed myself into a sitting position. Outside, the sky flushed with the bright hues of a budding dawn.

When my handmaids saw that my storm of pain had passed, they sprung up from the corners where they sat. They looked at each other, then one braved a step forward.

"Is there anything we can do, my lady?" she asked.

There was confusion and pity in their gazes, but I did not believe it. I knew now that any compassion I found in the royal city was always false. I wondered if when my handmaids talked about me, they laughed behind my back.

"Yes," I replied to the handmaid who had spoken. "You can all leave."

"Pardon?"

Something flashed across the face of a different handmaid, but when I turned sharply to look at her, it was gone. It moved to another handmaid, then another, each time disappearing just before I could catch it. It was a smile, I was sure of it. I could *feel* it. They were still laughing at me behind my back, right in front of me.

Resentment curdled within me. "I said get out!" I jumped to my feet so quickly that I startled my handmaids. "Get out. Get *out!*"

I reached for the thing nearest me—a bucket of vomit—and flung it at them. It narrowly missed them, crashing against the wall, its contents flying everywhere. They shrieked and scrambled to avoid the splatter, hurrying out of my hut.

Breathing heavily, I watched my vomit ooze down the walls and seep into expensive rugs. Mama Aláàfin believed whatever she had given me would prevent me from giving Àrèmọ an heir. I did not know if that was true or if it was just an old woman's superstitions, but it did not matter. I was not nearly as distressed by the possibility that she robbed me of children so much as I was by the simple fact she was able to try. When Kiigba had attacked me all those moons ago, I was a helpless witch. Now, I was officially the Aláàfin's wife, but the position had done nothing to protect me from being violated once again.

I sank to the ground, sitting against my bed and resting my head back on the mattress. I remained immobile on the floor, only knowing when the sun rose and set by watching the lightening and dimming of my ceiling. I did not feel the need to stand, not when I was already floating, free and newly untethered.

I wondered if Mama Aláàfin's potion had worked, if it was responsible for this new lightness. Having a son would not have been too bad, I reflected. It would have made Àrèmọ happy; he could have loved it, and slaves could have taken care of it. However, if I had a daughter, I would have broken her legs. I would have done everything I could to save her from having to walk

around in this world. Maybe then she would not have to feel
everything I had—or, worse, feel the nothing I felt now.

Eventually, I succumbed to sleep. I dreamt of fire, of red birds
falling through the air, and of silver flowers. When I opened my
eyes, Dígí was kneeling next to me. Another dream, no doubt;
another memory of a mistake I had made.

"Òdòdó, you're awake," Dígí breathed. She tilted my face to
her, inspecting me. Her warm touch dispelled the theory I was
asleep.

The whites of her large eyes were red, as though she had been
crying, or had not slept, or both. She wore the plain clothes of
a slave. I realized I had seen her wear the same thing before, in
my sleep, shortly after my near death at the slave revolt. But now
I realized that encounter had not been a dream. She must have
disguised herself so she could sneak in to check on me. She had
done the same thing now. It must have been incredibly easy; I
could not believe I had ever thought noblewomen were untouchable.

"I tried to come sooner, but the wedding made it difficult
to enter the royal city," she said. "I heard about your mother.
Well—I was there. At the execution."

When I did not say anything, Dígí continued, "I was going to
reunite you with your mother, truly. But first, I needed the strikes
to gain momentum. When your mother led her sisters away from
Timbuktu, days after the city had been claimed by the Aláàfin,
it seemed as though she was protesting Yorùbá rule. Blacksmiths
across Yorùbáland saw how Timbuktu struggled to cope with
their departure, and, for the first time, we realized the power we
could have. I was scared that if you returned to your mother, she
would return to Timbuktu. And if the first blacksmith to ever
walk away from her forge then returned to it, others would do
the same. But I didn't mean for any of this to happen. I am truly
sorry for all of this."

She gestured to me, then around the room. I realized that she
thought this state she found me in was because of the death of my

mother, as though that was still the only reason I had to grieve. I could have laughed.

Instead, I reached my hand out. Without hesitation, Dígí took hold of it. But I swatted her away, continuing to search for what I had been looking for until I found it tossed aside under my bed: a dagger, the one I'd had since confronting Kọ̀lọ̀.

Dígí barely moved in time to dodge my swing. With a surprised gasp, she fell back, landing hard with her hands behind her. I leapt to my feet, but my prolonged stillness had petrified my joints; my next swipe was even worse than the first, the dagger missing Dígí and embedding deep in a table behind her.

Dígí rolled out from under me, scrambling to her feet. I backhanded her across her jaw with my gold hand, metal ringing against bone, flinging her back. I used the time that she struggled to regain her senses as an opportunity to dislodge my dagger from the table.

"Òdòdó—" she slurred, still dazed.

She touched my shoulder. I quickly curled my arm up, driving the dagger into Dígí's left hand. With a pained cry, she released me. I turned, simultaneously kicking the back of her legs, sending her toppling down. But I caught her before she could fall completely, ramming my forearm into her collarbone and pinning her onto the table's surface bent over backwards.

I raised the dagger to finally rid my life of the nuisance that she was, but when I looked upon her face, I froze. She was smiling. For the first time since I had met Dígí, she was smiling. The wide smile unmasked spaced but straight teeth, the vibrance of which was not diminished even by her bloody lip.

The unexpected display of emotion from her was unnerving. "What?" I spat.

"You got up," she whispered.

The smile had transformed her eyes as well. No longer were they mirrors, more introspective of their beholder rather than their owner. The excitement she wore now was entirely her own.

It reminded me that we were the same age. Like me, she was

raised within the cruel conditions of being a blacksmith and had sought a better life. The opportunity that presented itself to me, in the form of escape, was Àrèmọ; the opportunity that presented itself to her, in the form of change, was the strikes. I understood the need to cling onto one's only chance to rise in life.

I reared the dagger up then plunged it down. Dígí flinched—but the blade landed harmlessly in the table, right next to her head.

"Leave," I said, stepping back from her. "Before I change my mind."

Dígí straightened, gripping her left hand, which bled profusely. It looked as though the stab wound had almost gone straight through it. "You are still my sister, Òdòdó. If there is anything I can do to make up for my mistakes, and to thank you for all you've done for us, you know where to find me."

My gaze strayed to the dagger. Dígí took the hint; she gave me a final polite nod then left my hut.

My heart still pounding in my chest, I looked around. If the grime on my clothes and the odor coming from the vomit stains on my wall were any indicator, I had been sitting here for a few days. With my new lightness, I had drifted through time, unresponsive to its passing. But now, after my scuffle with Dígí, I felt sore, my body regaining feeling and reminding me that I was, for better or for worse, still alive. Whatever else Dígí had done to me, she was the reason why, at least right now, I was standing once again.

I considered what to do next. My strongest desire was to repay Mama Aláàfin for what she had tried to do to me. But as soon as I thought of it, I knew it was pointless; Mama Aláàfin's entire life was Àrèmọ. So long as he remained unscathed, there was no real way to hurt her. Moreover, wives were replaceable in a way that mothers were not; if I tried and failed to penalize her, I would be the one to suffer the consequences.

I would have to determine if there was anything that could be

done about Mama Aláàfin in time. But right now, the only thing
I could do was keep moving forward.

Over the next few days, with the help of the twins, I caught up
on what had occurred in the royal city during my despondency,
both in the open and behind closed doors. The more I read-
justed to my routine, the more I wanted to have a say in state
affairs again.

Since Àrèmọ had still not returned, I offered my advice to
General Rótìmí; he had always been the only man, other than
Àrèmọ, who listened to me. It was on one of these afternoons
when Rótìmí extended an invitation to join the generals' daily
meetings myself.

I looked at him in surprise. "I would like to, but I am not
sure that is the best idea," I said. "I do not want to risk upsetting
Àrèmọ, or the other generals."

Rótìmí's vague smile flickered across his face. "As much respect as I hold for you, your majesty, I would never be so bold
as to speak for others. It was a unanimous decision to invite you
as the Aláàfin's proxy—we all remember your wisdom, and, as
the Aláàfin still lacks a second-in-command, it was the natural
choice."

After a moment, he added, "You'll find that not every man is
as stringent in his beliefs as General Ọmọ́sẹ̀wà. In fact, most are
quite willing to redefine their morals as needed."

"Well," I said, "I suppose I can help point the generals in the
right direction. Just while the Aláàfin is away, of course."

"Of course."

Unlike my first meeting with the generals, there was no
Aláàfin to undermine my place in the war room. It was a stark
change to be directly updated of military and political affairs,
but I quickly adjusted to moving from the shadows into the light.
As it turned out, our army had indeed triumphed in the Battle of
Gao; the Songhai were forced to retreat across the Niger, and for

those who had been unable to get out in time, they contributed handsomely to Yorùbáland's supply of slaves.

None of the reports spoke of the Aláàfin specifically. Naturally, it was assumed he played a role in our army's victory, but still, his lack of mention was odd. Or perhaps I was the only one who found it strange, alone in my fixation on him.

The first few days that I met with the generals, I walked around the war table during our conversations, or else hovered near the Aláàfin's seat. But one day, we were working through a particularly troublesome issue, and, in my deliberation, I sat. With a jolt, I realized I had sat in Àrèmọ's place. I quickly looked around the table, my heart pounding. But none of the generals, pages, or guards had so much as batted an eye. After a moment, when I was sure no one was going to object, I allowed myself to relax.

From that meeting onwards, I took my place at the head of the table.

When the day came that the Aláàfin was scheduled to hold court, and my husband had still not returned, I suggested that I stand in for him.

"Between the ivory situation and the wedding, it has been too long since the people of Ṣàngótè have had their grievances heard," I reasoned. "No one would know it's me. With the crown masking my face and the royal attire dwarfing my body, I would look the same as all Aláàfins have looked."

As it turned out, I did not need to make my case; by now, the generals trusted my abilities. They agreed without argument, and, when I held court the next day, it went just as smoothly as I had said it would.

Three days after that, Ṣégun arrived at the royal city. He was Ọmóṣewà's second-in-command and eldest son. Now that there had been a burial ceremony in Ìlọ́dẹ for his father, and a large celebration of his life afterwards, Ṣégun had been promoted to take his father's place as the general of Ìlọ́dẹ.

He was extremely handsome; he had smooth black skin, and

with his dark, meditative gaze, it was no wonder that gossiping noblewomen adoringly referred to him as an embodiment of the night. However, his was a beauty that could only be appreciated by someone who had never seen his father; the two men shared enough features that comparison was inevitable, but Ọmọ́ṣẹwà set a standard impossible to meet. Although, there was still a chance Ṣẹ́gun could age into that level of beauty—he was quite young, after all, being only three years my senior.

As he was so young and already at a high position, I knew he must have been a very talented soldier—which meant I needed his favor. The night before he arrived, I dined with Rótìmí and two slaves. As the general with whom Ọmọ́ṣẹwà had been closest, Rótìmí knew the most about him. As for the two slaves, they were chosen by the twins after I asked them to locate royal city slaves who had, at some point in their lives, served in Ìlọ́dẹ.

Thus, the morning that Ṣẹ́gun arrived, I knew precisely how to welcome him. He did not hate me as his father had, but there was a wariness in how he approached me. He was at a tipping point in his opinion of me; I simply needed to tip him in the right direction. I also could not help but note he had arrived with only a handful of slaves. He had no wives. That would make this easier.

As I concluded giving Ṣẹ́gun a tour of his new house—which I had only learned my way around the night before—I said, "By the way, General Rótìmí told me you recently went on a hunting trip in which you took down a full-grown lion by yourself."

Ṣẹ́gun frowned. "It has been years since I last hunted a lion."

"Years?" I echoed, prescribing a heavy dose of astonishment. "But that means you were just a boy! I know the Ẹgbẹ́-Ọdẹ are accomplished hunters, but I simply cannot believe you were so skilled at such a young age."

He shrugged, scratching the back of his neck. "Well, I admit, even for the Ẹgbẹ́-Ọdẹ, it is a bit unprecedented."

Ṣẹ́gun paused. We had reached the front door, but I made no move to leave, and he made no move to help me out. After a moment, he turned to me.

"It is true, though," he said. "I've had the pelt with me ever since. I can show it to you, if you like."

I smiled. "I would love that."

The moment his eyes lit up, I knew Ṣẹ́gun would be far less difficult than his father had been.

With each good decision I made, each ally I secured, I thought of how proud Àrẹ̀mọ would be once he returned and found that I had kept everything in order for him. But as time stretched on and there continued to be no word of him, a small voice rose within me. Like a mosquito buzzing in my ear, it would whisper: if things were going so well while Àrẹ̀mọ was gone, perhaps it would be best if he never came back.

The voice appeared when I passed by Mama Aláàfin, knowing Àrẹ̀mọ had not been here to protect me from her. Or it nagged at me when I returned to an empty bed after a long day. Or it surfaced when I glimpsed a mother and her daughter—two things the royal city seemed determined to make sure I could never be again. Each time I slipped into this darker part of myself, I grew into a fury unlike any I had ever known.

Where was Àrẹ̀mọ? Had he truly gone to Gao to fight, or had he been led there by a new "dream"? Was he searching for a woman right now, in that trading center, just as he had searched for me?

I was angry at him for leaving the royal city, for leaving me. And then I grew angrier that I doubted him. He was my husband, my Aláàfin. He had saved me from a lifetime of hard labor. I loved him—

But was this love? This twisting in my stomach every time I thought of him? The bruises left by my heart as it ricocheted within my chest whenever I heard his name? I could not sleep; I could hardly focus. I thought of him so much that I could no longer call my mind my own. I did not know if this feeling was love or if it was hatred.

No—NO! I did not hate Àrẹ̀mọ. I *could* not hate him; I had no choice. He had dragged me into this life, had trapped me into

loving him unconditionally . . . . Why couldn't he have done the
same for me?

I tried to hate him; I really tried. But every time I came close
to succeeding, I stumbled upon a metal flower I had gifted him,
carefully tucked under his headrest. Or I passed the field in
which he had so diligently overseen my training. Or I saw an
oddly shaped cloud that ridiculously reminded me of him. And
just like that, I was jerked back to where I started.

Loving him had become a reflex. Yet I was still so *angry*. It was
a pain so intense that I felt it would burn me alive from the inside
out. He had set my heart aflame, and if he did not soon return
to contain the fire, all I would be left with was a chest full of ash.

31

O ne month had passed since my wedding.

I was watching soldiers train when there came yells from atop the ramparts. A moment later, a rear gate of the royal city began rumbling open.

I frowned; supplies and nobles came and went through the main gate, at the front of the royal city. This gate, being near the barracks and the horse stables, was almost exclusively used by soldiers, and I had not heard anything about a unit being scheduled to return right now. Unless——

Àrèmọ.

I jogged to the gates. My heart pounded as the stone wall slowly parted. The soldiers, too, stopped their sparring to watch. From the anticipation drawing the air taut, I knew everyone was expecting their Aláàfin to be the one to arrive.

But beyond the gate waited neither Àrèmọ nor the men he had taken.

There was just one man, and he was not even riding a horse. As soon as the gates were wide enough, the man sprinted through. His head twisted this way and that so frantically that I wondered if the guards had just allowed a lunatic into the royal city.

The man's eyes locked onto me with such intensity that I nearly flinched. He barreled toward me, but before he could reach me, there were two soldiers at his side, their arms hooked under his own. The man was undeterred by his restraints; I was not even sure if he noticed them. His eyes remained on me, and his feet continued the motions of running, kicking up a cloud of dust as he was held above the ground.

"Your majesty," the man gasped, "I bring a message from the Aláàfin."

The words snapped me out of my shock. Only then did I take note of the man's appearance—the dust caked into his tight curls; the cracks in his lips; the sagging undersides of his sandals, on the verge of parting with his feet completely.

"You were one of the men who accompanied my husband?" I demanded.

At my signal, the two soldiers released the man. He stumbled forward before, apparently realizing that he no longer had to run, coming to a halt on wobbly legs.

"Yes," he said shakily—now that he had stopped, his voice grew faint, and his pupils were dilating at an alarming rate. "The Aláàfin assembled a team of one hundred men to join his army at the Battle of Gao. But we never made it there. On the way, we came across Ọ̀yọ́ who were also marching to Gao—to aid the enemy. We fought well . . . but . . . they had twice as many men—only a third of us survived, the Aláàfin . . . being one of them . . . but they do not know that, only that we're Aláràá soldiers . . . They have held us prisoner since then . . . they're now southwest of the Niger bend. I was the one who was the least injured, so I . . . was ordered to escape and run so I could . . . tell . . . tell . . ."

His mouth still moved, but no words came out, for his eyes had rolled to the back of his head. A breath later, he collapsed.

I had slaves fetch food, water, and the royal babaláwo, but I did not wait to see whether the runner survived his extreme exhaustion.

I went to the field where the senior-ranked soldiers trained, including the generals. I pulled Ṣẹ́gun aside and said to him, "I am leaving the royal city, and I do not know how long I will be gone. You have become familiar with my interests. Can I trust that, when you meet with the generals while I am gone, your contributions will keep my interests in mind?"

Ṣẹgun frowned. "Where are you going?"

Impatience roiled within me, but I forced myself to maintain a pleasant smile. "To attend to a family matter." I placed a hand on his arm, making my voice softer still as I said, "You have proven to be an incredible leader and friend. I feel as though you have become the general whom I trust the most. Will you be my voice while I am away?"

Ṣẹgun's gaze lingered where my hand rested on him before he nodded determinedly. "You can count on me, your majesty."

I squeezed his arm gently, and, as I turned to leave, I met the gaze of Rótìmí, who had planted himself nearby at some point while I had been speaking with Ṣẹgun. Curiosity was plain on his face, but feeling that I had no time to explain, I left the field. Nonetheless, he caught up with me, falling into step beside me as I rushed through the royal city.

"Did I hear correctly that you are leaving the royal city?" Rótìmí asked.

Unlike Ṣẹgun, who I had only flattered in order to secure his allyship, I genuinely trusted Rótìmí. So, I told him, "A messenger arrived earlier to inform me that my husband and his men have been captured. I am going to lead a squad to liberate them."

When Rótìmí opened his mouth, I felt compelled to add, "I do not care to hear any protests or alternative proposals. Know that I value your council, but this is one decision I will not be talked out of."

"When the elephant heads for the jungle, its tail is too small a handhold for the hunter who would pull it back," Rótìmí replied with his vague smile. "I mean to offer my support, not my opposition. As you know, I have my own squad of specially trained men, always at the ready for discrete operations."

My mind paused, thinking, as my feet kept moving. "Have

them at the elephant stables within the next hour," I told him at last.

With a nod, Rótìmí veered onto another path. I plowed ahead to the women's compound. I tore into my hut, exchanging my wrapper for a bandeau and a pair of trousers. Then, I donned my harness; even if I could no longer fight, it was still an important piece of my acclaimed woman warrior costume.

I still had the machete I had worn as decoration to the ivory raid and to my mother's execution. Strapping it to my belt, I flew out of the door, leaving the room looking as though a storm had just passed through.

Somewhere deep in the back of my mind, I acknowledged I was being too hasty, but I simply did not care. I realized now that the spells of intense anger I had experienced since my husband left had not come and gone; they were always there, only building and building and building. Now, the news of his capture ruptured the dam, sending a torrent of rage through me. I was too tired to swim against the current any longer. There was an odd relief in finally giving in to the destruction.

As I passed the newly constructed enclosure for my giraffe, I saw Rótìmí waiting outside the wall that marked the elephant stables. He—along with twenty other men—was battle ready, wearing cotton trousers and holding a spear. For a moment, I questioned our numbers. But then I remembered all these men had gone with Rótìmí to Taghaza—and all had returned. They would be enough.

Also gathered outside of the elephant stables were a few stable hands. The boys hardly took breaks, but, looking beyond them, I saw the reason why they took one now—Ajá was out of his stall, dining on bundles of grass.

I ignored the soldiers' greetings and the stable hands' deference, which quickly converted into shouts of alarm as I walked past them and vaulted over the short wall.

Yells followed, but I heard no footsteps behind me as I approached Ajá. From how his ears flapped around his head, I knew he had noticed me, but the haughty elephant made me walk a few paces forward before he finally deigned to outwardly give me his attention.

He looked at me with obvious boredom, his head shifting as he surveyed me. His intelligent golden eyes were like hardened honey lodged between his sleek black skin. Ajá took a step forward. When I did not move, he raised his trunk in newfound curiosity.

Then, he charged.

An earsplitting trumpet erupted from his trunk as he thundered toward me with alarming speed. A watermelon that had gone astray from a nearby pile rolled onto his path and was flattened under his massive foot, as easily as a man did a bug. I held my ground; I knew I would not die. I had already found myself outside Death's door once, begging to be let in, but it had remained shut.

Death would not come for me—and on the off chance that he did, well, maybe then I would finally be free of this anger.

Ajá abruptly came to a halt, so close that a gust of wind blew past me. I reached up and patted his cheek. "It has been a while, my friend," I said.

It was hard to decipher the expression of his elephant face, but I could have sworn the murder in his eyes gave way to humor as he tilted his head back and let out a noise that sounded suspiciously like laughter.

I looked back to the wall. The men and boys alike had gone silent, their eyes wide and their mouths slightly open.

"Get your horses," I commanded. "We're moving out. Ajá and I will lead the way."

It must have taken the runner the better part of a day to reach the royal city, for around half that time had passed once my squad finally spotted a camp located off the Niger, just where the runner had said it would be.

We could have arrived earlier if I had been on a horse like

the other men, but everything I remembered about my first time
riding a horse—from the act itself to the subsequent events—
was so unpleasant that I had no desire to repeat it. And besides,
as Ajá was the Aláàfin's steed, it seemed fitting to ride him to
save Àrẹ̀mọ.

Àrẹ̀mọ, Àrẹ̀mọ, Àrẹ̀mọ.

His name pulsed in my head, in sync with the rhythm of my
heart. I could hardly tell if I was angry for or at my husband, but
I had no capacity to think it through; as I dismounted from Ajá,
the only thing I knew was forward, no matter how exhaustible
the source of fuel.

"We're fortunate to have found their camp before they vacated
the area," Rótìmí remarked, dismounting his horse as, around
us, his men did the same.

Between us and the camp stood a hill. It was not very tall, but
it, the sparse Sahel trees, and the gradually increasing darkness
provided enough cover from the camp's possible lookouts. From
what I could see, peering around the edge of the hill, clusters of
tents were erected on grounds of reddish dirt. Roaming among
them, by torchlight, were about half the number of Ọ̀yọ́ that the
runner reported. Even assuming the rest were dead or injured
thanks to Àrẹ̀mọ and his men's valiant fighting, there were still
an imposing number of enemies.

Something that my soldiers noticed as well. "It looks like they
outnumber us four to one," one man pointed out.

I looked at him in annoyance. My irritation only increased
when I saw that the other men appeared to share his uneasiness.

"No," I said. "It is us who outnumbers them."

The other soldiers looked equal parts shocked and confused.
The first man exchanged a look with another, as though verify-
ing he heard me correctly, before he turned back to me with a
tentative, "Pardon, your majesty?"

"I said we outnumber them. We have more soldiers than they
can handle. When we storm their camp, they will believe they
are impossibly overwhelmed."

"We are to make them believe something that is untrue," Rótìmí said slowly. The flecks of gold in his brown eyes glinted in the day's dying light.

I nodded approvingly, for that was the very heart of it. It was one of the very first stratagems I had learned from Gassire: the art of deception. My mind traveled all the way back to that lazy afternoon as I announced the plan.

"Since the Ọ̀yọ́ are hovering here on this side of the Niger," I said, "it is safe to assume that they have heard of the Aláràá victory at Gao. Whether they are awaiting reinforcements to incite their own attack or the order to retreat, I do not know."

I thought of the woman who had not been Kọ̀lọ̀, and how her homesickness had been severe enough to sap her life force. "But," I continued, "I am willing to bet that now, weeks after the Battle of Gao, those men are becoming increasingly restless to return home, especially being positioned so openly in the middle of enemy territory.

"All we need to do is confirm their worst fear: that they have been found by an Aláràá regiment. We will storm the camp, on horseback, in three teams from three different directions. We will seemingly block off every exit except for one—the one they will think themselves lucky to have found and retreat through."

As I concluded, there was only the faint rustling of leaves and the distant voices of the Ọ̀yọ́. I looked around at my men, my impatience building with each blank face. Were these not elite soldiers? What was so hard to understand about what I had said?

I opened my mouth, ready to repeat the entire thing if need be, then paused. A light had shifted—within or outside me, I did not know—and I suddenly saw that these men's brows were furrowed more in preoccupation than confusion; that they fidgeted with their horses' reins more from uncertainty than from the discomfort of incomprehension. I forced myself to slow down and think back to the looks on their faces when we had first arrived and seen how outnumbered we were. It was the same look worn by Bámidélé and his regiment.

It did not matter that the men before me were infinitely more skilled fighters than those boys had been; if a soldier did not have something to fight for, the battle was already lost. For the first time, I felt a flare of panic—but it went as quickly as it came, for Àrèmọ had prepared me for this too. I had witnessed the speech he had given before the slave revolt, the speech that had converted those boys into real soldiers. All he had done was remind them why they were fighting.

"*Attention.*"

In Àrèmọ's possession, the word was a tangible thing, a whip that immediately straightened a man's spine. I did not try to emulate him; not only would it have failed horribly, but yelling would also put our position at risk. Instead, I put as much intention behind the word as I could. While the men did not assume attention in the blink of an eye, the word snagged their focus.

"Do you know who you are here to fight for?" When no one responded, I added, "I am not being rhetorical."

I waited patiently. After a beat, one man cleared his throat. "The Aláàfin," he replied.

I smiled, one that was more like a grimace—the mention of Àrèmọ out loud had sent a painful ache through me.

"Wrong," I said. "*I* am fighting for Àrèmọ. For as husband and wife, we are bound to go to such extremes for one another. A compulsion those of you with lovers and wives understand.

"And I know you understand, because, just like me, you are fighting for that bond," I continued, slightly louder as I paced alongside Ajá, who was beginning to shuffle impatiently. "Because if the Aláàfin is not rescued here today, Yorùbáland falls to his enemies. And if Yorùbáland falls to his enemies, none of the people who we love will be safe any longer. With every man you cut down, every man who you send fleeing, keep in mind the women you left behind. Keep in mind the half-filled beds waiting for your return."

I looked around the group, meeting as many pairs of eyes as

possible, as I declared, "Do not allow me to be the last woman whom you get fucked by."

Because of our proximity to the camp, the soldiers could not cheer, but their assent was given through the stomping of their spears against the ground, and in the determination shining with the silver starlight in their dark eyes.

I had no doubt Àrèmọ would have done better, but it seemed I struck a different nerve that had the proper effect all the same. Yes, I was beginning to understand the minds of men quite well.

"Rótìmí," I said, "you will lead a team to the north end of the camp. Choose one of your men to lead the second team east, and I will lead the third west. We charge into the camp on my signal."

Rótìmí nodded and beckoned to a man, who stepped forward. As the rest of the soldiers divided themselves into three equal sections, I told Ajá, "Up!"

He bent his foreleg, allowing me to use it to climb onto his neck. Once I had mounted him, I flicked my hands out on either side of me. Wordlessly, the two ends of our group broke off as Rótìmí and his chosen man led soldiers around the hill in opposite directions.

Rótìmí's team would take the longest to get into position. As I waited, listening to the men's horses behind me snorting and shifting, I looked up. Even sitting so high on Ajá, I was no closer to the stars strewn across the night sky than when I had been trapped underground. It was impossible to stretch high enough to reach one—which meant that by aiming for them, growth would be limitless. Àrèmọ's dream stopped at the sea, but if only he thought beyond physical boundaries for his empire . . .

Àrèmọ.

My anger returned tenfold. Newly determined to get him back, I pushed Ajá forward, signaling the direction by pressing my feet behind his ears. I led my men around the hill, maintaining a suitable distance from the Ọyọ́ camp so that we would not be prematurely spotted.

Upon reaching the west side of the camp, I brought Ajá to a stop, and my team settled around me. I peered into the night, searching for Rótìmí's team to the north. The camp's torches distorted the night around it, but if I looked close and long enough, I could just barely make out shadows shifting in the distance. He was in position; and if he was ready, I had to trust that my third team was set as well.

I leaned forward. Remembering all the nights when Àrèmọ had shown me how to ride his elephant, I leaned down. "Ajá," I said in one of the elephant's great ears. "Go."

The beautiful beast, bloodthirsty and brilliant as he was, understood immediately. Ajá raised his trunk with a giddy, almost juvenile excitement, and he blew a terrible trumpet. The savage sound ripped through the night, mangling the silence into shreds. As it echoed, Ajá surged forward.

The ground shuddered beneath me. Amidst the storm of horses and soldiers brewing around me, there rumbled the fierce battle cries of my men.

The camp came in fast. Something whizzed past my head, stinging my ear—an arrow. I sank low onto Ajá's back. But no more air assaults came, for in the next moment Ajá broke through the border of the camp, razing a tent to the ground.

I jerked up and down as the ground beneath us became uneven. With each step Ajá took, a bloodcurdling scream sounded from below. As I pushed him forward, I could only hope that none of the men he crushed were the prisoners we came to save.

My soldiers poured into the camp from what seemed like all directions, yelling at the top of their lungs. It really did feel as though we had five times the number of men than we did. The Ọ̀yọ́ soldiers were overwhelmed; they were like chickens with their heads cut off, scrambling for their weapons as my men cut them down with spears and machetes from atop horseback. Their fear was no doubt heightened by the presence of Ajá, who gave the illusion that the Aláàfin himself was leading this attack.

Galvanized by our success thus far, I stood on Ajá's back then leapt as far as I could from him, rolling as soon as I hit the ground to minimize injury, narrowly avoiding being trampled. I quickly scrambled to get out of the elephant's way; he had transformed into a golden-eyed black demon, tearing down five Ọ̀yọ́ soldiers at a time, targeting every man who was not atop a horse with his massive feet and violent swipes of his trunk.

I rushed through the camp, feverishly looking for any sign of Àrẹ̀mọ while dodging my men's horses and Ọ̀yọ́ soldiers as best as I could. Iron blades sliced at my arms and body. One even managed to graze my throat before one of my men took him down. I trudged on, my vision red with rage, blinding me from fear and even pain.

A foot rammed into my back. With a gasp, I was thrown forward. As soon as I hit the ground, I flipped over. My assailant was already on top of me, the point of his spear plunging down.

Instinctively, I splayed my hands in front of my face in a final, desperate attempt to block the attack. The spear collided into my palm; my arm vibrated, and my knuckle knocked against my lip so forcefully that it split.

Confused, I opened my eyes—to see that the spear had harmlessly embedded into my golden hand. The man was as stupefied as I was, but before he could retry his attack, a spearhead punctured a hole in his stomach from behind. Blood sprayed over me as the man's eyes widened. The spear was yanked back, and he swayed for a moment before collapsing on top of me.

With a grunt, I pushed his body aside and was met by the sight of a proffered hand. I allowed it to help me stand before I saw the man who the hand was attached to—Rótìmí.

"You're moving with a recklessness that's going to get you killed," he yelled over the tumult.

"That is, if Death deigns to show," I replied, extracting the spear from my hand and tossing it away. As we continued through the camp, I asked, "What is the situation?"

"It is as you planned—the more Ọ̀yọ́ we trample, the more of them who break away from the battle and flee southward. So far, we have not lost any men."

"And the Aláràá prisoners?" I asked.

"One man has reported seeing an odd-looking tent propped against a tree." He gestured behind him. "There has not yet been an opportunity to investigate, as it's on the very southeast corner of the camp—Òdòdó!"

The moment he had given me the direction, I had set off in it. Even as he continued yelling my name, I did not look back. If there was even the slightest chance that Àrẹ̀mọ was being held there, I had to check.

It had begun to rain. As I strayed further from the heavier fighting, the storm gradually became louder than the yells and clangs of metal until it was the only sound I could hear. None of my men were on this side of the camp, and the scattered Ọ̀yọ́ who I came across paid me no heed as they ran for their lives.

I searched frantically, blinking through the blood and rain streaming down my face. For all the tents I passed, none matched Rótìmí's description. Still, I ran from flap to flap, yelling Àrẹ̀mọ's name. He *had* to be here.

And then I saw it—a lopsided tent, slumped against a tree as though the trunk was one of its stakes. I ran to it and scrambled for the flap, but my hand only ran over smooth expanses of cloth. By now, it was raining hard enough that the soaked tent sagged, turning it into a jumble of gray cloth that nearly blended in with the mist.

With a surge of impatience, I sliced the tent with my machete. I widened the tear, pulling the cloth to the ground until I had created an opening.

Suddenly, lightning flashed in the sky, and, for a moment, night turned into day. In that split second, the scene before me was illuminated: a mass of men—their faces scruffy and bloody, their clothes grimy and torn—all chained to the trunk of the tree. Their brown eyes were impossibly wide.

The lightning passed quickly, flinging the world back into darkness as thunder cantered across the sky. But that single moment had been enough to see the scar over their left eyes and the three-headed elephant emblem fastening their capes.

I entered the tent and was immediately hit with an unbearable stench of unwashed bodies and human filth. I took another step forward, and, to my surprise, some men shrank back.

Then there came his voice—hoarse and tired and much smaller than usual, but his all the same.

"Ọya?" Àrẹ̀mọ whispered.

My eyes snapped to the corner of the tent, and a strangled sound of relief escaped me.

"Àrẹ̀mọ," I breathed, rushing over to him and dropping to my knees. "It's me."

The wariness drained from his eyes, the skin around which was tinged purple and green. "Òdòdó," he said in relief. Then, as if fully coming to realize I was here, his eyes widened, and he said again, "*Òdòdó!*"

His hands were chained together, but that did not stop him from trying to embrace me, nor me him. We became so tangled that it was impossible to tell who was being comforted and who was the one murmuring, "It's okay, I'm here, it's okay."

There was no room to fit around one another, but we tried. Oh, how we tried. My arms almost fit into the narrow space behind him, and he was almost able to strain enough from his chains to reach me, and my chin almost fit into the crook of his neck without bumping into the men packed around us.

For all my longing and for all my scars, there was nothing that had hurt quite as much as that almost, almost, almost.

32

As soon as we stepped foot in the royal city, Àrẹ̀mọ was whisked away by a sea of slaves, the royal babaláwo and his apprentices, and Mama Aláàfin. He suffered from several battle wounds, and he was further weakened by malnutrition and possible infection.

The other men we rescued were in just as bad of shape as he was, but I did not receive any updates about them, nor did I pursue the matter. They were not the Aláàfin, after all.

Four times I tried to see Àrẹ̀mọ, and four times nervous slaves turned me away at the base of the bronze stairs. On my fifth attempt, I got as far as to the front door—only to be met by Mama Aláàfin. She drew herself to her full height—which was not very much—and fixed me with a hard amber gaze as she said firmly, "My son's injuries are severe, but do not worry. We have experts who know how to properly heal him. I see no need for your witchcraft here."

Defeated at last, I retreated to the women's compound. When I finally sat down, my own exhaustion and injuries caught up with me. The twins fetched one of the royal babaláwo's apprentices. It took him hours to attend to my wounds, but even by the time he was done, there were still no updates about Àrẹ̀mọ's condition.

Although it was not a secret that Àrẹ̀mọ had led reinforcements to Gao, few people knew that he never reached the battle. After the generals and the royal city's high-ranking officers had been informed of the truth, they had sworn the men who returned with Àrẹ̀mọ to secrecy. That way, no one would know the Aláàfin had been so badly injured, not in valiant battle, but as a result of being captured.

This also meant it was not common knowledge that I had rescued them. And with the generals postponing their daily meetings out of respect for the Aláàfin's recovery, I had no choice but to return to my normal routine: exercising in the morning, lessons with the royal griot in the afternoons, and practicing music at night. I was the Aláàfin's family; I had saved him and his kingdom multiple times. Any other man would have been honored for such efforts—but I was not a man. I was a wife.

The passion that had driven me to rescue my husband had dissipated, taking with it any lingering illusions about the grandeur of being the Aláàfin's wife. When Àrẹ̀mọ had been gone, it was easy to fool myself into believing that everything would be solved if only I got him back. But it seemed by freeing him, I had only imprisoned myself.

Two weeks after I had returned to the royal city from rescuing Àrẹ̀mọ, I greeted the sunrise without ever having closed my eyes. Rather than sleeping on my bed—something I had been unable to peacefully do since the rescue—I sat on my rug with my legs tucked to one side of me as I crafted a golden daffodil.

Ìgbín had just left after dressing me in a vibrant red wrapper. I was using a knife to cut out stars from sheets of metal when I heard my door open. I knew it was the twins; they were the only ones who never knocked. Sure enough, a moment later, they dropped onto the floor on either side of me.

"Have we missed the flower song?" one asked.

"Can you sing it again?" asked the other.

"Later," I said, putting the flower aside. "Kẹ́hìndé, did you do as I asked?"

"She's arrived at the women's field," he replied.

"And Táíwò, did you do as I asked?"

"He's waiting for you outside," she said.

"Thank you, both of you."

I moved to stand, but Kẹ́hìndé prompted, "And?"

I looked at him in confusion, but his attention was on Táíwò, who frowned. After a moment, her eyebrows unknitted, as though she had just remembered something.

"And," Táíwò said, "one of the Aláàfin's guards told me to inform you that he is well enough to take visitors and has requested to see you."

My heart skipped a beat—I had almost given up on the prospect of seeing my husband before the moon had completed its cycle. I was not sure if I was prepared to see him—but then again, perhaps this was the best timing I could hope for.

"Thank you," I said again, though this time wariness clipped my tone as I watched the twins stare at each other. I wondered if Kẹ́hìndé had known to remind Táíwò because he could tell she had something more to say, or because they shared access to the same mind.

Shaking my head, I exited my hut, leaving the twins to their silent communication. Rótìmí waited for me outside the entrance to the women's compound.

"Your majesty," he greeted with a bow. "One of your twins informed me that you requested my presence?"

"Walk with me."

I looped my arm through his own. As the budding dawn lit our way, I said, "I hope you had a smooth recovery from our latest expedition."

He gratefully dipped his head. "Fortunately, I did not sustain any daunting injuries. Certainly not as bad as those which Taghaza gifted me."

"I can only imagine. Your elite squad is certainly skilled to have survived that."

I allowed silence to settle between us. Rótìmí's arm was slightly tense; we both knew I had not summoned him to merely check in. I, on the other hand, was calm. A tranquility played within me like a song, and I trusted the melody to guide me through the proper steps.

As we turned onto a path anew, I said, "Without you, I would not have gotten my husband back. Words could not do justice to how grateful I am for your friendship, Rótìmí."

"It is always an honor to serve you in any way I can, your majesty."

"I am glad you say that, because I am afraid I must take advantage of your benevolence once more."

Rótìmí cast me a curious glance. "Planning another mission?"

I laughed. "No, I am afraid that I have retired from battle. Do not take offense, but fighting like a man is incredibly exhausting and reaps little reward." I stopped walking, bringing Rótìmí to a halt and turning to face him. "I merely ask that you assemble the generals in the war room. The Aláàfin wishes to have a meeting immediately—there is much to discuss now that the generals will focus less on expansion and more on sustaining the present Yorùbáland."

Rótìmí's eyes seared into my own, his gaze searching. "As much as that excites me," he said slowly, "I also find it shocking. I have tried and failed many times in the past few years to point the Aláàfin in this direction."

"Winds shift without warning, then even the sturdiest of things can be blown another way," I said, smoothing a hand over his gold-lined collar. "I can guarantee the Aláàfin's time in captivity will bring this matter back onto the discussion table. Currently, Yorùbáland is a compilation of villages and towns who have little in common other than having been conquered. Now is the time to connect these different regions, and the best way to do that is through prioritizing trade, not war. Of course, this means that, central to this unification, and what will most be receiving our attention, are the six major cities—such as Wúràkẹ́mi."

Although Rótìmí maintained his poised demeanor, something like hunger shadowed his expression. "Then I trust your word. I will gather the generals right away."

He bowed and turned to leave, but when my hand remained on his shoulder, he looked back at me questioningly.

"One more thing," I said softly. "Bring your elite squad with you to the war room."

A slight crease appeared between Rótìmí's brows. But when I only smiled, he gave me a quick nod then whirled around. I watched him disappear around a corner before I continued to the women's field.

The royal city's noblewomen were already there, laughter ringing through the air as they played various sports and games. Standing under a tree watching them, some distance away, was Dígí.

"You are welcome," I greeted as I walked up to her, bringing her attention to me.

Her left hand was heavily wrapped in a cloth. With how badly I had maimed her hand, it was unlikely it would ever be useful again. But that did not dissuade her from dipping her head respectfully and saying, "Òdòdó. I was happy when you called on me."

"Of course. I wanted to speak to you. Yorùbáland needs its blacksmiths, Dígí. The strikes have gone on long enough. I summoned you to tell you they are ending today, and you will make sure of it."

Dígí released a long exhale. "I have said you may ask any favor of me, but you should know this is the one thing I cannot do," she said. "I do not possess the power to command the blacksmiths to return to their forges. And even if I did, why would I force my sisters back into the cages they only just escaped?"

A woman trotted a mare near the edge of the field. Moving so that I faced away from the field, away from the view of the noblewomen, I said, "Although you do not lead the strikes, I know how far your voice extends. Use it to announce that, if the blacksmiths return to their positions, they will find a new life waiting for them. One in which the state will treat them with the reverence and compensation they deserve. I had been planning to explain how I can guarantee that, but just recently, I have been given the opportunity to show you instead."

I turned and walked a few paces, then looked over my shoulder at Dígí. My own resolution was reflected in her eyes. Slowly, she nodded and followed behind me. I led her to the Aláàfin's chambers. As we reached the top of the great bronze staircase and the guards fell into attention at the sight of me, I informed them, "The generals and their pages will be arriving shortly. Let them through."

"Understood," they chorused as the front door closed behind me.

Once inside, I glanced at Dígí. She understood, walking away to blend in with the slaves who bustled about the house holding hot water, bloodied rags, or fine cloths. They knelt before me as I made my way to the Aláàfin's bedroom.

Àrèmọ's abdomen was wrapped in clean bandages, fresh bruises littered his bronze skin, and one of his eyes was swollen. Still, he was in better shape than I had expected; he sat up in his bed, shiny black curls falling around his face as he looked down at the dagger in his hands. Iron blade, gilded hilt—it was the one with which I had been made to kill my mother.

He toyed with the dagger, slowly turning it in his hands, but as I closed the door behind me, his gaze shifted to me. The sunlight reflected off his dark eyes, and my heart twisted; it was like finally stepping out of the shade.

"Òdòdó," Àrèmọ greeted softly. "Come here."

I did. I had barely reached him when he took my waist and hoisted me onto his lap. A small gasp escaped me as his lips collided into mine hard, impatient. He kissed me with the ferocity of a man starved; his lips made his way down my front—my neck, my collarbone, my chest.

"I missed you," he breathed, his hands bunching my wrapper over my thighs. "I thought about you every day. I had to get back to you."

I took the dagger from him and held it away, but that was the only semblance of sense I managed to grasp; in the next moment, he shifted, and my thoughts broke off into a strangled cry.

"You made me a promise," I whispered, burying my hand into his soft curls. "You said I'd be your first priority. Then you left on our wedding night."

I shivered as his hands found their way under my wrapper and ran over my bare back. "So we'll resume the wedding," he said. "Or we'll have another wedding entirely. One twice as long, with twice as many gifts. I will marry you every single day if you wish. Your wishes are mine to obey."

It was so familiar, him seeking my forgiveness within the folds of grand gestures, that I laughed. Àrèmọ grinned. He guided my hips over him, gradually quickening in tempo until, at last, a convulsion seized my body. I shuddered with a pleasure so deep that it bordered on pain—or a pain so deep that it was almost pleasure.

Panting, Àrèmọ gripped the back of my neck and brought my face to him until our noses touched. "My beautiful wife," he murmured.

"That's not all I can be," I said, pulling back just enough to meet his eyes. "While you were gone, I contributed to the generals' meetings. I would like to continue doing that as your second-in-command."

He laughed. When I did not join in, however, his amusement faded. "You're serious?"

"I know you still need one—the men with whom you've tried to replace Kiigba keep getting themselves killed in battle. I wouldn't need to see battle, I would just advise you. Like I've been doing, but in a more official capacity."

"I don't know, Òdòdó . . ."

"I discovered the traitor that none of your men could," I said. "Where do you think I learned of the second ivory camp? It was your first wife who was behind it. She was an Ahosi warrior, sent by Ọ̀yọ́ to dethrone you."

Àrèmọ sighed. "I am aware of your rivalry with her, but you need not make up any more lies about her. You have never needed to worry about my love for you being threatened, but especially not now that Kọ̀lọ̀ is dead—"

"She was not Kọ̀lọ̀. She was a *soldier*."

"She was a woman—"

"It was a woman who just rescued you!"

I made to move away from him, but his strong arms wrapped around my waist, keeping me in place.

"And I'm grateful for that," Àrèmọ said, kissing my shoulder. "Have I not just shown you how grateful I am?" He kissed my neck. "If you still do not believe me, I can show you again."

I closed my eyes. "Àrèmọ."

He pulled away, laughing. "Òdòdó." He said my name so adoringly that my eyes opened unwillingly. "The love of my life. Please, you are too beautiful to be upset, and you are certainly too beautiful to do a man's job. We are reunited—what more do you need?"

Àrèmọ bit his lip, awaiting my response. I tucked a curl behind his ear. I was sure it would have otherwise remained adrift; he never would have noticed it.

With his face unobscured, I looked at him—truly looked at him. I looked at the tenderness with which he regarded me; the same affection that had motivated me to cling onto life after he left me for dead, only for me to be immured and deemed insane. I looked at his black eyes, ever shifting like a restless sea; the same eyes that had watched me kill my mother at his command. I looked at his dimpled smile; the same smile he had given me before he had me dragged across the desert, ripping me away from the only home I had ever known, just for his enjoyment. And I smiled.

"Very well. I did not want to be second anyways," I said, which was true. I had asked knowing he would say no. But still, I had to give him the chance.

His eyes lit up, and he kissed me. I drank in his rain-filled scent. When I had poured him into every nook and cranny of my senses and memory, I pulled away.

And in one quick motion, I slid his gilded dagger across his neck.

Blood gushed out of him, spraying me and staining his fresh bandages. His eyes widened slowly. In a delayed response, a horrible gurgling sound bubbled from him as his hands flew to his throat. A flurry of emotions passed over his face—naked fear, murderous rage, heartache and betrayal.

"Shh," I said softly. "You'll be okay. I promise."

Then, there was acceptance; he struggled a moment more before slumping back against the wall. I caressed his hair, and he leaned into my touch. He almost looked content. So, in that way, I supposed our relationship would end as it had lived: one of us made a false promise, and the other pretended to believe.

Àrèmọ blinked slowly, drowsily. I helped lull him to sleep.

> *"You listen to her tale*
> *One her teacher always told*
> *Of roads his son walked*
> *Roads paved with petals of gold*
> *See them bloom, see them shine*
> *See this garden become a sky*
> *With a thousand tiny suns*
> *It's no lie, it's no lie*
> *Light the world through the night*
> *Keep this glow inside your heart*
> *Flowers wilt, lands dwindle*
> *But survival is in the art."*

At last, Àrèmọ's ragged breaths ground to a halt. His hands fell from his neck; his face went slack. The light in his eyes faded. I knew then that my world would be forever dimmed.

But I had no tears. It felt as though I had already grieved long ago. I had loved him, but so long as I belonged to a man, I would never have any power of my own.

Now, at least, I was free.

"Farewell, my love," I whispered, pressing a final kiss to his vacant face.

Silence roared in my ears as I rose from the bed. Blood still leaked from his neck. I had many loose ends to tie—tensions with Ọ̀yọ́ were only going to worsen, and Àrẹ̀mọ's many siblings, scattered throughout Yorùbáland, would come rushing back to Ṣàngótẹ̀ when they discovered he had died . . . *if* they discovered he had died . . .

But even now, I found myself approaching a variety of solutions. I would get to all of them, eventually; one step at a time.

Wedging the dagger into my gold hand, I walked around the bed to where a tall and thin wooden box sat, and I picked it up. Then, without a second glance back, I exited the room.

I found Dígí lingering in a hallway. When she saw the dagger I held and the blood covering me, her wide eyes became even wider, taking up most of her face. "Òdòdó, what have you done?"

"Guaranteeing I can keep my promise, so that you keep yours and put an end to the strikes," I said. "When you leave here today, tell as many blacksmith guilds as you can reach that they have a friend in the royal city. Tell them that friend has invited the heads of the guilds here. Perhaps if I meet them personally, I will be better able to meet their individual needs."

I did not know if I had forgiven Dígí for her part in my mother's death, but that did not matter. I could use her, and if I managed her correctly, I would reach eyes and ears not just throughout the royal city but across Yorùbáland. I understood now that this was the best way for friendship to work: it was not about blind faith, but rather trusting what they could do for you, and them trusting what you could do for them.

Dígí chuckled. Because she remained expressionless, I did not know if the sound came from delight or shock. Perhaps both. "I will, my sister," she said. "Thank you."

Mama Aláàfin came around the corner, nearly running into us. As she took in the blood I wore and the dagger in my hand, her annoyance shifted to confusion, which shifted to horror.

She screamed and backed against the wall, dropping the towels she held as her hands rose shakily to her face.

"Àbíkú," she said, her voice trembling. "Àbíkú."

I gave Dígí the box I had taken from Àrèmọ's room. "Take this to the war room," I told her. She nodded and turned around.

As she disappeared around the corner, I touched Mama Aláàfin's cheek. She flinched violently, but I merely inspected her paling features, tutting softly.

"You look frightened, ma," I said in concern. "I wish I had wine to offer, to ease your nerves, but it is a bit too early in the day for the rest of us. Guards," I said to two nearby soldiers, "Mama is unwell. Escort her home and keep a close eye on her. Inform me of any developments with her as they arise. I am invested in her health."

With a brief salute, the men took Mama Aláàfin's arms. They tried to guide her off the wall, but when it became apparent that her legs did not work, they dragged her as gently as they could.

I stepped in front of her, and, in a low voice only she could hear, I remarked, "I suppose that neither of our children will sit on the throne now."

She made a strange choked sound. I stepped aside, allowing the soldiers to pass. As she was taken away, the only thing she could say was "Àbíkú" in that same terrified drone.

I went to the war room. The six generals were seated around the table, just as any normal meeting. But this time, the pages standing around the room were joined by the men of Rótìmí's elite squad. The generals were quiet, glancing around at the unfamiliar faces, but as the door closed behind me, all eyes latched onto me.

The click of my sandals against the floor echoed as I walked to the head of the table. I sat slowly, my hands on the armrests, savoring every moment; the seat felt like a better fit than ever before.

After a moment, General Balógun cleared his throat, reminding me that they were still in the room.

"Your majesty, what is this?" he asked. There was a slight waver in his gruff voice. "Where is the king?"

My eyes found his. I noted the beads of sweat forming on his receding hairline.

I placed the bloody dagger onto the table with a small clatter. Dígí stood nearby, in the shadows, and when I flicked my hand, she sprung forward, the wooden box ready in her hands.

"The king is dead," I announced. Dígí slid the box open and extracted the long crown of the Aláàfin. A moment later, I felt its weight bearing down on my head. The beads susurrated loudly as they swished in front of me, mostly obscuring my face as I continued, "The Aláàfin lives on."

For a moment, there was only the sound of the swaying beaded crown.

Then Rótìmí stood, his chair scraping against the floor. Determination shone on his face as he gave me a small nod. "Long live the queen."

Ṣégun stood. "Long live the queen," he repeated fiercely. Although it was early morning, there were stars in his eyes as he gazed at me.

The four other generals looked at the two who stood. They looked at each other; they looked at the elite squad of soldiers lining the room; they looked at the bloody dagger I had placed on the table. Then, finally, they looked at me.

General Balógun was the first among them to stand. "Long live the queen."

I could almost hear General Àjàyí's bones creaking as he, too, pushed himself up from his seat and croaked, "Long live the queen."

Slowly, the remaining two generals, Yẹ̀kínì and Èmíọlá, rose to their feet. Each one uttered the same declaration, prompting their pages to do the same. The guards joined in, and the phrase was chanted throughout the room. Somewhat tentatively at first, but as more voices chorused it, the words gained more heart, more flesh, until they were as solid as anyone else.

"Long live the queen. Long live the queen. Long live the queen."

Long live the queen.

GLOSSARY

àbíkú "born to die"; a spirit child born into a borrowed body it will soon desert to return to its unborn playmates

agbádá a traditional attire worn by men, which consists of four pieces: a large loose-fitting outer dress, an underwear jacket, drawstring trousers, and a traditional cap

Aláàfin "man of the palace"; traditionally the title of the king of Ọ̀yọ́

àṣẹ the divine energy which *Olódùmarè* manifests as; runs through all things, both living and inanimate

aṣọ òkè "top cloth"; a handwoven fabric specific to the Yorùbá people, typically regarded as an esteemed material

babaláwo "father of secrets"; a figure of religious authority

balafon a xylophone that has gourds as resonators

egúngún "masquerade"; a rite performed in order to make visible the ancestral spirits

Èṣù the trickster and messenger *òrìṣà*

gèlè a head tie

griot a West African oral historian and repository for the traditions of the people he represents

guembri a three stringed box-shaped lute

ìró and bùbá "blouse" and "wrapper"; a traditional attire worn by women, most commonly worn with a *gèlè* and a shawl or shoulder sash

kora a long-necked harp lute

Ọbà a minor Yorùbá river goddess and the first wife of *Ṣàngó*

Obàtálá the Yorùbá god of wisdom who created humanity

Ògún the Yorùbá god of iron and war

Olódùmarè the Yorùbá Supreme God who maintains the universe

òrìṣà a Yorùbá deity

Ọ̀ṣun a Yorùbá river goddess, associated with love and fertility

Ọya the Yorùbá goddess of winds and tempests, also associated with death

Sahara refers to the large desert that stretches across the African continent, from the Atlantic Ocean to the Red Sea

Sahel refers to the semiarid portion of the Sudan, which is the transitional zone between the *Sahara* to the north and the grasslands of the south

Ṣàngó the Yorùbá god of thunder and lightning

Savanna refers to the long band of grasslands south of the *Sahara*

talking drum an hourglass-shaped drum that can imitate human speech

Yorùbáland refers to the West African region of the Yorùbá people

ACKNOWLEDGMENTS

In Yorùbá culture, true death occurs in the face of obscurity. In this sense, I believe the undertold histories of precolonial West Africa are dying. This was my primary motivation for writing *Masquerade*—to help breathe life into these rich histories by sharing them. Thus, first and foremost, to whoever is currently holding this book: thank you for reading this story. You are the "you" Òdòdó sings of.

To Larissa Melo Pienowski, the first person to believe that Òdòdó's story deserves to be heard. Thank you for never wavering in your faith in me and my writing. This novel would not be what it is now without your encouragement and insight.

To Robert Davis, whose enthusiasm for *Masquerade* is so great that it renewed my own excitement about it. Thank you for understanding this novel's creative direction without me having to explain it, and for your careful expertise while polishing this story. And thank you as well to Troix Jackson for your editorial support.

To AM Kvita, who allowed a random freshman to latch onto them and interrogate them about all things publishing. Thank you for being my first guiding light on the dark and twisty road that is this industry. And thank you to the rest of The Raft—Casey Colaine, Sulagna Hati, Shay Kauwe, Amanda Helms, and Samantha Bansil—for providing a warm and supportive space. I can't wait to watch you all set sail.

To Professor Adélékè Adéèkó, who graciously fielded my millions of research questions. Thank you for your time and wisdom, and for your help with the Yorùbá language.

To Professors Wendy L. Belcher and Nathan Alan Davis, in whose classes I was first exposed to African literature and African drama, respectively. Thank you for planting seeds of inspiration that would grow to become *Masquerade*.

To Micaela Alcaino, the incredible illustrator who designed *Masquerade*'s cover. Thank you for creating artwork that so beautifully encapsulates this novel. To the team at Forge and Macmillan: Alexis Saarela, Libby Collins, Heather Saunders, Russel Trakhtenberg, Rafal Gibek, Jeff LaSala, Jim Kapp, Jennifer McClelland-Smith, Anthony Parisi, Eileen Lawrence, Julia Bergen, Linda Quinton, and Jeané Ridges. Thank you all for your help with bringing this novel into the world.

Lastly, to Desire, Jazmine, and Ashley, who cheered me on while I was querying; to Yusof, who is always willing to talk for hours on end; to the members of the "2024 publishing children" Discord, who make being a Gen Z author feel less lonely; to Cassandra—aren't you glad we didn't chicken out and go to law school? Writing *Masquerade* was a solitary process, but at different points along the road to publication, I found these kind writers. Thank you all for your support.